# Re- Collection

### ✦ A Novel ✦

# Laura West Hall

Printed by Amazon Kindle Direct Publishing
Cover art by Laura West Hall
Cover model – Shelley Kreusch

First printing, 2023.
ISBN: 9798375524146

Follow Laura West Hall on Facebook and Instagram.
Find more content at lwhallauthor.com

## By Laura West Hall

*Permission Not Required: Poetry and Prose for Kickass Women*

*Of Broken Things: A Collection of Poems and Ponderings*

*Two Cries and a Laugh: A Collection of Three One Act Plays*

*To the teachers…*

# 1 ~ Before

I shut off my computer--disgusted, starving, and throbbing from head to toe.

Croft poked his head in my classroom door. "Did you get your lesson plans approved on the parent portal yet?"

I rolled my eyes and chuckled. He always made me laugh, even over things that ticked me off. "Don't get me started. Did you get the memo on the new book bans?" He snorted and grabbed my coat, always the gentleman, holding it out for me to slip on. "Seriously, Croft, when is it enough?"

"I don't know, but I think we've both had enough for today. Come on, let's go get a drink before the school board meeting."

"Anson's bringing the kids up here before his appoint..."

The phone cut me off. "Janie?" Michele, our secretary was on the other end. I could hear the tension in her voice. "Anson just pulled up out front. He's in the bus lane."

"Ok, thanks, I'm on my way down."

"Um, there's something else. Your mother just parked in front of him, and it looks like they're having words."

"Oh crap. I'm on my way."

I hung up and dashed for the door with Croft close behind. I ran, my feet sliding down most of the stairs, to get out front before things got ugly. Two young men waiting for rides flipped the doors open for me to fly through.

"Thanks boys," I blurted out just in time before the flash, and the debris hit my body.

# 2 ~ Empty

I came to consciousness with a violent headache. Draped over a bed railing, my drool stretched to a bucket on the floor. My body lurched and flung me back. Struggling to get my bearings, and grasp something familiar, I glanced around and noticed a high window with white bars. *Bars!* A thud of consciousness slammed my chest. My eyes opened wider and landed on the profile of a russet-colored man. He turned to face me. I studied him, checking for familiar features, but nothing. He leaned in trying to communicate, and wisps of his wavy hair enticed me to reach out, but my limbs were too heavy.

Squinting to read the words forming in his mouth, I stared intently, but all I could hear was the rasp of my own breathing. I wanted to focus on his eyes, but his inaudible words became more frantic. The tension made me tremble. I was disjointed, shaking violently. *What the...?* My body had reached its limit.

Everything went dark.

A tidal wave of sound jolted me into clarity. *I could hear.* There was a pinging alarm, rhythmically thumping the beat of my headache. The only thing that distracted me from the pain and urged me to open my eyes, was feeling the man lift my legs in the air. His eyes flooded with relief. Setting my legs down, he cradled my face, and kissed me on the forehead, his lips white with desperation as he pulled away.

Scared and confused, I wanted to look around, but stared only at him. His voice broke through the fog.

"Janie, we have to go! Shit!"

The thud of a large metal door startled us both. I panicked, but instantly felt groggy.

"Hold on, hold on. Keep your eyes open."

The alarm grew louder and throbbed through my head. Snapping me out of my haze, he yanked the sheet from over my legs and I saw my body

6

for the first time. I was pale--really pale. My skin was dry and flaky, and covering my legs were coin-sized bruises, symmetrically spaced down each leg.

"I know it's a lot to take in right now, honey, but we need to go."

*Honey.* He reached into a bag on the floor and grabbed a gray, bulky sweater, pulling it over my head and down over my torso with my arms trapped inside. My eyes closed. A pungent odor stung my nose while his fingers snapped in front of my face. Lifting my lids, I zeroed in and noticed his crystal blue eyes for the first time. Concerned, and so blue.

"Janie, stay with me, sweetheart." *Honey. Sweetheart.* "Put your arms in the sleeves." I quickly squirmed around in the sweater and found the openings. It was such a chore to push my arms through the tight knit, but I finally freed my fingers.

Reaching in the bag again, he handed me a pair of faded blue scrub pants. "I'll close my eyes while you pull the gown out from under your sweater."

Without question, I set the pants down and pulled, but the gown didn't budge. Sensing the struggle, he cracked one eye open and reached around me with both arms to untie the ties up inside my sweater. The soft, wide-wale corduroy of his brown shirt tickled my sides.

I noticed his smell for the first time. Until then, all I had smelled was the metal after-taste of the oxygen, but I was overcome with the aroma of a woodsy musk an inch away. His arms enveloped me like a warm blanket. One of his hands seemed to pause on the small of my back. I startled, and he quickly pulled away and closed his eyes again.

"Hurry now!" I yanked the gown free. "Put your hands on my shoulders," he instructed with a whisper. I stalled, looking at the top of his mosaic hair. It looked so soft.

BANG!

The sound echoed from the metal door across the room. He looked back to me with creases between his eyebrows. I knew I must move. He closed his eyes again and held the pants out in front of me. Needing no more instruction, I put my hands on his shoulders, pulled up my knees and slipped my feet into the pant legs.

"Careful, Janie, you haven't been vertical in a while."

My name was Janie. I didn't recognize it. I wanted to shout a question, but no sound came out. *Janie.* I let it sink in as I slid down into the pants. He pulled them up over my hips before opening his eyes, preserving my modesty the whole time. As my feet hit the floor, I went limp. The black spots returned, and blood rushed to my face. He grabbed my waist with both hands to steady me while my arms slid around his neck for balance.

BANG!

The second time we both jumped as something hit the metal door. He turned his head to look over his shoulder and then I saw it--three dots on the side of his neck. I knew something instantly. I didn't recognize my name or where I was, but I knew those dots. I had seen them before.

# 3 ~ The Mission

Trey's deep brown head reflected the autumn sun. Hairless, except for his eyebrows, his square jaw and wide head gave him a stern look, though his charming smile made up for it. Sabine had what she would call a "hard crush" on Trey. From the moment he guided her hands in the garden to show her how to pick the beans, she was tragically smitten. She watched him perform menial tasks, with her mouth hanging open—a fact her friends mercilessly teased her about.

"Never pick the favas until the shell and stem are dry. Dry beans last longer," Trey coached.

To Sabine's ears it sounded more like, "Hey gorgeous."

Trey was indifferent toward Sabine. His passion was the Growing Community. The GC, besides educating people outside of the Government Collection cities, helped supply food for the Sentries and the network. After growing and harvesting, the GC was responsible for canning, storing, and moving the food. Each time the Collectors found the current farm, the GC would hide the food in large compactors so it could be moved to the next scouted location. The compactors suggested garbage, so the cargo could go unnoticed.

Trey was a dedicated farmer in the GC. He was known for talking to the plants like children and watching the sunrise every morning. If there was no sun, he was not himself. To his satisfaction, most days of the calendar had become hot and warm. The oldest Sentries still mourned the temperature changes of the seasons, but Trey was young. At twenty-seven, he never knew anything different than hot and less hot. The winter storms still engulfed the north and made year-round sun worship difficult, so Trey wasn't pleased when he got the message from Croft to head north to help with the next rescue.

Sabine sat on the porch of the GC storage building staring at Trey who was worshipping the setting sun in the soybean field. He was kneeling with his arms outstretched, letting the breeze lap the plants up onto his hands

9

like waves in a deep green ocean. He hummed in meditation as Sabine debated whether to tell him how she felt before he left on his rescue mission. She had just decided, when Trey rolled back on his heels and stood up in one powerful movement. Her heart raced in anticipation as he turned to walk toward her. Trey glanced up and then back at the ground. His eyes were tight, and his lips pressed hard together, signaling not to approach. It was not the time for confessions.

# 4 ~ Fragments

I'm not sure why I opened my eyes. I was alert, but my body was depleted. Images flashed through my head--my legs crashing into metal carts, and pain as I knocked them over, bright sunlight, followed by blue sky. The details were like random puzzle pieces floating around in my mind, and I hadn't yet found the piece that made them all fit together and make sense. It hurt my brain, so I let my eyes focus and take in my new surroundings.

Beyond my feet, two arched windows, six feet high, each a solid pane with no lattice work. The deep window well sparked a memory of running my hands across the cool smoothness. The most striking contrast of orange maple leaves against black bark were all I could see outside. On an adjoining wall was an alabaster fireplace, and above it, a large mirror. From my angle, it reflected nothing but white ceiling. Hints of things I knew tugged at me to remember. I didn't have many memories, but I had feelings attached to this room.

I grabbed the green chenille blanket covering my body and pulled it close to my chin. It was gently worn, and the bumps and patterns teased my brain to make pictures out of the chaos. My eyelids became heavy, and I finally gave into sleep once more. *Janie, my…name…is J…*

A sweet cinnamon smell nudged me awake. It was later, almost dusk, as the orange leaves appeared burnt and red. A light source from another room and the reflection of a fire, covered the smooth ceiling and walls in a pink glow. I stretched my face and limbs and found new strength in my body. A sense of purpose took over. I needed to know where I was and why. I needed to know who I was, and to connect the images in my head to the real world.

As I attempted to sit up, a tray appeared at the table next to the couch. I followed the hand holding it to the corduroy sleeve and on up to the eyes I

11

remembered from my rescue. A smile started in his eyes and traveled through his whole face. Instinctively, I smiled in return. He blushed a little as his gaze diverted me to the tray holding a giant sweet roll. My mouth salivated uncontrollably but I knew not to reach for it.

"You must be starving. Take it slow though, it may take your stomach a while to recognize food again."

As I tried to boost myself up to a sitting position, footsteps distracted us both. A young woman entered the room and set a glass of water on the table.

"She's awake!" She grabbed the man's arm and shook it in excitement. "I think she knows who I am, Croft."

Dressed all in black, her angular haircut was short in the back and longer in the front. Dark and silky, it framed her stunning green eyes that danced in the glow from the firelight. Her porcelain complexion highlighted a few tiny freckles on her nose. I knew this woman. I felt instantly attached to her.

"Give her a minute, Sagie. She hasn't been able to move on her own for over a year. She is still very weak."

*A year.* I tried to concentrate, but nothing was tangible. She was familiar but I couldn't place her. The man had called her Sagie. I opened my eyes again to try to focus on her face, but she had turned on her heels and walked around behind the couch. Twisting to follow her, I noticed the narrow bit of room behind me. She sat down at a baby grand piano that barely fit in the space. It looked old, and I knew immediately that this was also a piece from my past. The woman began playing. Her fingers were deft and quick, but the music was tranquil like a rocking ship. I closed my eyes to the music's sedation and started to sway. A lullaby fell over my whole body, each note a gentle trickle that danced on my skin.

Then, a vision--my head, buried in long auburn hair, and I was being rocked, but I was not a baby. My childlike legs were long and almost touched the floor. My face was wet, and in my daydream, I felt a poke on my calf. I turned to look and a small child with long dark hair and green eyes tugged on my dress.

"Itz'okay Janie, come pway wif me."

Then the voice of the woman rocking me interrupted, "Sage, she is fine. Go outside. She will be out soon." The woman turned to me and wiped the tears from the wells under my eyes. She smiled and touched her nose and forehead to mine. *Mommy, I love you.* Contentedly, I stroked her hair.

The music became unexpectedly louder and faster, trying to pull me back from my reverie. SAGE! Sage was my sister! I turned more of my body on the couch now to face her. She looked at me with anticipation while her fingers robotically moved on their own across the keys, inviting snippets of memories.

12

"Are you my sister? Yes!" I answered myself before she could respond. "You're my younger sister. Aw, Sagie. We had matching dresses..." More pictures of us sitting together on a twin bed crept in my mind. "...and we shared a room. You were funny, a little stinker." She laughed and kept playing. It was such an odd sensation to have affection for her as a child, but no memories or emotions attached to her as an adult.

The man laughed and nodded. I had almost forgotten he was there. His laugh triggered something deep. He seemed so sincere and encouraging, and it made me want to focus on him, but the other woman with the long dark hair kept entering my mind.

"Our mother..." I stopped because the fragments of her were not complete enough to form a coherent thought. Sage's eyes widened as she leaned forward and played more furiously. She and the man exchanged several hesitant glances, but he nodded again for her to continue. "We played in a creek, and you fell into the water, and when I pulled you out there was blood on my leg." She nodded.

Her playing softened so I didn't have to strain but that's all I had. My mind searched for more details, but I couldn't conjure up another scene. It felt like I was beginning a race over and over again, but I couldn't make it past the starting line. Sage closed her eyes and kept playing, almost willing me to remember. The soothing music turned stormy and tightened around me trying to choke out a memory.

"Why don't I remember more of you?"

I asked the question quietly to myself trying to figure out the answer. The music stopped abruptly. She looked at the man, I think hoping for him to answer in her stead. He met her gaze, and I knew they had a secret they weren't yet willing to share.

She stammered, "Well, it's hard to explain."

"Try, please try."

Suddenly a loud buzzer interrupted the moment. It was harsh and relentless. Above my head on the ceiling a series of pinpoint lights appeared--three green lights in the center and groups of five or six red lights moving toward them on two sides. Sage and the man called Croft looked at each other in a panic. She stood frozen. Croft gently grabbed my legs and swung my feet off the couch. Then holding me by the arms, he coached me.

"Can you stand, Janie?"

"I'll try. I think so."

My legs straightened. I could almost feel the blood circulating and reminding them of their job. I was dressed in the same blue scrub pants and gray bulky sweater Croft gave me before, at that place. As I looked down to confirm I was upright, long strawberry blond hair fell in front of me and covered one eye. My hair! It was abnormal to have to acknowledge myself as its owner. Croft reached up and tucked it behind both ears. He stroked down the length of it as he let go. It occurred to me that I had not yet seen myself in a mirror. I tried to take a side-step and stumbled a little.

"Janie, I'm sorry, we have to leave. I thought you would be safe here. I just never thought she would send them here--with your sister." I could barely hear him above the buzzer. "No matter now. We have to go."

I pulled from his grasp just enough to take another step to my left so that I was directly in front of the fireplace and looking in the mirror. I had the same green eyes as my sister. We were a match, except for the hair. Sage walked to stand next to me and put her arm around my shoulder, looking only at our reflection and not me. The light flickered up from the fire and cast devilish shadows on our faces.

"Do you know your face?" she asked the mirror.

I turned to look her in the eyes--the eyes that reflected my own better than the mirror.

"Yes."

She took hold of my hand and squeezed with a reassuring smile, "Good! Then, let's go!"

# 5 ~ Road Trip

The GC truck rumbled on the broken road. This time Trey had a driver, so he could plan and eat on his journey. Still stewing about Croft calling him to the north, Trey could only think of one Sentry for whom they would risk a rescue. Janie McAvoy had been the impetus for the creation of the GC and their whole philosophy in general, but she had been under the control of the Collection for over a year. It was possible she was brain dead, but she was valuable, so it was worth the risk.

Bodhi Burch, though he had been driving since he was ten, hadn't driven long for the GC. He was only nineteen, but Trey spoke for him because he knew Bodhi's experience. It was something that made him invaluable since most young adults no longer knew how to drive. And while he tried to hide it, Trey enjoyed Bodhi's quick wit.

"Trey, hey you still with me? You look like you're in love with your celery or something. You've been staring at it since we crossed the 40° N."

Trey chuckled, "Yeah man, I'm just going over details in my head."

Bodhi's body longed for muscles to hug on his post-adolescent frame. Still scrawny, he was starting to fill out like he thought a real man should. Always a little overconfident, he was not bothered by his slightness. He compensated for any lack of strength with his mind. Well-read for his age, he also never let his intelligence get in the way of admiring himself. He glanced over to the sideview mirror and flashed himself a seductive smile in appreciation. Then he pulled his forearm up enough to see the faint glimmer of a bicep form in the mirror.

Trey rolled his eyes. "If you're done cooing to yourself, Croft said we are meeting at 41°04'50" N and -85°08'21" W, so you might want to start consulting the charts."

"Dude, I can't help but be distracted by perfection," Bodhi said, winking at himself in the mirror.

"Hey, pay attention. We need to keep an eye on the weather too. The sun will be going down soon and then we only have the network to rely on.

It should be okay this time of year, but it's farther north than I've been since I was a little boy. Gran-mamma used to say tornados were rare in this area, but now it can be prone to some vicious storms."

"Wow, I never had you pegged as a chicken."

"Cluck, cluck."

Bodhi wheezed a laugh which helped Trey loosen up.

"I'm not scared of tornados. I don't think. They wouldn't happen this time of year anyway." Bodhi shot him a skeptic glance. "Summer lasts longer and longer every year, but fall is so unpredictable. It's being stuck in ten feet of snow that I'm worried about. Not having doppler or satellite communication anymore puts a serious damper on things."

"We have techs that can link up sat com. Heck, I could probably do it remotely, but the quote, unquote government is so good at jamming our signal now. We're stuck with hundred-year-old technology. We need that satellite back. We could do so much with a satellite."

"First of all, that old technology is the best defense we have. The Collection has no idea what it is or how to use it. As far as the satellite goes, we don't even know if it's still functioning. Plus, that would mean going even further north to the Lakes. That's the only command center that could be remotely accessible."

"Trey, we could do that! Get Croft and that girl, drop 'em off at Euro City and head on over to the command center."

"Mm, not in the plans."

"What is the plan then?"

"You'll know when I know."

"I think you know."

Trey smirked. "Ok, well, you'll know when I tell ya."

"So ya don't know."

Getting more exasperated, Trey slapped his hand on the dash. "Bodhi, it's for your protection. Croft will tell us what we need to know when we get there."

"All right, all right! It's a simple question, you freak, and besides I was just trying to get this part of the trip over with so we can go nab us some satellite."

"Not gonna happen this trip. I will be sure to let the Sentries know you are on call for the next suicide mission though."

Bodhi rolled his eyes and shook his head as he flung the map across the dash. "Man, can you imagine? We could finally get rid of this ancient crap and plug in. I mean like really plug in! You can't tell me that idea doesn't excite you?"

"Okay, it does, but we all have our jobs to do."

"You sound like the New Congress. 'Do your job and don't question anything, you sweet, brainwashed little robots.' What a bunch of bull," scoffed Bodhi.

"No, you know I don't subscribe to that rhetoric. I heard enough of it growing up. Plus, I don't even like calling them the 'New Congress.' There is nothing congressional about what they do, even though—never mind."

"For the life of me, I can't believe so many people bought that shit and stayed."

"It's called fear, and it's very powerful. The problem is that most people either have too much of it, or not enough."

"So, what about me?"

"What?"

"Too much or too little?"

"What, fear?"

"Yeah."

"Too little, definitely too little!"

Bodhi considered Trey's words thoughtfully in silence as the monotonous landscape rolled by. The sun was setting to the left of the old highway and radiated through the windows. Most of the time Bodhi didn't like the heat, but evening sun was nice. The hilly road was flattening out and the crumbling infrastructure of the old regime arose in the distance. Trey glanced up from the map he had been studying. Shock pushed him back to his seat.

"Stop! Get off the road!"

"What, what? I thought we still had about fifty miles to go?"

"We do, but we're getting close to a check point so that means road and sky patrols will be out soon."

"We're picking them up at a congress city?"

"No, it's technically after the city. I think the Collectors are starting to get wise, but they haven't figured out where the people are yet. They just started putting up check points to catch anyone who's careless."

"Are there GC here?"

"Yes, but they're not in the Collection. That's how they have evaded them. Sentries plant garbage, food containers and other trappings of congress cities around the south side of the city to keep them guessing. Funny they haven't figured out we don't live like that anymore."

"It seems like if they knew the truth…"

"Don't go there, man, we're not converting anyone today," Trey cautioned. "Now, get off the damn road!"

Bodhi slammed on the breaks hoping Trey might lose a little arrogance and smash into the dash. Trey anticipated Bodhi's move and braced so he didn't move an inch.

"Look, we're on the same side! You don't have to agree with me, but if you want to go on rescues, you do need to listen to me."

Bodhi smirked, "Just messing with ya. Don't be so serious."

"This is serious though. We need to focus. If you can't do this, let me know now and I will drop you off and pick you up on the way back."

"Naw, I'm in, I'm in! Where should I go?"

"You see the path on the other side of those trees over there? We will start there but I'm gonna scout on top. Once you get through the tree line, I will get out and get on the roof, but take it slow so you don't knock me off with a tree branch or something." A devilish grin crept across Bodhi's face. "Hey, before you get any clever ideas, remember you need me as much as I need you."

The compactor rattled off the main trail. The clearing through the trees was once a dirt road but it hadn't been tended to in many years. When the truck stopped, Trey climbed up the ladder on the side until he got to the top.

"Hope you don't bounce off," Bodhi yelled as he hit the gas.

# 6 ~ Running

The window closest to the fireplace shattered so violently the glass fell from the frame like sand. Sage and I were leveled to the floor in the blast. I tried not to inhale for fear I would breathe in glass. Holding my breath, I turned my head to the side to let the glass slide off my face. Sage, frozen, stared at the ceiling. A two-inch shard of glass was lodged right below her left cheekbone. Tears welled in her eyes and dripped out the corners down a trail to her ears. She didn't move and I briefly wondered if she felt like I had when Croft found me. I could feel her pain in my own cheek. I touched my face to make sure there was no glass, but I could not ignore the pain. It burned and made my eyes water. I shook my head to try to reset. The pain didn't leave, but I refocused on Sage.

Croft kicked a pile of the glass aside with his foot and then bent down, unsure of whom to tend to first.

"I'm fine!" I shouted above the buzzer.

He had me hold her hand while he quickly slipped the shard of glass from her cheek. The cut didn't seem to be too deep but was profusely bleeding. I yanked the napkin from my tray of food, guiding her hand to push it on the wound. Croft sprang up and ran around behind us. Scooping an arm under each of ours, he helped us both to our feet.

Right as we gained our posture, another small window behind the piano shattered. A low rumble started emanating from the door to the right of the fireplace. Croft glanced to the ceiling to see the red lights getting closer to the green lights. As the rumble grew louder, Croft put his hands on our upper backs to guide us forward, gently but firmly. We ran into an adjoining room that was the kitchen. A few familiar objects caught my eye, but there was no time to soak in the details. Croft reached for the silver stove as we ran by and turned a blue gas knob. The buzzer stopped. It was only then I realized the low rumble was footsteps growing louder and faster.

19

When I took another step, I noticed an intense pain. No shoes meant I had been walking on glass, now imbedded in my feet. I bit my lower lip to deflect the pain, knowing I had no time to stop and pick out glass. Croft opened a cabinet that revealed a black and white screen. Running his hand across a scroll bar at the bottom, a panoramic view of what looked like a forest whipped across the screen.

"Good, we have to hustle now, girls."

He shut the cabinet and opened a thick door, next to the stove, which led into a small dark closet. A blue light filled the close space.

"Get in, Janie."

I didn't remember being claustrophobic, but I knew instantly I was. My chest felt heavy. Croft stepped in first, lifting a pack from the wall and slinging it over his shoulder, then grabbed my hand to yank me in. I turned to pull Sagie into the cramped space, but her blood-soaked hand slipped out of my grasp. As I reached for her other hand, the door next to the fireplace broke open and men dressed in dark camouflage fell on each other as they burst into the room. Sage looked over her shoulder and then back at me, slipped off her short boots and pushed them into my chest until I grabbed them. Then she shut the door between us.

*My sister!* The only answer to my enigma, was on the other side of an insignificant piece of wood. The woman whose memory I needed and the comfort I craved, felt a thousand miles away. Possibilities of our future together were quickly melting. The door rattled violently. Sage screamed and then there was silence. Searing pain crept up the back of my neck. My shoulders rose to compensate for the throbbing, but to no avail. More banging and then the sound of a drill broke my spell of pain. My face grew hot with anger. I couldn't breathe for a brief moment until Croft pulled a chain hanging from the ceiling and the floor dropped away.

We fell fast, probably about fifteen feet to a net so well camouflaged by the earth below, I didn't know it was there until it gave way under our weight. We were suspended in the net about two feet off the ground. Croft grabbed a handle that looked like a ripcord and the corners of the net fell. We slammed the last two feet to the ground, harder than expected. I pushed myself up and winced when my feet, full of glass shards, felt the earth. I tried to brush off my raw feet and shove them inside Sagie's boots. Sage was still up there. I felt like she was still alive, but maybe I was deluding myself. Tears pooled in my eyes and clouded my vision.

"Sage," I whispered in eulogy, hoping I was wrong.

"I know," Croft answered. "I'm sorry, honey. Sage is either captured or…we have to go." I could tell he was heartbroken to admit it.

My feet were stuck half in and half out of the boots, so Croft bent forward, slung me up over his shoulder and started running. No more than five steps later, his foot caught in the net. As he flew forward, I was flung down on my back. I could tell he was hurt, but he wouldn't acknowledge the pain. My knee began to throb even though I hadn't hit it, and then curiously, I saw him rub his knee. He helped me up, and as I stood, my feet slid painfully down into the heels of the boots. Putting one arm around my back and one behind my knees he scooped me up again and ran.

It was mostly dark now, but a full moon lit the enormous stone house. Three large oak trees supported half of the house and the other half pushed into a hill. Two knotted ropes hung down from the suspended half. My body knew those ropes and remembered climbing on them, but that was all I could pull from the stubborn files in my head.

"It's okay, I can walk."

"I've got you, don't worry."

"I know, but this will slow us both down."

"You're still recovering, and we need to move fast." I knew he was right. I didn't argue. Pain, fear, exhaustion, and sadness convinced me to let him work for both of us.

"Keep your eyes out for any kind of movement, Janie."

Croft was strong. I could feel it in his resolve. Not huge in stature, his physical power came from sheer determination. Tripping on the net had only made him more focused and single minded. He held me with complete confidence, barely jostling me as he ran. I studied his profile as the moon flashed the shadows of the trees on his face and hair. I felt drawn to this man.

Reflexively, I reached up and stroked the hair on the back of his head. The softness reminded me of something. I was suddenly lost in a dream of a little blond girl on my lap. Feeling my touch, he turned to look at me, and abruptly the movie in my head disappeared. Croft's eyes searched mine for answers to my thoughts. Funny, what a futile gesture it would prove to be.

As we ran, with woods in every direction, hints of memories invaded my brain. It was so much darker in the thicket of the trees I didn't need to close my eyes to focus. Croft was still holding me, but I was transported back in the room where he rescued me. My head was heavy and bobbed up and down on his shoulder, but I was conscious enough to see them--a row of about twenty beds with unconscious people hooked up to bags and machines. That must have been what I looked like before he pulled me off the table. Straps over their waists, and wrists, I couldn't help wondering who they were and why we were there. Carts with data screens were at the end of each bed, but they were scrolling too fast for me to read any names.

When we were almost to the end of the long room, my foot hooked the rail of the last bed cart and spun it around. The paper-thin tech screen slid off and shattered on the floor. The cart, in turn, pulled the sheet to the side revealing a black grappling hook that attached to both legs of the young man on the table. The multi-prongs of the hooks were hollow, and a liquid flowed through them and into the legs of the person on the table. Croft looked at me with concern in his eyes and then ran full tilt to the door and rammed us through. As the door opened, bright sunshine assaulted my eyes and the alarm we heard inside rose in pitch.

We were halted by a metal spiral staircase. Croft almost launched me over the rail while trying to stop his run.

"Janie, you're going to have to make it down these stairs on your feet but wait a second."

He set me down and put my hands on the railing. From the pocket of his shirt, he pulled out a small plastic cylinder, flipped open the top, and touched the nozzle to the crack between the door and the frame. He tipped the bottle and a light mist emerged as a greenish liquid oozed out into the crack, expanding and creating a foam substance that traveled around the door, sealing it to the frame.

Croft made eye contact with me for reassurance. "Okay, honey, put your arms around my neck." Once I did, he grabbed my hands for extra security and began running down the stairs. My feet couldn't keep up, so I let them drag down each step to keep pace with Croft. When we were almost to the bottom, there was a loud thud on the door above. I turned to look through the maze of winding metal to the top of the staircase. "Don't worry, that door is sealed."

I hate being chased. As the thought became conscious, I was brought back to the reality of the woods and my second escape of the day.

"Janie, do you see anyone behind us?"

"I don't know, it's so dark."

I squinted and strained my eyes to scan the woods. Trees and the occasional glimpse of the moon stretched out in every direction. The wind was strong and biting, and I shivered uncontrollably.

"Hang on Janie, we…are… almost there."

Croft panted as he talked. I could tell I was beginning to be a real burden on him. I begged for him to let me down, but he acted like he didn't hear me. Then, we stopped. Croft tried to set me down without falling but his knees buckled and hit the ground. Wincing, he leaned forward and gently set me on the ground. His arms stayed under me, and his head rested on my shoulder. My knee hurt again. I couldn't figure out why, until I realized it was his pain I was feeling.

Confused, I lowered my head to try to catch his eyes.

"Are you okay?" He lifted his head so abruptly it knocked my cheek. We both laughed a little.

Still a bit winded he answered. "Yes, yes, I'm fine. Are you okay?"

We chuckled again. As the nervous laughter faded, I looked into his eyes. I couldn't see their stunning blue, but I had adjusted enough to the darkness that I could catch their expression. There was a past between us. I didn't know what it was, but I felt safe with him, even in the middle of the cold darkness, not knowing who was chasing us. I couldn't fathom how I could be lucky enough to warrant this type of dedication and care. A

22

familiar churning of excitement twisted my stomach enough to realize it was empty. Without warning, a loud grumbling erupted from the core of my body. We both looked at each other in surprise and laughed again. The moment was gone.

# 7 ~ Anticipation

"Miss Charlotte, is she really coming?"

"I can't believe we are going to get to meet her."

"When will she be here?"

"Calm down everyone." Charlotte tried to control her own excitement, so she didn't further energize the crowd of young people waiting for the arrival of their icon. "Yes, she was rescued, and they are on their way. No, we don't know when they will get here. Yes, you will get to meet her. No, you will not bombard her with questions when she arrives. Now, let's get back to work, we still have prep to do."

# 8 ~ Tuning In & Tuning Out

Croft pulled his arms from beneath me and reached out for my hands to pull me to my feet. Oh, how I had forgotten the stinging in my soles. He put my arm around his neck and walked us toward a birch tree directly in front of us. As he reached up, I noticed a thick wire wrapped around a low branch. It was so camouflaged into the bark of the birch, no one could have seen it unless they knew it was there, especially in the dark. While he uncoiled the wire, Croft had me retrieve a small metal stake from the ground by the base of the tree.

"Put it right in front of my foot, Janie."

Then he pulled the wire down and wrapped it around the stake. From inside his backpack, he pulled out a keypad with a loose wire, and attached it to the wire from the tree.

"Croft? Is it okay if I call you that?

He nodded. "Yes, please do."

"What is that? Is it dangerous?"

"No Janie, it's communication."

He continued, talking aloud to himself, "What's today? Um, cypher three, no cypher four. Yes, that's it. Keep scanning the woods, Janie."

Croft began typing furiously on his keypad. I strained to see through the trees as the moon was setting and the real darkness was falling in around us. The small glow from Croft's keypad made it difficult to see in the immediate area, so I took a few steps away. Croft startled at the motion and looked up.

"Don't wander off now. You can get lost easily in these woods."

"I'm just trying to see past the glow."

Then it happened--a small, almost imperceptible movement about thirty yards away. Croft tuned in to my discovery and swiftly glanced around. I stepped forward, wincing, and whispered, "To your left, past that row of spindly pine trees."

As I squinted to confirm what I saw, my vision blurred, and I was transported out of the woods again. I was kneeling next to a small blond child and holding her hands to shape the dirt in a garden at the base of a wooden fence. She looked up at me with a smile. Blue-green eyes squinted with love, and she reached up to touch my face with the dirt on her hands. We both laughed. The laugh choked in my throat as I had the biggest revelation of my new life. *I'm a mother.*

Croft shook me and whispered frantic instructions I didn't understand. My conscious world was beginning to crumble. My head hurt. My feet hurt. My legs hurt like someone was drilling holes in them, and my brain hurt with a thousand questions no one could answer. It was all too much. Not an hour earlier I had been reconnected to a sister I barely remembered, before she was taken from me. Now, I was on the run with a man I didn't remember, from people I also didn't know or remember, that apparently wanted to harm me.

I questioned whether I was hallucinating, but more than that, I questioned reality itself. I looked around in a panic, hoping to grasp onto something concrete. Straining in the darkness, I saw a flash of someone moving toward us in black. Fear grabbed my insides and wrung them like a towel. I struggled to focus, but inside me was a volcano bubbling over with shards of memories, questions, and pain. I wanted it to stop! Finally, in a last-ditch protective mode, my body shut down.

"Janie, look at me. Stay with me. Your knees are buckling. Try to…"

With that, I looked down at my knees to see if he was right and everything went black.

# 9 ~ Indie City

Delilah's short flaxen hair glistened in the sunlight. Entertained by the smallest things, she twisted her head back and forth to catch the glimmer. She was happy to be outside on such a beautiful day. Indie City had declared safe outside days for three weeks--no U.V. warnings, no flares, and no storms, so most of the GC who resided there were enjoying the weather.

One parking lot remained undamaged, though it looked like a graveyard of carbon beasts, faded to pale shades of blue, peach and gray. Young adults sat in them and dreamed of what it must have been like to drive. But, for a small group of teenage Indies, it was a 'beach' day as they had sprawled across them to worship the waning sun. Ahanu whacked the side of Delilah's chosen metal companion for the day.

"Wow, look at this classic. LINCOLN TOWN CAR. It's hard to believe they had technology for these things in the 1900's." Without invitation, Ahanu jumped up next to Delilah and tried to stare at the sky with her. Seconds passed before he yawned. "Yeah, so, um, this is boring. D'you wanna try to get the coaster going again?"

"No, I want to stay outside, Ahi. We'll be cooped up inside soon enough. I want to soak up every bit of sun I can before it's gone. Why, don't you like the sun?"

"I like it well enough. I just don't want to lie around looking at it all day. "You coming for dinner tonight?"

"Sure, I'll be there."

Delilah flashed her best smile. She was happy to have a friend, especially a good one like Ahanu, but even with the brilliant sunshine and the company, she couldn't shake her sadness. She had many who wanted to take care of her, but no family. So many questions still lingered about the death of her father and the rumors of her mother. All she had was a sister, whom she thought she would never see again. The day mocked her, and every smile reminded her of the faces who were lost to her forever. Still, Delilah was not one to mope.

"Come on, Ahi, let's race," Delilah shouted as she slid off the car and into the driver's seat. Ahanu skimmed through the non-existent passenger door into the seat next to her. Grabbing his invisible steering wheel, he looked at her with a competitive grin. They raced in their play-mobile, making motor hums and screeching brake sounds until they had the attention of most of the surrounding sun bathers. The young Indies gathered around them, taking sides to cheer on one or the other.

Delilah's fans outnumbered Ahanu's four to one. She was championed by a variety of personalities that admired her, pitied her, and envied her, but none that knew her. Since she had come to Indie City two years before at the age of fourteen, she still hadn't really found a place to fit in. Delilah's enthusiasm for racing began to fade. She stopped steering and stared off into the distance. Ahanu knew Delilah's mood instantly.

"Come on, let's walk." He reached for her hand and pulled her through the passenger side.

They left the crowd behind and walked hand in hand across the broken pavement toward the safe inner haven of Indie City. It had once been a shopping center, the largest in the country, where people purchased things with currency. It was the crowning achievement of the consumerism that ruled society for over one hundred years in the old United States until the war in 2042, finally broke the country and forced everyone to choose sides. The capitalists, having priced everyone out of what they were selling, all retreated to the Collection to lick their wounds and rebuild bigger and gaudier. The Sentries in Indie City, and throughout the GC network chose to start again as minimalists.

The former stores in Indie City had been converted into living quarters, hydroponic food centers, studios to learn and practice the fine arts, repairing and repurposing, and library areas for gathering to socialize and read what was left of paper books. The rotundas served as education centers and think tanks. One whole level was devoted to science and research including a small group trying to rebuild an internet system. Several outside and inside gardens lent themselves to meditation and spiritual enlightenment, but no formal religion was introduced or supported.

"Do you want to hang out before dinner, Delilah?"

"I don't know. I might take a nap."

"I know that face. What's wrong?"

Delilah didn't answer. Still holding hands Ahanu swung her arm forward and back in a playful childlike gesture. She squeezed his hand in appreciation and leaned in to kiss him on the cheek. Ahanu blushed and Delilah instantly regretted it as she realized she may have conveyed a message she didn't mean to send. As they approached the entrance, warning lights flashed, and the doors flung open.

"Come on, kids, there's a threat approaching." Old man Ryker's voice bellowed.

Young Indies came running from every direction. Ahanu and Delilah picked up pace to not get trampled in the stampede. Delilah, a faster runner than Ahanu, dragged him to keep up with her until they reached the entrance. As the last of the teens shoved in behind them, the large metal barricade slid across in front of the glass doors. Inside, lights continued to flash in warning. It was not a weather threat. A silent warning meant Collectors were nearby.

# 10 ~ Hit the Ground Running

The sun had set, and what was challenging terrain in the daylight became almost impossible to navigate in the dark. The only light was in old Fort Wayne to the northeast. It was obvious to Trey that Collectors were occupying the city because the streetlights were the awful orange of his childhood. Trey was lying flat on the roof of the compactor to avoid being scraped by hanging tree branches. Shivering from the chilly wind, he tried to imagine the warm southern sun that so many detested.

"Hey, I got a ping! I got the ping," Bodhi yelled through the open window.

The rumble of the compactor was so loud, Trey could not hear him, so Bodhi stepped on the breaks to get his attention. Trey's body lurched forward, and Bodhi jumped as Trey's upper torso slid down part of the windshield.

"I GOT THE PING!" Bodhi yelled again through the glass, and laughed.

Trey, not as amused grabbed the wipers to pull himself down the length of the windshield and onto the hood of the truck. Leaping off the side, he landed with the grace of a super-hero and jumped back in the passenger seat.

"It's about time," he yelled as he punched Bodhi in the arm.

Bodhi rubbed his arm. "Hey what was that for?"

"For slamming on the breaks."

"I had to get your attention somehow."

"Did any message come with it?"

"Yeah," Bodhi fumbled with the display, "here it is, F.O.X. 911. I don't know what that means."

"That's okay, I do."

"Since we're so close, I'm assuming FOX is the old Fox Island Park. Is 911, like, 9-1-1?"

"Yeah, emergency. We need to park this thing in about another three miles and then I'm going to hike in the rest on foot."

"What about me? I'm going too."

"No, you are staying here and guarding the beast. We won't get far without it, so you have to stay behind."

"What if someone comes? How do I defend myself? My ninja's a little weak."

"Tell 'em a joke. That'll kill 'em."

"How 'bout I show them a picture of your face."

"Okay, listen, you have to stand your ground. I know you have never been in a situation like this, but you can't let anyone get this rig. If you see someone coming, just drive. Get the hell out of here."

"I'll do what I have to."

"Pull over here. If we're not back in three hours turn around and go home. I mean it! You can't be here when the sun comes up. This thing will stick out in the daylight and the Collectors could be tuned into your radio signal by then."

"I got this. Now go!"

Trey jumped out of the passenger door and hit the ground running. In his pack, he had some medical supplies, a small red light and bear scented spray to ward off any unfriendly animals. His favorite item was his twentieth century antique knife his gran-daddy had given him. He had both dreamed of and feared a time that he would have to use it.

Luckily, Trey was in excellent condition. He had run two miles before he started feeling winded as he broke the barrier of Fox Island Park. He was excited to finally get to see the ghost city, or Fox as it had been nicknamed, in action and to see if his suspicions had been right about whom they were rescuing. He knew it was a long shot that Croft and the girl would be able to make it the seven miles to the western border of the park. She would be weak and perhaps unconscious. Still, Trey knew he was their only hope. So, when he heard the subtle ping in the trees indicating they had made it to the first extraction point, he resolved to run as fast and hard as he could to get there.

Trey figured that it must be Janie McAvoy, or else Croft wouldn't have first taken her to the tree house. It was known in the GC that the tree house was Janie's childhood home. As he tossed the information around in his brain, he noticed a small bluish light ahead. The frequency of the ping through the trees increased as he ran toward the light. Trey's anticipation was already palpable when thirty yards away, a woman with long light hair caught his eye. She stumbled toward him and fell, but caught just in time by his mentor, Croft.

# 11 ~ Breathing Dirt

I startled awake into complete darkness with a hand covering my mouth. I kept re-opening my eyes to see if I had opened them at all. Croft's familiar musky smell was near which comforted me, but it was mixed with sweat and weeds and sand. I felt the presence of someone new in this dark place. I tried to peel his hand from my mouth. He resisted but I knew there was a reason. Croft flashed a small red light between us. He took his hand from my mouth and used it to signal silence. I nodded and looked quickly around to see who was with us. It's an eerie feeling to see the outline of a person without being able to see the actual person.

My eyes adjusted to the red glow. Above us was a jut of rock and cascading all around us were tree roots and grass. Underneath us was cold, wet sand. Fear seized in my throat as I realized we were underground. I recognized the feeling from when Croft had pulled me into the closet in the stone tree house. My chest tightened. My limbs stiff. I couldn't catch my breath. I suddenly felt I was breathing in no air, only sand and grass. I looked around for an escape and then that someone touched my leg.

He was dressed in all black and just far enough away that he had to lean in for me to see him. He glistened slightly in the red light, which gave him glowing orange eyes. His presence distracted me from my panic until we heard footsteps above our heads. We were indeed underground. Croft turned off the red light and put his mouth so close to my ear it sent shivers down my side. He whispered, "Close your eyes, honey. Try to slow your breathing if you can. Imagine you are lying in bed and nodding off to sleep."

As Croft continued whispering in my ear, my mind wandered at his suggestion. I was in a bedroom with periwinkle walls and sheer white curtains blowing in the wind through the open windows. It was night, but there was a light coming from the outside, maybe a porch light. Under a plush comforter, I sank deeper into my bed. I felt peaceful and content. There were two small white cribs against the far wall, but I couldn't see

33

what was in them. I turned to look next to me and spotted a beautifully sculptured shoulder. Following his form down to the line of the blanket, his silhouette caught me off guard.

I searched my mind for the emotional connection to this man that matched the physical connection. I followed the defined lines that separated his muscles like rivers flowing upward to his neck. Then, soft golden hair--it was my husband. Anson. I knew instantly. Anson was not just gone, but he was dead. I don't remember how or when, but I knew it in my core. I didn't have any specific memories of him to recall, but I remembered his presence. Hard poisonous tears stung my eyes and ran down the sides of my face warming my cold skin.

"Janie, sweetie, we will get out of here soon, I promise. Don't cry." Croft's soft voice broke and caught itself in emotion.

I wanted to tell him where I'd been and what I remembered and that the tears weren't about our current situation, but sometime in my past. My insides ached for that past. A past I knew. I wished I knew how and why I arrived at that moment hiding underground with one stranger and one...Croft. I felt myself slipping again as if I wanted to leave my current reality and escape. Escape that place and escape that life. My self-pity expanded in my chest, exacerbated only by the rank musty air I was trying to breathe. The pot boiled, churning my insides and the tears came faster and harder. The more I tried to stop them, the more vehemently they escaped my burning eyes.

Croft began stroking my hair and put his head on my shoulder in frustration. The stranger at my feet patted my leg. Then, the tears changed from noxious to cooling, from painful to cleansing. I was disgusted for feeling so sorry for myself. I had at least two people, three if I counted my sister Sage, who would risk their life for me. I couldn't let them down and give in to the fear and exhaustion. I wasn't afraid anymore, just angry with myself at my fragility. The crying stopped abruptly as I shook my head in disgust. This panic, this weak whelp of a person I had been portraying was not me. I knew it was not me.

My cold hands reached up to find Croft's face in the darkness. I think I surprised him a little. I turned his head slightly so I could whisper in his ear. "I'm okay, Croft. I'm fine. I will be better now. I am not scared anymore. Just hold on to me and tell me what to do."

His sigh relieved a thousand fears for both of us as he wrapped his arms around me in an embrace I would remember for the rest of my life.

# 12 ~ Departure

Old man Ryker motioned for everyone to return to their apartments. As Delilah walked with the crowd, he grabbed her arm, "Not you, missy. You come with me."

Ahanu was still holding her hand and turned to walk with her, but Ryker, in an overly forceful move chopped his arm between the two of them to break the hold. Ahanu's posture changed from confused to challenged. He charged at Ryker who laid him out flat in one swift arm movement. Ahanu was winded and bewildered at Ryker's aggression. He tried to sit up, but Ryker's boot on his chest forced him back to the ground.

"I'm gonna tell you this one time only. I need to take the girl and you need to go home. This ain't a negotiation. Now if you wanna continue contesting my decision, my foot would be more than happy to take the argument to your face."

Ahanu didn't move, but his face twisted in anger.

"It's okay Ahi," Delilah interjected.

Ahanu stopped struggling and Ryker grabbed Delilah's arm to move her along. Delilah looked back at Ahanu as they walked away. She didn't know why, but she knew this could be the last time she ever saw her friend. Seeing her expression, he took a step to follow, but stopped short. Ahanu stood still in silent protest as the girl he dreamt about nightly walked out of his life and into the Kodachrome file in his head.

# 13 ~ The Collectors

The footsteps we heard above had vanished and only the wind whistled through the cracks of our hideaway. I was lost in Croft's embrace for what felt like hours. Memories tried to intercede, but I focused on the comfort I felt in Croft's arms. Then, the voice of a stranger that I had almost forgotten was there, whispered in the darkness.

"Croft, we need to leave while they are downhill. We only have about a quarter mile to the entrance."

Croft pulled away slightly, "I don't know, Trey, what if one of them is standing by? We can't take the chance. Janie may not make it. She is still weak."

I felt a stab of betrayal as Croft doubted my resolve to overcome my weakness, "I'm NOT weak, I can run. I can do whatever I need to."

I could feel Croft shaking his head, but the stranger came to my defense, "Come on, we've got to let her try. The longer we wait here, the lighter it will get and if we are not gone by daybreak, we may not get out at all."

"Okay," Croft resigned.

With that, the man called Trey lifted a carpet of grass hanging down from the rock ceiling we were under. Dirt and debris rained down all around us. Trey rolled to the outside and Croft crawled over to help him hold the dense earth and lift it up over the rock. He motioned for me to come, and I crawled past him into the open air. I tried to take a deep breath but ended up snorting in some of the dirt that had landed on my face. Coughing, I looked around anxiously wondering if I was too loud. The carpet of sod that had been covering the entrance to our small cave would look out of place in the daylight but blended in at first glance in the subtle darkness.

"Let's go." Trey motioned to follow as he took the lead.

Without waiting for guidance, I ran after Trey. *Ah, my feet.* Croft quickly caught up to me. We ran along the side of a giant dune to the right

36

that leveled off under our feet and continued sloping downward to our left. Trey made a sharp right around a bank of trees that looked like the end of the dune, as it flattened out to more solid ground.

As I curved to make the turn, I saw Trey's legs on the ground and a figure kneeling next to him with a gun pointed at his head. I stopped abruptly and Croft ran into the back of me propelling us both forward. I fell on top of Trey, and Croft slid over the top of me forcing the man in sandy colored camouflage to the ground. His weapon fired as he and Croft struggled for control. I wriggled out of the Trey/Croft sandwich filling I had become. As soon as I freed us both, Trey pounced and secured the weapon. I leaned in and pushed the man that was now on top of Croft jabbing my elbow between his shoulder blades. He arched back and rammed his head into my nose. I fell back instantly and tasted blood as it trailed down my face. Seeing me covered in blood, Trey put the barrel of the gun to the man's head, closed his eyes and pulled the trigger.

Within seconds we were surrounded by more men in tan camouflage. Croft covered me as Trey fired several shots at them. Yet, as they fell, more came from behind. One tackled him flinging the gun several feet away. Two men peeled Croft off me, and only then did I notice the spider insignia on their uniforms. I recognized it immediately. It was the sign of the Collectors. A memory tried to invade my mind, but I pushed it out. I was confident in what I knew. I could examine why later.

I'm not sure if I first heard Croft's yell or felt a hand on my head, but when I looked up, a man knelt behind me, grabbed my hair, and twisted it until his knuckles hit the nape of my neck. I tried to reach for his hands to yank them off, but he pulled and torqued my head. A burning sensation ran down my scalp as the roots of my hair started to give way. I begged in my mind for it to stop, but I tried not to give him any satisfaction by making a noise. I just wanted him to pull out my hair or stop. The anticipation was unbearable.

I had a choice to make. Instead of pulling away I leaned back into his hands and used the resistance to stand. I pushed so hard that he had no choice but to stand with me. He twisted my hair tighter, but the steps I needed to take lined up for me like a blueprint in my head. Feeling a sense of calm, I lifted the heel of my beautiful sister's boot and kicking back, I drove it right between his legs. He yelped and loosened his grip. I didn't let up. I swung my elbow back and landed a blow to his side. Letting go of my hair completely, he grabbed his ribs. Then I raised my elbow slightly higher for one more jab to the face. As he stumbled back the two men holding Croft released him and leapt for me.

I was caught between an angry man that I injured and two more lurching toward me, so I dove to the side and let the men pounce on their own commander. Croft reached out and grabbed the gun. Pop! Pop! Pop! The sound made me close my eyes. A burning smell filled my nose. I opened my eyes to see three men lying on the ground with single holes in their foreheads. Croft killed for me. I didn't know how to feel about that.

Trey finally kicked off the man who had tackled him, and as the man lunged at him again, Trey reached to the strap on his side that held his granddaddy's knife and pulled it up in front of his chest. The man in motion fell on the knife. His face was inches away from Trey's as the life left his eyes. Trey pushed him off. I could see in his expression that that type of death felt worse than shooting a gun. Croft dropped the gun. I fell to my knees next to him and wrapped my arms around his neck and hugged him tight. Trey lay on the ground, stunned, with the bloody knife in his hand. A single tear ran a path down his dirt covered face to the ground below.

Croft turned to him, "Are you okay?"

He sat up silently for a moment. "I killed, like…fifty people." Trey's voice was thin but filled with emotion. Croft let go of me to scoot next to Trey and offer him some counsel.

"Not fifty, more like five, but you had to defend yourself, and you saved us too. I killed too. Don't be too hard on yourself, kid."

"I just never imagined myself killing someone before. I'm a farmer, not a killer. Besides, it wasn't me that saved us. It was that girl with the big cajones next to you that turned this around. Otherwise, we would probably all be dead."

Croft laughed harder than the comment warranted. It was a cathartic laugh that we all felt deeply. He turned to me and tried to wipe the dirt and blood from my face.

"You're a mess!"

"You're not winning any beauty contests either today, Croft," Trey interjected.

We all laughed. We needed that laugh. Trey extended his hand, "Hey, I'm Trey, nice to actually meet you."

"Hi, they tell me I'm Janie."

There was a strange connection when we shook hands. It was exciting and uncomfortable at the same time. I glanced at Croft and could see that he saw something in our exchange as well that he didn't like. Trey broke the awkwardness with his laughter.

"Man, girl, I thought we were all worm food until you kicked that damn spider's ass."

I giggled but Croft tuned him out completely and helped me to my feet. "Let's get going. We probably need to hide your rig before we go to the city."

"Aw no, I totally forgot about Bodhi."

"You brought that kid with you? What were you thinking?"

38

"You don't know him. He's a good kid and a good driver. Plus, he made it possible for me to come get you quicker than I might have otherwise."

"Well, no one consulted me. This was an important rescue, probably the most important rescue we've ever had. I don't like being kept out of the loop."

"There just wasn't time."

I suddenly felt like this argument had more to do with me than the driver. I dared to interject, "Croft, let's go get him. It doesn't matter why he's here. We can't leave him out there by himself. He came to help me, didn't he?"

"Of course, you're right," he conceded.

I was relieved but still confused at the subtle animosity between them.

# 14 ~ Fox Island

The approaching dawn made me uneasy. As the night yawned its farewell and the sky brightened, we alternated jogging and walking to get to Bodhi and the compactor. Hunger consumed me. Visions of the giant sweet roll I never got to taste haunted my stomach, but I knew we had to get to him before we could rest. I felt like everyone was counting on me to keep going, but one thought lingered. Two cribs--I saw two cribs. The question formed itself in twenty different ways, but never made it out of my mouth.

Finally, I saw the beautiful spring green color I would come to know as representing all things related to the GC. The compactor was much bigger than I expected, dwarfing some of the trees in the immediate area. As we approached, I could see the empty driver's seat. Trey sprinted the last few yards, climbed up to open the driver's door, and leaned back to show us blood on the steering wheel. He jumped in and checked the entire cab for clues.

"Trey, maybe you shouldn't..."

Trey ignored Croft entirely. "Let's check the compactor. Maybe he hid in there for the night." After hitting the big red button on the console, he jumped down, and all three of us ran to the back of the giant metal monster. It groaned with every inch of movement. As the jaws opened, my heart raced with anticipation of what we might find, but nothing was there, save a few blankets, a jug of water, and a crate of peaches that looked to be a little over ripe. Trey smiled and climbed in to push all the supplies to the edge.

I grabbed a peach, despite its pungent smell and devoured it. At first, I tried to peel a little of the skin with my teeth, but then I gave in and gulped it all, sucking the pit for any last bit of flesh. My stomach lurched with its first real food. Trey opened the water jug and offered it to me first. As I grabbed it, he went out of his way to touch my hand. It was awkward and obvious, and Croft seemed bothered by it too. We each took a blanket and

40

wrapped it around ourselves as the sun poked its head up from the east. It was hours away from being warm, but even the thought of it was encouraging.

"Bodhi is obviously not here. However, the fact is, we came here for Janie, and we got her. We need to get her to safety. Bodhi probably left to find the city."

"Come on, Croft, you know that's not what happened. If anything, he left to find us, even though he was specifically told to leave without us. I don't know about the blood, and I don't want to know. He knew what he was in for on this mission. Let's ditch the rig and get to the city before the patrols find us. I'm sure those Collectors are missed by now. If Bodhi comes back and finds the rig gone, he will know to look for the ghost city."

"You're right."

Trey closed the back of the compactor and jumped in the driver's seat. I climbed up and sat in the middle between him and Croft. The landscape was an interesting mix of sand, trees, grass and low-lying creeks and swamps. As we drove close to the big dune where we had hidden, we veered left to keep to the trees and noticed the bodies of the Collectors were still there. It was a sickening reminder of what we had gone through and the lengths we took to save ourselves, but it was also a relief that they had not been discovered. Croft and Trey discussed hiding the bodies but decided time was too short. They would be found soon enough.

Eventually we came to a thicker mass of trees. To our right was the far side of the dune which covered the top of a large cave. The compactor could not fit completely in the cave, but it was the best cover we had. Trey noticed that the radio relay display was still on the dash which gave us some hope Bodhi was not taken by Collectors. We grabbed the radio and Croft and I jumped out so Trey could wedge the passenger side into the rock. We gathered some of the branches that had broken off from the impact of the rig and threw them over the end and top of the compactor. It was not a good cover if someone was near but from a distance it would suffice.

Judging by the height of the sun, it was around 8:00 a.m. We jogged through the trees for about a mile. My whole body throbbed with pain, but the hope of finding a place to rest propelled me farther than I thought I could go. I tried to suspend my pain with the memory I had in the woods the night before. I was a mother. I clung to the hope that once I found safety, I could also find my children, and remember my life as a mother.

As we came to a clearing, I noticed a house that looked like it had sprung from nature. Windows and a few pieces of concrete and wood were all that signified it as a building. A small waterfall cascaded out of the side of the natural stone structure. Evidenced by the moss and ivy, it was long forgotten as a dwelling. A cobblestone path, sinking into the landscape, led to a sign for an historical landmark - 'Fox Island Museum, Once the home of the Agri-Culture Intellectual Society.'

"We're here!" Trey crowed as he and Croft high-fived over my head.

They led me up the moss-covered stone stairs. Absent a door, ivy hung down like a curtain over the old doorway. After we stepped through, Croft carefully pushed the vines back into place, so they looked undisturbed. Once inside I could see that only the front windows remained. The back of the structure looked to have been all glass at one time but now was open to all of nature's tourists. Birds, rabbits, frogs, chipmunks, and a variety of flying insects now haunted the main room. Through the back I could see what looked like a swamp covered in moss and surrounded with high grasses and cattails. I walked to the front window to view part of the waterfall from above. It led to a stream that looked like it flowed under the building.

The beams that supported the ceiling branched off like a canopy of trees. The ceiling rounded from one branch to the next in a dance of architecture and nature. Croft chuckled, watching my curious face as my boots clicked on the slate floor. The room felt warm even though it was open and still early in the day. Several hallways forked off in each direction. I wanted to explore, but Croft pulled me toward the longest and narrowest hallway. The hallway contained a network of intricately woven spider webs, so thick they were nearly opaque. Yet as we walked through them, they didn't stick to us. Glancing behind me, the first of the webs we traveled through were all intact.

"A projection?"

Croft shushed me with a finger to his mouth while he nodded and smiled.

Finally, we came to a small room with a wooden desk and boxes of old papers. On the desk were brochures from the historical house. Trey grabbed the radio device from the compactor out of his pack. He pressed his thumb on the screen and a small keypad appeared. After he typed a short message, the floor began to vibrate beneath our feet. Croft reached his arm across in front of me to have me back up a few steps. One end of the table rose taking the floorboards with it, and I noticed the brochures on the tabletop stayed firmly in place. The table arched back until it was perpendicular to the floor to reveal a wooden staircase underneath.

Trey reached for my hand to guide me down the stairs which seemed to dead end into a wall. The familiar feeling of walking into a closed space arose in my throat. Croft followed me, grabbing my other hand. I don't know why, but the thought of the two of them trying to protect me irritated me so much I forgot my uneasiness and pulled my hands back from both, crossing my arms in front of my chest. When we got to the bottom of the staircase Trey punched in some more digits. Nothing happened. Croft reached past me, gesturing for the keypad, and when Croft's thumb touched the screen, the faux wall in front of us lifted and we entered a large, light space bustling with people. This was the ghost city.

An older woman dressed in a white gauze shirt and long flowing flowered skirt approached us. She had platinum shoulder length hair, that was almost translucent, and the kindest hazel eyes I have ever seen. She walked straight to me, ignoring the men and grabbed my hand. Her thin skin was soft and creped, but warm to the touch.

"You made it. I'm so glad you made it, my love. We have all been waiting to meet you."

I looked confused at Croft and then Trey who both beamed, as if they brought the prize turkey home for dinner.

"I'm sorry, where are my manners? My name is Charlotte."

"Janie."

"I know dear, I know."

"Come on now, everyone is waiting for you."

Croft interjected, "Wait Char, can we let the poor girl catch up a bit? We have been on the run since yesterday. Twenty-four hours ago, she was still in the TRC. She is starving, and I'm sure, exhausted, too."

I wanted to tell Croft I could speak for myself, but I was glad he spoke up for me. I was too tired and overwhelmed to express what I needed. *TRC?* Another question to add to my ever-growing list.

"Yes, oh yes, I'm sorry. You all must need a good shower and a meal. Follow me."

As we walked, I silently tried to remember my older questions as new ones leapt to the front of my mind. Unsure of what exactly was going on with Croft and Trey, I turned my queries completely to Charlotte.

"Are we underground?"

"Yes, can you believe it?"

"No, it's so light and airy feeling."

"The filtered fresh air gives the feeling of being outside. Some of the light you are seeing is natural and reflected but some of it is artificial. Oh dear, I almost forgot."

She backtracked a few steps to a table and pressed her hand on the glassy white surface. A screen appeared that showed her the room we had just been in above. After sliding her finger across the screen with triumphant command, small tubes in the ceiling sprayed a fine brown powder over the room and created a new layer of dust to cover any disturbance we had made. *Genius.*

"All right then, that should do. Let's get you comfy."

Walking through the space, I noticed the light came from everywhere. The great room branched off in so many directions I could not call them hallways but more like causeways. Directly ahead was a tall archway that led to another large room. In that room a myriad of natural-colored tiles swirled in the center of the floor. As they spun out to each side, they presented colored pathways down even more corridors.

"You are all red path. When you get to the end you can pick any room with an open door. I'll tell the council you're going to rest and wash up. I'm sure they will all understand. We can gather tomorrow."

Nearing the end of the path, I could hear rushing water. Croft sensed my question and answered before I could ask. "We are close to the creek bed."

I nodded absentmindedly. Then I stopped abruptly and grabbed Croft's sleeve. What had been such soft corduroy earlier was now crunchy with blood and dirt. His face was dusty with lines of sweat streaking down his hairline. The slight reflection in the walls confirmed that I was equally grubby. I sighed as I pulled some grass from his hair. He smiled back as he pulled a twig from mine.

"I am so tired, but I don't know if I can sleep without some of my questions being answered."

"Janie, I will answer any questions you have, after we get cleaned up."

Our eyes connected and I knew I didn't have to say a word. Not to be overlooked, Trey's eyes searched mine for confirmation that his presence was acknowledged. I gave him a polite, noncommittal smile. I held nothing against him, he just made me feel—uncomfortably intrigued. I turned back to Croft. "Can I come to your room after I shower?" He agreed.

We came to the hallway of rooms. It was darker than the color path. The lighting suggested peaceful rest, but I think it was to save power. Two rooms were open to the left, and one was open to the right corridor. Croft guided me to the left while gesturing for Trey to go right. Trey smiled at me, defeated, and I thought I caught a bit of a dagger eye toward Croft.

"I'll see you later," I offered as condolences.

I wanted Trey to know I appreciated his help with my rescue, but it didn't seem right to say it in front of Croft. Trey stood there, stone-faced, waiting to see if I would indeed go with Croft. I did. When we got to the rooms, Croft stopped at the first door with me and kissed me on the forehead.

"Will you be okay?"

"Yes, I'm fine."

I tucked his hair behind his ear, walked in my room and shut the door. I didn't want to admit it, but I was scared to be by myself. I looked for some type of music to calm my discomfort. Next to the bed was a nightstand with a black glass surface. I touched it and a lighted menu flashed on the tabletop. 1. Music 2. Lighting 3. Temperature 4. Communications 5. Help. I quickly found a relaxing selection mixed with sounds of nature and adjusted the lighting to give the room a warm glow. I'm not ashamed to admit, I cranked the temperature up to eighty, since I was still cold from the night. As I walked into the washroom, a robe hanging in the closet reminded me I didn't have any clean clothes.

There was a small kitchenette to the left of the bed. I was thrilled to find some cheese in the cooler and broke off a piece shoving the whole thing in my mouth as I headed back to the bathroom, spying a shower directly in front of me. Imagining the warm water running over my body, I couldn't get my clothes off fast enough. The sweater I had been wearing was full of dirt that splattered debris everywhere as I took it off. There was no trashcan, but there was a chute, so I figured it would work either way. I deposited both the sweater and the pants I had been wearing and decided to fill the large tub while I showered off most of the muck and washed my hair in the shower.

As the bath foam filled the tub, I turned the faucet on trickle, so it didn't overflow while I enjoyed my shower. I felt privileged and out of place with a choice of shower and tub, like I didn't deserve either. I stepped in the glass shower and shut the door to notice a full-length mirror facing me from across the room. There was a small moment of horror as I saw the debris on my body as well as numerous bruises, cuts, and scrapes. I turned the pressure of the stream to high so I could feel every drop massaging into my skin. There are no words to describe the sensation of that shower. Closing my eyes, the steady stream took me briefly to another world--a world where I didn't have to think, to reason or to remember. I was just me, Janie. Of course, I didn't know then, how little I knew the real Janie.

After the tub was mostly full, I turned off the shower and tiptoed to the tub. It was a comfortable scald that warmed me through. Sinking in the cushion of bubbles, I leaned my head back, the soles of my feet stinging as the glass cuts from the day before, reopened in the soapy water. I had almost forgotten about that chapter in my first day of alertness. The sting reminded me of putting my feet in the boots. The boots that belonged to my sister who had either died or was taken. I squeezed my eyes tight to remember her beautiful face. I ached inside and out.

I tried to remember anything about Sage, but the harder I tried, the less it felt like real memories and not fabrication. I began to recount the last day as if it were a week. Weary from the process, I rolled to my side and pulled my legs up to cuddle in my bubble bed.

I must have fallen asleep. I don't know how long I stayed there or how I got out of the tub, but I awoke in a downy bed wrapped in the robe from the closet. I looked around the room, which was darker now, and noticed Croft asleep in a reclining chair. It startled me so much I gasped and sat up straight. I stared at Croft. His subtle wrinkles were highlighted by his sunken posture. Squinting in the dimness, I saw his face relaxed for the first time. I wanted to reach out and touch him, to hold his face in my hands. His presence comforted me. Still, I wondered if he had taken me out of the tub. He would have some questions to answer later, but for now sleep was my only option.

# 15 ~ Haircut

Aviva sat at her desk flipping through papers, not comprehending anything she read. Her recently cut hair hanging by her chin reminded her of her latest outrage. Since her teen years she had prided herself on her long auburn locks, but the week before, she had slammed her brush down and picked up the scissors. It had been a day. She needed a change to help her find her way.

As the wealthiest, and most powerful voice in the New Congress and the founder of the Collection movement, Aviva Chandler wielded power over everyone she met. She had an uncanny ability to anticipate every rival's next move. She wasn't psychic, Aviva just knew how to manipulate. Her first move, as part of the old congress, had been convincing the remaining states that hadn't folded after the pandemic, to fire all public-school teachers across the country. Teachers were especially vexing to Aviva since they were the ones encouraging young minds to think for themselves. It was a move that rocked the country and led to massive rioting but was also the beginning of her real power, a power that had not been challenged until the appointment of Taurus Roma, by the Fair Tax Party.

Aviva was suspicious of Taurus from the beginning. His tax reform proposals and briefs had bolstered lingering resentments in the Collection. Unlike most of the New Congress, Taurus saw rebates and reform as the only way to prevent the upheaval of the twenties. Recent rumblings had once again turned to soap boxing in several more liberal corridors of New Congress City and Aviva blamed Taurus Roma for all of it.

Aviva was secure in her belief that she could quell dissension to her weekly address with a flush. After successful trials in Detroit, she thought of the idea as a general populous control. Simply flush the water system with a psilocybin and compliance was almost guaranteed. After each flush, the status quo returned, but while she knew she could maintain order in

New Congress City, she wasn't sure about the handful of Collections spread around what used to be the Midwest.

One Collection city called New Fundamental had fallen only a year before. The people had simply walked out of the city into the wilderness, abandoning everything they owned. Since the fall of New Fundamental, Aviva had been sending out Collectors to gather information and grab any remaining Sentries. She knew without a doubt that the people of New Fundamental were somewhere, and someone was helping them. She had just started convincing the New Congress of that information when Taurus rose to power in his district.

Taurus had a large booming voice and an austere presence, especially when dealing with Aviva. Even though he had a history as a public figure, he was still a freshman in the New Congress. He had revamped the education system after the expulsion of the teachers and was credited with the success of the program schools. With immediate employment in a government chosen field guaranteed for students after graduation, Taurus was dubbed the savior of education.

A hero to the Collection, especially the young adults, his charisma overshadowed his mixed message of Collection loyalty and change. His speeches radiated strong with the people, but he was on the verge of a change even he couldn't predict. His schools had begun to morph into think tanks of innovation and ingenuity. Unknowingly, Taurus had hired former teachers as facilitators of his new program, right after the war. Some of those teachers were Sentries from the GC. The students loved him because they thought he was an innovator, yet with almost no oversight, he had empowered the Sentries to be able to finally start reforming education.

Aviva could see the seeds of doubt growing in the young people, just like before the war, and she didn't want independent and creative thinkers. New Congress City was to set the example of the Collective way of life, and there was no room for errant thinking.

After Taurus's last brief, Aviva had had enough. She stood before her bathroom mirror examining her aging face. She snatched the scissors from her desk, walked back into the bathroom, grabbed a lock halfway up the length of her hair, and cut. She cut hard with equal purpose and disdain. Six inches of hair fell in her sink. Aviva pulled her fingers through her lighter locks. Triumph. It felt like the key to her new resolve. She was going to take back the Collection.

A flush was in order, but the city water had to bypass the filtration system and make its way to Taurus and others in Congress Village, a bold move that Aviva had never attempted. The last several weeks replayed in her head and convinced her, it was going to be expensive, but it had to be done. She went to call for her assistant, but before she could, Ingrid burst through the door with news that would add urgency to her plan. There had been another escape at the TRC.

48

# 16 ~ In Dreams Awake

Slowly, I walked to the cribs, afraid of what I might find. The wind was cool and gave me goose bumps. I looked back to see Anson sound asleep with a peaceful expression, but I walked with trepidation. The ten feet to the cribs felt like ten miles. It was taking so long. I looked back at Anson again, and this time he did not appear to be asleep. As I approached the bed, he rolled from his side to his back. His arm flopped to the mattress, and his eyes were open and fixed. Suddenly, his color changed from pale blue to deep orange in a matter of seconds. The color intensity under his skin grew luminescent until it finally burst into flames. I screamed in horror and wanted to run toward him but stopped short. The babies! I turned, and a wall of flames shot up in front of the cribs. I began to scream, not knowing what to do next. My body was shaking, not of my own accord. I couldn't make it stop. I closed my eyes to escape.

When I opened them, I was screaming at Croft, but he was holding my shoulders and calmly saying my name over and over. "Janie? Janie, sweetheart. Janie…"

My head fell on his chest, and I started sobbing. He rocked me for a moment until I froze and resisted.

"They died. They died in a fire, didn't they?"

I pulled back for reaction and answers.

"Didn't they Croft? You tell me right now!"

"Yes, but…"

"Anson, my husband's name was Anson. Did I have twins? Were they blond? What were their names? How old were they?"

"Hold on Janie, one at a time. Yes, you were married to Anson McAvoy for twelve years."

He swallowed to catch his breath and decide what to say next. I flared and pushed him back away from me. "Don't lie to me, Croft. You better tell me what happened."

50

In a calm whisper he spoke, "I'm not lying to you, Janie. I've never lied to you. I will tell you everything you want to know. The council thinks it may be too soon, but I don't care. It has to be torture trying to remember your life. Just take a deep breath and ask me one question at a time. I will try to elaborate where I can. But you have to trust me if I tell you there are some things you need to remember yourself in your own time."

"That's fine, as long as you tell me everything I need to know."

Croft shook his head knowing his last advice would go unheeded.

My eyes welled with tears again. "Tell me about my family."

"As I said, you were married to Anson McAvoy for twelve years. You had twin daughters named Delilah and Sequoia. Yes, they were the most beautiful little blond girls. Delilah had sparkling green eyes like her momma and Sequoia had one green eye and one that was more aqua colored. She was quite stunning to see in person. Sequoia's hair was a little more strawberry and always stuck to the side of her head. Sequoia was funny. She made everyone laugh. Delilah was much more serious. She loved to talk to people. You know, like an old soul."

He smiled a fond smile like he knew her.

"How old were they when they, um, died?" I could barely choke out the words.

"Your husband was bringing the girls to meet you at your school."

I raised my eyebrows in question.

"Do you remember that you were a teacher?"

I tried to recall. I could not grasp a specific memory, but I remembered the feeling of it, of standing in front of a class and young people looking to me for answers.

"Sort of, continue…"

"Anson was a teacher too, but his school let out early that day for a state sports tournament or something. You were scheduled to pick up the girls but had an important school board meeting to go to. He had an appointment, so he picked them up from their school and drove to your school. He had switched cars with you that morning so he could recharge your car. Anyway, he pulled in front of the school, and the office called to tell you he was there. As you walked out of the building, the car…"

He stopped and rested his head on his fingertips, squeezing his eyes tightly shut to stop any tears that might escape.

"The car WHAT?"

"…exploded."

As Croft got to the last word, I felt a flash of hot air on my face followed by the memory of a very hot wind and debris blowing toward me. My hair blew out from my face, and it felt like I inhaled black smoke. I closed my eyes and saw my husband burn. I couldn't see the children. They must have been too short to see their heads. The hope of being a mother, now extinguished.

My words screamed in my head but came out barely audible. "They all died. My family--burned. This can't be real. My little girls, my--and Anson."

I fell forward onto the blanket and sobbed. I wheezed in and out. *Breathe...don't forget to breathe.* The truth was like venom invading my heart and filling it with new poison. I pounded my fists on my head to relieve the pressure of this new-found memory. Croft grabbed me by the wrists until I stopped and stared at him. He pulled my wrists up around his neck and then slowly put his arms around my waist, pulling me closer to him. As his arms coiled around me, I sunk into his embrace and let my arms slide around his neck. He was my balm. I didn't try to analyze what it meant, I just let his presence tranquilize me into a newer peace.

My brain didn't rest long. "Is that why I don't remember anything?" I asked into his shoulder.

"No Janie that was only the beginning."

I distanced myself enough to see his face. "The beginning of what? My God, what else is there?" I shook my head trying to decide if I really wanted to know. "Better or worse? Does it get better or worse?"

He put his hand on my hand.

"Better...and worse. Your life has not been easy, but you are a scrapper. You never give up on anything. Janie, you are the reason the GC exists. Your words and actions have been the voice of reason amid the chaos." He spoke with such reverence it scared me. I didn't know how to answer. "Never mind, we don't need to get into that now. You need to know that your life is not all terrible and once you remember, it will all make sense. It will be okay."

"How can this be okay? My whole family died. How can that be okay?"

"That's not what I mean. What I mean, sweetheart, is that you have already been through this. You have already grieved. It breaks my heart to see you have to experience it again, but you made it through the first time. I think once you remember you won't have to do all of it again. I mean your grieving period should be shorter."

Suddenly something felt strange. "Wait, how do you know me? How is it that you know so much about my family and about me?"

"You are my best friend." Croft shyly dropped his head as if there were more and then suddenly looked up. "We taught together for almost 20 years. I was there when you met your husband, and when you married him. I was there for the birth of your babies. I was there for their deaths too. Well, for...never mind."

"What? Why did you stop?"

"I probably shouldn't tell you this, because it may be insignificant, and I don't want to encourage any false hopes, but you knew it before, so what can it hurt? They didn't find all the bodies."

"What do you mean?"

"Several witnesses saw your girls in the backseat of the car, but their bodies were never recovered. The coroner offered some feeble excuses as to why they weren't found, but Janie, some still believe your girls are alive."

"What? Maybe you should lead with that."

"It's not fact, it's a hypothesis. I mean there are rumors, but nothing concrete."

"So, my children are alive?"

"No, I'm not saying…we don't know for sure, Janie."

"And Anson? Did they find Anson?"

"Yes, it is certain that Anson died that day."

My fleeting hope vanished. I knew it was false hope. The image of him burning in my mind was seared into my soul. How did I survive that image before? I didn't even remember him or why I loved him, but the loss of him was profound.

"Okay, but go back for a minute. You said he switched cars with me that day?"

"Yes, the council believes the explosion was meant for you."

"Me? Why would anyone want to kill me?"

"Oh sweetheart, I want you to take this as a compliment. Believe me when I say, A LOT of people want to kill you."

I don't know why, but this made me laugh.

"And there is one more thing I think you should know right now…"

Suddenly there was a loud pounding on the door. "Croft, do you have her in there with you? Where is she?"

Croft bounded to the door and jerked it open to find Trey sweaty faced and agitated.

"She's fine, she…"

Trey leaned to look over Croft's shoulder. Noticing him, noticing me in nothing but a robe sitting on what was apparently Croft's bed and not mine, my face turned crimson. I didn't know why I should be embarrassed, but I sensed that Trey was not happy to find me there. Trey had tried to forge some claim on me, the likes of which were too difficult to figure out in the aftermath of Croft's words.

"Charlotte sent me to get you both for dinner." Trey's voice got suddenly softer as he leaned into Croft's ear. I pretended that I couldn't hear.

"There have been some new developments in Indie too."

Croft almost turned to look back at me but then thought better of it. I knew it must have something to do with me or something they didn't want me to know yet. Trey leaned back and looked coolly around the room. The solidarity ended there. They wanted to be on each other's side so they could both be on my side, but a rivalry had started that would not soon be ended.

"Um, I would love to go eat, but I'm sort of lacking clothes."

Croft laughed.

Trey wanted to laugh but forced a smile instead, "I was pretty young, but do you remember when we actually bought clothes at a store?"

"They still do in the Collection," Char interjected as she joined them in the doorway.

Even though I don't think Trey meant it in a derogatory way, Croft was bothered.

"Well, I wasn't quite as young, but I do remember. I remember working my ass off for less money and less respect every year. I remember watching friends and family join the Collection, regardless of who was left to pick up the pieces. I remember countless friends leaving education during the pandemic, or worse dying. I remember..." Croft stopped his tirade as he looked at Char and realized for the first time she was there. "Hi Charlotte, we just got your message. I ran into Sparky a while ago and he set me up, but can you tell me where to find some clothes for Janie?"

"No, but I can tell Janie where to find them. Come on, dear."

She held her hand out to me and grabbed mine as I came near. Charlotte Gage was petite but mighty. I quickly gleaned that people didn't mess with her. She shot a suspicious look at both Croft and Trey, then holding my hand walked us between them. As we walked past and into the hall, she forced her gaze forward, not acknowledging their presence.

"See you at dinner, boys." Then she looked at me out of the corner of her weathered sweet eyes and winked.

54

# 17 ~ Here's Granny

Delilah followed Ryker willingly but cautiously through Indie City. She was so distracted and irritated by him, she could barely make sense of her thoughts. She didn't think he would hurt her, but Delilah didn't have the luxury of trust to frame the experience.

Ryker commanded attention. He was three inches shy of six feet, but his stockiness was all muscle. His forearms were wider than Delilah's thighs and covered in tattoos and gray hair. One tattoo in particular stood out to Delilah. It was a large tree whose roots began above his elbow. The lowest left branch curled down and around toward the trunk to form the letter G and the lowest right branch curved around to form the letter C. In between the branches were several different scientific symbols. The tattoo was an oxymoron to the personality of Ryker. His brawn often overshadowing his brain.

He was walking as fast as his burly frame would carry him. Delilah was skip-walking to keep up. She knew she could outrun him, but she didn't want to seem too anxious. She kept trying to get a better glance at his tattoo. She wanted to ask what it meant, but every time she caught up, he increased his gait. Delilah finally slowed a bit in protest to see if he would slow with her. Noticing his short white hair grazing over the scalp rolls on the back of his thick neck made her silently chuckle. Ryker was a funny combination of a man, but she would never laugh in his presence. As her eyes squinted in thought, she saw three unusual dots across the right side of the bottom neck roll.

Young Indies speculated in hushed tones over the meaning of the three dots since they had seen them on others. Delilah flashed back to the last day she saw her father. He had been taking her and her sister to meet their mother. From the back seat, she noticed three dots on the side of her father's neck. They looked like small moles, but she had never seen them before, and they were in perfect symmetry to each other. She was getting ready to ask him what they were when her grandmother approached their car.

"Anson, I need the girls for a minute. I have a little something for them in the car."

"We are picking up Janie. Why don't you bring it over?"

"I don't see why they can't come to my car?"

"I don't think Janie would like it. I guess…"

Sequoia kept talking to Delilah, so Delilah couldn't hear the whole conversation, but Anson finally gave in and told his girls to hurry back. When they got to their grandmother's car, a tall black van drove up and blocked the view of their father's car. Four men jumped out and grabbed Delilah and her sister. Her grandmother willingly got in the van.

As they drove away, the girls kicked and struggled and called for their father. Grandma Chandler told them that their father and mother were in some trouble and that she was going to take care of them for a while. She tried to be soothing and calming, but that had never been her grandmother's forte.

"You have to trust me that this is for the best," Delilah's grandmother had insisted.

"Did they tell you to take us?" Sequoia had asked. Her Grandma Chandler didn't answer.

So much had happened since then. Delilah knew she couldn't rehash any more of the last four years at that moment, but the three dots on Ryker's neck made her afraid. Besides Ryker, everyone she knew who had the three dots was dead.

After walking through the first-floor library, they entered a system of hallways. Stairs led in every direction. Delilah remembered playing in the east stairwells when she first arrived at Indie City. Suddenly, the flashing lights in the corridor changed from yellow to red. Ryker turned to grab Delilah's arm. As he glanced back, Delilah saw his conflicted expression. His narrowed eyes hid his emotion. He was hurried and scared and maybe even confused. Delilah thought he seemed angry too, but then Ryker was always cross with someone.

"Where are you taking me?"

"Listen young'un, we don't have time for questions. Just keep up."

"No!"

Delilah stopped abruptly and yanked her arm away from Ryker, massaging her wrist.

"You're hurting me. Where are you taking me?"

"You are your mother's girl, aren't you?"

Delilah began to tear up at the mention of her mother. "What do you know of my mother?"

"Probably more than you, Dee Dee," Ryker snapped with sarcasm.

Delilah froze at the mention of the nick name her mother had given her. How could he have known that name?

"Where did you hear that?"

Ryker started walking. Delilah quickly followed.

"Wait, I'm talking to you."

"Well, you better keep up then."

"Why can't I go back to my pod?"

The off shoot of the corridor made a sharp left. Ryker heard Delilah's footsteps and didn't even look back to see if she was still following. As the hallway ended, he flung open a large metal door. Delilah was blasted with sunlight. Ryker turned to grab her hand again.

"Come on girl, we gotta hustle now."

He dragged her across a small courtyard. The remnants of an old overgrown garden tripped her as she ran behind Ryker. On the far side of the courtyard was another metal door. Ryker kicked it three times with his boot, and someone opened it from inside. A young man dressed in a bright green jumpsuit held the door for them to walk through. Delilah stepped through, into a loading dock with large metal doors that rolled up into the ceiling. Lining the outer walls of the space, were immense trucks with jaws in back that opened into huge compartments. Teams of people in green jumpsuits unloaded wooden trays of fruits and vegetables and put them on large rolling carts that Delilah recognized from the food storage area.

Ryker grabbed Delilah's hand and yanked so hard her hair flew out behind her. He dragged her through a maze of trucks, carts, people, and large support posts. She called to Ryker, but he couldn't hear her over the white noise of the massive over-head fans. Finally slowing to catch his own breath, Ryker motioned with his free hand to a small antique truck painted with gray urban camouflage that was parked outside the large roll top door labeled BAY FOUR. It sat very low to the ground. The windows were darkened, and any markings or insignia had been removed.

Outside, the noise of the fans was barely noticeable. Delilah couldn't get over the fact that she had never seen this area of Indie City before. She could see the old remnants of a large sign across the vast cement lot. A star with swirls on either side, sat on top of it. Underneath was a sign with some letters missing, MALL OF _ _ERIC_. Ryker continued dragging Delilah toward the vehicle.

"Yer chariot awaits, young'un."

"Wait, stop dragging me! Stop giving me orders! You are going to tell me where I'm going and why, and you're going to tell me right now!"

Ryker turned to Delilah, got close enough for her to name his eyebrow hairs, and whispered, "Granny's in town."

# 18 ~ Celebrity

Charlotte took me through a maze of corridors to a beautiful room with a tall ceiling and glassy orange walls. Lining the walls were natural wood drawers and mirrors. The middle of the room had orange velvety seats and long racks of clothing with the markings of numbers and letters. We walked between the rows of beautifully hand sewn garments. The craftsmanship and artistry of each piece was impeccable.

"Let's see now, you're taller than I thought, you must be about an H10. Do you see anything you like?"

"Yes, all of them." I laughed faintly.

"Well, pick out a few outfits, at least five or six for now."

"I can just take them?"

"I'm sorry dear, I forget you haven't officially been in a GC since..."

"Croft said that earlier. What is a GC?"

"Oh my, we do have a lot to catch you up on, don't we? Nevertheless, you can take what you want. I think this lavender smock and denims would look lovely on you. What a compliment for your strawberry locks and green eyes. You are quite pretty. I can see why the boys are fighting over you."

"What do you mean?"

"Oh, come now, you must see how even young Trey can't take his eyes off you."

"Trey? How old *is* he?"

"Twenty-seven."

"Twenty-seven. Oh, how old am I?"

Char put her hand on my face and stared at me with a look of pity I don't think I could ever get used to. "Janie, you are forty-seven."

"Really? I don't feel forty-seven."

"What do you think forty-seven feels like?"

I giggled, "I don't know."

"Well, then you're doing pretty well, aren't you?"

58

"Forty-seven, I never would have guessed that--and Croft?"

She smiled and her eyes narrowed in approval. "Forty-seven."

I hugged the three outfits I had picked out and buried my face in them.

"Sweetie, are you okay?"

"I don't even know how old I am. How pitiful is that?"

Charlotte put her hand on my shoulder.

"I forget how old I am all the time."

I smiled at her efforts. "Yes, but you know your name without anyone having to tell you."

"Most days." She grinned. "It's okay, I know this is overwhelming, but you are too hard on yourself. It takes some escapees months to remember."

My look of surprise startled her, and Char shook her head in disgust with herself.

"I'll tell you what, let's take you back so you can get dressed. We can always come back for more clothes later. I want you to meet with the GC so you can get some answers that will satisfy you."

"That sounds perfect."

On the way out of the orange room, Charlotte touched a small black shiny screen by the exit and spoke into it, "Gather the council, she is ready."

Croft met us in the hall on the way back to my room, his sweet blue eyes filled with concern. Smiling briefly at me, he turned to Charlotte in a hushed voice.

"I heard the announcement. I don't know if she is quite ready yet."

I shoved between them. I wanted to correct him, but his expression wouldn't let me. And his smell, I don't know what it was, it just smelled like home--as if I knew what that was. I was heady with his aura as I stared into his eyes and almost forgot what I was going to say. Summoning myself I stepped back to collect my thoughts. I glanced at the red tiled floor and then lifted my eyes without lifting my head.

"I *am* ready."

My conviction was suddenly so strong it made me shake.

"Croft, she needs some answers. It might help her to remember."

"Or we could end up with another Lucky Pete."

"She is much stronger than that."

"Thank you, Charlotte, for the vote of confidence."

Croft looked at me with sincerity, "Of course you are strong, honey. Janie Chandler McAvoy never backed down from anything. You have accomplished everything you ever set your mind to. I know you can handle this too. Forgive me."

"Forgiven."

Croft's light eyes reflected even the dimmest light in the hallway. He held out his hand, "Shall we?"

I smiled unconsciously and grabbed his hand. He squeezed mine with delight. Charlotte smiled to herself, pretending not to notice. When we turned the last corner to my room, I noticed Trey sitting on the floor outside my door. Looking up at my hand intertwined with Croft's, Trey's eyes caught mine. I was embarrassed and indignant at the same time. Croft, almost jubilant now, spoke. "Trey, my good man, I wondered where you had wandered off to."

"Just collecting my thoughts. I wondered the same about all of you."

"I needed some clothes." Lifting the arm with the outfits draped over it. "Now, I'm going to get dressed and then get some answers." I turned to Charlotte. "Will there be food at the council meeting?"

Charlotte and Croft laughed, but Trey remained silently staring at Croft, then me, then our hands. I let go of Croft's hand, opened the door to my room, looked back at all of them in silence, and closed the door. I could hear muffled talking outside the door but couldn't make out what they were saying.

I went straight to the bathroom to get dressed. Finding a brush and hair accessories in a drawer I brushed through my still damp hair and put it back into a low ponytail. The floor was cold on my feet, but it was comforting to their soreness. I glanced down at the white tile and noticed the dirt from my sweater was gone. My guess was Croft cleaned it up. Realizing I didn't have underwear, I went back into the bedroom. On a whim, I opened all the drawers in the dresser by the bed. Each one was filled with undergarments, socks, and personal items. I glanced at the door, wondering who had done this and saw several pairs of shoes lining the wall by the door. Next to the door was a small desk and chair. On the desk were books, paper and pens, a tech screen and box of tissue. Wow, someone had been busy.

I finished getting ready in the outfit Charlotte had picked out for me and slipped on a pair of gel filled sandals. My damaged feet relished the sensation, and my pain was instantly relieved. As I opened my door, Croft, Trey, and Charlotte abruptly stopped their heated discussion and smiled strained smiles at me. I stared briefly, with a blank expression. "Everyone ready?"

I don't know why, but I was feeling bothered, so I walked past them to get away from whatever drama they were embroiled in, and then realized I didn't know where I was going. I stopped to let Char take the lead. I didn't understand why I was feeling so childish. I liked Croft, a lot, especially for someone I didn't remember. Maybe I was just infatuated with Trey, since he was so good looking, but I couldn't get over the fact that he seemed to be attached to me. I can't say I didn't like the attention from them both, and yet I was annoyed by it too. While it was flattering and fun, it also reminded me my husband had died. I missed Anson, even though I didn't remember much of him. I hoped I wasn't always surrounded by so much drama.

As I walked in the middle of the pack to the council meeting, my eyes filled with tears. I didn't want anyone to see. I swallowed hard and tried to swipe my eyes quick to get rid of the evidence. It felt like everyone was looking at me. Taking a deep breath, I choked down my questions, my mourning, and my confusion and buried it deep to awaken at what I was sure would be an inopportune time in the future.

# 19 ~ Dodging

The unrepaired road was aggravating Aviva who detested riding anywhere. In the Collection she had a fast, smooth ride, and the means to fly for longer trips. However, she knew she couldn't get near her destination without being detected in anything that flew, so the last few miles had to be on the road. It couldn't be helped. With recent news her daughter was taken before the re-programing sequence started, she was in a snit, and determined to find her runaway granddaughter.

Collectors had been gathering intelligence in old Minnesota for several months and could sometimes intercept radio static. They couldn't decipher it and they couldn't pinpoint it. Every time they thought they had found the source they came up with nothing. Tired of second-hand information, Aviva believed she had the nose to sniff out the truth. She could not possibly know how close she was to Indie City and the unraveling of at least part of the GC.

Delilah shuddered at Ryker's words. In the past few years, she had learned many things about her grandmother that shocked and scared her. But more than any rumor was the hard truth of what her grandmother had done to her sister, Sequoia. Delilah and her twin had lived comfortably, but not peacefully with Aviva Chandler for two years. The answers Aviva gave to their many questions about their parents, had not been enough to appease the girls, especially Delilah.

She had just started to feel at home in Indie City, and now had to face the possibility of seeing her grandmother again. Suffice to say, Delilah's last conversation with her grandmother was not something she wanted to re-live. Fear and anger twisted her insides as she thought about what she would say and what she would do if she ever saw her grandmother again.

Delilah was still jogging to keep up with Ryker as they approached the gray truck. Delilah grabbed his arm, and her thumb touched the trunk of Ryker's tattoo. She stopped herself from yelling at him, thought of the meaning of his tattoo and the meaning of the three dots on his neck, and changed her approach.

"Please, I know you're trying to help me. Everyone wants to help me, but no one wants to give me answers. Please Ryker, please tell me where I'm going. People have lied to me for years. I want the truth. Don't I deserve to know?"

Ryker's eyes softened.

"Miss Delilah, it's not a question of deserve, but we're shy of time. I'm going to tell ya what I can in the next two shakes. Yer grandma weren't always so mean. It wasn't 'til yer grandpa passed, rest his soul, that she flipped. Her sadness swallowed 'er up, and she became meaner than a chicken in heat. Now that's no excuses, cuz I know some of what she put you through, I jist wanted you to know. W'tever fond memories I have, or you might have…"

"I don't have fond memories."

"Either way, I'm tellin' ya, she is not that girl. I don't think she'll find Indie City, but if she does, you can't be here. Yer the prize pig, and you best be leavin' 'fore she gets here."

"But what I wanted to know was…"

Suddenly the large bay doors began to close. Ryker looked around nervously and opened the door to the gray truck.

"Listen Dee, ya got a great driver here. You'll be safe. I know this ain't enough, but it'll have to do. Hop in now."

Delilah turned to look inside the cab of the old truck to see a slender handsome young man. She turned to ask another question and Ryker was already running back to the bay doors.

She called across the lot, "But where am I going?"

"Lord willin' and the creek don't rise—safely away!"

Delilah, confused and feeling betrayed, stepped up into the passenger seat. The lanky boy smiled more happily than warranted and reached across to shake her hand.

"Howdy, my name's Bodhi."

# 20 ~ Under a Microscope

The meeting room for the Growing Community Council was spectacular. Before we even got to the entrance an intoxicating aroma of orange spice grabbed me. As I walked in, I was struck immediately by the contrast of the oak floor with the centerpiece of the room, an enormous round white table. Seemingly growing from the center of the table was a twelve-foot silver tree with niello washed carvings. Leaves carved of pine and turquoise hung from the branches of the metal structure.

I was so taken with the tree, I didn't realize the conversation had stopped, and all attention was on me. I wanted to appreciate the beauty of it but was distracted by an inscription on the trunk of the tree:

*"...We must be tenacious, or as we have seen, truth dies with comfort. We, each one of us, are the sentries of truth and knowledge. The keepers of the past, and the shepherds of the future. That is our calling. We can't give up now. Who will be left to share knowledge and inspire the curious, if not us? You say you don't know where we start to fix this? That is where we start! We don't go back. We bring the past with us, and we start from here."*

*~ Janie McAvoy*

Suddenly I was alone in the center of the room. I felt the room spinning around me as I twisted side to side scanning the sea of faces along the edge of the round room. I could not make sense of why words attributed to me were etched on the tree. My pulse quickened and a fine sweat broke out on my forehead. Then, as if he had been summoned Croft was at my side.

"Janie, look at me."

I heard his words but couldn't look. He gently put his hands on either side of my face and turned me toward him.

"Janie, look at me."

His pale blue eyes soothed me. *Oh la mer.*

"I know this is a lot to take in. I was hoping to talk to you more before you were brought here, but I didn't want you to think I was keeping

64

anything from you. I want you to have the answers you need, but everyone will understand if you need some time to digest this."

I closed my eyes and soaked in the peace I felt near Croft. Taking a deep breath, I decided I must move forward. I could cry and collapse and be overwhelmed again but that would get me nowhere. This was my life. This was my past and my future, and the sooner I listened and learned about it, the sooner I might remember my whole life story.

Croft knew all my revelations in my crooked smile. I placed my hands over his and removed them from my face but didn't let them go. Charlotte was suddenly standing next to me.

"Come on, Janie. Let's sit down and get you something to eat."

I hadn't even noticed the food that had been laid out around the table at each place setting. I dropped one hand and held on tightly with the other as Char led us to some seats. Croft sat on my left and Charlotte stood behind me giddily whispering in my ear.

"Normally, we serve ourselves, but we had so many volunteers that wanted to get a glimpse of you, we decided to let them prepare the meal and serve it."

Croft interrupted, "Char, is that necessary? She is already overwhelmed. She doesn't need any gawkers. Can't we ask those not on the council to leave?"

"We could, but that would mean Trey would have to leave too and I don't think he will go without a fight."

Croft grumbled, "Well, that's up to Janie. He can only stay if she wants him to stay."

I should have known Trey was not far away. He must have been there the whole time. I don't know how I could miss a 6-foot-4-inch chiseled ebony statue, especially in the glowing light of the room's rotunda.

Trey jumped in. "Oh, I'm staying all right. I mean, if it's okay with you, Janie? May I stay? I want to stay. I think I should stay, for you."

I nodded absentmindedly. Trey tried not to smile but he couldn't help himself. He grabbed a chair and attempted to sit to my right when Charlotte purposely stepped in front of the chair and sat down. "Trey, you are such a gentleman. Thank you so much." Thwarted, he grabbed another chair to sit to the right of Charlotte.

I don't even remember what I ate. I know there was some type of fish and lots of beautiful fruits and vegetables. While eating, I found myself slowing and listening to the discussion around me. Trey enthralled everyone with his dissertation on the merits of the wax bean and he squeaked like a little girl when a tray of kiwi appeared. His expressive face made the lackluster subject matter so much more appealing.

I was lost in the moment until Croft scooted so close to me, we were touching from ankle to shoulder. The hint was obvious. I leaned back and looked to the floor to remember the man who had rescued me--the man who had been a part of my entire adult life. He was my best friend and my guide, and something else. And Trey? Well, Trey was cute. I hoped I wasn't this fickle all the time.

I couldn't look Croft in the eye. I knew I would get lost in the deep galaxy of intention behind his stare. So, I shoved most of a roll in my mouth instead. My eyes watered a bit as I realized the enormity of the roll and my inability to chew it. I could see a smirk on Croft's face out of the corner of my eye which I tried not to acknowledge but when he snickered, I almost spit out my roll.

Trey mistook our giggling as an evaluation of his story and stopped abruptly which was more obvious than he intended. I looked around to find a topic to fill the void and my eyes once again landed on the silver tree. My tunnel vision returned, and I knew exactly what I wanted to say. I motioned with my head to the silver tree as I swallowed the remains of my roll.

"Did I really say that?" Their silence answered my question. "And why is it carved in a tree?"

Croft offered first. "I told you, honey, you are important to a lot of people, to the cause."

"What cause is that exactly?"

Char jumped in. "Let's back up a little. Do you know that you were a teacher, Janie?"

"Croft told me."

"Well, you and almost everyone in this room were teachers at one time."

"Are they not anymore? Am I not anymore?"

"There are no more teachers, well not like before. We all became too big of a threat to the politicians."

Croft interjected again, "Well, at first it wasn't teachers that were the threat, it was the unions. However, the politicians saw we weren't going to slink into the woodwork and got nervous. Legislation after legislation passed without discourse and then all hell broke loose. You see there was an undercurrent all along, a campaign if you will. The object was not even re-election, it was annihilation of all opposition. It wasn't only teachers that were targeted at first, but the whole of the middle class. Janie, you told me once that money was power, but not as powerful as the people when they rise up together."

A shiver went down my spine. Those words felt familiar but still not like my own.

Croft continued, "So that's what the teachers did, they rose up."

"How could teachers be a threat to anybody?"

Croft answered again, "Because we're the purveyors of knowledge. More importantly we taught students how to find it themselves. It's harder to deceive a well-educated public, so get rid of the educators and the knowledge goes with them. Or so they thought."

"What do you mean? It's not like all knowledge is in schools. Can't students at least read books or search on the internet?"

"Well sure, there are books approved by the New Congress and government-controlled information systems."

"So, why did the public accept that?"

Charlotte jumped in before Croft could answer. "By the time it happened Janie, teachers were thought to be greedy and evil, with a diabolical plan to indoctrinate their students. They were called Marxists and labeled as puppets of the government, and yet also against the government, depending on which side you were on. Rumors, conspiracies, and misinformation pumped through social media, and the issues around the pandemic, just exacerbated all of it. They—we had been so vilified in the public arena that it was a relief when we went away."

"Went away," Croft scoffed. "When we were fired, fell ill, and taken away was more like it."

"I don't understand. How could the people, the students, the parents stand for it?"

"The older students revolted at first, but they were subdued with threats and brainwashing," Croft continued. "The college students, well they had it rough. They were so passionate because of…let's just say because they stood up to be counted. Many of them died."

I felt a resentment growing deep inside that felt familiar. I sat silently processing for a moment and shaking my head. "I can't believe this could happen. Didn't anyone speak for us and for the students?"

Simultaneously Croft, Charlotte and even Trey exclaimed, "You did!"

"Oh. I did?"

"Yes, and people listened to you because you had more to lose than anyone. I mean you had already lost so much," Charlotte corrected, "and in spite of it all and in spite of your mother, you were not afraid to speak out."

My eyes widened as Croft looked past me to flash Charlotte a look of warning. He then grabbed the sides of my chair and turned it, so I was facing him. I looked deeply into his eyes and almost wanted to laugh at his intensity.

I chuckled. "Aaaaaand what about my mother?"

Croft lowered his head. I supposed he was relieved I wasn't falling apart. He then leaned back with a wide smile, and I smiled back waiting for his answer. He just kept beaming at me. My heart started to flutter.

"You were saying?"

Croft roared in delight, "This is my Janie. I can feel you coming back."

Still smiling, I reprimanded through my teeth, "So, is it like me to get agitated when someone avoids my question?"

"Yes, completely."

Finally Charlotte slid her chair around next to Croft, so she was facing me too, followed by Trey. I had my small fan club surrounding me smiling, but still no one offered an answer to the question hanging in the air. *Who was my mother?*

# 21~ Subterfuge

"Pull over!" Aviva barked. "What is that monstrous building ahead?"

"Nothing, it's abandoned," stammered Braeden.

"How do you know this?"

"We've searched this area extensively. There is no heat signature, no movement, no energy spike, nothing. Plus, no one is stupid enough to come this far north anymore."

"Has the building actually been searched?"

"Um, yeah, as much as we can."

"What do you mean, as much as you can?"

"Well, there are some old civil riot barricades still up at several entrances."

"Several? Don't you find that odd? Are you sure they are old?"

"Yes, mom, geez. It's been addressed already. And no, it's not odd. This was one of the last battlegrounds in the war before the New Congress was formed."

"If you were my employee and not my son, you wouldn't be talking to me like that. Don't you sass me, Braeden. I've got no patience for it today. I think we should take a look. There have been a number of communication static interceptions from this area, and this is a viable place for a large group of people to live. This is the only monument we have seen in miles that is even remotely close to the last trail of…"

"Mom, listen, there are still land mines and booby traps at places like this. Sentries are not gonna hide someplace this obvious. It's not worth the risk. We have checked it all out before. I think we should move on!"

"Braeden Horace Chandler, I will tell you when it's time to move on. Now, pull over right now!"

Braeden slammed on the breaks. Aviva pushed the button on her arm rest to lower her tele-communication screen from the ceiling of the car. As she talked with her Collection advisors on the screen, she ignored the events unfolding right in front of her. A small dust cloud appeared in the distance. Braeden squinted and focused on a vehicle approaching. Panic grew in his stomach. Knowing Aviva would soon make the same discovery, he raised the black shield between the front and back seats. She was too busy in her discourse to notice. Suddenly, the approaching vehicle stopped and turned off the old broken interstate and into the wilderness. Braeden took a deep breath and let his mind wander. He knew it was probably a GC vehicle and he shuddered at the thought of Aviva's discovery of such. Placing his sweaty palms on his knees he recalled the last time his heart pounded with such anticipation.

It had been six months since he had accidentally stumbled upon his sister. Janie wasn't closest to him in age, but in relationship they were "bread and butter" as she used to say. He loved his sister Sage, but it was Janie who mothered him, especially after the death of his father when Braeden was only four years old. Braeden barely remembered his father, or the mother that Janie had talked about from her younger years. It was Janie who raised him, so he was naturally traumatized to see his sister's lifeless looking body in a room full of unconscious patients strapped to their beds. Braeden had been told his sister was missing and presumed dead. He never imagined that his mother could be responsible for kidnapping and drugging her.

For months Braeden had felt uneasy about his mother's dealings. He had begun a quiet investigation under the guise of wanting to learn more about every aspect of the business. It was an accidental discovery that brought him to the truth. At that point, Braeden Chandler broke ranks and began a silent revolution of his own. It started with his plea to take over what he knew as the Transient Reprogramming Clinic, otherwise known as the TRC. Aviva did not like giving up any control, but since her daughters had already been such a disappointment, she welcomed her son's interest.

Soon after Braeden took over, a barely known member of the Collection became the newest employee at the TRC, Charles Farrell Merot. Many thought Charles was a convert from the New Fundamental Collection, though no one else from New Fundamental had found their way to another Collection. His anonymity was what allowed Braeden to slip him into the position so easily. Braeden tried to forget Charles' real name, even though he had heard it and spoke it many times over the years. Charles was his contact. And though Braeden could pay him handsomely, Charles never took a dime from him.

Braeden visited his sister often, with Charles' help, though Aviva was unaware he knew of his sister's imprisonment with other high-risk figures in the country ward of the TRC. He had stumbled upon it quite innocently on an errand with one of the Collectors who assumed that being Aviva's son, he would know of it. Braeden remembered being completely annoyed at having to stop and see the man's cousin that was an anesthesiologist at the TRC. Not impressed, Braeden reluctantly followed the Collector into the building to use the restroom and discovered an unusually high-tech world inside. Curious, he had asked for a tour.

The lower levels looked like a research lab and offices. Seeing nothing of consequence and bored with the tour, he almost gave up on the last flight of stairs, but his tour guide nurse urged him to see the advances in the upper ward. To his horror, as they stepped into the mint-colored room, he saw rows of unconscious people hooked to several types of machinery. At the TRCs he had visited previously, there had only been conscious, and what he assumed were willing, participants taking part in rehabilitation from the wild into the Collection. His guide bragged of the mind-altering and mind-wiping drugs they had developed to reprogram the most defiant resisters.

Braeden's heart raced at the reality of the situation. He noticed the bars on the high windows and wondered at the crimes of these poor people for them to deserve such intense consequences.

"Why are these patients unconscious? What did they do?"

"Do sir?"

"Yes, why are they strapped down and unconscious?"

"They were teachers, of course."

"Teachers?!"

"Yes sir. What did you think the T stood for? This is the Teacher Reprogramming center, after all."

Braeden felt even more duped than before. He looked down the first row to examine their faces and make up stories in his mind that would absolve his mother when, to his surprise, he saw a swath of long strawberry-blond hair. Trying not to seem too eager, he gently pushed past the nurse to get closer only to discover that the weak, defenseless body hooked up to wires and machinery was his big sister, Janie.

Braeden left knowing he was powerless in that moment. For hours that night, he pounded his fists into his bed. Wiping away tears, he wondered what he could do to save his sister. When he finally fell asleep, he slept restlessly. Finally, waking in a cold sweat, Braeden sat on the edge of his bed with his hands in his wet, sandy brown hair.

*"How could mother do this? My God, Janie…all this time. I'm so sorry. I'm so sorry I didn't know."*

Braeden whispered aloud to himself, trying to make sense, trying to convince himself he hadn't seen what he had seen.

*"It's so fucking hot in here. Why is it so fucking hot in here?"*

He paced back and forth through his bedroom until he felt like he was suffocating. Finally, Braeden threw on jeans and a T-shirt and ran down the long hall of the city home he shared with his mother until he reached the east stair. He raced down the stairs so fast, his feet barely touched the steps. Quickly deactivating the alarm at the east entrance, Braeden burst into the open and choked on a gulp of cool night air.

He ran across the small garden leading to the stone wall and followed it to a fifteen-foot-high iron gate. Waving at the security guard, he pushed through the gate as it opened and ran straight into the busiest street of New Congress City. Luckily, there were few transports at four in the morning. Braeden didn't stop to look for traffic but kept running across the street and into the park facing the east side of Chandler Manor. He may have kept running had he not passed through a small thicket of trees and slammed right into a man crossing his path.

The two men fell hard to the ground.

"Oh shit!"

"Oh shit, is right."

"I'm sorry," Braeden pleaded as he jumped to his feet and offered the man his hand.

The wavy-haired gentleman reluctantly took Braeden's hand. As he stood up into the overhead cast of the orange walkway light, Braeden stepped back in recognition.

"No way, you're…"

"Call me Charles for now."

"Charles, right, okay. What the hell are you doing here, um, Charles? Do you know I live, we live, right across the street?"

"Yes, that's why I'm…"

"Oh my God, do you know about my sister?" Braeden interrupted.

"Do *you* know about your sister?"

"Yes, I mean I didn't until--but now I do. I still can't fucking believe it."

Braeden sat down on a wooden bench next to the walkway. The man who called himself Charles sat next to him.

Braeden turned to him in a panic, "It's not safe for you here. If my mother finds you--oh my God, if she found me talking to you, holy fuck."

"Braeden, I know about Janie, it's okay. I mean, it's not okay but I came here to find you."

"I don't even know what to do. I've got to get her out of there."

"I know, I know, this is what you're going to do…"

Three hours later Braeden ate breakfast with his mother and begged her for some new responsibility, a chance to prove himself as future New Congress. His acting was superb and his back story of wanting this opportunity for years was convincing enough. Aviva's secret hopes were finally realized when her only son volunteered to oversee the TRC.

Suddenly loud, impatient knocking on the glass behind him shocked Braeden out of his memory. He lowered the glass shield afraid his mother had read his mind.

"Why did you raise the security glass?"

72

"Um, well, I heard you on a tele-conference and thought it might help keep the glare down so you could see better."

"Oh, well thank you, son. It turns out you were right. There is more investigating we can do at this location, but there is good concern for snares and even ambush. This is more than you and I can handle. More importantly, Taurus Roma thinks my absence is a convenient time to incite the crowds with more anti-tax rhetoric. We need to get back to the airstrip. We're going to have to hunt for your niece another time."

Braeden breathed a silent sigh of relief that his new friends in the GC would have a little more time. His warning had worked. Luckily, their camouflage was extensive, and from what he could see, it looked abandoned. There were indeed traps had she ventured too close. Knowing what he knew, he felt he could snare his mother if he had to, but it was too dangerous until he knew whether Charles had rescued his sister. All he could do was hope.

# 22 ~ Like, Dude

"I don't mean to be rude, but can you tell me where we're going?"
Bodhi's instant smile and crooked glance put Delilah at ease. He wasn't
bad to look at. In fact, she thought he was nice on the eyes. But her world
was still spinning around her, and she didn't want her driver to distract her
from her question.

"Oh, yeah, sorry. We're going--well, I'm not sure if I'm supposed to
tell you. They have all these stupid rules and whenever I find out
something cool, it's like I'm not allowed to share it anyway. This all just
happened you know. This was never a plan or anything. I guess I was in
the right place at the right time."

"The right place for what?" Delilah insisted.

"Well, I had to drive this arrogant friend of mine on a rescue, and we
were supposed to bring this girl south, but then we got called to the Fox
and he left me and didn't come back. Then these creepers in camo with big
spiders on their shirts, Collectors you know, snuck up on me when I was
taking a leak. I turned around and sprayed them by accident..."

"Ew!"

"Wait, it gets better. I scared the shit out of them too. When I sprayed
them, this tall dude with a white buzz cut jerked his arm. His gun went off
when he jumped back and nailed the other guy in the leg. Then that guy got
so freaked out, he fired back at buzz cut. One of the bullets even took off
the top of my hand."

Bodhi anxiously took off a fingerless glove on his right hand and lifted
the bandage to show Delilah the battle scar, "Look, isn't this cool?
Anyway, before I knew it, they were both dead. Sweet, huh? I mean, not
that they were dead, but that I wasn't and that I still had my hand and uh,
pardon me, my uh, ya know, wiener." Bodhi whispered the last word as he
pointed downward and then burst out laughing. Delilah was amused but
didn't show it. "Sorry, but that was a close one you know." He side-eyed
Delilah and winked.

74

"Anyway, I heard more footsteps, so I ducked behind some bushes. Then these four dudes that didn't look like Collectors--they were wild looking you know, came running up to the truck. They were high fiving and when they saw the dead dudes, they took their clothes and weapons and pushed the bodies down into a ravine. They wanted to take my truck, but I heard 'em talking and none of them knew how to drive. So, they just ran off with plans to come back later.

I was like, *phew*, another close one. I had just got back in my truck when this bad ass chopper flew overhead. It was dark, so I couldn't see it, but I definitely heard it. I was gonna take off, but then I thought maybe they don't see me in here, so I ducked. Two guys repelled down about thirty yards away with some sick looking weapons, so I snuck out my door, slid to the ground and took off running."

Bodhi smiled proudly and nodded at Delilah waiting for her reaction to his story before he continued. Delilah was entertained and annoyed at the same time.

"Wow, that is quite a story. I didn't understand most of what you said, but it sounded exciting. Now, where are you taking me?"

"I'm getting to that, seriously. Anyway, I ran about mile until I came to the enemy camp." Bodhi raised his eyebrows as his injured hand panned across the dash in mime of his discovery. "I was like, shit, cool. There were like twenty guys sitting around a campfire eating, surrounded by a ring of tents. I peeked under the big tent closest to me. Not a soul, but there were a ton of weapons. I grabbed as many as I could carry and made off into the woods when I heard them discover my dastardly plan. *Bum-bum-bum.*" Bodhi sang the last words. "That's when I found this sweet ride. The keys were inside, so I threw the weapons in and took off. They ran after me for like a mile or something until they gave up."

"That actually is a pretty good story, but you're going to have to forgive me. I just left my home, well the place I live, and I'm in a car with a funny, albeit interesting driver, going--I still don't know where. Can you please just tell me where…"

"I know, I know, *where are you taking me*? I'm getting to that." Bodhi mocked in a high-pitched voice.

"Well, I drove all night. I didn't know where the hell I was going. So, I drove north because I knew they probably wouldn't follow me north. I finally came to a groomed field. I knew it had to have been planted, so it must be GC. I found the GC farmer, because I know where to look, you know."

He winked again at Delilah who sat stone-faced.

"Anyway, he directed me here, or back there to Indie City. Now, here is the exciting part, the part you have been waiting for…I am on my way to the big lakes to capture a satellite, and you get to go with me."

Delilah felt no more satisfied at the end of Bodhi's ramblings than she did at the beginning. She couldn't understand why she had to leave with him. She remembered Ryker's words and they twisted her stomach. *"Granny's in town."*

"I'm sorry Brady, why am *I* going with you to get a satellite?"

"Bohhh-deeee." Bodhi ticked his head to the right and then the left as he said each syllable. Then he turned toward Delilah, tipped his head down and peered up as if looking over spectacles and stared at her in disbelief.

Delilah chuckled. "I'm sorry, okay? Bo-deee." She couldn't talk without laughing.

"S'all right. We cool. Here's the thing, I'm not sure why you are going with me except that I was going anyway and then that scary old dude Ryker, with the GC tat said you were in trouble and needed to leave and I was gonna drive you and be like your bodyguard or something. So, I said, cool."

"You're going to be my bodyguard?"

Bodhi didn't own the insult. "Hey, I am more rugged than I look. Besides your friend Ryker told me I was the perfect man for the job. Plus, I am supposed to steer you away from trouble, kinda like I did back there."

He motioned behind him and smiled a triumphant smile. "Did you see that big black beast on the road? That thing was wicked. I knew there were Collectors in the area, but that creeped me out. I have never seen a ride like that before. I want one."

Delilah could tell that Bodhi often talked to fill space, but she was much more introspective. She didn't find use for a lot of endless chatter, but she admired people that could do it as if it were a skill to possess.

"I'm sorry, I didn't mean to imply that you were not up to the job of defending me."

"Yes, you did. But that's okay. You'll see. I'm pretty handy to have around."

Delilah giggled.

"So why a satellite?"

"Aw dude, this is so exciting. I can't believe they are even gonna let me do it. Well, I don't know if the old man got it officially approved or anything, but I think he figured if I was dumb enough to try, why not let me go for it. Seriously, we have been in the dark ages for too long. We need some serious long-range communication, not the stupid tree radios, so we can talk to all the GC and see what is going on out west and everywhere else in the world. No one seems to know where the rest of the world went, and the satellite is the only way we can find out."

"But doesn't the government control all of the satellites?"

"Well, yes, most of the few that are left but there is one control center, in the old Michigan territory that is thought to be abandoned. Well, we don't know for sure, but I gotta find out. This is our best chance."

"So, if you are taking me to a control center that is possibly occupied by the Collection, is that really protecting me?"

"No, but you're not going all the way with me. I'm dropping you off in Euro City."

"Dropping me off? Like a package?"

"Well, yes, kind of I guess?"

"I'm not a package. I'm so tired of being thrown around wherever. You can't tell me where I can go and where I can't go. I don't have to do anything you tell me to. I could get out right here if I wanted."

Bodhi came to a complete stop. The road they had stumbled upon was not in terrible shape considering there had been no road repairs in over thirty years in that region. However, surrounding the road on either side was an endless forest of pine trees.

"Be my guest." Bodhi touched a button on the dash and the passenger side door flew open.

Delilah looked at her surroundings in every direction and then looked at Bodhi to see if he was serious. She inched over like she thought she was being forced out. Bodhi pounded his fist on the same button and her door slammed shut.

"STOP! Geez, I'm kidding okay. You can't leave. Ryker would totally kill me. Listen, I'm not trying to tell you what to do, but I can't take you to the control center either. It's way too dangerous."

"Well, what are you going to do? Go by yourself?"

"No, I'm hoping I can round up a GC posse or something in Euro City."

"What exactly is the GC?"

Bodhi's head flung to the right to stare at Delilah in disbelief. *"What is the GC?!"*

"Yeah, well I've heard it talked about in Indie City, and then I saw Ryker's tattoo and now you keep saying GC, GC, GC, so it must be important."

"Um, yeah, you could say that. GC, the Growing Community? Ring a bell?"

"Not really."

"Where do you think all your food comes from?"

"Uh, I guess I thought it was grown at Indie City."

"Some of it is, yes, but there are small Growing Communities splattered all over the mid-west and the south and even here in the north. I mean, it's more than farmers though. The GC are a state of mind--a philosophy of living. All are equal. All are one in the GC...GC...GC...Ohmm."

Bodhi pulled fake strings from the ceiling as his hands formed into a meditation pose.

"That's not possible?"

"What?"

"All people aren't equal. Some have more talents and skills or more deficiencies than others."

"Wow, back it up. Where did that come from? Just because they are different doesn't make them unequal."

"Um, yes it does, actually."

"Geez Louise, what is equality to you, then? All are equal means no one person is less important than another. It doesn't mean we all have to be the same."

"I'm sorry, I forget myself. I know that--I do. I sometimes, mix things up inside my head. I have had a, well you could say, a confusing upbringing."

"You're confused all right," Bodhi mumbled.

They sat in silence for a few moments while Delilah reflected on her grandmother. Her grandmother had a unique way of talking so Delilah always ended up agreeing with her. Delilah's actions in her grandmother's care were often in direct conflict to the beliefs of her mother and father and to those taught to her in Indie City. It was a struggle to get that thinking out of her head when she first came to Indie City, but she had come far in two short years. She finally broke the silence.

"Bodhi, I'm sorry for interrupting. Will you tell me more about the GC?"

Unsure of how to proceed, Bodhi sat in silent protest for a moment. He wondered who this girl was and how she could be from Indie City.

"If you wanna know, the GC is a lot of things. This lady first started it to feed people after the war, but then it became like this whole other thing where people learn stuff, and it became like a way of living. You've been part of the GC, whether you know it or not."

"Why do the people in the Collection not know of the GC?"

"Because they are not allowed to, uh, duh."

Delilah didn't answer because she knew that was probably true.

Bodhi continued, "We would all, for real, be wandering in the wilderness without the GC."

"How does everyone stay together? I mean, who is in charge?"

"Are you a spy or something?" Bodhi asked the question comically, but it was a serious concern.

Delilah laughed, "No, I'm just curious. This interests me, and it helps me."

"Well, Miss Curious, there is no one in charge. I mean we're all sort of in charge, of ourselves."

"That sounds good on paper, but who takes care of business?"

"Some say the GC also stands for Governing Council."

"What? Like the government?"

"No, no, not like that. They are the smart people who help organize everything and keep us all connected. You know there are like scientists,

78

some master craftsmen, good builders and technicians, some doctors, a couple dentists, veterinarians, mechanics, of course the teachers, and…"

"That sounds like a ship with a lot of captains."

"Think of it like one street in a town. No one is really in charge of that one street. People do as they please."

"Yes, but someone has to make sure there is food in the stores, and trash pickup, and plowing snow in the winter and running traffic lights."

"Ok, or, we all grow our own food and compost, and have a party to all shovel the road together, and well, there isn't any traffic anymore. But yeah, I mean, that's how it works in the GC. It's like a bunch of little micro societies."

"But still, someone must be in charge."

"Ok, if you're gonna keep pushing, I guess the closest to 'leaders' we have are the Sentries. They started the whole thing. They protect the knowledge base."

"What do you mean 'protect' the base? Do they keep it from everyone else?"

"No sugar pie, that's what the Collection does. The Sentries are teachers. They teach what they know and make sure everyone has access to information. They teach us how to think for ourselves."

"So, the Sentries are in charge?"

"No, you're not getting it. They are leaders, but they lead by example, not by bossing people around. None of them feel more important than any other in the GC."

"So, they're communists."

"Woah, what's with the labels? No man, we are past that shit. Ya know, people can live together peacefully, when there isn't rhetoric being shoved down our throats."

Delilah was impressed Bodhi knew the word rhetoric. "Yeah, that's how it is in Indie City--everyone helps everyone. It's so different from how I lived the four years before that, though."

"How did you live before that?"

"Well, I lived in the Collection with my grandmother."

"You lived in the Collection?"

"Yes."

"So, did I, when I was younger."

"You did? You lived in the Collection? Where?"

"I grew up in New Fundamental until the second elimination. And why do you say "you" like I am a virus or something?"

Delilah wheezed out a laugh. "I just mean you don't seem like the Collection type. What's the elimination?"

"Ha, ha very funny."

"No, I'm serious, what is an elimination? Elimination from what?"

"Um, duh, from the Collection of course."

"How do you get eliminated from the Collection?"

"Where did you say you grew up?"

"New Congress City."

"Oh, well, that explains some. I guess I assumed when you said you used to live in the Collection that you were eliminated too."

"Um, no, I was sort of, uh, it's a long story. Anyway, why were you 'eliminated'?"

"You've seriously never heard of an elimination? Well, I guess that's not so strange. I never knew of them either, until I got eliminated. The only people that never had to worry about it were the super-rich. Were you super rich?"

"Yeah, I guess you could say that. Well, I wasn't, my grandmother was."

"Lucky you. Anyway, everyone in the Collection has to pay taxes you know--well except for the super-rich. But once you reach a certain age and you can't work and contribute, you are no longer valuable to the Collection. Families drop off their elder relatives at the retirement transport. The families know they can't ever see their relatives again, but all the geezers still look forward to it because all their needs are met, and they get to have fun gran-n-gramp parties. What the Collection doesn't know is that all the old people are driven out into the wilderness and dropped off to fend for themselves."

"What? No, that can't be true. There is no way that anyone would do that? I mean, no one would drive a bunch of old people out and just leave them."

"Oh, you bet they would. They get paid a lot of money to do it."

"But it's wrong!" Delilah shook her head in disgust. If that had happened, her grandmother would know about it, and Delilah couldn't believe even Aviva would do something so horrendous.

"But you said old people. You're not old."

"No, but the same is true for children. I mean, there is an exception for children until the age of twelve. I started working at my grandpa's orchard when I was five, but my taxes never amounted to anything until I turned twelve."

"You had to work when you were five?"

"Yeah, didn't ya--oh no, 'super rich,' I forgot.

"That's not fair."

"You're right, it's not. It is definitely not fair. I prolly could'a stayed and kept working if the government hadn't taken over the orchard for genetic testing and put my grandpa out of business. He was getting old, so it was convenient for them."

"But how...?"

"The send-off party rocked. We saw videos about all the cool things we'd get to do. My grandparents were okay with it 'cuz they thought it

80

somewhat made up for the orchard and they were getting tired anyway. We left everything we had because we were told that stuff would be waiting for us. We didn't have much anyway. Dude, I was super excited. I had nothing to lose. Still, it was a little sad that nobody came to say goodbye to us."

"What about your parents?"

"My parents died when I was two. If I had any other relatives, I never knew 'em."

Delilah thought of her own parents and was sad that she and Bodhi had something else in common.

"So, it was just me and my grandma and grandpa. There were prolly about twenty old fogies celebrating and a few other kids besides myself. Most of those kids had some serious problems though--you know mentally. That part was sad. Poor kids, it wasn't their fault. But they were gonna be taken care of, so everyone thought it was okay. Anyway, after the party was over and all the relatives left, we were all loaded on to this huge truck with windows. I think it was like a school bus.

We must have gone a hundred miles or so. Everyone kept looking for a village or big building, but there was nothing. Finally, the truck stopped, and they told us to get out. I still remember the faces of the people trying to grab us from the truck. They had bright yellow uniforms. I think it was supposed to be like the happy-mobile, but psych, nope we're the baddies. It kinda helps, ya know, not to think of them as real people, I mean who does that?"

"So, what happened?"

"Everyone was confused and some of the old ladies and kids were crying. They pushed us, the fuckers- with guns at our backs, right off the truck. My grandpa tried to refuse. He sat there holding me tight, with his legs wrapped around the seat. Two big guys pulled me off and held me. It took three of them to get him off the bench and..." Bodhi stopped and swallowed hard. His eyes narrowed and he shook his head to flick off the tears threatening to break free. "...then they threw him. They threw my grandpa right out on the road."

Delilah quietly reached over and put her hand on Bodhi's arm. She took a deep breath, not knowing what to say. She realized her grandmother was the oldest person she knew in New Congress City. She had never thought that strange until that moment.

# 23 ~ Fanclub

Three beautiful faces sat in front of me in the council room. Charlotte, whom I had known for less than a day but whom I felt I could trust to be completely honest. I wanted to say she reminded me of my mother, but the truth was, I didn't know if that were true. Trey, a tall and impressively handsome man who exuded some strange kinetic energy over me that made me uncomfortable. Then there was Croft--*my* Croft.

I was lost in a daydream of him while he stared at me, turning all my senses backward. It became harder to concentrate on what he was to me as I plunged deeper into the pools of his blue eyes. I wanted to know this man, to know him like he knew me. I couldn't yet understand to what depth of human emotion this would push me. Tumbling off the cliff was what I feared, but I wanted to go anyway. I wanted to jump, with him.

I had just opened my mouth to ask a question of Croft when a hand poked through between Char and Trey.

"Hi, I don't mean to interrupt, but you're her, aren't you?" Not realizing I had been leaning forward, I startled and sat back in my chair. A bright young girl with ochre skin, smooth black hair, and brown eyes smiled at me in anticipation. "Gosh you are pretty," she continued.

"Funny, I was thinking the same thing of you."

She grinned wider until Charlotte pushed the girl's outstretched hand down to her side. All faces followed from the girl's face to Charlotte's and then back to mine. I felt it was my volley, but the girl interceded.

"I'm so sorry. I hope it's okay, I wanted to meet you. You have been such a…"

"Malina!" Charlotte scolded.

"No, it's fine," I interrupted. "Hi, Malina. What a gorgeous name. I'm Janie."

Her voice hushed in embarrassment. "It's *so* nice to meet you. Sorry again."

She slunk away as quickly as she appeared, but others followed, each reaching in to shake my hand. I had not realized that so many people were still in the room and moreover were focused on me. Croft, Trey, and Charlotte stood, and Croft put his arms out to gently move the other two back to give me more room. At least forty people of varying ages approached, each one tiptoeing in gingerly, so as not to crowd me. It was sweet at first, but after a while, my eggshell exterior began to crack.

I glanced up a few times to see the reactions of my small crew. Trey watched with keen eyes, following my movements. Charlotte fumed. I could feel her protective shield around me. Finally, Croft, who so often sheltered me, stood beaming from ear to ear. His proud smile made me giggle and remember I was stronger than I thought.

I noticed that the youngest admirers left the room after they spoke to me. When all was said and done, about fifteen people remained and sat around the large table. The oldest was Charlotte and the youngest was Trey. Charlotte called the meeting to order and asked everyone to rise. Croft, who had moved to my right, grabbed my hand to prepare me for something. Then in unison, the entire room began reciting the words on the silver tree--my words.

I realized that how I acted at that moment would define me to the group. "I'm sorry. I don't know what your procedures are here, but I don't really know what to say to all of that. If those are my words, I don't remember saying them. If I know you, I apologize, I don't remember you either. All I know is that the more I see and hear, the more confused I become. I want to tell you all that I understand, this, thing. I don't, but I want to. Does that make sense?"

Everyone laughed sympathetically.

"If it's okay I'd like to ask a few questions."

"Of course, of course you do," a meek voice on the far side of the table suggested.

A slight, older man stepped to his left, so the tree was not obstructing our view. He wore tan pants, a white tee, and a dark plaid jacket. His dark donut ring of hair was frosted in white and did not continue across his forehead. His beautiful black eyes and sienna skin were glowing in the light of the room.

"Hi Janie, we did meet once, but you probably wouldn't remember me anyway. I am of no consequence." The small crowd guffawed. The man smiled in appreciation as he walked toward me around the great table. "I am Chul-moo. I want to offer you some counsel if you would have it. I have walked before in the shoes you walk now."

"You have?"

"Yes."

"You mean you didn't, I mean, couldn't remember anything?"

"No, they didn't syphon my memory, but I was held captive like you. What I have to tell you may help you and it may not. Would you like me to…"?

"Oh please, I would love to hear whatever you could tell me." The whole room was still silent. "Were you in that hospital place--what's it called?"

"TRC," Croft interjected.

"Yes, but I was one of the first. I was gone before you arrived."

Charlotte spoke up, "Chul-moo actually escaped on his own."

"How is that possible?"

Chul-moo continued, "I was one of the first in the TRC. I had some military training when I was younger, and their drugs were weaker then, so the mind control techniques did not work on me. I think I was the reason they opened the country ward. Avi…, I mean that woman…"

He stopped and looked to Croft for approval. Croft shook his head and I immediately felt something was being kept from me, but it was not the right time to ask. Chul-moo looked nervously back to me and continued.

"They couldn't accept failure, so they had to move us to a more remote location away from the Collection. When we first arrived at the country ward we were strapped to gurneys and injected with a saline solution on the initial round of I.V.s. I saw a nurse coming down the row with the heavy stuff and I fought the urge to give up. I'm not inclined toward resignation, you know.

I could see the others, some of whom were my friends, go limp. I was the last bed, so I had a little time to think. I conjured up a few scenarios but being strapped to the table made those impossible. The nurse was only two beds away when she was called out of the room. I roused my friend next to me. His name was Moreau, Jack Moreau, my old friend. We served in the Syrian War together. Anyway, we decided our best chance was to pretend that we had already been injected and hope she forgot. It was a long shot, but since we were strapped down, we had no other choice."

A picture flashed into my head, and I interrupted, "But what about those black claw things I saw attached to the other's legs, to my legs?" I pulled up my pant legs in confirmation and the group gasped as they saw the symmetrically spaced bruises down my shins. They had grown since the day before and the center of each was now dotted with a scab.

Croft came and sat next to me. "Janie, they didn't have those when Chul-moo was there. They were installed as extra security after the first few escapes and as a more efficient way to deliver the drugs."

I let my pant legs drop. "I'm sorry to interrupt. Please continue."

Chul-moo patted my hand in appreciation. "Let's see, where was I?"

"You were playing dead I think."

He smiled. "Yes, we were playing dead. The nurse came back, and we had taken the slack posture of the others. She was confused and pulled up

84

Moreau's arm. He flopped to perfection. She jabbed him with a needle, and he didn't flinch. My poor friend. The worst was when they came to install the catheters. I had to take my mind to another place."

All the men in the room collectively flinched.

"Even with your eyes closed it's much harder to pretend you are not paying attention than you might think, but we listened hard as we let our bodies go soft. At that time, the drugs were only administered every other day, we had overheard, so we knew we had twenty-four hours to make a move. On that second day, they removed our restraints. Luck smiled on us. I guess they thought there was no need to strap down a vegetable. Heh, heh. We waited until the ward was quiet. It was dark in the room, except for the data screens and a low light on the floor. Moreau and I instinctively moved at the same time, disconnecting our wires. There was a door only five feet to my left, but we didn't know where it led. I had seen no one go in or out of that door, so we assumed it could be a way out. As I opened it, the lights in the room suddenly turned on. It was some type of silent alarm. I stepped down onto a bumpy, cold metal staircase."

"I remember that staircase," I shouted. Everyone looked at me in surprise. "Sorry, go ahead."

Chul-moo nodded. "Oh, it was dreadfully cold that night. My bare feet almost stuck to the landing. As Moreau followed me out the door, we heard someone yell, "stop." Then his gown turned red before I even heard the gunshots. It doesn't matter how many people you see die--it breaks something inside you every time, especially a friend like Jack."

Chul-moo paused, and the room bowed their heads. His words pierced an old forgotten wound. He acknowledged the room and continued. "As Moreau fell out of the door, it closed behind him. I turned to him. He was already gone. I hated to leave his body, but I could hear voices in the distance outside and I knew I had to run. My feet slid down those stairs so fast, I almost lost a toe on one of the last steps. I hit the cold ground hard as I tripped and it felt like I broke my nose, but I got up and ran anyway. The soles of my feet still ache when I think of that cold ground.

I had probably run a couple miles when I heard dogs in the distance. I ran through a marsh and a creek so they might lose my scent. I never thought I could be so numb and still run, but I knew I couldn't go much farther in that cold. I was losing feeling in more than my feet. I thought my only hope was to climb a tree and hope I could wrap my thin gown around me until the danger was gone. As I made it to the third rung of branches, I felt a strange subtle vibration. I reached around and cut my hand on a rusty wire. Following the wire, I found a small transmitter. Fearing it was some type of warning system for the TRC I smashed it and threw it some distance away.

That's how he found me. I was half naked and shivering in that tree with the sounds of the dogs getting closer when this old hippie drove up on one of those, um, pardon me, two-wheeler things..."

"Motorcycles!" Croft yelled out jovially.

They both laughed.

"Luck was with me that night. No luck for Moreau but much luck for me. Croft says it was the interruption in signal that helped him find me, but I think Moreau somehow sent him to me."

"Croft saved you too?" I asked.

"Croft has saved many," Charlotte offered.

"I can see that." I stared at him. My savior, my friend. His soft expression cushioned my uneasiness in that room of strangers. I suddenly wanted to be alone with him. I wanted to cuddle up with him in my room and talk. I didn't know what I wanted to say, but I wanted to be out of the spotlight, and I only wanted to be with him. I had more questions for Chul-moo and Charlotte and the others, but all I needed right then was Croft.

Suddenly I felt like the whole group knew my intentions. I pried my eyes away from Croft to address Chul-moo. "Thank you so much. I do want to hear more of your story, but I think I'm just tired and I maybe need some time to process everything."

"Completely understandable."

I turned to address the room. "I know you are all as curious about me as I am about you, but can I go rest for a while?"

Charlotte piped up, "Of course you can. Do you want me to walk back to your room with you?"

I turned to look at Croft. Instinctually, he stepped forward and Char stepped back.

Faces around the room smiled except for the eerily quiet Trey. Croft offered no apologies or salutations. He walked over and reached out for my hand, and together we left the room. Everyone watched us walk away. It was odd and uncomfortable, but at the same time, I liked it. As we stepped into the hallway, I realized I hadn't taken a deep breath in hours. Breathing felt good. I turned and pled to the group, "Thanks everyone. Please don't say those tree words anymore. It's weird." They all laughed. Croft squeezed my hand and pulled me away.

We came to the red path. On each red stone, I placed a quiet hope for my new life. With each hope I tried to imagine how Croft fit into my ever-expanding world. How could I have such strong feelings for this man I barely knew? Then, without warning my face flushed and I felt something deep in the pit of my stomach. A memory dashed through my conscious mind. A touch. It was Croft's hand touching my face. He stared into my eyes and then I saw him lean in to kiss me. I quivered and closed my eyes. I stopped walking and let go of his hand.

"What's wrong? Did you remember something?" he asked, observing my reaction.

"Well, yes, sort of, but I'm not sure I want to talk about it. I'm not sure if it's real or not."

He turned me to face him. "It's okay Janie. It will help you to talk about it. Just ask me. I may be able to tell you if it is a true memory."

"Um, it's kind of complicated. I mean, it's about you."

Croft grinned. "Come on." He grabbed my hand, and we jogged the few remaining steps to my room. As we entered, he kicked the door shut with his foot and my heart began to race. He led me across the room to sit on the bed and grabbed my other hand.

"Janie, there are a few other things you need to know. We…"

"I saw you kiss me," I interrupted.

"Yes. That is true." A silent pause hammered my fluttering insides. "What else do you remember?"

"That's it, except for…" I didn't know how to finish.

"Except for what?"

"Well, I find myself staring at you a lot and I have these feelings that I can't explain. I mean, you said you were, or are, my best friend, but this is kind of embarrassing. These don't feel like friend emo…"

His thumbs skimmed back and forth across the tops of my hands and stopped my thought. I glanced down and allowed myself to feel the velvet of the moment.

"You're still so soft."

"Still?"

Croft smiled a warm loving smile and scooted closer to me. He didn't speak at first, but his eyes voiced all our ancient secrets.

"Janie, we were dating, I guess you could say. I mean, we were starting to fall, uh, just starting things when you were taken."

"Oh, well that explains some things then. I do feel something for you, but I'm not sure what I can offer you right now. It's hard to explain. I mean I feel for you, but I don't remember feeling for you. Does that make sense?"

"You don't need to offer me anything. All you have to do right now, is what makes you comfortable. I don't want anything from you Janie, except for you to be happy and to get your memory back."

"Thanks. I just don't know what to do next."

"Janie, you have been in the conscious world for less than forty-eight hours. For now, concentrate on getting some rest and getting your strength back. I have faith that your memory will come back. You have already done so well, and I know your spirit. You will not give up. You will remember and I will be right here by your side, or as close as you want me to be."

"Right by my side," I confirmed.

"Okay, good. Now why don't you get some rest?"

Croft stood, and I panicked. "Can you, I mean, I don't know if it's okay to ask you, but will you stay with me?"

"Stay?"

"Yes, I don't really want to be by myself. I mean, I would like you to stay."

"Of course, sweetheart."

This 'sweetheart' felt different than the one I heard during my rescue. It was not the friendly gesture of a stranger. It was meant for me. I was *his* sweetheart. Croft reached around and took out my ponytail holder and stroked his hands through my hair to free it. It felt familiar, like he had done it before. Then unconsciously, as if by rote, I leaned forward and kissed him. I startled Croft and myself. We both leaned back away from each other and stared at each other with equal surprise. I giggled and then he giggled but soon I felt the pull again as if our mouths were magnetized.

I was lost in his kiss once more--truly lost. I was no longer grounded but floating somewhere unearthly watching the cluttered path of my life. Then just before I plummeted to oblivion I was suddenly in his embrace. His strong hands held me firmly to him. Such were the next few minutes that stalled as slowly as hours. His lips were so soft, so, so soft. He kissed me harder and then gentler until we stopped and pressed our foreheads together. I felt good. I was happy and confused. I had never felt such passion and love for someone, that I could remember. He pulled our bodies close and rested his head on my shoulder. Contentment.

Croft began to shake, and I could feel him sob. I wanted to ask if he was all right, but I didn't want to let go. I let my arms around him talk for me. He buried his face in my neck and kissed behind my ear. I felt a shiver down that side of my body. Then, increasing the shiver he tenderly spoke. "My God Janie, I still can't believe you are here. I can't believe we made it out of there, and you are here. I have missed you so…"

He broke off and sobbed again. I wanted to talk to him and console him, but I didn't want to spoil the moment, so I continued hugging him in silence. I wanted to remember missing him too, but I couldn't. I didn't know that feeling. I didn't miss anything but my memory. I reached deep and the dream of my husband and daughters rose to the surface. I couldn't even remember missing them specifically. I had no emotion for them beyond the pain of their loss. It made me feel suddenly sad. Knowing me better than I knew myself Croft pushed back and held on to my arms.

"Are you okay? I shouldn't have said all that. I have held it in for so long and my emotions got the better of me. This is too much for you right now."

"No, that's not it. I just wish I felt the same way."

His mouth turned down in disappointment.

"No, that's not what I mean either. I feel great right now, with you. I only wish I remembered missing you and..."

"Your family," he reluctantly offered.

"Yes, how did you know?"

"It's okay Janie. That's how it should be. You will remember them, and hopefully me too eventually."

I smiled and locked my fingers around his waist.

"I don't need to remember right now. I just want to enjoy this time with you. It feels good and I hope when I do remember I can make sense of it all, but for now, well let's just be in the now."

"It's funny Janie. You used to talk like that--living each day in the now. Even though you can't remember your personality, you can't escape it."

I laughed, "That could be good and bad."

"There is no bad in you. Challenging yes, but no bad."

"How can there be no bad? Every person is good and bad."

I found myself talking and philosophizing as if I was coming to consciousness in the middle of my words. Croft kept nodding.

"What?" I stopped and chortled again.

"I like when you talk. I think you will find yourself that way. You can't help but be who you are, the person so many people love. The person who I..."

I touched my index finger to his lips to stop him.

"I don't know if I am ready to hear that yet."

"What, that so many people love you?"

"Yes, and what you were about to say."

"I know. I'm sorry."

He bowed his head. I tipped his chin to force his eyes upward. "Look at me, blue eyes."

He laughed a little.

"It's not that I don't want you to feel that way--to love me. I just want to feel like I deserve it."

"You don't think you deserve it? Everyone deserves to be loved. You said that all the time, about your students, and about people in general."

"I think I do believe that. That feels right to me. But does anyone ever feel like they deserve love, unless someone shows them they do? They should, but do they?"

"You're so smart Janie. You are right. No one feels they deserve love until someone shows them. So, am I not showing you?" We both laughed as two people who shared a long history would laugh. Impetuously, I lurched forward and flung him back on the bed and kissed him several times on the cheek.

"Yes, yes, you are."

We stared at each other. How strange it was to feel such passion and emotion for someone I had only known for two days of my new life. I dared myself to stroke the copper and grey mosaic hair I had admired. It felt like home. As I breathed in his enticing musk, the years that I didn't remember weaved around us and bonded us together. I drank in the moment and let it breathe.

"Okay, let me try again. It's not that I don't think I deserve love, I think it's that I want to remember why you love me. I want to remember what about me deserves your love, and I want to remember loving you."

"That makes perfect sense. I wish you could know the Janie I know. I am overwhelmed right now with my feelings for you. I can describe you with all the right words, kind, smart, fierce, passionate, driven, beautiful. I could go on and on, but labels do no justice to the real Janie. I hope you understand when you remember yourself." Then he smiled in his own reverie. "...and you are also a great debater with a sarcastic and devilish wit."

"Ooo, that last part sounds a little scary."

"You asked me to tell you why I loved you. I adore that part of you. I haven't yet met someone who can out-reason you. I try, but you always win."

"Aw, but I don't always want to win."

"Yes, you do. You don't remember that you do, but you do." He smiled. I frowned. "No, you mistake me. You are not argumentative, just tenacious. People listen to you. They need to listen to you. You have great ideas. Those are only some of the reasons I...love you."

"I want to tell you that too."
"There's no rush."

"Have I told you that before? What I feel right now makes me believe I have."

"In so many words."

Questions bombarded my mind, about him, about us. I leaned away from him and smiled. I used my thumbs to wipe away the remnants of tears on his cheeks and then leaned in for one more salty kiss before I spoke. "Do you have any children?"

"No."
"What about other family?"
"No, I had a younger brother, but he passed away."
"I'm sorry. As a baby?"
"No, it was...an accident."
I stroked his cheek again. "So, what did you teach?"

"Well, I was first a history teacher and ended up teaching everything from web design to art."

"Wow that is quite a jump. I can imagine all your students trying to impress you. Oh Mr. uh...this is embarrassing. What is your name? Is Croft your first name or your last?"

His mouth dropped in surprise, and he seemed instantly nervous. Sitting up, he turned away from me. I felt cold and anxious.

"Um, my first."

I sat up and stroked my hand through his hair. "Oh, okay. So, what is your last name then?"

He breathed a heavy sigh. "My last name is McAvoy."

I felt a knife twist in my stomach. "Wh--what do you mean?"

"Anson was my brother."

# 24 ~ Conflicted

I leaned away. I couldn't speak. I couldn't think. I had just kissed my dead husband's brother. Croft looked at me questioningly.

"You lied to me!"

"No, Janie. It's not like that. I didn't lie--I mean, I didn't intend to keep it from you. I just wanted you to be ready. I was going to tell you before when Trey came and pounded on the door. Then, there really wasn't a good time. I wanted to tell you, but I also hoped you might remember on your own." The warm feeling of the moments before, was gone. "I'm so sorry Janie. This is a big thing. Do you understand why it was hard for me to tell you?"

"I don't understand anything right now." Croft tried to grab my hand. I didn't push it away, but I didn't reciprocate. "Did I--I mean did we--before he died?"

"No, no, it wasn't like that. I mean we had a long history yes, but you would have never. And I would never--I would not have hurt you or my brother like that." I shook my head, hoping for answers. "Janie," he said defeated, "it will be okay, I promise."

"How is this okay? How would I ever agree to this?"

I suddenly felt used and cheap. Croft, the person I idolized seconds before, had lied to me or deliberately kept the truth from me. It didn't matter. It didn't make sense. I got up and ran for the door. Croft yelled after me, "No please, Janie, can't we talk about this? I have more…"

I paused at the door but didn't turn around. "More? I can't handle more right now."

I left my room in a fog. The low hallway lighting was even dimmer than I remembered. Croft did not follow me. I was glad, for a moment. Then I became angry that he didn't follow. I wondered if that was all the fight he had in him. If I was important to him, he would have followed. No, I chose to leave. He was respecting that. Maybe I should have gone back. He said there was more to the story. I wondered what else he could have possibly said.

My eyes stung fighting back the tears. I leaned against the wall in defeat. I was nauseous and hot. Black dots crowded my vision, and my legs grew weaker as I started sliding down the wall. The last thing I remember was Trey rounding the corner and running for me with outstretched arms.

~~~~~~~~~~~~~~~~~~~~~~~~~~~~~~~~~~~~~~~~~~~~~~~~~~~~~~~~

I awoke with my face in a damp pillow. As I rolled to my side, I heard a male voice ask if I was awake. *Trey.* Confusion swirled in my brain as details of my last moments with Croft solidified.

"Why am I here?"

"Janie," Trey sat on the bed next to me, "you had a rough night. I found you in the hallway in the nick of time. You were about to pass…"

"Where is Croft?" I interrupted.

"Well, you told him to leave you alone."

"I did? When?"

"Last night, when he came to check on you."

"He came to check on me?"

"Yes, but you told him to stay away."

"I don't--I don't remember that at all."

"Janie, I don't know all of what happened with you two last night. I mean you two left the council room like you were eloping." My face flushed. "But then I found you and when you recovered you were crying and begging me not to let him see you."

"Why can't I remember that?"

"I don't know for sure, Janie. I have heard of this happening to other rescues. Sometimes, it takes a while to get all the drugs out of your system."

"But then how do I know what is real? What if I have been dreaming everything? What if this is a dream right now?"

"It's not a dream. It felt like it last night. But no, this is totally real."

"What do you mean, last night?"

"Um, yeah, well that is a little hard to explain. You really don't remember? I mean you were in bad shape and when you kissed me, I didn't know what to do, so I went along with it."

"WHAT?! You kissed me?"

"Well, technically you kissed me."

"…and while I didn't have my memory?"

"Wait now. I didn't know you weren't going to remember. It actually kind of hurts my feelings that you don't."

I sat up and put my head to my bent knees.

"Janie, I'm sorry. I wasn't trying to take advantage of you. You seemed to be into the moment, and I don't know what it is about you, but I can't stop thinking of you. I mean, I do know what it is, but I can't really control it."

"What are you saying?"

"I mean, I know why we are drawn together. Er, I don't want to speak for you, but you were pretty drawn to me last night and you kept telling me how you felt 'electric' around me."

"Oh my God! I did?"

Trey grinned. "Yeah, it was pretty cute."

"This is not cute. It's not cute at all. How could I? I am leaving tornadoes in my wake."

"Hey now, I'm not that bad."

"No, you're not. I'm bad. I am apparently a nightmare."
"What?"

"Never mind, this is too much for me right now."

My head was throbbing. I ran my fingers through my hair and tried to massage my scalp to make it go away. Trey tried to rub my back and I stiffened. I didn't want to like it, so I made myself shiver but it made me even more relaxed. I wanted to tell him to stop. I knew I should tell him to stop, but I didn't.

"I've had a headache today too," he offered as his palms swirled a tantalizing message on my back.

I hated him for making me feel better. I imagined him lifting my shirt so he could massage the bare skin on my back. My body continued to relax, and as my shoulders loosened so did my restraint. I leaned back into his proficient fingers. I wanted arms around me, so I leaned back even further until I felt the tranquilizing warmth of his chest. In my mind a mantra began: *I love you, I love you, I love you…Croft.*

As I said his name in my mind a pinch of reality hit me that I was not in Croft's arms, but Trey's. I bolted upright and turned my head to look at him and confirm. I knew there was pain in my expression, but I didn't care if I hurt his feelings. I was going full tilt on my emotional treadmill, and I no longer cared who I ran over.

"Look Janie, I know you are completely cognizant right now and I also know that was not me you were just imagining."

"I'm sorry Trey I am mentally bankrupt right now. I don't even know what I am doing. I can't even cry about it anymore."

Without thinking I rubbed my temples.

"Here, let me do that." His hands replaced mind. "Close your eyes and breathe deeply. Just relax and keep breathing."

I tried to keep my mind as blank as I could and let his fingers do their magic. He traced small circles all over my face. Finally, as he pushed his thumbs up under my eyebrows my head pain started to ease.

"Ahh, how did you do that?" I felt intoxicated with the pain relief. "Seriously, you have good hands." After I said it aloud, I immediately

94

wanted to take it back. It lingered in the air uncomfortably which brought me back to the issue at hand.

"What did you mean when you said you knew why we were drawn together?"

"Well, I asked Charlotte to be sure, but I had the feeling you were one when I met you."

"You had the feeling I was what?"

"An empath, like me."

"What's an empath?"

Trey sighed, "I'm not sure how much I'm supposed to tell you about yourself. I mean Croft said it would be better for you to remember on your own."

"Yes, I'm sure Croft did say something like that. He would prefer to not tell me anything, but that didn't work out so well for him, or me. So, tell me already!"

"Okay, okay..."

"What is an empath?"

"Well, empaths feel what others feel. It's like you mirror other's emotions. Sometimes empaths can even feel the physical pain of others. I think you are one of those empaths."

"Really?"

"Yes. I've seen you experience other's pain. Right before the meeting yesterday Charlotte had told me how the arthritis in her hands was bothering her. When you first came into the council room, I noticed you were wringing your hands. At first, I thought you were just nervous, but the look on your face made me think your hands hurt."

"I do remember my hands hurting but I wasn't aware of it, you know. I was kind of overwhelmed with everything."

"Crowds are often tough for empaths too because there are so many conflicting emotions. It can be overwhelming."

Suddenly I felt the truth of Trey's words. I had felt exactly that in the council room the day before. More examples popped in my head. Feeling Croft's knee pain, and the glass in my sister's face. Then the thought occurred to me, if I was a mirror of other's emotions and pain how was I to know when my own emotions were real? Maybe the love I thought I was feeling for Croft was only a mirror of his love. Maybe the attraction I felt for Trey was only a mirror of his attraction. I shook my head in disbelief that I could be so easily influenced.

"Trey, what exactly happened when I came to, or should I say when you brought me to your room?"

"Well, when you woke up you were quite weak. I was about to get help, but you begged me not to. You drank like three cups of water and some hot tea and then paced around the room mumbling to yourself. It was sorta creepy." I could feel my eyes roll. "Anyway, then Croft pounded on the door. He demanded to see you, but you kept yelling, "No Trey, don't let him in. Don't you dare." You were completely unhinged. He looked like he had been crying."

"He did?"

"Yeah, I almost felt bad for the son of a bitch, but I was more worried about you. Then after he left, more mumbling and pacing until Charlotte came to see you. She tried to talk to you, and you completely shut down. You sat in my chair and stared at the ground. Charlotte eventually gave up.

Finally, after she left, you came and sat next to me and apologized and then started to cry. So, I wasn't sure if I should, but I hugged you because you looked like you needed it. After that I sort of lost my common sense."

"What the hell does that mean?"

"Well, you pulled back and put your hands on my face and stared at me for a long time. I was unsure, Janie. I didn't know what to do. I didn't want to pull away, but I knew you were in an emotional state. I told you I cared about you and that I was worried about you and then you jumped on me and kissed me. It was crazy. I tried to pull away, I did, but you had me in a strangle hold and you just kept kissing the hell out of me."

"Okay, tell me right now. Am I a mental patient? Is that what this place is, an underground asylum?" Trey tried to cover his snicker. "I mean, I don't remember anything. Maybe people are telling me I lost my memory to placate me and cover up my real issues."

"What issues, Janie? There is nothing wrong with you except that you have been under the influence of some serious drugs for a long time. They are bound to mess with your brain. Don't sweat it. It will get better."

"I know, I know, everyone keeps telling me it will get better. But in the meantime, I am making a real mess of things. I'm sorry I kissed you."

"Seriously? Don't apologize. It was a little violent at first but then I pretty much enjoyed it." I punched him in the arm and he laughed. "See, like that? I tried not to like it, but I couldn't help myself. You're a good kisser. You're good--at a lot of things."

Then the horror of what he said, slid the lump that was building in my throat, down to my stomach.

"I'm almost afraid to ask, but what things are you referring to?"

"Janie, don't punch me again, okay?"

"WHAT THINGS?!"

"I just mean that you have a way about you. You are so sensual. I think it's because you can read people so well, especially me."

"Trey, please tell me this is not true. I couldn't--I mean I didn't. We didn't, did we?"

Trey's eyes were transparent. He spoke no words and inched away from me on the bed readying for a getaway. Then the devil dared to verbalize my fears, "It's, um, complicated. Hard to explain."

I felt fire flash from my eyes. "TRY!"

96

"I think I better leave and give you some time to yourself."

My hands flew to my face. *Tornadoes in my wake.* I stood slowly and walked to the door. I have no idea what he said to me on the way out. He was talking, but nothing registered.

I left Trey's room and walked down the hall to my room with my senses completely muffled. Several people passed me in the hallway. I saw their mouths move. I acknowledged no one. When I reached my room, Croft was walking out of his room. His face was a myriad of conflicted emotions, surprise, joy, anguish, contempt for himself, and relief to see me. For the first time since I was awakened from my oblivion, I looked past the beautiful, tortured eyes that saved me without looking into them. I caught only a small glimpse of his devastation. I was a shell. A shell of someone I didn't even know.

I walked into my room and locked the door.

# 25 ~ Like Bees to Honey

New Congress City was abuzz with solidarity. Taurus Roma had the entire congregation of spectators on their feet. "Roma! Roma! Roma!" they cheered as Aviva Chandler and her son passed the outskirts of the enormous crowd that had gathered in Chandler Park. Aviva's rage was introspective, as she sized up her opponent. Her face burned red trying to plot her next move.

She spoke, almost calmly, "An assembly without prior authorization, and in my absence. That's a lot of nerve, don't you think?"

Braeden was lost in thought.

"Don't you think?"

Braeden answered only with an obligatory head nod.

"Braeden! Braeden!"

Suddenly forced back to reality, he answered nonchalantly, "Yes mother."

"Are you listening to me?"

"Yes mother."

"Don't take that droll tone with me. We need to take Inner City Line #7."

"Yes mother, I have been here before."

Braeden pushed the course alteration button of their pod on the city transport track. The track had been a gift from Congresswoman Chandler to the city of New Congress at the official city renaming ceremony after CW II. The track suspended twenty feet above street level to avoid the few remaining vehicles that still traveled the lower streets. It was convenient. It also allowed Aviva to peer down on her constituents.

Only the New Congress still owned vehicles that were street sensor capable, but with the crowds that day Aviva wanted the efficiency of the transport. Traveling in a circle around the city, tracks called Lines weaved to the center of the city like spokes on a wheel. Line #7 led to the Congress

98

Hall of Statutes and Chandler Manor. The crowd began at Line #5 and stretched far past Line #9. There had not been a crowd that size since the Collection naming ceremony and the size of the crowd angered Aviva.

Unlike other Collection cities that had been built around the rubble of Civil War II, New Congress was a completely new city built with technology. Before the construction, it had been rural land in the southern half of old Ohio. The goal, according to Aviva, was for other cities in the Collection to aspire to the innovation in New Congress City.

As soon as the transport pod stopped, Aviva walked past Braeden without a word through the habit-trail that led to Congress Hall. The massive white stone structures of the old state capitols were avoided when designing Collection buildings. The New Congress Hall of Statutes had a completely glass façade. When Braeden neared the end of the glass tunnel, he caught a glimpse of his mother's expression reflected in the mirrored building. While fearful of the sour carving on her face, he became angry with himself that she could still affect him so, especially considering what he had come to know about her.

Upon entering the building, Aviva's entourage of assistants surrounded her and crowded out her less important son.

"Mrs. Chandler, may I take your coat?"

"Here is your coffee, Mrs. Chandler. Would you like anything to eat?

"You have a meeting at 5:00 p.m. with Congressman Heath. We should discuss some other changes in your calendar."

Braeden used the opportunity to slink into the background and head for his suite while muttering under his breath, "Would you like a kick in the head, Mrs. Chandler? Here, I've poisoned your coffee for you, Mrs. Chandler. Here are your messages, Mrs. Chandler. Oh look, they all say, 'fuck you,' Mrs. Chandler."

Braeden's elevator to the underground tunnel leading to Chandler Manor, was especially slow. Still mumbling when the door opened, Braeden was shocked by a surprise visitor. A young woman with wispy brown hair and a small scar on her right cheek startled him. Sabine's dark eyes sparkled in the fluorescent lighting of the tunnels. She wore the burgundy suit of the congressional assistants sharply and convincingly. In her lapel pocket was a bright green pen. Braeden stepped back uneasily as Sabine pushed a note scratched on New Congress stationery up to his face.

"Mr. Chandler, I have a message."

"From?"

She took the bright green pen from her pocket and used it to point to the note.

TO: Mr. Braeden Chandler
FROM: Charles Ferril Merot
MEMO: The package has been delivered to your specifications.

Braeden's bitter mood lifted, and a broad smile spread across his face, as he read the memo over again. Finally, he thought the charade could end. Sabine's expression cautioned otherwise.

"Mr. Merot requested that you finalize a few details per your agreement."

"I'm sorry, what was your name?"

Sabine thought of the surety of surveillance and answered tentatively, "Sabi...Sabrina."

"Thank you, Sabrina. I'm exhausted from my trip. Would you be able to accompany me to the Manor so I could change and grab a quick bite while we discuss the details?"

"Of course, sir."

Sabine followed Braeden with a giddy click-step of her heels down the long, echoing hallway. As they emerged from the tunnel, Sabine noticed the bright blue light of the security passage.

"Stand completely still," Braeden instructed. "You don't have any--never mind, of course you don't."

The body scanner traveled up its trajectory to the ceiling and beeped a short 'all clear' tone. Braeden then rested his chin on the cradle for the retinal scanner. The armored door for Chandler Manor opened automatically, but as Braeden tried to hold the door for Sabine a loud voice boomed.

"I'm sorry sir, but all congressional aides must be scanned before entry."

Braeden raised his voice to the speaker in the ceiling, "She is with me."

"I understand sir, but she has a code for authentication that must clear before we can let her through."

Sabine's cheery smile hid her fluttering heart. Braeden didn't pause. "Look, it's not like we're going to a briefing room or something. This is *my* house. I am in a hurry, and she is with me! Got it?"

Muffled voices argued softly in the speaker. Braeden tried to make idle conversation with Sabine to ease both of their minds while they waited. Sabine did not disappoint with her inquiries about Braeden's trip and a few comments about the weather. Finally, they were interrupted, "Um, very good Mr. Chandler. Welcome home sir." Braeden wryly recognized the privilege of being a Chandler.

"Thank you," Braeden responded in a more gracious tone than his thoughts intended. Turning to Sabine, he proposed, "Sabrina, I am fairly sure the contract is in my room. Why don't you come up with me and if you wouldn't mind, you can make us some coffee while I change."

"Absolutely sir."

The main staircase of Chandler Manor stupefied Sabine as they approached. Never had she seen such luxury. The marble stairs were twelve feet wide at the base and tapered to a six-foot expanse at the top. A railing of carved mahogany lined each side and split the largest steps down the middle at the bottom of the staircase. Once on the upper floor, Sabine had to catch her breath to keep up on the long trip down the hallway to Braeden's suite.

Braeden supposed there were hidden cameras and microphones throughout his five-room suite, as there were in every other room. The only secure location that he had recently designed and outfitted himself was his ten by ten-foot closet. Sabine almost flew out of her tall gray heels as Braeden whisked her in the room and dragged her to a large metal door with a relief carving of the nearby mountains. He tried to put his arm around her on the trip to serve as a visual alibi should his mother ask about the girl in his suite. Sabine played along to perfection.

"Stand back a little now, okay?"

Braeden put his wrist on a metal plate next to the closet door. A red pinpoint laser above the door fanned out and the array scanned down Braeden's body stopping at his chest. Suddenly an image of a beating heart with numbers above it materialized on a small screen above the door.

Sabine stared and wondered, "Is that your heart?"

"Yes," Braeden whispered, "But it's a little fast. Shush, now while I concentrate."

Braeden stood very still and took a long deep breath. Staring intently at the screen he breathed again exhaling more slowly the second time. The numbers on the screen slowly decreased until the screen turned blue with the word, "MATCH" blinking in the middle of it. The heavy metal door slid open in a flash revealing a wall with the outline of another door. Braeden whispered a series of numbers and letters and the seam popped. He touched it and it mechanically opened wider. Once they were both inside Braeden closed the laser cut door to his closet, which sealed, allowing no light or sound to escape. The outer door then closed behind it.

He led Sabine to the large black velvet dressing ottoman in the middle of the room and invited her to sit next to him. Never being too cautious, he whispered, "Tell me everything. Is she okay? Is she conscious? Does she remember anything?"

"Whoa, slow down," Sabine interrupted. "I don't know any details."

"And, what about Sage? Did he say anything about her, or my niece? Did they get my niece yet?"

"I don't know, all I did was transcribe the message from your friend Charles."

"What do you mean, my friend? Don't you know him? I thought everyone in the GC knew each other?"

"Well, mostly we do, but I don't know Charles."

Then the obvious occurred to Braeden. Only he and the other employees of the country ward knew the name Charles. "My mistake. Did Charles give you any details?"

"No, just what you read and..."

Braeden abruptly tuned out. He turned and pushed the shirts on a bottom rack to the side revealing an almost imperceptible white door. From inside the door, he grabbed a large duffle bag filled with clothes. He also pulled a small black case from the space, unzipped it, and checked the contents. Sabine noticed a hatchet, a small tri-fold shovel, a fire laser, water purification drops and some first-aid supplies.

"Wait, wait, uh..."

"You can call me Braeden."

"Okay, thanks Braeden. But you can't leave yet."

"What do you mean? I am going to see my sister."

"No, Charles said you have to stay until you contact the Black Horse. He said you would know who that is and that you had to tell him about the flush. I don't know what any of this means, but he was very adamant that you do it."

Braeden slumped back down on the ottoman and looked around at all his trappings. He despised his life of excess. Now that at least one sister was safe, he wanted out. He wanted to live a natural and unencumbered life in the GC, away from the Collection, and away from Aviva.

"Getting close to the Black Horse isn't going to be easy or quick. How can he ask me to do that now?"

"He gave me the impression that you had already agreed to it."

"Well, we talked about it, but I guess I thought it would only happen if the opportunity came up. Creating the opportunity is another story. How can I contact Charles? Did he tell you? I need to ask him a few questions."

"No, but that is way too risky anyway. I'm assuming by what you said that the package that was delivered was your sister. I am also assuming your sister was the high-profile rescue that just occurred. My friend Trey is probably the one who pulled it off. So, if that is the case, I can understand why you are anxious to see her. But Charles said..."

"I know, I know what Charles said. I'm going to do it, okay? I just don't want to do it."

"Do you know where to find him? The Black Horse?"

"Yes, but that is not the problem. Getting close to him without my mother finding out is the issue."

"Why do you care what she thinks if you're leaving anyway?"

"Well because I want to make sure I still can leave after I'm done. I've been able to fly under her radar until now, but I know what she's capable of, and she is not above sacrificing her family to get her own..."

A faint knocking interrupted Braeden's thought. He looked desperately at Sabine and quickly shoved his packed bag back into its hideaway, sealed the door and then readjusted the clothes.

"Let me do the talking okay?"

"Obviously," she said with a nervous smile.

102

Braeden waved his hand in front of a small sensor to open the inner sound-proof door. He grabbed Sabine's hand and raised his eyebrows in question if the act agreed with her. She nodded and brightened up her smile. The knocking was now a loud pounding.

"Braeden! Braeden! Open this door! I know you're in there!"

Braeden waved his hand again in front of the sensor and the outer door opened.

"Hello mother," he offered in his most deadpan voice.

Aviva's face was even more beat red than usual as she scrutinized Sabine.

"Who is this?"

"How welcoming. This is Sabrina, mother."

Sabine stretched her free hand out in greeting. Aviva stared at it with contempt.

"I mean, what is she doing here, in your room?"

"I am an adult mother."

"Yes, my dear I am aware of that. But she is an…an assistant!"

"Careful mother. I wouldn't want any proletarian to rub off on you."

Aviva slapped him across the face, and he stepped back in shock. Sabine tried to let go of his hand, but he squeezed it tight.

"Don't talk to me like that. This is my house!"

Braeden gritted his teeth. "Yes, I am aware this is your house, but this is my room, and I can have who I want in here."

"Not her. It's not appropriate for a congressional assistant to be in our house."

"Except for your assistants, right?"

"That's business. This does not appear to be business."

"Well, it's not your business." He braced for another slap. "She is not an assistant, okay? I got her the uniform so she could be here without questions from security."

Aviva's shoulders relaxed slightly at the realization that Sabine was not a servant, or an assistant, which was only slightly better in her mind. She was quite fed up with social climbers. Yet, she still didn't give Sabine the courtesy of looking her in the eye.

"What were you doing in there with the door locked anyway?"

"Making cookies. What do you think?"

Sabine blushed in embarrassment even though it was all a ruse. Aviva, though enraged, decided it was more prudent to befriend her son's new girlfriend.

In her best estimation of a motherly voice Aviva apologized to Sabine. "I'm sorry. I'm not used to my son having friends over."

"Seriously, mother?" Braeden burst in. "You act like I'm a hermit crab or something."

Ignoring him and still addressing Sabine, Aviva continued, "No, I just mean he doesn't have too many girlfriends. In fact, I can't even think when..."

"Okay, that's enough. Excuse us mother."

Not waiting for a response, he sidestepped his mother and pulled Sabine along with him. As they walked to the exit door of his suite, Aviva tried to lean in and inspect the mysterious room to which she had no access. As Braeden opened the hallway door, both doors to his closet automatically closed and almost clipped Aviva's nose. She stumbled back in surprise and then turned to him with a look of disapproval.

He held the door open with a phony smile, "After you, mother."

Aviva swished past Braeden and Sabine. Sabine called after her, "It was nice to meet you."

Braeden spit out a laugh. "You're brave!"

Sabine didn't dare laugh until Aviva was out of ear's range. The two ran down the hall holding hands and giggling. They followed the same path that Braeden had taken the night he ran into Charles. When they reached the gate to the street, he was stunned by the number of people still milling around.

After the usual security scrutiny, Braeden and Sabine were released into the heart of New Congress City. He felt a new freedom as they breached the crowded street. The thought of disappearing into the crowd and never coming back excited him. He looked at Sabine with an impish smile like he had been paroled.

The unseasonable wind whipped through the street. "You must be freezing in that getup."

"I'm okay," Sabine answered through chattering teeth.

"I'm freezing and I at least have my legs covered. Come on, follow me."

Braeden pulled Sabine behind him. He didn't want to lose her in the crowd, and he was growing fond of holding her hand. They made their way to the conveyors that ran as a moving sidewalk in front of the businesses that lined the street. Riding under the spokes of Line #7 and Line #8, Braeden saw their destination. "Time to get off!"

Still holding hands, they stepped off the conveyor into the heart of the shopping district. Sabine was stunned at the number of shops and the people walking around with full shopping bags. Growing up in the GC, she had been too young to remember much of life in a real city, and it was her first time in the Collection. She had been born when the states still had their names in a city called Defiance, Ohio. Appropriately named, it was the center of many protests right before the second Civil War.

Though stunned and a little disgusted, Sabine was curious about life in the Collection and lingered to look in the shop windows. Braeden, on the other hand, wanted to nudge her along.

104

"It's cold, let's keep moving. So, Sabrina? Is that your real name?"

"No, it's Sabine."

Braeden smiled broadly, "Beautiful!" Sabine was unsure if he meant her or her name, but she didn't want to ask.

The wind outside took on a new bite as they walked down the street. After an art gallery called Sequoia's, they came to a clothing store named Delilah's Treasures. Once inside, Braeden told Sabine to find a warm outfit and a coat.

"I only have a few coins with me to get me through town. We should save them."

"You don't have to pay for anything here."

"Why not?"

"My mother owns it."

"Of course, she does."

Both smiling they walked to their respective sides of the store. Sabine picked out black leather pants, an all-weather silk shirt, a cream-colored cable knit sweater and black riding boots. She stepped out of the dressing room and Braeden blushed when he saw her.

Braeden's mussed sandy colored hair looked more designed than wind-blown. His pale complexion was still ruddy from the wind, which made his light eyebrows glow. He had switched his business shirt for a long-sleeved muscle hugging evergreen tee. His navy dress pants had been replaced with form-fitted black denims and short zippered army boots.

"Will you be warm enough," she asked.

"I'm pretty warm right now," he said flirtatiously.

She tried to pretend she didn't get the inference. Braeden didn't want to come off as creepy while playing the role of boyfriend. There was something he genuinely liked about Sabine. Trying to fight the urge to flirt, he grabbed a black suede jacket and matching cap and headed for the door.

Back in character, he held the door. "Ready, sweet pea?"

"As ever, buttercup."

They both laughed at their cleverness on the way out.

After downing a hot tea from a street vendor, they wound their way through the crowd to the front steps of Congress Hall where Taurus Roma was speaking. A loudspeaker amplified his deep booming voice as he assured the people that he had been working on their behalf to find new ways to lower taxes and still increase city services.

"With the right tools, each of you can learn to grow your own food again and to trade some of the services that you now pay for with your hard-earned wages. Let's get back to a simpler way of life…"

The crowd burst into applause at Taurus's words. The wealthiest in the crowd looked disgusted and whispered with indignation. Braeden recognized several faces from cocktail parties and government meetings that ran late into the night at Chandler Manor. Their curiosity had been satiated past comfort.

Suddenly an immediate solution to Braden's situation occurred to him. He grabbed Sabine's hand again and dragged her through the masses to the steps of Congress Hall.

"Where are we going?" she yelled over the crowd.

"Come on, I have an idea."

Remembering that Taurus always shook hands with constituents in the first row, Braeden pulled Sabine as they ducked under and around obstacles in the thickening crowd. Braeden panicked as the speech ended and he noticed Taurus descending the steps to make his way to the crowd. He shoved through the stubborn bodies until he lost Sabine's hand. Panicked, he glanced back to find her.

"It's okay," she shouted with a smile. "I'll catch up, keep going."

He nodded and tried to drive through the final barrier of the front row. A young couple holding hands in the front wouldn't budge. "Excuse me," Braeden offered politely.

They laughed. "You're crazy, buddy. He gives out government tokens when he shakes hands. No way you're getting in front of us."

Braeden quickly pulled out his wallet, emptying several coins into his hand to show the couple. "Silver or gold?"

They answered in unison, "Both."

Braeden started to put them in the man's hand and then handed them to the woman.

"Ooo, I like you." She cackled and pulled her partner out of the way right as Taurus approached.

His greetings seemed genuine, though he rarely looked at people's faces. "Thank you for coming. This is a small token of my appreciation for your struggles." He placed a coin in Braeden's hand as he shook it and attempted to walk by, but Braeden wouldn't let go. Still not looking up he continued, "Thank you, son, I need to move on now."

Braeden countered, "I heard you have a new black horse in your stable."

Taurus Roma's heavy lids flashed up in surprise and then panned a double take as he realized he was shaking the hand of Aviva Chandler's son.

# 26 ~ Boy Wonder

"Jumpin' Jupiter," Bodhi leaned forward and yelled. "It's getting dark." He wiped his eyes with the back of his hands. "We've gotta get moving."

Delilah played along to keep his mind off his grandparents. She wanted to ask what happened, but Bodhi's body language told her to save her questions for another time.

"We're not going to make it to the Lake before tomorrow anyway, and I am getting pretty tired after the last couple days. I retro-fitted the headlights on this old beast with night vision cameras."

"What does that mean?"

"Well, dear Delilah, it means no one can see us coming in the dark, but we can see them."

"That's a great idea."

"I know, pretty awesome, right?"

"How do you turn it on?"

Bodhi tapped on the screen to show her, "Right here, but it's still too light, unless you want to roast your eyeballs for dinner."

"Um, no, I'm good." Delilah spoke mindlessly as her thoughts lingered on Bodhi's last word - dinner. She hadn't eaten in hours and her stomach loudly protested.

Bodhi laughed and took the initiative, pulling out a plastic pouch from a box on the floor. "Hungry?"

Delilah grabbed the pouch to find dried apricots, and pineapple pieces. "Yum! Perfect!"

"There's some nuts in the hatch too."

"The hatch?"

He pointed to the box on the seat between them.

"Oh, this is good for now. This is one of my favorite snacks."

"Cool, these are one of my specialties."

"What, you make these?"

"Yeah, I'm somewhat of a fruit scientist."

Delilah tried hard not to roll her eyes. "Hey Einstein, is there any heat in this thing? It's getting a little chilly in here."

"Also my specialty. Do you see that smooth part of the arm rest on your door?"

"Uh huh."

"Put your hand on it."

As Delilah pressed her palm down, the surface changed color, first red, orange, yellow, green, then blue.

"Wow, you are cold. Keep your hand there for a minute."

Delilah kept her palm pressing down and noticed the air temperature rising. As the air changed and her skin warmed, the display screen evened out to a light orange color.

"Ooooo," she squealed to Bodhi. "That's amazing."

"Yeah, another one of my upgrades," he smiled proudly.

"You actually are a scientist, or at least a good mechanic."

"A little of both Miss Delilah Marie."

"My middle name's not Marie."

"Oh, it's not? Well, it should be. I like it." He started to sing, "Deliiilahhh Marie, I do decreeeeee. You're smart, it's true, but your lips are blue, so I guess you still need meeeeeee."

Delilah grinned and shook her head.

"S'gonna take about seven hours to get to Lake Michigan and we can't drive that whole distance in the dark, even with night vision. Plus, it's too sketchy out here in the wilderness at night. Many of the small lakes have dried up but we still have several bridges we will need to cross, and I don't want to take my chances on some raggedy-ass bridge in the darkness."

Delilah stared blankly at Bodhi and sarcastically added, "Wow, the scientist boy genius is all of a sudden mister business."

"Anyway, too risky," Bodhi added before he realized what she had said. "Besides Delilah Marie, if we cross farther north, we should be able to make it to a ghost city in the next two hours."

Delilah smiled at the return of playful Bodhi. "What's a ghost city, like in the old west?"

"Not exactly, it's a former city that looks deserted. A lot of GC hang in ghost cities."

"Like Indie City or Euro City?"

"No, not that big of scale. Usually only a couple hundred or so live in a ghost city."

"So, you're saying if I stumbled on a ghost city, I wouldn't know anyone lived there?"

"Right-O."

"Have you ever been to a ghost city before?"

"Almost, right before I met you."

108

Delilah tried to acknowledge with a smile, but a yawn forced its way out instead. Bodhi held the steering wheel with his knee and took off his jacket. He wadded it up in a ball on the box between them and patted it with his hand. "Here, go ahead and take a little nap. We have about an hour before I need your help."

"Wow, you make fruit and pillows. You are amazing."

Bodhi smirked. "Wow you make jokes. Maybe when you get good, they'll be funny too."

Delilah smiled and curled up in the wide seat, resting her head on the makeshift pillow and pulled her legs up to her chest. Her blond hair cascaded over her face. She tried to blow it out away from her mouth. "Wake me up, when you need me."

"Sure thing, Delilah Marie."

# 27 ~ Reflection

No one locked doors in the underground ghost city, but my door was locked. In self-imposed exclusion, I stared at the lock to make sure it didn't move, and yet I hoped it would move. I rolled back to stare at the ceiling.

I couldn't cry. I couldn't get angry. I just lay there, my brain spinning over what I had done to myself. I couldn't help but feel it was all my own doing--the reason I was being held captive in the first place, Croft, the indiscretion with Trey, and deep inside I even felt my family's blood on my hands. All I could do was close my eyes and try to force myself to sleep. *Breathe*. I wanted to clear my mind, but images of Croft and Trey and Anson and my children forced me to stay conscious. *Breathe*. Frustrated, I ran to the bathroom and decided to take a warm bath. I filled the tub and slid down so the water line was inches below my nose. *Breathe*. As warm and comfortable as the water was, the longer I sat there, the more I ruminated on the guilt, the pain, and mostly the dark space in my mind that swallowed up my memory. I wanted nothing more than to remember and nothing more than to forget.

Scooching up on the edge of the tub, I squeezed the excess water from my hair and found the plush robe I had worn earlier. I wrapped myself in the robe and jumped under the covers while I was still damp. It was a dark day, and it was time to say goodbye to it. Cranking up the temperature, I finally let go, and quickly drifted off to sleep.

I don't know how long I slept, but when I woke, I felt as if I was still in my dream. It was so vivid I wasn't sure if it was a memory. The same scene played itself over and over in my mind. I was looking through the slits of my eyes and I was back in the TRC ward. Croft was sitting next to the bed and exercising my legs. Lifting them up and down, bending both at the knee, I could see the grotesque black claw that dug into each shin. He was softy humming and smiling at me.

Then he would cup his hand on the side of my face and get close enough to whisper, "Don't worry Janie, it won't be long. Close your eyes now."

Each time I replayed that part of the dream in my head I shivered. That lovely man saved me. He must have spent months planning and executing my escape despite the threat to his own safety. I couldn't think of him as my husband's brother. I didn't remember him in that role. My only memories were of Croft my caretaker, my cheerleader, my friend, and my something more. I'd been too harsh with him. *Damn it.* He had obviously been traumatized by all of this too. He had lost his brother, and me for a while.

I wondered about his relationship with his brother, my deceased husband. I didn't get the feeling that they argued or that his pursuing me was an act of spite in any way. However, the fact remained that he hadn't trusted me enough to tell me the truth. Even though I could understand why, it still made me mad as hell, and helpless. And even though I had been practicing it a lot, feeling helpless was not a comfortable emotion for me.

Suddenly, the only thing I could think of was getting answers. I jumped up and stretched each part of my body. My still damp hair clung to my back. I reached over to check the time on the table screen. 7:14 a.m. I had slept all night and felt refreshed.

I ran my fingers through my hair and thought of the appreciative look Croft had given me when he did the same. After brushing and braiding across my hairline to my ear, I secured the rest with a tie and let it cascade down my side. Excited, I remembered my new clothes and ran to my closet. I pulled out a long sleeved, persimmon shirt with brown leather frog buttons, and a pair of drawstring khaki pants. White slip-on canvas shoes waited by the door. I put them on and ceremoniously unlocked the door to the rest of my small new world.

As I opened it, a gush of cool, fresh air rushed into my room. My body was accustomed to the balmy temperature, but the air felt good and right. I stepped out with authority only to almost trip on Croft who was sitting propped up on the wall next to my room, sound asleep. I wanted to bend down and stroke his hair and tell him it would be okay, but the truth was, I didn't know what would happen. Croft would have to wait.

Trying not to wake him, I gingerly stepped over his legs and tiptoed a few steps further before looking back. I was relieved to see he was still asleep, but I felt sad and childish for trying to slip away unnoticed. I wondered if he had slept there on the floor all night. Oh, my Croft.

I turned away. Of course, the last person I wanted to see sat on a wooden bench as I rounded the corner from the red path hall to the main hub of the underground city. The lights were brighter in the rotunda and reflected fiercely off Trey's perfectly moisturized skin. My heart sunk. Why, why, why did I have to run into him?

I glared at him and kept walking. "Janie, I'm sorry. I am so sorry," I heard as I walked away. I ignored him expertly and kept walking, feeling his profound sadness with every step. It weighed heavy on my heart, but I couldn't entertain anyone's feelings but my own. I pretended like I had an important mission even though I didn't know where I was going or why, so I just kept walking.

Soon I found myself in a gray hall with no colored path on the floor. At the end of the hall was the mouth of another great cupola. As I stepped into the room, I looked up. I could see the sky, yet it wasn't the sky. I was looking at what appeared to be the underside of the forest floor. I could see tree roots, sod and even animals, yet above that, I could also see the pink clouds of the sunrise in the sky.

Fascinated, I walked to the center of the empty room and lay down on the floor looking up. Leaves blew across my view, and small animals scurried back and forth from tree to tree. I was so mesmerized I didn't notice Char come in until she lay down next to me on the cold floor.

"Captivating, isn't it? I never get tired of looking at it."

Keeping my gaze on the sky above me I agreed. "Mmm hmm. I can't stop staring. Is it a projection?"

"No, this is a holo-turf room. We call it the Turf-dome because it's the biggest."

"What is holo-turf?"

"Well, if you think of how a hologram can create a three-dimensional looking object, that is what it looks like from above. From beneath it is a very thick piece of glass, so what you are seeing is what is up there above this room, but from the topside it appears to be the forest floor. You cannot see the room below."

"What does it feel like? I mean what happens if you step on it?"

"Well, that is the tricky part. It appears to be dirt, or grass, or a combination of the two, but it's smoother to the touch. We try to rough up the texture and put as much natural foliage around as possible. Do you see the dirt and leaves blowing across? That helps make it look more natural."

"Have you ever seen anyone walk on it, someone that wasn't supposed to be there?"

"We saw you."

"You did? I don't remember feeling anything slippery or unnatural."

"Looks like it works then, eh?"

"Looks like."

Char turned her head to look at me, "Are you okay? I wanted to check on you again, but it seemed like you needed some space."

"Trey told me."

"How are things, with the two of you?"

"Who? Trey and I?" She nodded. "There is no Trey and I."

She tried to hide her smile and feign confusion, but I knew her plan instantly. "Oh, I assumed since you were in his room, and he said…"

"What?! What did he say?"

"Just that you two were trying to work things out and that you wanted to be left alone."

I rolled on my side to face her. "Char, I really messed things up. I mean, things were messed up, but I didn't know what I was doing. I don't want to make excuses. I don't think I am the type of person to do that, but I don't remember anything, with Trey and I, I mean. He told me what happened, but I can't believe it. I'm so stupid. I mean I was angry with Croft, but I would have never--in my right mind, done anything so stupid."

Char rolled on her side to face me and motioned to someone who happened to be walking by another entrance to Turf-dome. Instantly a young boy of about twelve brought over a soft blue chambray cushion from one of the benches along the side of the room. Char tucked the long cushion under both her head and mine.

"Do you need anything else Miss Charlotte?"

"No thank you, Graham. Go get yourself some breakfast."

"On my way," he answered. He then tipped his chin down at me out of respect and uttered a soft, "Mam."

"Thank you," I called back over my shoulder as he jogged out of the room.

Charlotte put her hand on my arm as we turned back to face each other. Lying in the middle of the huge room on the cold floor with our heads on the same pillow felt like something I would do with my sister or my mother. Still, it was nice and comfortable with my new friend Char. Even though it was cozy, it made me wonder about my poor sister Sage. I didn't know if anyone knew if she were alive. I had been too busy messing up my new life to even ask.

Char and I both began to speak at the same time. "No, you go first," I conceded.

"Janie, don't be too hard on yourself. You said yourself, you were not in your right mind. Besides Trey is young and impulsive and you can't blame him for being attracted to you."

"I don't blame him. Well, I guess I do a little bit, for taking advantage of the situation, but I am the one to blame."

"You were in a different place, mentally. This type of thing may happen a few more times. The drugs you were on in captivity are very strong. Plus, I don't think Trey realized you were in an altered state, or he wouldn't have…"

"I am not so sure he wouldn't have, but whatever. Besides, he knew I was upset. Couldn't he see how upset I was?"

"Wait a minute, I thought you said you blamed yourself and not him?"

We both laughed. "Yes, I did say that."

Char turned serious again. "What about Croft?"

"I don't know what to do about Croft. I mean there was something starting between us, but then no, it had started before apparently."

"Janie, Croft loves you, and you love him."

"I know, I mean I feel like I do, but I don't remember that I do. Does that make sense?"

"Perfect sense."

"Then why am I so confused and so angry with him? Never mind, I know why I am so angry with him. He kind of forgot to mention that I was his sister-in-law."

"Janie, Croft has loved you his whole life. You two have been friends forever. You were inseparable at one time. You did everything together. Everyone thought you two were in love until one day when his dashing younger brother came into town and swept you off your feet. Croft had been trying to find the courage to tell you how he felt when Anson asked if it was okay for him to date you. Croft assumed you had already agreed and weren't interested in anything more with him. You assumed that Croft wasn't interested since he gave Anson his blessing and so you decided to go ahead and date Anson. None of this was discovered until years later, after Anson passed away."

"You mean until after he was murdered?"

"Yes, I'm sorry."

"It's okay. I know I'm sad when I think of him. I remember the car burning and seeing other bits and pieces, like snapshots of him. I have the new memory of the shock when I remembered that he had died. I just don't have any memories of interacting with him. Did I love him, Char? I feel like I did, but that's what makes this even more confusing."

"Yes, sweetie. You loved your husband, and you were devoted to him, but your pretty green eyes never lit up for Anson like they did for Croft. Anson was your nest, but Croft was your wings."

"My wings...yes." I rolled back on to my back and put my palms on my forehead. I imagined Croft with wings to cocoon around me and hold me. "Wow, so I was in love with Croft during my marriage?"

"You never admitted as much dear, but we all thought you were."

"Did we know each other back then--you and I?"

"Not really. We spoke on the phone, but we never met."

"So, how do you know all of this?"

"Croft and I have had many conversations in this same spot. Ironically, this is one of his favorite things to do, but he prefers to lay here at night with the lights off and stargaze. It's very much like a planetarium at night."

"Char, he has been here, lying on the floor talking to you too?"

Char smiled broadly, "Yes!"

I rolled up on to my elbow, "Char, how long after Anson died did he, I mean did we…"

"Is that what you are worried about?" I nodded. "Janie, it was several years. You and Croft were newly rediscovering each other and finally honoring your feelings when you were kidnapped."

"Is that how I got to that TRC place? Who kidnapped me, Char?"

Suddenly I heard footsteps behind me. I turned to see his sparkling blue eyes shine through the red swollen lids that surrounded them. "We can't keep it from her anymore, Char."

"Keep what from me? Who kidnapped me?"

"Your mother."

# 28 ~ The Red Doors

Roma's handlers tried to move him along, but he resisted. He looked cautiously into Braeden's eyes wondering if, as the son of the most powerful woman in the Collection and possibly the continent, he could be trusted. Still, he had heard the code word that could only come from one person. Taurus shook Braeden's hand vigorously, "It's good to see you. How are you?"

Sabine cautiously approached from behind. As she took her final step to get closer to Braeden, she found herself dwarfed in the opposing shadow of Taurus Roma. His near seven-foot frame literally blocked out the sun, exposing the aura around his dark silhouette. Sabine, though mesmerized, smiled, and Taurus just winked back at her.

"I need to talk to you," Braeden whispered as soft as he could over the roar of the crowd.

Taurus, still holding Braeden's hand patted him hard on the other arm and nervously scanned the rest of the mob who looked on with hungry eyes waiting to get a piece of the politician.

Taurus leaned in. "Farley's--it's in the domestic district. Do you know it?"

"No, but I will find it."

"Seven o'clock, and don't be seen." Braeden nodded. "Go to the red door."

Taurus let go of Braden's hand and triumphantly waved to the restless mass. He continued shaking hands down the row, "Sorry about that, folks-- an old friend."

Onlookers turned to see who was important enough to warrant so much time, but Braeden had already grabbed Sabine and slipped away. As they reached the edge of the crowd, he noticed a military presence beginning to form. Several Collectors taunted bystanders, trying to entice them into reaction. He knew it was his mother's idea to find some tactical reason to break up the crowd.

116

Sabine looked anxiously at Braeden, "Is it safe here?"

"Technically it is safe for me, and probably for you too since you are with me. Collectors wouldn't mess with us, but I also don't want to draw their attention. Time to disappear for a while. Are you hungry?"

"Yes, famished!"

"Good, me too."

They dipped through the fringe of the crowd. Finally, they reached a side street leading to a part of town that looked foreign to Braeden. The main thoroughfares narrowed into alleys shadowed by tall buildings on both sides. Each of the brick paved alleys spread out like fingers on a glove from a center hub. Painted on a black light-post in the center of the hub were the words, "*The Nucleus*".

The Nucleus was a small area where people openly traded on the streets. Generally, trading in New Congress or any Collection was frowned upon because if people were trading, they weren't buying. Traders were villainized on the weekly Collection broadcasts for being old fashioned and even dangerous to a stable economy. Yet, all the dangerous people were there, clinking glasses, laughing, and helping each other clean their booths for the evening. As Braeden stood in the center of The Nucleus he marveled at the life of the residents and wrote their histories in his head. Often, he had ridden the transport peering down on the inhabitants and wondering what life was like in the real city.

"This is not far from where I was two days ago," Sabine offered. "I stayed in a room at a GC safe house in an alley right past the next merchant circle."

"They have GC safe houses in New Congress City?"

"Of course, they do. How do you think I was able to come here?"

"Isn't that dangerous though? I mean, there are imaging devices everywhere."

"Do you think the Collection holds all of the world's smart people?"

"No," Braeden answered.

"Besides teachers, the GC council is made up largely of scientists and technitions. You don't think one of them could figure out a way to bypass a security camera?"

"Yes, of course. I just mean my mother has virtually endless resources."

Sabine grabbed Braeden's hand and pulled him to a stop, "Money can't buy everything you know, or everyone."

"I want to believe that. It just hasn't been my experience."

"Well, it's a good thing you met me then, isn't it?"

"Best thing that's happened to me in a long time."

With the setting sun, the wind turned frigid as it whipped through the alleys. Even their new warmer clothing was insufficient, so their search for food became a priority again. Most food in the Collection was genetically engineered. Sabine had already noticed in the few days she had been in

117

New Congress City that much of what she ate lacked color and taste, but her stomach was audibly growling so she was ready to agree to anything. Braeden for other reasons, was also used to better fare, in that most of his food was grown or manufactured at a separate Chandler estate in the country.

Happily, they soon stumbled upon a small café with a red door. Mulling over Roma's instructions, Braeden stepped out from under the portico and glanced up, but the sign didn't say Farley's. In fact, it appeared that the letters had fallen from the façade and all that was left was an outline of four words, The Red Horse Tavern. With his curiosity piqued, Braeden insisted this was the place they should eat, and Sabine whole heartedly agreed.

Inside, dark wood booths lined the walls of the cramped space. They took a seat near the window. Braeden didn't want to take his eyes off Sabine's radiant complexion in the glow from the pendant lights, but he was nervous about whose eyes were on them. He scanned the room cautiously and was met with more questions. The few people in the establishment were not like anyone he had seen before in New Congress.

Braeden leaned in to whisper to Sabine, "What do you notice about the people as you look around the room?" Sabine shrugged her shoulders. "They look so healthy."

"They look like GC," Sabine countered.

"How can you tell?"

"Because they look healthy!"

Both chuckled. Braeden put his hand on the table and Sabine set her hand next to his. They stared at each other in silence. Sabine's mind wandered back to her home in the southern most GC settlement. She was so eager when asked to go on her first mission, though the excitement came from thinking she would run into Trey. However, to her surprise and relief she hadn't thought of Trey all day. With Braeden's company, she finally accepted that Trey had never even noticed her. Crush extinguished.

"Excuse me," a waitress set glasses of water down and directed their attention to the interactive menu screen in the middle of the table. Braeden nodded, and she walked away.

Sabine picked up her glass to drink but Braeden gently guided her arm back to the table. "Hold on. Don't drink that." He pulled out a small vial from his pants pocket and after scanning the room dropped two drops into each glass.

"What is that?"

"Give it a minute. The water is not safe to drink."

Sabine wondered about the water she had drank the last couple days. "Oh great, what am I gonna catch? Botulism? Salmonella?"

Braeden stared into the distance as he answered, "No, it's not disease you have to worry about."

"What then?"

Braeden continued to look past Sabine as he whispered without moving his mouth, "I don't think this is the best place to talk about it."

"Why not?" Sabine tried to turn her head to see what Braeden was staring at, but he tapped her hand to keep her attention.

A tall red-haired man with a pharaoh goatee sat in a booth on the other side of the room. Braeden noticed the man cupping his ear.

"What are you staring at? What is going on?" Sabine insisted.

"There is a man over there with a listening device," Braeden enunciated slowly and quietly, expecting the man to make eye contact when he heard him.

The man didn't look up but acted nervous. Suddenly the front door flew open, and a gush of cool air escorted in a white-haired woman with a crisp green jacket and white linen pants. Her hair was long and fell loose down her back. Two tiny braids adorned her face on either side. Braeden got a good glimpse of the woman's necklace. Charms, crystals, and small vials crowded the chain around her neck, as well as a prominent red zigzag design Braeden recognized as The Prime Helix.

Sabine interrupted his gawking, "What are you staring at now?"

"Shhh, I'm not sure. That lady that walked in is an Apothecary. I recognize the charms on her necklace. I'm trying to figure out what she is doing here."

"Um. Maybe having dinner, like us?"

Braeden ignored Sabine's jab and tried to listen as the lady sat down at the booth with the red-haired man.

"Hey," Sabine jerked Braeden's hand to force him to look at her. "Why are you staring at those people? They seem perfectly harmless?"

Braeden resented that he couldn't afford to be that trusting anymore. "I'm trying to figure out why Wintergreen is meeting Red Beard."

"Wintergreen? Red Beard? Seriously, let them enjoy their meal."

"Shhh, one more minute..."

The lady Braeden had called Wintergreen was loud and boisterous. She pulled a small vial from her handbag. "So, this is a special mix of Rosemary, Thyme, and Thieves. It should clear that earache right up."

The man pulled his hand from his ear to grab the vial. He glanced up just in time to notice Braeden staring at him with a heated glare. Without warning the man slammed the vial down on the table, jumped up and took four giant steps over to Braeden's and Sabine's table. "Why do you keep staring at me?" They both sat silently. He leaned in to get closer in Braeden's space, "I know who you are. Why are you here?"

Braeden wanted to speak but was distracted by a lariat around the man's neck with a red horse on it. Braeden whispered his realization, "Red horse."

The stunned man stepped back, acting flustered, "Yes, this is the Red Horse Tavern, so what?"

"No," Braeden answered. "Are you the Red Horse?"

The man stepped back silently, giving no answers.

"I noticed your red door and I have a meeting later at a place called Farley's that I understand also has a red door. I am meeting the Black Horse there. Do you know the Black Horse?"

The man leaned in close and whispered, "Come with me."

Sabine and Braeden followed him back by his table where he thanked the Wintergreen woman and told her to order what she wanted. He led them through a leather door next to the bar, and down a long dim hallway to a door with a keypad next to it. Punching in a twelve-digit code, he opened it and ushered them in.

"Have a seat."

The room was small and painted dark teal. The facing wall was covered with a display of eight different projections showing data and charts, one of which Braeden recognized as a map of New Congress City and another was a diagram of Chandler Manor. Braeden's chin dropped. Noticing his reaction, the man touched a pad on his desk and the data disappeared.

Getting right to the point, the man sputtered, "You're Aviva Chandler's son, aren't ya?"

Braeden didn't answer.

"Check. So, why are you here and what do you know of the Red Horse?"

"I don't know anything of the Red Horse. I didn't even know there was a Red Horse. I just guessed when I saw your necklace."

"Hmm, well, what do you know of the Black Horse then?"

"I told you, I am meeting him later tonight at a place called..." Braeden stopped himself. Why did you have a diagram of my mother's house on your wall?"

"I don't answer questions, I ask them. You waltzed into my establishment and if you want to waltz out, you're going to answer my questions."

Sabine, feeling threatened for the first time, grabbed Braeden's hand under the ledge of the desk. He squeezed her hand without looking. "I'm meeting the Black Horse at Farley's at 7:00."

"Why?"

"I have a message from a mutual friend."

"Who could possibly be a mutual friend of you and the Black Horse?"

"C.F.M."

The red man's eyes opened wide. "*You* are a friend of Cr..."

"Charles!" Braeden emphasized.

He eyed Braeden suspiciously, but confirmed, "Charles, yes."

Sabine's stomach growled so loudly both men startled and turned to look at her. Braeden and Sabine laughed, but the man didn't say a word.

"Well, little lady, it sounds like your stomach has betrayed you in this clandestine meeting."

"We are pretty hungry. That's the only reason we stopped here, to eat."

"Yes, well I can do something about that." He pressed the touch pad on his desk again and scrolled through screens projected on his wall until he got to the one labeled MENU. "Here, pick what you want, it's on the house."

He flicked an accusatory finger at Braeden, "I'm sure you can afford to pay, but we don't accept coins here anyway."

"You don't?" Sabine asked.

"I mean, we'll take it, but we prefer trades."

"Yeah, speaking of that," Braeden interrupted. "I am sorry about staring at you before. I thought you were holding your ear because you had an earpiece. But then I saw the Apothecary symbol on that lady's chain."

"Oh, know your symbols, do you? You must have worked closely with…Charles."

# 29 ~ Wilderness

"Hey! Hey! Delilah, are you okay?"

Delilah's eyes flew open. She screamed and shirked as she realized she was screaming. Bodhi, who had been trying to shake her awake, was so startled he screamed at her scream.

"Are you okay?" Delilah didn't respond. "Seriously Delilah, you're freaking me out. You were screaming in your sleep and now you're not talking."

"Mmm, I'm fine. I'm just trying to get my bearings."

"I pulled over so I could snooze while you were napping, and you just started yelling. What were you dreaming about? Your body was like, rigid."

"It was my sister." Delilah swallowed hard to keep from crying. "There was also a white tiger, but it was like the tiger was trying to keep her away from me." Her voice trailed off as she realized the tiger was probably her grandmother.

"You have a sister?"

"Yeah, she's my twin."

Bodhi kept asking questions, but Delilah tuned him out to concentrate. Since leaving New Congress City, she had assumed that Sequoia wanted to stay with her grandmother. Sequoia had changed. She was cold and mean and not like herself. Even though they had been arguing about everything, Delilah couldn't believe it when Aviva told her Sequoia asked for her own room on the other end of Chandler Manor.

She had reluctantly helped Sequoia pack her belongings, though Sequoia's blank stare left her angry and afraid. Delilah had had many nightmares of that day, but her current nightmare of her sister was different. It made her wonder if her sister had left their room willingly, or had been brainwashed? It sounded so far-fetched, but it never seemed plausible that her sister could have become the person she was right before Delilah left.

Bodhi had started driving again. His voice became audible and pulled her out of her trance. She giggled silently as she felt like she was eavesdropping on Bodhi's dissertation to himself about rude people that ignore someone who is obviously talking to them.

"Hey, I'm back," Delilah interrupted as she sat up.

"S'bout time. Where'd ya go?"

"Sorry, I was trying to figure some things out." Not giving Bodhi time to comment, Delilah switched topics. "So, what do you know about Aviva Chandler?"

"Wow that came out of left field. Well, I guess besides the fact that she's a badger from hell who scammed the entire Collection, brainwashes people with propaganda, and sends old people and children out into the wilderness to die, she is probably an okay person."

"Bodhi, I've been wondering, but I didn't want to ask, what ended up happening to your grandparents?"

"Well, when the Collectors threw gramps out on the road, his head hit the pavement and he died in a split second. My grandma was so upset she ran as fast as her legs would carry her and tried to jump on one of the Collectors. He pushed her off and shot her in the head."

"Oh, my goodness, Bodhi. They shot her?! You must have been terrified."

"Those of us left were so scared. I felt like a ghost following the pack. I didn't think. I didn't even worry about eating or staying warm. A couple of the old ladies tried to take care of me and the other kids. We wandered around in the boonies for four days. Some of them collapsed and died from the cold. We had to leave them there--alone." Bodhi shook his head in disgust. "Eventually, there was an abandoned town and we tried to camp there, but it was still cold with no heat. We built fires, but the nights were R-U-F-F. I've never gotten over being that cold, so voila, my awesome temperature control system."

Bodhi paused to pan the cab of the truck to display his handiwork. Delilah smiled but said nothing, the resentment of her grandmother festering.

"When they found us, there were only six of us left. One cool couple that wanted to adopt me as their grandson, two old feisty dudes, a kid about my age who I am pretty sure was schizophrenic, and little ole me."

"Who found you?"

"Two Sentries from the GC saw the smoke from our fires. They gave us a couple choices of where we could go to be safe. After how cold we had been, we all chose the south. The large GC farm in old Tennessee is where I have been ever since, well, until ending up in Indie City."

"I'm really sorry Bodhi. You have been through a lot."

"S'okay, I am a lot better than I used to be. Now, why were you asking about that old Chandler beast? I feel like you keep trying to ask me a question, but then you ask me other questions to avoid asking what you really want to know, ya know?"

Delilah froze at the thought of Bodhi figuring out her past and her family. She tipped her head down in reverence to Bodhi's grandparents and her parents and everyone else she believed her grandmother had harmed and decided to tell the truth.

"Do you know who I am?"

Bodhi sang, "Delilah Marieee from Tallahatchieee or Indie Cityeee or..." He stopped abruptly, "Hey what is your last name?"

"McAvoy."

"Delilah Marie McAvoy," Bodhi confirmed.

"Actually, it's Delilah Jane McAvoy."

"Cool, named after a famous person. Did your mom like Jane McAvoy?"

"My mom is, uh, was Janie McAvoy."

Bodhi took his foot off the gas and let the car coast to a stop. It was the first time Delilah had seen him speechless. He turned to stare at her, leaning his elbow on the steering wheel and rested his head on his hand. He then leaned back to his seat. Four positions and twenty silent questions later Bodhi finally made the connection.

"So, if Jane McAvoy is your mother, then Aviva Chandler..."

"...is my grandmother."

"Aw snap. I would like to say sorry for everything I said about her..."

"I wouldn't expect you to say sorry. I knew my grandmother was not a good person, but I didn't know how bad she was until talking to you."

"That's just my opinion. Seriously though, I'm sorry."

Delilah tried to laugh, "Sorry about what you said or sorry that she is my grandmother?"

"Yeah, you right, both. So, how did you get out of the Collection? Did you run away or something?"

"People don't often run away from the Collection."

"Truth, especially a congresswoman's granddaughter, I'm sure."

"Exactly! It had been bad for a while. My sister had--wait, what did you say a while ago about brainwashing?"

"Uh yeah, well that was your grandmother's master scheme. She began weekly, and sometimes daily speeches to the Collection about stuff like loyalty."

"Yes, but couldn't you turn off the monitors? It's only brainwashing if you listen to it."

"True, there were some that were smart enough to do that. That's why she started the flushes."

Recognition hit Delilah's brain. "I remember hearing that word--flush."

"She couldn't take it, ya know, that someone might have an opinion other than hers. She dug up some info about mind benders they used, like a hundred years ago."

"Mind benders?"

"Yeah, ya know, drugs that make people tell the truth or get them to do what you want. I think the main one was called Devil's Breath and then she added some mushrooms or something and changed a few things."

"I guess you can do that when your family has unlimited resources."

"Right? So, anywho, she thought about creating some type of 'vaccine' but there was so much hubbub over those during the pandemic, she knew she still wouldn't get everybody, so she schemed up a delivery system that could reach everyone."

"But what could reach everyone?"

"Think about what flows into every single home in the Collection."

"The water system?"

"Ding, ding, ding. We have a winner."

"Okay, but is mind control really a thing?"

"Well, yeah, but this new formula works different. It relaxes the impulse to disagree."

"But if it was in the water supply, how was I not affected? How was she not affected?"

"I'm sure Chandler Manor had its own water supply."

"Okay Bodhi, this is what I am trying to figure out. My sister…"
"Yeah, I almost forgot, you said you had a twin sister."

"Yes, anyway I think she might have been brainwashed, but I am trying to figure out why I wasn't."

"I don't know. Did she spend a lot of time out of your house?"

"Not that I know of." Then the answer slapped Delilah's brain. "Wait, she had been drinking these awful immune boosting shakes. She, and my grandmother kept trying to get me to try them. I had a sip once, but they had a horrible aftertaste and I remember feeling weird afterward. I thought I was maybe getting the flu or something. My sister said she felt that way too when she first tried them, but she said the shakes made her better."

"I think that's how the drug works. It makes you feel gross at first but then it's like, addicting. The flushes make people, like, super thirsty, so everyone wants to drink more water which makes the drug stronger in their system. New Fundamental never had flushes, but we had injections into our food supply. That's the reason they wanted my grandparents' orchard. I had been drugged for years and didn't even know it until the elimination. I think that might be why so many died in the wilderness. Besides being cold, or old, we were all going through withdrawals."

Delilah leaned forward and rested her head on the dash. "How could I be related to such an evil person? How does someone do that to so many people?"

"Greed," Bodhi responded almost inaudibly as he put his hand on Delilah's back. She nodded in acceptance. Bodhi noticed the darkness that had slipped down around them. "We better get going. Tell me now if you have any more big announcements. I need you to watch the monitor and help me troll for anything moving."

Bodhi tapped the monitor to turn it on, and he and Delilah both startled as they saw a red figure fast approaching.

# 30 ~ Devil in the Details

"My mother? What do you mean, my mother?"

Croft stepped back as I rolled up onto my knees with determination.

Char intervened, fearing for Croft. "Janie, you were not ready to know this before. I know you want all the answers right now, but you're going to have to trust us. We've been through this process before with others. You can easily get overloaded and we…"

"Do you mean you're not going to tell me anything else?"

"No, no that's not what I mean. We couldn't tell you more, before this. You are still fragile until all that poison gets out of your system."

Croft appeared frozen, not knowing whether to move. I tried to relax my face and reached up to grab his hand. His surprise changed his face so much that guilt hollowed out my insides. What I had done to this poor man. I squeezed his hand, and he squeezed back as the tears, which hadn't been absent long, reappeared in his eyes. He knelt in front of me and put his free hand on my cheek. It felt like home.

He whispered intently, "Janie, I'm so sorry. I never meant to hurt you or keep anything from you. I…lo…" He sighed heavily. "I care about you more than you know. I only ever wanted to protect you. You have had so much pain in your life. Even though I want you to have your memory back, I wanted to save you from re-experiencing the hard stuff again."

I let my chin fall to my chest. I could not still be mad at that man, but I also couldn't give him what he needed. He took a breath to speak, and I put my hand up to his mouth gently to stop him. I couldn't yet look him in the eyes because I knew I would fall prey to their blue persuasion.

I whispered, "Croft, I'm not mad at you. I am sorry I was. The whole situation, our situation, was not what, I mean--it was a big surprise."

Char interjected an "mmm hmmm" and acted like she was going to speak, but Croft put his hand in the air to stop her.

"I didn't know how to think of our situation. I still don't, but I know you lo…"

"Loves you," Char interjected again. We both glared at her.

I scooted closer and dared to look into his eyes. "I can't even express all that I feel for you right now." He smiled like a blossom to the sun. I paused to not ruin the moment and to drink in his expression. "I just can't...I mean, I don't even know who I am."

Surprisingly he kept smiling, "It's okay Janie. It's my fault. I would have never--I mean you can have all the time you need. And if in the end, you decide that you don't want this, or me, I will understand."

I tried to smile as reassuringly as I could, "That's why I know you love me. That's why I love you." I stunned myself so much as I said it that I couldn't think of anything else to do than to wrap my arms around his neck so that I didn't have to look at him or say anymore.

Suddenly Croft and I both noticed Char, the fly on the wall, had been tiptoeing across the room to the exit. Croft and I broke our embrace and then simultaneously begged her to stay. All three of us laughed in the moment.

"No, you kids have some catching up to do," she conceded.

I jumped up and ran across the room to her. "Char we want you to stay. It's going to take a while to figure all of this out."

Croft joined us and put his hand on her shoulder. "Charlotte, we need you to stay. You have some of the answers I don't, and Janie needs both of us right now."

"Well, when you put it that way, I guess." Judging by her awkward smile, Char loved that she was needed. "Why don't we take a walk outside? It's beautiful today."

I looked apprehensively at them both. "Is it safe?" Croft put his arm around me and guided me to follow Char as we talked. "So, I'm guessing that's a yes?" They both laughed.

Char turned to speak over her shoulder as we walked swiftly down the gray corridor. "It's safe Janie. Normally we would be on high alert with you here, but we just installed more eyes in the sky. We have cameras in a mile perimeter around the city now."

"That leads me to a question..."

Croft interrupted, "I promise Janie, we will give you all the details about your mother."

"My mother, I had almost forgotten. Yes, yes, I do want all the details, but I had another ques...wait. Am I this flighty normally?"

They both looked at each other and emphatically responded, "No!"

"Okay good. Anyway, I have heard this place called the ghost city, the underground city and just the city. Does it have a real name?"

Char took over, "We had never intended for it to become a city, more of a layover really. Proximity wise, it's much too close to Collection developments, but people kept coming and we had to keep expanding. It turns out that it's a good location for us to keep an eye on Collectors that

128

frequent old Fort Wayne, which I think they call Fort Promise, or something else ridiculous like that. The biggest change in our little city was when Chul-moo and my brother Chauncey came."

"Smart men, smart, smart men," Croft mumbled to himself.

Char continued, "They both had so much knowledge and experience. They have revolutionized our technology to ensure our safety here."

"So, long story short, we call this place Fox Island," Croft interjected.

"Yes, thank you, Croft." Char confirmed as she patted his arm.

I smiled at their interplay. "So how did you come up with that name?"

Charlotte finished. "It's under an old park of the same name. Plus, foxes are cunning and often outwit their predators. It seemed to fit." I nodded at the logic in it.

We had been walking through corridor after corridor. I was so focused on our conversation I hadn't paid much attention to where we were going. I noticed the rushing water I had heard before, but we were in a new hallway with a greenish-blue cast. As we walked, the sound of water became louder, and the floor and ceiling danced with patterns of light. Finally, the walls disappeared, and I realized we were under, and surrounded by the stream, in a glass tunnel that seemed to cut right through. The play of light from the sun above the water was mesmerizing.

Croft grabbed my hand and led me through the glass tube about forty feet to a door at the end of the tunnel. Charlotte was already punching in a number code on a keypad that opened the door to a dark staircase that twisted with a landing halfway up. My chest tightened hard, and my pulse was racing. Still holding Croft's hand, I stopped at the bottom of the staircase. Char turned. "What's wrong?"

Croft immediately jumped into action. "I got this," he said confidently. Bounding up the stairs, I heard noises and then a light from the top appeared. He hollered down, "Better?"

"Yes," I squeaked. I still didn't want to go into the stairwell, but knowing there was an escape, and Croft, at the top made it bearable. Twelve steps up and then a landing and a turn. Once we got to the turn, I could see the top.

As we walked through the opening, I realized we were emerging from a tree. The door closed after we stepped out and left behind a seamless tree trunk. Char and Croft both smiled at my amazed expression. "How does the tree stay alive?"

Croft interjected, "The trunk is man-made, but what appear to be the big branches up top are actually dwarf trees that are grown from a hydroponics chamber above the stairwell we were just in."

"That's incredible. It looks completely flawless and alive."

Char smiled at the accomplishment of the secret world she helped develop.

The park was buzzing with birds and squirrels. A cool breeze wrapped around me and sent a shiver up my spine. Croft put his arm around me to warm me. It prompted a flash of a memory with Croft.

"Have I been here before? I remember standing some place like this with you, and your arm was around me."

Croft was introspective. "Yes, it was very similar to this. You were finally getting to a good place, where you could smile again, so we decided to venture out into the wilderness to get away. We camped for weeks, living off the land and making plans for the future."

"The future?"

"Yes, our future, our friends' future, everyone's future. You had a thousand ideas for how to jumpstart a new movement in the country."

"I did?"

"You did," interjected Char. "Janie, we all looked to you."

Suddenly that familiar weight I had felt in the council meeting room returned. I took a few steps forward and sat on a fallen log. Croft and Char sat on either side of me with questioning looks.

"I'm going to stop you Char because I know that conversation is too big for me right now. What I need you both to tell me, is everything you can about my mother. The world can wait. I need to get myself figured out first."

"Always so smart and in tune with yourself, Janie," Croft said with reverence. His kind words and tone reminded me of the day before when I wasn't so smart or in tune with myself. I knew I had to tell him about Trey, but I couldn't do it then.

Char pierced my thoughts. "Janie, why don't we start with the questions you have about your mother?"

"Well, the obvious question is why would my mother kidnap me? And also where is my father in all of this?"

Croft pulled my hand over to his. "Sweetheart, you and your mom have been at odds for many years. It began way back when society started to fall apart. Let me back up some more. Your father died in 2019. He was a good man, a very good man. He was a scientist. He was kind, could talk your ear off, spiritual but not religious, jovial. His laugh…"

"I can't believe I have to ask this, but what was his name?"

"Avery Chandler. Avery Braeden Chandler."

A glimpse of a tall broad man looking down at me raced through my mind. "Did he have red hair but more of a tan complexion than most redheads?"

"Yes, exactly. Do you remember seeing him?"

"I have a picture of him in my head. I don't know why I knew it was him."

"Very good," Charlotte praised. "That's how it starts, small memories, pictures, feelings. Your memory is trying to come back."

130

I nodded and smiled. "How did he die?"

Char looked at Croft to field the question. "Avery was in his lab. There was an explosion. That's all we know." His sudden silence made me suspicious.

"Was the explosion accidental?"

"That's really all we know."

I wanted to feel sad about my father, but I remembered nothing of him except his appearance. I felt ill that I couldn't. I closed my eyes and begged again for the darkness to release itself, but when it refused, I opened my eyes with new purpose.

"Okay, I'm going to have to revisit that later. Now tell me about my mom."

Croft continued, "Your mother was different back then too. She was the head of a renewable energy company. She was powerful, but gracious. Then the corporations started to unite. The CEOs formed a union of sorts-- the very thing they despised. They fired the lobbyists and organized and rallied congress themselves. It infuriated you because they weren't asking for better pay or working conditions for their employees, it was all based on greed. They wanted more money for themselves and found every legal loophole possible to get what they wanted. Their greed was insatiable. What they couldn't get legally, they 'purchased' or stole."

"Yes," Char interrupted. "But it was more than greed. Ultimately it was about a quick grab for control of all of the country's resources."

Croft nodded. "Your mother stood for everything that you opposed, and you became very vocal about it. As the corporations took over, they bought the rest of the politicians to strip away every civil liberty possible. As the rights were stripped from the middle class, so were the money and the power. At first you and others spoke out quietly about the trends that threatened us all, but as the first round of riots broke out around the country, the CEOs and their puppets in Congress began to crack down. Most of Congress and the Supreme Court were bought and paid for by then, and the election laws had been rigged so extensively that the last officially elected President of the United States was a mouthpiece. He had no more power than a figure head, and no way to turn the tide. That's when your mother became ruthless. She stopped talking to you and tried to get your brother and sister to turn you in, every time you spoke at a rally."

"I have a brother too?"

"Yes, I will get to him shortly. I need to get this out first, for your sake and mine. Your mother hatched a plan, a truly horrible plan to keep you in line. She was responsible for the car bomb that killed your husband, my brother." Croft's eyes dilated with emotion. "We had suspicions that she didn't kill your children but kidnapped them instead."

"But why, even if she was mad at me, even if she didn't agree with me, would she kill my husband and kidnap my children--and me? What type of awful person does that to her own family?"

Char added, "She did it to keep you in line, Janie. We now know that she threatened to harm your children if you didn't stop speaking out. You didn't believe her, so she took them instead and faked their deaths in the explosion. None of us thought that your children could still be alive back then. After that, you tried to step out of the spotlight, but she realized you were trying to empower other people to step up and speak. The only way to stop you was to kill you or to kidnap you too. I think she had high hopes of trying to reprogram you like she tried with your sister and brother."

"This is so much to process. I see why you were worried about telling me. I'm glad I can't remember her. If I'm this angry without even remembering her, I can't imagine how I'll feel when I do."

"I can," Croft mumbled.

For some reason, it made me laugh. "But wait, you said earlier and now again that my daughters are alive. Are they alive?"

"I'm so stupid, Janie. Your brother and I had many conversations, but we never had time to talk about more than your rescue. I could have found out months ago if I would have just asked." He shook his head berating himself.

"So...?"

"So, it has been confirmed, that a girl matching Delilah's description has been living safely in Indie City farther up north for a few years now. We're pretty confident it's Delilah. Her identity was kept secret to protect her, so she was not discussed on any channels that could be intercepted. She is on the move now, and we are hoping to reunite you within a few weeks."

"Croft, I'm obviously happy I will get to meet her, er, see her again, but why didn't anyone tell me, for several years, that my daughters were alive?"

"Janie, we didn't find out until after you were taken that it was even a possibility. I would have never kept that from you."

I wanted to believe him, so I chose to. I tried to instead focus on Delilah, and the face of the little blond girl I had seen in my fractured memory.

"How old is she?" I felt embarrassed I didn't know right after I said it.

"Sixteen."

"Sixteen?! How much time have I missed?"

Char joined the conversation again, "Your girls were taken when they were ten. We assumed them dead for four years when rumors of them in New Congress City began to surface. Delilah had apparently become defiant toward your mother and allowed herself to be seen in public several times. It was then that a Sentry was able to get her to Indie City, but he

132

thought it safest for her to keep her identity hidden. Like Croft said, all of this was just confirmed since she was being moved."

"I wanted to go see for myself Janie, when I heard the first rumors about her being in Indie City, but you had just been kidnapped and I couldn't focus on anything but finding you first. Besides, if it was her, I feared she might recognize me, and I had no idea what I would tell her about her mother."

"So, my daughters knew you well?"

"They used to call me Uncle Crock," he chuckled in a melancholy way.

"Oh, that's right, you are my—their uncle." I paused to breathe and once again review the spider web of our tangled relationships. Croft was gloomy. "Why is your face so sad? Is it something about Delilah?"

"Janie, she is fine, I promise you. I just miss her. She was my little buddy."

"That is sweet. Is that all though?"

"I always thought of your girls, Anson's and your girls, as my girls too. When he was alive, the five of us spent a lot of time togeth..."

Croft couldn't finish the thought. I looked to Char, but she was artificially busying herself with a small family of squirrels a few yards away.

Croft took a deep breath and tried to finish, "It's not that I ever wanted to replace their dad. Despite everything I still wish he were alive, even though the implications of that are hard to swallow. I just…"

"Wish they were yours in the first place?" I offered.

"No, no--well, yes, I guess there have been times I thought that. I'm sorry Janie. I miss my brother more than you know. I was so happy for you both when the girls were born."

"It's okay, you don't have to say any more. I think I get it. Char told me more about what happened between us."

"She did, did she?" Croft eyed Char suspiciously.

"Yes, I understand now how hard all of this has been on you. I'm sorry. So, during that whole time, did you marry or date anyone else or have any children?"

"Hell no, everyone thought he was gay." Char shouted up to the sky while keeping her back to us. "He had all kinds of women chasing him. He was the total package, you know. But he never glanced at one of them. He only had eyes for you."

Croft looked at me and smiled at her intrusion, "There were not women chasing me."

Char was suddenly near us again, "Oh yes, yes there were many interested in Croft McAvoy, just not the one who mattered."

Char walked on past us as she patted me on the shoulder. Her gesture, for whatever reason, sparked a new thought, "But what about my other daughter Sequoia? Is she still alive?"

"Yes, we know now that she is still with your mother--by choice," Croft confirmed.

"By choice? But does she know who she is with? I mean why is she still there?"

"We are hoping to get those answers when Delilah gets here. Everything is more complicated now, Janie. We can't just make a phone call for information. It has taken many years to establish lines of communication and to figure out who we can trust. Now that you are safe, I feel like we have more time to concentrate on moving forward with a plan."

I knew he was right, so I relaxed my shoulders. Croft breathed deeply and wrapped his arms around me. His embrace spoke words he wanted to say and words I wanted to hear. We inhaled and exhaled in unison for several minutes, and I closed my eyes to feel the rhythm. It was the first moments of real peace I had had since my rescue. Croft and I were friends again, and I was going to see my daughter. Hope was replacing fear, and I knew everything was going to work out.

Then, without warning, the peace left me, and my stomach felt queasy. I was so on edge, trying to figure out what was going on. Then it happened again, a vibration in the ground beneath me. "Do you feel that?" I put my hands down on the log to validate.

"What? What's wrong?" Croft asked worriedly.

"Vibrating, can you feel the vibrating?" I got up and walked toward the stream. The water buzzed with tight ripples. "Look, do you see that?"

Croft and Char ran to my side. The look in Char's eyes was pure panic. "Oh my, they've found us."

"What do you mean Char?" Croft asked incredulously.

"I mean, that vibration in the water is from one of our newer warning systems. The alarm sounds below, but because of Janie's heightened senses, she can feel it up here. It means the city is about to be breached. I'm not sure how they found us, but, wait…" Charlotte's voice trailed off.

"Char, I know we weren't followed, and we watched you follow the safety measures to cover our tracks."

"Yes, Croft, but remember you took her sooner than you had planned to because of the orderly pulling the alarm at the TRC. She still had so much of the drug in her system."

"And?"

"And that means the compound they use for tracking is still strong in her bloodstream."

"Of course," Croft berated himself. "That is probably how they found us at the tree house. I just assumed since it had been Janie's home, Aviva guessed we were there. I didn't even think of the tracking protein."

I swallowed hard. "D'you mean, they are here because of me?"

134

Croft put his hands on my shoulders to reassure me, "It's okay Janie, it's not your fault."

Char interrupted abruptly, "There is no blame. Forget that. We just need to get underground right now and hook up a transfusion cocktail."

# 31 ~ Tunneling

"So, do you have another name besides Red Horse?" Braeden persisted.

"To be sure, but I won't be telling you now, will I?"

"What should I call you then?"

"Mmm, I don't know. How about something like Hot Tamale?" he offered slyly.

Not amused Braeden countered, "I'll just call you Red."

A knock on the door broke the awkwardness in the room. A young woman with short spiky red hair entered the room carrying a large tray of food. Her features indicated some relation to Red. The woman placed two crocks of French onion soup, two small salads and a large loaf of crusty bread on the desk. She uttered a name and a bony youngster with dark hair and bulging eyes stepped into the office carrying silverware, napkins and two beers.

"Alcohol?" Sabine questioned.

"I can get you water, if you like," the young woman offered unapologetically.

"No, no it's fine. I have only had it once and I probably drank it a bit too fast. I will drink this slower."

Braeden leaned back behind Sabine, out of eye shot and mouthed, "How about some water too?" The girl nodded.

Red interrupted the exchange, "So tell me again why you are meeting the Black Horse?"

"I don't think I told you in the first place, Braeden answered sloppily while sipping his soup.

"The Black Horse and I are very close."

"Well then I guess he will tell you after the meeting."

Red threatened, "I know some people that must be looking for you. It would be a shame if they found you here, or in the alley out back."

"If you were a friend of the Black Horse and Charles, you wouldn't be threatening me, you would be offering to help us."

136

"Help a Chandler? You've got to be kidding."

Sabine interrupted, "He's not like the rest, er, like his mother. He is leaving and joining the GC."

Braeden's look cautioned her to stop. Red jumped up and clapped his hands. "Aye there, there's that Chandler face."

"I'm telling you," she stopped to chew and swallow, "forget about his last name. He cares about people. He is a good man."

"Known him a long time then?"

"Long enough. He is trying to help…"

Red quickly sat back in his desk chair and spun away from them. Braeden could see him typing on a small blue screen, then Red got up and abruptly left the room.

Sabine leaned in to whisper to Braeden, "He gives me the creeps. We need to get out of here."

"I think you're right."

They hurried to drink down their soup and took a bite of bread. As they stood to leave, the door opened. Red walked in with a man dressed in the black and burgundy security uniform worn in and around Chandler Manor. Sabine gasped and Braeden struggled to recognize the man. The security officer closed the door and stood in front of it with his hand on his holster. Braeden glanced at Sabine and then eyed Red who responded with a feigned gasp.

"Yah, come on boy. There's that Chandler venom."

Braeden lashed out, "You're questioning me, and you walk back in with a Collector?"

Red pointed at Sabine, "You, I can account for. I can verify you." Then he pointed at Braeden, "But you, you are not accounted for. There's a lot of confusion in the network over you."

Sabine interrupted, "Well a spy doesn't have contacts with everyone do they? They are usually only connected to one or two people in an organization, or they wouldn't be spies, would they?"

"That's true Miss Sabine," Red countered. "But wouldn't you think a spy would know the true identity of his contact if he was worth his spit?"

"Not necessarily."

Red tried to speak again but Braeden interrupted him, "I never said I didn't know my contact. I told you his name is Charles."

"Yes, but that is not his real name, boy."

"I know that!" Braeden replied indignantly.

"You do?" Red answered at the same time Sabine questioned, "It isn't?"

"Yes, and no," Braeden answered to each of them respectively.

Both Sabine and Red started rapidly firing off questions until Braeden slammed his hands down on the table and yelled, "Enough!" Their silence amplified the rustle of the safety guard removing his weapon from his hip and pointing it at Braeden who froze upon realization.

"Chill, chill, put that thing away. Can we all calm down?" Braeden took a deep breath as the man returned his weapon to its holster. "I do have answers, but I have just as many questions. Why is one of my mother's goons here?"

Red flopped down in his chair again, "No, no, no I tell you nothing until you tell me Charles' real name."

Frustrated Braeden blurted out, "C.F.M. is Croft Frasier McAvoy! There, are you happy? Now tell me why he is here," pointing to the security guard.

"Don't get your panties in a bunch. This is one of our field agents. We like to call 'em Weeds in the GC. You know, they get in there and work their way around the garden, slowly killing off the competition."

"Field agents? Killing? That doesn't sound very GC to me."

"My thoughts exactly," Sabine added.

"Well, we don't live in la-di-da land here. This is the front line. What we do makes it possible for all of those gardeners to live in peace and harmony."

"Don't bore me with your speeches. Something about this operation is not right and I'm going to find out what." Braeden grabbed Sabine's hand and attempted to sidestep the security guard. The guard looked to Red for permission to let them go and Red nodded. As the guard stepped aside Braeden asked, "And why don't I recognize you, if you work at my house?"

"His first day is tomorrow," Red offered.

"Ah, well good luck with that." Braeden opened the door with more force than was needed and almost hit the guard. Sabine glanced at a clock reading 6:32 p.m. on the wall in the hallway as they left. She nodded for Braeden to notice, and they both picked up their step, knowing they still needed to find *Farley's* before seven.

As they neared the door to the main dining room Red yelled from behind, "When you see the Black Horse, tell him time is running out."

Braeden and Sabine pretended they didn't hear and pushed through the doors to an empty restaurant. Feeling an immediate panic Braeden cautioned Sabine before she opened the door to the street. Ducking down in a booth by the main window where they sat before, Braeden could see Collectors running down the street.

Suddenly a door on the other side of the bar opened and the girl with spiky red hair burst through whispering in a panic, "No, no you can't go that way. Come with me."

Seeing no better option, Braeden and Sabine followed her into the kitchen.

"Come on now, we have to hurry." As she approached the far wall, a double decker built-in oven turned on by voice command. She set the time on the oven to 2:22 and a seem popped next to the oven. She grabbed the side and pulled, revealing the entire unit was not an oven, but a hinged door. The girl motioned for them to walk through. Once they were through the door, she pulled it, shutting them all in complete darkness.

"I'm sorry," the girl confessed. We need two to use the tunnel. I wasn't thinking. Do either of you have clearance?"

"I'm not sure, clearance for what?" Sabine asked.

"Here, let's just try it." The girl reached in the dark until she found Sabine's hand, fumbling to get to her thumb, and then placed it on a small pad on her wrist. The pad lit up, flashed red and then beeped. "Uh oh, well I hope yours works or we may be stuck here a while until the streets clear." She then reached out for Braeden's hand and repeated the process. The pad lit up and turned red, then blue then red again before it finally turned green. After it turned green the girl quickly put her thumb on the pad to verify, and abruptly the lights turned on revealing a short staircase followed by a long tunnel with canned lights down the middle of the ceiling.

Braeden raised his eyebrows at Sabine. The girl burst through between them and ordered them to follow. As they descended the stairs, they could hear commotion in the kitchen behind them. "Don't worry, they have never figured this out," the girl snarked over her shoulder.

"Is Red your father?" Braeden quietly inquired.

"Mmm'yeah, I wish I could deny it, but I'm stuck with him."

"Is he going to be okay?" Sabine asked, though she didn't really care.

"Oh yeah, he is already gone, not really chivalrous, you know. But he knows I can fend for myself."

Feeling sorry for the girl, Sabine tried to keep the conversation going as they made their way down the hall. "Did he know what was going on outside?"

"He knew it was coming, he just didn't know when."

"Why didn't he tell us?"

"He worries about himself and his own--well more like just himself. Sorry about that. I came back for you though."

"Yes, and we appreciate that," Braeden confirmed. "So where are you taking us?"

"Through the red door network. These tunnels connect all the red door establishments."

"Why couldn't your father have told us that?"

"Again, not so worried about you, he wanted information from you first and I guess once he got it--well, that's my dad." She shook her head in disgust. "Listen, once we get to Farley's you don't have much time. The spiders are out."

"I can't let them get Sabine, but I've been around Collectors my whole life. They don't scare me, then again they have never been after me."

Sabine patted him on the back, "Soon, my dear, soon." She smirked.

"More than Collectors, these are the elite fighters. There is no arguing or fighting, you just die if you are in their way."

Before Braeden could comment the red-haired girl shushed him. They had reached a fork in the tunnel. One of the tunnels was dark and quiet while the other was bright with green light. The green tunnel was loud with voices and music. Turning down the green hall, they all listened intently to the voices above them. If laughter was heard, they kept walking. Braeden counted four branches of the tunnel. Two were green, one was dark, and one tunnel was red. The red light spilled ominously into their space as they approached. The girl put her arms out to block Braeden and Sabine from going forward. Crouching down, she peered around the corner and pulled a concealed gun from an ankle holster under her pant leg. Braeden peered over the top of her head to see for himself. The tunnel was so long that the red light made it difficult to see detail. What he did see was bodies on the floor and what looked like some movement. Both he and the girl startled back. Braeden tripped and fell into Sabine who caught him effortlessly.

"Quickly, we have to do this quickly." The girl whispered as she grabbed Braeden's hand and pulled him back to the opening. Accelerating footsteps approached from the red haze. The girl held her small wrist pad up to a four-inch pad on the wall next to the tunnel entrance. A red laser pulsated to sync the two pads. Once it stopped, the girl put her thumb on her wrist pad and then grabbed Braeden's thumb to do the same. As soon as the pad turned green a door started to slide across in front of the tunnel opening.

Hearing two sets of running feet, Braeden's curiosity trumped his common sense and right before the door closed, he peered through the shrinking gap. He saw a young girl running for the door. "Uncle Braeden!" she shouted as the door closed. In horror, Braeden put his ear up to the closed door only to hear gun shots and a body fall against the door.

# 32 ~ Eagle Crossing

Bodhi put the truck in gear right as the figure approached the cab screaming and banging on the windows. His first instinct was to drive, but the man had white shoulder length hair and a green shirt with a GC emblem. He lowered the window to hear him.

"Go! Drive! Up that way, through those trees. That is the easiest way out."

"Okay, okay, sheesh I'm going. What is the big deal?"

"The big deal is that you are in a dried-up riverbed that's not going to be dry much longer."

"Really? Why?"

"There is a new Collection forming about twenty miles from here and they are getting ready to release the dam."

"At night?"

"Yes, they don't want anyone to know what they are doing. They want it to look like an act of nature. Now, come on, drive. We'll chat when you're out of the ravine."

Bodhi motioned for the man to get in the back seat, then turned on the headlights and shifted the gear for the terrain. He yelled to Delilah over the noise of the shaking truck, "I didn't even realize the road ended, did you?" Delilah shook her head. "There must have been a bridge here back in the day."

Delilah squinted to see through the dark window as they drove, "Yeah, there is a lot of grass and weeds. This must have been dried up for a long time."

"Hey, there it is!" Bodhi pointed to the steep embankment which appeared to be their best option. "Hold on!"

Delilah screamed, "What are you doing?"

"Well, we're either gonna make it up that hill…or we're not. Pedal to the metal baby."

"What? What does that mean?" Delilah shrieked.

"It means you seriously need to hold on."

The man in the backseat added a "Whoop, whoop!"

Delilah let out an accidental yelp as the truck lurched forward. Bracing against the dash, she closed her eyes and began humming to compensate for the thrill of the speed. Just as she thought they couldn't go any faster, the truck slammed hard on to the embankment, and she felt the truck tipping up and almost backward. Delilah opened her eyes in time to see them clear the line of trees at the top of the bank. Looking down to her side to see how steep the climb was, she was relieved she hadn't watched.

"Wa-hoooo!" Bodhi yelled. "I can't believe we actually made it."

The man in back joined in the celebration. Still breathing hard, Delilah nodded without saying a word.

Bodhi turned to the man in back. "Thanks, man. I don't know how long I would have driven around trying to figure out how we got in there and how to get out."

"Sure, sure, no problem. My name's Foster."

"Hey there, I'm Bodhi and this is Delilah. You're GC, yes?"

"Yes, I guess the green shirt gave it away huh? Your truck had me a little confused at first though. I saw a Collection rig like this not too long ago, but as I got closer, I could see it's been souped-up like the GC would do. I wish I could meet the people who modify these things. We could use some help with some of our rigs."

"Yer lookin' at him."

"No shit?"

Delilah leaned over to interject, "It really is amazing what he has done with this thing. It warms up to match your body temperature. It can see people in the dark."

"It can leap tall buildings in a single bound," Bodhi added as he slapped his knee laughing at himself. Delilah's look made him suddenly feel awkward, which made Delilah and Foster burst out laughing at his self-deprecating manner.

Foster patted him hard on the arm, "Just gibing ya, son." Then focusing on Delilah, Foster reached forward to shake her hand, "I'm sorry miss, Delilah did you say?" Delilah nodded. "I've been rude. Are you okay after that thrill ride?"

Delilah forced herself to smile. "Yes, I'm fine."

"All right, well good. Are you two hungry?"

Bodhi and Delilah both shouted, "Yes!" All three laughed again.

"Our town is only about a quarter of a mile east of here."

Bodhi fantasized about what foods were waiting for him.

"All right kiddo, do you see that road with the broken pavement ahead?"

"Yeah, is that the road where the bridge used to be?"

142

"Sure is, but you don't want that road. It's in rough shape. Drive to the right of it until you see a tree or something and then drive around the tree."

Bodhi side-eyed Foster sarcastically.

"Don't worry, there's not many trees."

Bodhi scanned the dark horizon which appeared to be trees in every direction, and then raised his eyebrows at Foster.

"...next to the road." Foster added.

Bodhi drove toward the road calling out every tree in his path. Delilah and Foster smirked at each other over Bodhi's comedic wit. As they approached the road, a small green light on the dash of the truck started to blink. Bodhi rolled down the window slightly so they all could hear the faint ping through the trees which everyone, but Delilah knew was part of the GC network of warning and information. Bodhi explained to her that a green light with a ping alerted them that someone in the GC was approaching. A yellow light indicated uncertainty and a red light was most likely danger.

Foster continued to explain to Delilah, "Even though your light is signaling green, showing the GC network, your light to us showed yellow because of this morphed vehicle that your friend created."

Delilah smiled appreciatively at Bodhi who was suddenly mesmerized by the dance of the cab lights across Delilah's face. She mirrored his comedic style by raising her eyebrows and tilting her head in question of his staring. When she turned to glance back at the road Delilah mimicked Bodhi's droll tone and said, "tree".

Foster laughed and Bodhi broke from his trance, shaking his head in confusion. Delilah gestured ahead with her hand insistently and yelled, "Tree!" Bodhi looked up just in time to swerve around a set of maple trees.

Foster guffawed and slapped his thigh, "Wow, she is good--mostly because you don't see her coming."

"Yeah, she's a quick one," Bodhi mocked satirically. "Maybe next time she'll be quick enough to point out the tree," he paused for effect, "a little soooooooner."

"I thought you were the tree whisperer. I was just helping out," Delilah added without missing a beat.

Bodhi relaxed as the trees thinned and they came to a deserted town. There were streets after streets of dark houses with an emerging city center in the distance. Delilah saw a green road sign that read, "La Crosse – 1 mile." Foster had Bodhi turn left down a street that had four houses lining a cul-de-sac.

"Pull over to that one on the right," Foster ordered. As they drove into the driveway Foster opened the door before Bodhi could come to a complete stop. He disappeared around the side of the house. Suddenly the garage door opened, and on the inside of the garage was Foster, hoisting it up with an old shovel. Once he got it high enough, he moved to the side and motioned for them to drive in. Then, he carefully let the door back down so it wouldn't crash.

Bodhi got out of the truck. "Yeah, who would ever expect to find a working car in a garage these days?"

"That was my thinking," agreed Foster. "Let's wedge this door closed just in case though."

After securing the door, Bodhi and Delilah followed Foster into the house. Bodhi stood nostalgic. "Wow, I can't even remember living in a real house."

"I can," Foster added. "And as much as I love the GC life, it always saddens me when I think back."

As they walked through the living area, Bodhi spotted a few blankets folded on a couch. He looked to Foster for permission.

"Sure, take them. You two are definitely not dressed for the temperatures tonight."

They continued walking through to the kitchen where Foster closed the window he had crawled through. Foster made his way out of the back door on to a large, raised patio. Delilah and Bodhi stopped abruptly at the back door. Ahead of them were eight city blocks of burned out and destroyed houses.

Foster, who realized they were not still walking next to him stopped and turned back. "It's okay, it's not dangerous anymore. This was a big battle ground in the war, ya know?"

Bodhi and Delilah stood motionless. Foster walked back to Delilah who was crying.

"I knew it happened. I mean I know it happened, but I never saw firsthand how awful it was? Why would the government, my gran…" Suddenly she realized that everyone may not be so accepting of her family connections.

Foster quelled her fears. "We don't care who your grandmother is." Delilah was shocked he made the connection. "We are much more interested in who your mother is."

"Was, you mean." Delilah corrected.

"No, IS!"

"I'm sorry to tell you but my mother is dead."

Foster beamed. "No, I'm happy to tell you she is not."

"What? What do you mean? How do you know that?"

"We got word earlier tonight that she has been rescued and that her daughter may be heading this way."

"I knew it," shouted Bodhi. "Trey, that sneaky little bastard. I knew he knew. It was her after all." He picked Delilah up and swung her around. "That must be the best news all day."

Delilah pulled away, sat on the patio steps that descended into the yard, and sobbed. The almost full moon cast a distorted shadow in front of her.

144

Through her tears, her emotional pleas sounded especially direct. "I hope you know this for sure. I hope you would never tell a girl something like that if it wasn't true."

"It's true," Foster confirmed.

Delilah sobbed harder. "But where is she? Where has she been?"

"Sure, I know you want to know everything, but the sun will be up in about an hour and with those Collectors nearby, we need to get to a more secure location before daylight comes knocking on our door and says, 'I told you so'."

"Fine, we can go, but please tell me where she is. Is she here?" Delilah demanded with hope in her voice.

"Delilah," Bodhi intervened. "I know this has to be a big shock but hows'about we take this conversation on the road. I think Foster is right. I would just as soon get somewhere safe before sun-up." Bodhi held out his hand to help Delilah stand.

She cautiously looked around and put her hand in Bodhi's. "You're right. I'm sorry. I still can't believe my mother could be alive. Why would they tell me she was dead?"

"I don't know all the answers Delilah Marie, but I am guessing it was for your safety. Come on now, get a move on, little lady."

Bodhi and Delilah followed Foster through yard after yard of rubble, burnt and dilapidated houses trying to be reclaimed by the earth that was growing up around them. Delilah felt the sadness of all the people who lost their lives there. She silently wished them well, and the pain embedded in the rubble waned enough for her to keep walking. Feeling lighter, she remembered the news that her mother was not among those she had to mourn anymore.

"Why hasn't anyone cleaned this up?" Bodhi wondered aloud.

Before Foster could answer, Delilah interjected, "This is a burial ground of sorts. It would be like disturbing the dead. Plus, it's a good reminder of what happened, what so many gave their lives for."

Foster and Bodhi stopped and stared at Delilah, admiring her words. "Your friend is right," Foster added. "Add to that, if Collectors have been to the area and we move the rubble they will know people are here. We try very hard to make it look like no one lives here anymore, for safety."

The faint tease of daylight crept into the horizon behind the city. Foster led them three more blocks to the right where the lines of rebellion and capitalism began to blur again. On the block facing them, the store fronts were damaged and graffitied. Foster stopped at a store with boarded windows and a sign hanging from one corner by a chain that read, Phelp's Organic Grocery. Foster reached between the wooden slats that covered the door. After a series of beeps and a popping sound, he grabbed the left side of the door and pulled. The entire door with slats attached opened at a hidden hinge.

Once the three stepped through, the door closed behind them and sealed, pushing out a small cloud of dust in its wake. The inside was filled with flowerpots, seeds, growing lights, and shelves that looked like they once held produce. A thick layer of dust covered all. The room had only a few slits of light shining through from the rising sun. Foster walked to the row of growing lights. Pulling out a small black cylinder from his pocket, he plugged the lamp into the end of the device. The ultraviolet light lit up the room. Suddenly Delilah felt a vibration under her feet. Foster pulled both her and Bodhi to the center of the room and the floor lowered like an elevator. After about six feet, Delilah saw light around the edges. Voices, and what sounded like a busy day in a city burst through the silence. As the elevator touched down, they were both stunned to be standing in a large well-lit dome with people bustling through from corridor to corridor. "Welcome to the ghost city. We call it Eagle Crossing."

# 33 ~ Accomplices

Aviva flung open the door to her granddaughter Sequoia's bedroom. "I just spoke with Damien. He tells me his serving staff said you weren't drinking your protein shakes anymore. Why would you stop doing that?"

Sequoia didn't answer.

"You always talk about how great they make you feel."

"I know gran, but that's the thing. I haven't been feeling well, and I think the shakes are making it worse. My stomach hurts every time I drink one and I feel like I am in a fog or something."

"That's nonsense. Part of the problem is you haven't been drinking them on a regular basis, and your system is starting to get confused."

"I don't know, maybe I caught a cold or something."

"No one has been sick in this household in more than fifteen years."

"Gran, don't you think that is odd?"

"It's not odd at all. I pay a lot to keep you healthy, which is precisely why you need to keep drinking your shakes. If you are actually sick, it is probably from those other congressional brats you like to hang around."

"Gran, they're not brats. Besides, I need some company since my sister left. You're busy all the time, and Uncle Braeden is always gone with his new job."

"Yes, your sister did leave. She left you. She abandoned you, like your parents did. Don't get me started on your ungrateful uncle. I am the one who stayed. I am all you have. The one who has always had your best interests at heart."

"I know, gran, I know, but it's still so weird Delilah left. I mean I know we weren't getting along but there is something about it that never made any sense. I just remembered it when I stopped drinking the shakes."

Sequoia startled as Damien, Aviva's personal chef appeared next to her in the doorway and handed Aviva a large glass of purple liquid. Aviva dismissed Damien with a flick of the hand and walked toward Sequoia.

"I don't know what fairy tale you have yourself talked in to, but the truth is that you and I only have each other. I can't afford to live in a fantasy world, and neither can you. Now, drink this up, and I think you are going to feel better."

Sequoia leaned away from Aviva, disgusted that she was not listening. "Ew, no gran, what even is that?"

"Damien found a way to synthesize all of the vitamins into a purer liquid form. I bet it will be easier on your stomach. Come on now, Quoi, let's get you feeling better." Aviva moved the glass in Sequoia's direction. Sequoia slid herself off the end of her bed and her bedspread slid to the floor bringing with it a pile of books. Hearing the thud, Aviva set the drink on the nightstand, walked around the end of the bed, and picked up one of the books.

"Books? Where did you get these relics?" Aviva scanned the title and read it under her breath, *"The Chemical Conspiracy."* Aviva's look of horror caused Sequoia to take a few steps back. "This is garbage young lady. Do you hear me? Where did you get this? It was someone from that little group of yours, wasn't it?"

"Sheesh gran, relax! I haven't even opened it yet. What is the big deal? I was just curious. Besides I thought it might give me a little information. You never let me tell you about Delilah. She said…"

"Listen to me," Aviva wagged her finger in Sequoia's face. I am not interested in anything that little brat had to say. She showed her true colors, didn't she? Now I'm not going to let you get dragged down with all of this propaganda." Aviva reached for the other books on the floor.

"No, wait. Stop gran! Listen to me. Before Delilah left, she kept saying I was acting different. I thought it was her that had changed. I didn't want to believe her, but now I'm not sure. Some of my friends…"

"See, I knew they had something to do with this," Aviva interrupted.

Sequoia ignored the interruption, "Some of my friends said they never drink water in the city. One even said her father warned her not to, that it would make her sick."

Aviva's face turned bright red as she tried to collect her thoughts. "First of all, as children of congressional leaders they have no business cavorting about in the city anyway. It's not safe. Second, I don't know why their parents would fill their heads with such stories. I'll be looking into it. On the other hand, your sister has some mental issues, like your mother did, and neither of them ever had any common sense. Delilah apparently inherited some of your mother's foolishness. She has always been jealous of your even temperament. I am sure she, in her twisted sense of logic, just wanted to say anything to make you go with her. She knew better than to say such nonsense to me, being the only voice of reason here, and that is why she slunk off like a snake in the middle of the night."

148

"Gran, that is what I am saying, it was almost like Delilah had to get away from me. Thinking back on it, things didn't get bad between us until I was drinking those shakes a few times a day. Maybe there is something in them or something in the water. She kept saying I wasn't acting like myself."

"The only one who wasn't acting like herself was your sister." Aviva set the books down and sat on Sequoia's bed and patted her hand on the mattress inviting Sequoia to sit by her. Struggling to keep a calm façade, she tried to talk how she thought other grandmothers might. "Come here Sequoia. Let's talk."

Sequoia hesitantly approached her bed and sat down next to her grandmother. Aviva put her arm around her which immediately made Sequoia nervous, knowing that her grandmother was not the affectionate type.

"I'm sorry this has all been confusing for you and I'm sorry that you haven't been feeling well. But do you see how some of your bad decisions have led to this? You listened to your crazy sister and your misinformed friends, and you stopped drinking the vitamin mix that helps keep you healthy. Of course, you are not going to feel well and of course you are going to be confused. Let's set this straight right now. You are not allowed to hang out in the student lounge anymore."

"What? No gran..."

"I'm not finished. You are just too impressionable. Also, there will be no more of these antiques in here," Aviva continued while kicking the books on the floor. "Anything you need to know is on our intra-net. Most importantly…"

Sequoia interrupted again, "but I can't find that information on the intra-net. One of my friends even said the intra-net used to be called an internet and allowed people to connect all over the world for information. Can you imagine? Do you remember that gran?"

"Yes of course I remember. It was awful. There were no rules or restrictions so people could say whatever they wanted and call it the truth. People can't handle that much information. They need to be guided as to what is appropriate to read and discuss. That's why our intra-net is so helpful because it gives answers that have been discussed and approved so there is none of this nonsense about a government conspiracy to poison the water."

Alarmed, Sequoia leaned away from Aviva. "I never said it was a government conspiracy. I thought maybe there was radiation leakage, or like a parasite in the water system or something."

Realizing her misstep, Aviva smiled broader to cover her fury and began to unconsciously speak through her teeth. "Well, I assumed since one of the books was about a conspiracy. Usually a conspiracy implicates the government, no?" Sequoia sat silently trying to assess her grandmother's truth from fiction. "Anyway, back to my earlier point, we need to get you back on the proper course." She grabbed the glass of purple liquid from the nightstand with one hand while firmly holding her grasp around Sequoia's shoulder with the other hand. "This will make you feel so much better. Now drink up."

As Aviva moved the cup toward her mouth, Sequoia realized that only the drinks from Damien made her sick and Damien didn't make a move without Aviva. Suddenly Sequoia started to shake.

"See, you are so ill, you're shaking. Come now, let's get this in you before you get any worse."

Sequoia put her hand up in front of her mouth as the glass reached it and said, "If you are sure gran, will you show me how confident you are by taking a drink?"

"Don't be ridiculous! Besides, I already had mine today."

Preying on Aviva's silent admission in her shifting body language, Sequoia subtly pounced back. "I'm sure a little sip won't hurt. You know, now that I think of it, I don't think I have ever seen you drink it before."

"That's because I drink mine when I first get up. Now, I have had enough of this. You are going to drink this without any more arguing. I know your little game."

"And for the first time, I know yours." Sequoia's voice was an arrow.

Enraged, Aviva grabbed a chunk of Sequoia's hair, pulled back, and as Sequoia screamed, she tried to pour the liquid into Sequoia's mouth. Sequoia knocked the glass to the floor with her free hand, spilling the drink into her open closet. Aviva stood and a beastly expression transformed her face. Shocked and scared, Sequoia stepped back. When her grandmother tried to lunge for her, Aviva slipped on the liquid and fell into the closet. Sequoia shut the door quick and locked it. Immediately, she second guessed herself as her grandmother screamed through the door.

"Sequoia Sage McAvoy, you open this door. You will regret this, young lady. You will regret this." Her voice was panicked but firm.

Sequoia knew Aviva meant it and would make her regret it forever. Her only option was to leave and try to find her sister. Grabbing her white down coat, she slipped on a pair of short white patent leather boots. She knew she wouldn't have much time to get away before someone discovered the wild beast in her closet.

Sequoia approached the hallway door and decided to slip through it as quickly as possible to muffle the noise. Once on the other side she walked with a quick pace smiling at anyone she encountered in the hallway, so to not raise suspicions. Expecting she might be questioned at any of the normal routes off the grounds of Chandler Manor, Sequoia decided to walk the habitrail that looped past the student lounge in the Hall of Statutes.

As she rounded the sweeping hallway of the fourth floor, Sequoia passed the one person who might question her more than any other--

150

Damien. He didn't look up until she was almost to him. She smiled so politely and inconsequently that he did not initially realize it was her. "Thank you for the new drink. I feel much better now."

Damien smiled a confused and unconvinced smile but nodded his head and continued walking. Sequoia, knowing she had to walk with purpose, then quick-stepped to the habitrail exit. Always friendly with the guards at that exit, she promised another delicious treat from Rockman's bakery in the student lounge. Obligingly they let her through unquestioned.

Once in the habitrail Sequoia ran until meeting the second set of guards at the other end. They paid her no mind since their job was not to keep her in, but to keep others out. She made her way swiftly to the student lounge where her two best friends Tilly Heath and Howard Roma were sitting next to each other whispering nervously on a red couch. Seeing her approach Tilly almost squealed, "Quoi!"

The friends scooted apart to make room for Sequoia in the middle. "Listen, I don't have much time. My grandmother found the books." Tilly and Howard looked sternly at each other.

"What did you tell her, Quoi?" asked Howard.

"Don't worry, I didn't say much, I just told her I got them from friends."

"What, are you crazy?"

"Never mind that, that isn't even the half of it. She found out I stopped drinking the shakes." Tilly gasped and put her hand to her mouth. "She tried to make me drink this gross purple stuff that smelled horrible and said it would make me all better."

"You didn't drink it did you?" asked Howard.

Sequoia noticed several guards gathering at the habitrail entrance. "I have to go."

"Wait, what do you mean?" Tilly panicked.

"I don't have time to explain. Can you guys get me out of here?"

Tilly looked around nervously. "Switch me coats."

A confused Sequoia obliged. Tilly then took off her aqua hooded jacket and wrapped it around Sequoia. Sequoia put it on, zipped up and pulled up the hood, tucking in her hair.

"Let's get going," Howard commanded. "I know where we can go."

The girls followed Howard past an elevator, where they would surely be on surveillance, to a set of stairs that led to the street.

"Where are you taking us?"

"You know my dad has a lot of connections, right? I'm going to connect you."

Winded from the cold and their quick pace, Sequoia asked, "Connect us? With who?"

"You're gonna have to trust me. I know your grandmother doesn't like my dad, but he is trying to change things. He will help."

"I don't care who my grandmother likes anymore. Plus, she can't disagree while she is locked in my closet."

Tilly and Howard stopped abruptly, looking at her in disbelief and then both snickered.

"Savage! Well, I guess we better hurry then," Howard added laughingly. "Girl, you got some balls."

"I wish I would have found them sooner."

Howard led the girls to an unremarkable storefront. He motioned for her and Tilly to go to a side door and nodded at the clerk as they entered. The sizeable space looked like a library. Before Sequoia could ask, Howard confirmed that that was where he got the books. They walked through ten more aisles before they came to a wall made of marble. Digital displays played underground news on the wall. Sequoia tried to read the captions, but they came and went too quickly.

In the middle of the wall was a pedestal with a large book that looked to be six inches thick. The dusty cover read, 'Merriam-Webster Dictionary: Unabridged.' Howard laid his hand flat on the page and pushed. Suddenly a crack formed down the middle of the marble wall in front of them. Two panels separated and opened into a dark space barely illuminated by the library room.

"Shoot. I forgot," Howard pronounced.

"I got this." A voice startled them from behind. An elderly woman with thin white hair walked between the friends into the dark space. "Come on. You must be in a hurry. I heard there's commotion over at Chandler Manor. Howard looked nervously at Sequoia and walked forward to join the old woman. Lifting the sleeve from his gray thermal, Howard revealed a small wrist band an inch wide. It was green and iridescent. He put his thumb on the band until it turned a brighter green and then the woman followed with her thumb. The dark space in front of them lit up with a cautionary yellow light. Howard looked at the old bookkeeper.

"You still have time," she answered to his silent question. "Just hurry and be careful."

Ahead of them was a metal staircase. The friends descended quickly and began to jog down the long hallway. Tilly and Sequoia giggled as they raced each other through the tunnels. Howard stayed cautiously behind to keep watch until they rounded the sixth corner and lights in the tunnel turned red. He whispered for them to sprint. Sequoia took the lead as she was the fastest runner. She didn't know where she was going but was comforted by the footsteps of her friends behind her. Realizing the steps had multiplied, she turned to look back just in time to see several men in all black approaching from behind.

"I know, keep running," Howard yelled. Sequoia noticed a cross tunnel ahead with white lights. She figured this was their best bet. The foreign footsteps sounded closer. Her panic made her run faster until the footsteps behind her stopped. She looked back again to see two large figures hovering over Tilly and Howard who were in a clump on the floor. Howard called in a pained voice, "Don't stop Quoi. Keep runni..."

His words were stopped by a boot to the head. Sequoia cringed and stopped, not knowing what to do. "Go Quoi!" screamed Tilly who also took a foot to the face. Sequoia thought for sure she heard Tilly's neck break from the blow. She gasped, but the fear inside would not let any tears escape. She turned and ran toward the white tunnel which seemed farther away than ever, when an unbelievable glimmer of hope flashed in front of her. She screamed, "Uncle Braeden!" as the doorway to the tunnel closed off and the lights went out.

# 34 ~ Secrets Revealed

Braeden slid down the door to the floor in disbelief, replaying the whole scene in his head over, and over again in slow motion. Sabine knelt at his side. "Braeden, who was that?"

He didn't speak. Sabine could see his frustration build in the flush of his face. Braeden vigorously rubbed his eyes. "What was she doing here? What on earth was she doing here?" Turning to Red's daughter, he asked the girl to open the door.

"I can't do that."

"You have to! That was my niece on the other side of the door!"

"Yes, *was* on the other side of the door. I'm sorry, but either she has been taken or she is dead. One way or the other, the only thing on the other side of that door is trouble."

"I don't understand." Braeden pounded his fist on his head, trying to find an answer he knew wasn't there. "Collectors wouldn't have shot her. They would know who she is."

"Maybe it wasn't Collectors. Maybe she was in the wrong part of town and some people, not so accepting of Chandlers got her."

"Or maybe she was trying to escape," Braeden barked back.

"I don't want to say it doesn't matter, but right now it doesn't matter. You have a meeting in three minutes with the Black Horse, and you are pretty much the only one who can make him understand what is going on. We are running out of time."

Conflicted to his core, Braeden stood, knowing she was probably right about everything. "Okay, how do we get there?"

The girl took off running down the tunnel. Braeden pulled Sabine to her feet, and they ran after her. Not forty feet ahead was the end of the main tunnel. The girl put her thumb on her wrist pad and Braeden followed without instruction. A heavy metal door slid open exposing an elevator. The girl stepped aside to let them pass. Holding the door open with her hand she lowered her head to collect her thoughts.

154

"You need to tell him about the flushes."

"That's our plan."

"But do you know how it all started?"

"What do you mean?" Braeden asked.

"I mean do you know about the first flush?"

"No, not really. I guess I hadn't thought of it before."

"The first flush was Detroit."

"What?"

"It was what everyone thought was the tenth wave of the pandemic. Remember how it had mutated so much, they didn't even recognize it? Well, so many had been crying conspiracy about the vaccines, your mother decided to capitalize on that idea, but with a faster delivery system--the water."

"But wait, the New Congress was not in control back then. We were still the United States of America. How could that have happened?"

"Who do you think owned a pharmaceutical company, the privately contracted public works system, and had the drain commissioner in her pocket?"

Sabine reacted to the shock on Braeden's face, "Did you really not know any of this?"

The girl interrupted. "You two can discuss this more later. You have to go now. Tell him, tell him everything. The Black Horse is the only one with enough power to do anything about it." She stepped back and as the elevator door closed, the tunnel lights turned red.

The elevator doors opened into a bustling kitchen. A server with ear length green hair stopped and set down her tray. "'Bout time you got here. He is pretty agitated." Music and raucous laughter emanated from the next room, contradicting the mood the server had indicated. "Follow me."

Braeden and Sabine followed her into the main dining room of *Farley's* Pub. Dark oak walls were broken up by raised panels of sculptured metal. A small band of musicians played in the corner. Most people were gathered around standing-height, blue glass tables that dotted the room. A few large booths lined two of the walls.

The laughter in the room was subsiding, and Braeden first thought it was because of his entrance until he realized a buzz of information was spreading around the room. The middle tables cleared, and patrons laid down government coins and other tokens as they left through the front red door. The crowd thinned and Braeden noticed Taurus Roma sitting in a corner booth that was separated by a half wall. The short wall was painted black and covered in relief carvings of horses.

Feeling the panic in the room, Braeden and Sabine walked swiftly to the booth and sat down across from Taurus.

Taurus eyed Sabine suspiciously. "Who's this?"

"Don't worry. She is GC, she is fine." Braeden countered.

Acting as if he didn't hear Braeden, Taurus continued, "So let's have it. What is this all about?"

"Croft sent me."

Taurus' wide-set eyes closed to slits of suspicion. "I figured that, so what's up?"

"I'm leaving, for good, but before I go Croft wanted to make sure you knew everything my mother is up to."

"Oh, I think I have..."

"Shut up, no listen." Braeden scanned the almost empty room and lowered his voice to a whisper. "My mother is responsible for drugging...everyone."

"Drugging? What do you mean?"

"In the water system. It's called a flush. It's a type of tasteless solution that makes the human mind very susceptible to influence."

"I've heard rumors. We don't drink the city water, but really, how could she pull that off?"

"Unlimited power and resources. Haven't you ever wondered why people accepted her word, without question, in those inane weekly addresses?"

Taurus muttered under his breath, "She obviously had help, which means others know too."

Bending down to catch Taurus' eyes again, Braeden glared intently and talked slowly to convey his seriousness. "This goes back to the late thirties. I didn't even realize how far back it goes."

Sabine, anxious to make the point interrupted, "Chandler Pharmaceuticals was doing this way back at the end of the pandemic."

"What, can you prove that?"

"Probably, but that's not the point. Do you remember when that big mob of white people that had never been known to be white supremacists before, descended on Detroit and started messing with those college kids that were protesting? That was all at her bidding. She drugged anyone who wasn't protesting, to fight against the protesters. Those riots essentially led to the Civil War."

Taurus seemed unconvinced. "Do we know they weren't that way before? There's a lot of closet Nazis out there."

"Yes, I know people can hide who they are, but usually there are signs from family or friends, but with this group, it was middle of the road people, you know blue collar average people, with no history of hate. I remember a lot of them worked for Chandler Energy. I thought that was strange, but it makes even more sense now."

"But why would she do that?"

"Well, I'm sure the protesters were hurting her bottom line, but more importantly, she wanted to do a trial run on drugging large masses of people. Honestly though, I think it's all because of a dispute with my

156

sister." Braeden ran his hand through his thick course hair as he swallowed the implications of what he just said. "The Collection has no idea what is being done to them. Not only are they being subtly poisoned, but they are being controlled. It's not that people wouldn't want change if they knew. You must see it in the eyes of people who attend your speeches. There is an energy, a questioning in the crowd that the people can't even put their finger on. They listen to you because they know you are right. They know there is a better way, but they are powerless to do anything about it. Unless they are in the New Congress or undercover GC, their mind is not their own in the Collection."

Taurus sat silently, adding up the evidence in his head.

"The biggest news is my mother. I can hardly even call her that anymore. Congresswoman Chandler is raising the stakes. She sees resistance in you and others. Until now the water in the congressional buildings and residences has been clean, but she is going to be 'flushing' all water, except for Chandler Manor. I wouldn't be surprised if she hasn't done it already. She has been holding secret cabinet meetings for several weeks now."

Taurus' eyes grew bigger and bigger as Braeden spoke. "So why does Croft want me to know?"

"Look, let's not play games. I don't agree with everything you have done, especially when it came to the schools, but Croft thinks, and I agree, you are our best chance."

"Best chance for what?"

"To change it. To change everything."

"How am I going to do that? I am one person."

"I don't know. That is for you to figure out. I am just here to give you the information."

"And then what?"

"Then, I mean now, I'm leaving. My sister has been rescued and I need to get to her."

"Rescued?"

"Yes, rescued from the TRC. Tell me you don't know about the TRC either?"

As Taurus shook his head a loud commotion erupted in the street. All three jumped up and ran to the next booth with a window to the street. Braeden pulled the curtain to the side to reveal masses of people running and screaming. Then the screaming dissipated, and the middle of the street cleared. Taurus rubbed his eyes and strained to see, hoping that his initial observation was wrong. It was not. Walking in formation down the center of the street were four Collectors. One Collector panned the spectators with a weapon as a warning. One carried the limp body of a young girl and two others fought to control the kicking and squirming of a young male prisoner.

Taurus Roma choked back anger as it became evident that the bloody body being dragged through the street was his son Howard. He lurched toward the window, almost going through it. "Howard, my boy. How did they get him? Why?"

Braeden shook his head at the depravity of his mother once again. "Obviously, my mother knows something. This is only the beginning. We have to get him back right now or she will have exactly what she wants." The men looked intently agreeing with each other and flew out of the booth toward the front door. Sabine, who had been lost in her own mind mumbled at the window to herself, "My God, he looks just like Trey."

Roma stopped abruptly and turned back toward Sabine. "What did you say?"

Sabine startled out of her haze and looked confused at Roma. "I said he looks like my friend Trey."

"Trey Roma? How do you know Trey?"

"How do you know Trey, sir?"

"Trey is my eldest son."

# 35 ~ Captivity and Croft

We descended into the stairway hidden in the tree. A red flashing warning light was pulsating through the corridors of Fox Island. Croft was pulling me to keep up with Charlotte. Breathlessly, I grabbed his arm, "Croft, what did she mean transfusion?"

"Janie, we have to clean your blood, but there may not be time for that right now. For now, we just need to get you safe."

Once through the tunnel under the creek, Char took a sharp right turn through a short hallway until we reached an arched metal door. She opened the door to a beautiful apartment. There were soft white and blue lights from a variety of lamps throughout the space that highlighted the dark teakwood floors. Straight ahead was a kitchen area with wood and chrome furnishings and a small open fire pit in the center of a raised island. To the left, a living area with voluptuous purple furniture bathed in the glow of soft white hanging pendant lights. Several closets and small rooms branched off from the main room.

Char busied herself with important tasks I didn't understand. Croft helped her as I walked, mesmerized, around the room. I filled my lungs with the fresh purified air and closed my eyes to try to absorb the comfort of the place. Char and Croft muttered softly and discretely as they peered through a hanging glass pane that displayed surveillance footage. Their busyness gave me the freedom to keep exploring.

I was drawn to a large dividing wall next to the living area with several framed documents: *Charlotte Tanner-Teacher of the Year-1999, Joined in Holy Matrimony- Charlotte Elizabeth Tanner and Henry Gerold Gage-2004, Charlotte Gage- PhD-Principal of the year 2016, Dr. Charlotte E. Gage-State of Michigan Board of Education 2018.* On a small table, underneath the documents were three picture frames of a small boy with a bright smile and Charlotte's eyes. The third was matted in a frame with the inscription: *Evan Tanner Gage 2006-2010.*

A lump formed in my throat, and I teared up at the thought of Char losing both her husband and her son. I sat on the arm of one of the purple couches.

Charlotte whisked past me. "I'll send a med tech."

"But wait, if a transfusion would clean everything out of my blood, why didn't you do it when I got here?"

Char stopped in her tracks and turned to face me. "Janie, I'm sorry. We didn't think of the tracking compound until now."

"But would it help me to remember faster if we get the drugs out of my system."

"Yyyees, but, well it's not that easy."

Croft was instantly by my side. "I'm tired of beating around the bush. Sweetheart, it could be dangerous to flush the drugs out too quickly. That is why we usually let them clean out on their own."

"What do you mean dangerous?"

"We tried it with the first couple rescues, and it didn't go so well."

"You're still beating around the bush. What happened?"

"You may remember some references to Lucky Pete, well that was one attempt. Some think he had a lot of issues to begin with, but the transfusion sure didn't help."

"And, the other?"

Croft said nothing and just shook his head silently warning me not to ask again.

"So, what makes it safe now?"

He grabbed my hands. "Nothing, nothing except you. You' re the strongest person I know, Janie McAvoy. If anyone can do this, you can. I was weaning you from the drugs several days before most people we rescue, but I didn't think about the trackers. Not everyone gets tracking solution, only the important guests. It's my own stupid fault. They must have been injecting you with tracking solution when I wasn't there. I can't believe I was so dumb. But you have a head start on the drug evacuation. It should almost all be gone on its own now. Still, we have to get the trackers out or there will be no place you can hide. The tracking solution could take weeks on its own."

"So, it's safe then?"

Char and Croft looked somberly at each other but neither answered. He started pacing, going over the details.

"Stupid question, I know the answer. I am going to do it. This is what I must do to protect the city and the people. I can't have my presence lead to any more deaths. I could never live with that." I rubbed my hands on the purple plush of the couch. I knew the implications of the agreement, but I also knew that this was my chance to set things right. Maybe making it safer for the inhabitants of Fox Island would somehow compensate for

160

how I failed to protect my family. Then I shook my head, knowing I could never ditch that burden.

"No!" Croft burst from across the room. "We can't do this Char. I can't let you do it, Janie. I can't believe we even considered it." He put his hand on his head and suddenly looked up, "We'll run. We'll keep running until you're safe."

"Croft, you know we can't do that. How will we know when it's safe? I won't put anyone else in jeopardy. More importantly, I will not risk you. You have sacrificed everything for me. I will not allow it. We will do the transfusion. That is the only way. You're right. I can do this. I feel strong. I know it will be okay."

"How do you know?" His words were soft.

"I know because I have you." I put his hand on my heart and covered it with my own. I smiled. "And we both have Char to…" I reached out my hand and looked to where she had been standing but she was gone.

Before I could speak, a bell chimed and the screen next to the door turned on. Croft walked over to touch it, not letting go of my other hand. Charlotte's face appeared. "Listen you two, there is no time for the transfusion right now. We are under attack. The warning system was right."

"Char, how did you sneak out? What is going on out there?" Croft and I blurted in a staggered round.

"We've had a breach of the outer ring, but we are taking care of it. You both need to stay there until I come to get you."

"What? No, I want to help," I yelped.

"You cannot help. You would be in way too much danger, and there is nothing you can do."

"I can fight!"

Croft smiled proudly, but his tone was more like a big brother. "No, Char is right. It will be better for you to stay here."

Charlotte interrupted, "I didn't say for her to stay there. I said for both of you to stay there."

"But I…"

"Yes dear, I know you want to help," Char scolded Croft. "But your biggest job is to protect our Janie, your Janie. You can do that best by staying there. Besides I sealed you in, just in case you had any funny ideas."

"Charlotte!" insisted Croft.

"Hush! You will be safe. There is virtually no way for anyone to get to you. I collapsed the tunnel to my pod. There is one more thing you need to know." Char's attention was drawn to something else in the room. She stepped away from the screen to reveal a control room behind her. When she stepped back into view she was speaking, but we couldn't hear her. Her face looked panicked as the screen started to pixilate, and then suddenly it went black.

Croft let go of my hand and put his arm around me pulling me close in one swift move. Neither of us took our eyes from the screen for several minutes. Abruptly, Croft let go and I realized my side was numb from where he had been holding on to me. He feverously tried to manipulate the technology to get us out of there but to no avail.

"I guess all we can do now is wait," he offered as he slipped down to a squat, resting his elbows on his knees for new perspective.

We took turns pacing, wringing our hands, and slumping in defeat for the next several hours. Finally, as my stomach threatened to devour itself from the inside, Croft suggested we eat something. I didn't want to think about food, I just didn't want my body to remind me anymore. Croft found some fresh black berries and a loaf of thick sweet-rye bread. We dipped the bread in olive oil and ate the berries one by one savoring each as if they could be our last meal. I drank the remainder of a glass of water and yawned.

Croft reached across the counter and put his hand on my cheek. I closed my eyes and rested my face on his hand. "You have been yawning for a while," Croft offered as his hand left my cheek and stroked my hair.

The suggestion made me yawn again as I spoke, "I knooooow, but I don't think I can sleep, not until we know what is happening out there."

"Yes Janie, but we can't get out until Char comes to get us. We may as well rest while we can."

I had no more answers and no reason to argue with his logic. Neither of us spoke as he led me over to Char's large white bed. I flopped on to the cushy down spread. Croft pulled a throw blanket from the end of the bed and draped it over me as if he were tucking me in. I looked up, surprised, "Aren't you going to rest too?"

"I might. I want you to get some good, undisturbed sleep though. I'll crash on the couch if I get tired."

"Oh, so you didn't want us to rest, you wanted me to rest."

Croft smiled. I looked up at him with seductive eyes and patted the bed next to me. He was so taken aback, it made me embarrassed I had made the gesture. He sat down on the edge of the bed and stroked my hair again. "Janie, I don't want to hurt you anymore. I want you have your memory back before we…"

His implication made me even more embarrassed until I realized I really did intend to imply what he thought. Abruptly I sat up and kissed him with conviction. This was not the kiss of a frightened girl, but a fierce woman who saw what she wanted in front of her and pounced on her prey. Initially he tried to break it off, but then wrapped his arms around me. I melted as he kissed me with the yearning that I thought I should expect from my long-lost love. I could scarcely breathe, but I didn't want to break

162

away. Finally, our lips parted just enough to make me want more. I took a breath, ready to claim my prize. I opened my eyes briefly, and when I closed them again, I gasped as I saw Anson, inches from my face. His smile was slightly more crooked than Croft's, but his teeth were amazing. I guess I had a thing for teeth. Weird. His eyes squinted the same but were a much darker blue than Croft's. I shook my head but could not clear his image. I knew he was not real, but my emotions were all over the place as he stared at me lovingly.

I tried to open my eyes, but my head bobbed and drooped. Suddenly a muffled voice emerged in the darkness. I thought my body was convulsing. I heard my name over and over, but it sounded like someone talking through a pillow. I opened my eyes again and saw Croft shaking me. Then I closed my eyes and saw Anson's face. Open - Croft. Closed - Anson. I had to decide where I wanted to stay. Open - Croft. Closed - Anson.

Finally, I opened my eyes and fell back exhausted on the bed. Croft busied himself like a mother hen, checking my pulse, feeling my forehead, and turning the lamp shade near the bed to check my pupils. I didn't respond to anything he was doing. I just lay there silently recovering from my episode. Croft's eyes watered as he tried to blink the tears away.

"Janie, I'm sorry Janie. Are you okay? I…"

"Wow that was some kiss." My attempt to lessen his worry didn't work. He kept caressing my hair and his eyes darted back and forth nervously trying to assess my condition. "Did I love him?"

He finally smiled but his body language showed confusion.

"Anson--did I love him?"

"Janie, that's not for me to say, but I think you did, yes."

"I saw him."

"What do you mean, when?"

"Just now."

Croft tried not to show disappointment, but his shoulders slumped in defeat. "Oh. So, you mean the kiss--you thought you were, er, it was him?"

I realized my vagueness was creating new webs to untangle. "What? NO! You. I was kissing you. I wanted to kiss you. It was just when I closed my eyes, I saw him."

"I don't know what to do with that, Janie."

"I don't either, but Croft..." I put my hands on his cheeks. "I was kissing you and only you. Okay? I can't even remember him, let alone remember kissing him. I'm sorry, I…"

"Don't be. You didn't do anything wrong. It's just your memory. It's fighting to come back. Just let it come."

"It was weird. I felt like if I closed my eyes, I would stay with Anson forever."

He looked down, "You were definitely someplace else for a while."

I scrunched down to get in his view and then sat up forcing his eyes to follow me. "But I opened my eyes. I chose you."

Croft tilted his head, "You shouldn't have to choose Janie. You should have it all. A complete life with your husband and your kids by your side."

"I should have chosen you in the first place. I can't say I regret my life with the family that I don't remember, I just wonder how things might have been different if I…"

He put his finger to my mouth. "Don't go down that road. We've been there many times. You don't remember, but we have guilted ourselves into oblivion with 'what-ifs.' We can only move forward."

"I know. It's just that I feel like we can't go forward until I go back."

"Wait. What if…"

I shook my head and teased, "You said no what-ifs, remember?"

"No, not that type of what-if. What if you don't try to force it? I know you want to remember, but maybe you don't have to go back and rehash every detail. Maybe we just leave the past where it is for now and once you remember you won't have to experience all the negative things again. Maybe your past, including all of those emotions that you have gone through will be there in a neat little package when you come to complete consciousness again."

"Do you think it could be that easy?"

"No, not really."

"Me neither." We both laughed heartily. "Okay then, if we can't solve our problems, let's brainstorm about what we can do."

"I like the way you think Mrs. McAvoy."

"Same to you, Mr.--uh, McAvoy."

# 36 ~ Villain Within

I awoke with a start, then pacified by the calm, darker room. The lamps had been extinguished but there was a faint natural light, surely mirrored in from somewhere. I rolled over to see a tuft of blanket bunched up like a croissant offering up the head of a strange and wonderful creature I had come to know as Croft. The medley of his hair fell naturally about the pillow he was buried in. His face, solemn in slumber.

I carefully slid out from the covers and crept to find which door led to the bathroom. As I walked in, a natural pinkish light turned on. I examined my face in the mirror. Forty-seven. It seemed like a sentence more than a reality. The subtle lines, still not bad for my place in life's timeline. I wondered at the memory of my younger self, and how I felt about my face through the years. Part of me thought I might be one of those people who truly didn't care about the streams carving their way into rivers around my eyes and mouth. My complexion was an acceptance speech of the lessons that life had doled out, and I was going to wear it proudly.

Still, looking at my eyes, I could see my sister. I just couldn't accept that the Jane I had always been, was someone who let others sacrifice and die for her. I racked my brain for what I could do to find Sage, (if there was still a Sage) and so decided on my new occupation of forgetting about myself while I tried more intently to find my family that remained. My sister, my daughters, my brother and maybe even the monster they called my mother.

I splashed some water on my face. I needed to shower, but I was too excited with purpose to bother with it at the time. I bounded back to the bed trying to think of a legitimate reason to wake Croft and tell him my plans. I was almost disappointed to see he was awake and sitting up in bed. I had thought briefly of kissing him into alertness, but it was probably better I didn't have to make that choice. He smiled contentedly as I rounded the corner. Mmm, yes, sleep agreed with him.

His expression changed as he saw the look of determination on my face. His stunning eyes narrowed in question, even though he kept smiling. He wanted to speak but waited for me.

I leapt to the bed and pounced next to him.

"Croft, I can't stay here any longer. I have let too many people sacrifice for me. I am stronger. I know what you're thinking, but I am. I may not have my memory, but I can't wallow any longer. Sitting around is not going to bring back my family any faster. I want to go look for my children, and my sister, if I still have a sister, and my brother. Isn't that something I would have done, before?" He sat silently.

Croft dropped his head to think, probably about how to let me down gently. I was ready to refute, but I reminded myself to give him time to voice his objections. He leaned forward and touched his forehead to mine. His eyes, only inches away, drilled their answer into my brain. I had to convince him. Part of me knew I would go without his blessing, but I wanted him with me. I wanted him to say, "Excellent idea Janie." I wanted him on board.

"What is the last thing you remember Janie, apart from the time since the rescue?"

I sat back and was forced inside my brain again. "It's all confusing bits and pieces."

"Forget your personal life for a minute. Do you have memories of what the world was like before you were taken? Do you remember teaching? Do you remember the war? Try not to associate it with people."

I willed the stubborn fog in my brain to dissipate so I could peer through at anything tangible. The images felt like a strobe light that was slowing down, revealing the scene behind it. I was looking at a wooden floor and feeling sweat drip down my face. I glanced up and saw a multi-level carpeted area covered with teenagers. Each student held a tablet of some kind and in the space between us was a holographic image of the world. The area I knew to be the United States was red, but smaller than I had thought. Pockets of red illuminated from various countries around the world, but most of the land mass was blackened out. The water shown as blue, but the areas surrounding most of the continents were green. The northern polar ice cap was almost non-existent.

As I moved my hands, the earth spun, and the students laughed. I could only see and not hear them in my silent bubble. The students raised their hands and anxiously begged to ask questions. I felt myself smile, in both realities. "Did I teach geography?"

"Yes, some, but mostly political science," he could hardly say the words he was smiling so wide. "D'you remember?"

The vision faded but didn't leave. I tried to recall it several times and it came back each time more clearly than the time before. I continued scanning my classroom. Frames encasing digital screens surrounded the

166

room. Posters and announcements flashed like billboards. Two of the screens I could see from my vantage point had rolling obstructions in front of them. I instantly knew the obstructions were there to lessen student's exposure but also to move quickly should anyone question their placement. Those two screens alternated test taking strategies with government slogans and propaganda. I tried recalling the images as if they had been branded on my brain from repetition throughout the day.

"You look as if you are watching a movie in your head."

I still couldn't focus on Croft but only hear his voice. "It's funny you say that because that's exactly what it is like."

"How are you able to do that?"

"What do you mean?"

"I mean, how do you remember things that way? When I remember something, it is usually like a picture with a feeling attached."

"I don't know if this is all one memory or a bunch of memories running together."

Questions and thought-provoking images kept popping into my head, not as if I was seeing them in that specific memory but as if I was recalling them as part of my long-term memory. Song lyrics and snippets of poems began to fill the void where my memory had been held hostage. "Croft, was I a rebel?"

Croft laughed and clapped his hands. "Oh Janie, you have no idea. There was not a cause you didn't support, except for the causes the administration or the government wanted you to support as a molder of young minds."

I liked his analogy of me. "That does sound rebellious. Ha. Was I a good teacher?"

"What do you think?"

"I don't know if my students learned much, but I feel like I loved teaching."

"That is why you were so good. You never thought of yourself as a 'molder of minds.' You were just authentically yourself and had a passion for learning that spilled over to your students. The powers in charge, especially your mother, didn't like your influence. She thought you were cavalier, but you were anything but cavalier. You had an agenda. They just couldn't figure it out." He boasted proudly.

"I don't like that word, agenda, it makes me sound like my mother."

"Janie, everyone has an agenda. Yours was not a scheme, like your mother would hatch. It was more like an outline of what you believed in and how you lived your life."

"But who is to say I was right, in my agenda?"

"It's not a question of right or wrong. It's a question of information. You are very well-read, and you talk to people, and more importantly, listen. You never told them what to believe or how to believe. You simply gave your students the information you had, and the critical thinking skills to formulate their own conclusions. That's why they trusted you and worked so hard for you."

Suddenly I felt introspective, like a question I couldn't articulate was nagging at me. As I pondered it, a nauseous knot grew in my stomach as I remembered something Croft had told me before. "When we were in the GC council room you talked about the first rebellions, and you said that many college students died." Tears multiplied in my eyes. "I know I taught high school, but did I have something to do with that?"

Croft was very still. Suspiciously quiet, he asked, "Why do you ask that?"

"Please tell me, okay? I keep seeing crowds and posters." My stomach lurched. "I see myself watching the news and I have this overwhelming feeling of guilt like I murdered someone or did something terrible."

Croft leaned forward and tried to hug me. I pushed him back. "Don't try to console me. What did I do? Why do I feel this way?! Did children die because of me?"

His demeanor changed. "Janie, you are no monster. I have seen that look in your eyes. You didn't *DO* anything. You blame yourself, but all you did was tell the truth."

"So why do I feel this way?"

"Take a deep breath. I will tell you everything, okay?"

I breathed deeply. It was refreshing, but the feeling didn't leave.

"It was Labor Day. There was always a big celebration in town, and you ran into several of your former students while we were watching the parade. You asked them how school was going and if they kept their scholarships. They talked about the rising student loan rates and inflating tuition. Their scholarship money wasn't enough, and student aid had tapped out. One of them, Ezra, I think his name was, had dropped out of college because he couldn't afford it any longer. Another boy, Mitch, what a good kid, anyway he just accepted that he would never be able to pay off his debt and tried to laugh about it. You were infuriated because the government could have spent less money paying for everyone's education than it did on grants, or even worse, on lobbyists."

I interrupted, "but what does…"

Croft countered, "Be patient Janie. I'm getting to it. It was the third girl that really affected you. You had had her as a student for several different classes and she was always one of your favorites. Her name was Delilah. I am pretty sure you named your Delilah after her." Suddenly a flash of a short, red-haired girl zipped through my mind. Croft continued, "She said she was doing okay because she had made friends with someone in the financial aid office. After you pressed her for more information, she admitted…"

"She was sleeping with someone who was 'making all of her numbers work out' for her," I finished his sentence. "I remember the conversation. I was furious. I don't know if I was more furious at her for basically prostituting herself for an education or at the system for forcing her into that situation."

Croft nodded. "What happened next? See if you can remember."

"Did I run out into the street and stop the parade?" My eyes were wide as saucers hoping it wasn't a real memory.

Croft laughed, "Yeah, I have never seen anything like it. Our friend Dalton was driving a truck with a small rock band in the back end. I still don't know what you said to Dalton or the lead singer, but Dalton turned his truck sideways, so the parade had to stop, and the singer gave you his microphone. You got right up on top of the cab and Dalton cranked up the amp even louder. At first the crowd thought it was a stunt or part of the parade but within minutes you had the crowd on their feet, cheering and hanging on your every word."

"I vaguely remember being on the truck. Oh my God! What did I say?"

"What didn't you say? It was brilliant, like you had rehearsed it for years. I recite parts of it in my head whenever I get discouraged or disillusioned that change can happen."

"That's overwhelming. What parts?"

"There were a few hecklers in the crowd, mostly people that were afraid of change, but everyone knew you were right. You could see the desperation in peoples' faces. There was some lead-up about why Labor Day started, and you talked about some of the crazy things that have happened in the last few decades, but this is the part I always remember. You said,":

*"We are drowning. We are drowning in work, in poverty, in sickness.*

*What does our government do? They put weights on our ankles and make us grovel for even more water. They keep us so busy trying to stay afloat that we don't notice them plucking the life rafts from the water one by one. What they don't realize is that every now and then, in our floundering, we touch bottom, and it gives us hope. There comes a time when no water will extinguish the fire that is brewing beneath the surface. Then we will stand up--and only then will the waters recede."*

"You remember all of that?"

"Yes, I do. Of course, I also watched the news casts of it and re-played it on the internet a hundred times." He chuckled, but I couldn't laugh.

"Croft, did those kids somehow die because of what I said?"

"Janie, your words were what everyone needed to hear. They started a soapbox movement around the country. Many people, including your students, took your words to heart. There had already been demonstrations and riots for several years. Some states had receded and, sheesh, we had already built a wall down the middle of the country by then, to keep the peace. But the soapboxing was different. It was hopeful, and mostly young people fighting for their future. Of course, with all rebellion there comes a turning point of decision and sometimes it turns the wrong way."

"Croft," I said, desperately needing to hear the answer I already knew.

Croft nodded at my question. "They died, Janie. All three of your students we saw that day died and many, many more. Students had begun skipping class to soapbox and it was getting uncomfortable for authorities. A nationwide curfew on college campuses was instituted, but the more they cracked down, the more the students rebelled. It was as if no one learned anything from Kent State. Roughly thirty thousand students from campuses all around the country died in those rebellions."

I plopped back down on to the plush bed. "Thirty thousand." I was a monster. I was worse than my mother.

Croft rolled over and turned my tear-streaked face toward his. "But...*BUT*, regardless of what you thought back then, and regardless of what you think now. It was not your fault!" I sobbed harder. "You have carried this weight around on your shoulders for too long. They didn't die because of you. They all made their own choices. You weren't the only one speaking out, Janie. It's just that Delilah and Mitch quoted you in some of their speeches, so you felt responsible."

"I am responsible." I muttered under my breath. Surprising even myself, I jumped up and ran around Char's pod looking for some way to escape. I needed to get out of that place and out of my head, or I thought I would explode. Croft followed close behind me not knowing what to do to calm me.

"Janie, stop please and listen to me. You are not the villain. You did not create the awful situation that caused thousands, if not millions to want to rebel."

I couldn't hear his words anymore. I couldn't hear anyone else telling me that everything would be okay. It wasn't. "Croft, I can't sit here any longer wondering about my past. I can't fix it. I can only make amends. The first people, to whom I must make amends, are my family. We need to go find them. How do we get out of here? I need to get out of here right now! Do you think there is another way out?"

"I never thought of that, but I bet there is. Char does not strike me as a one-option kind of gal."

We felt along the walls and checked every door and closet. I tentatively sat down on the purple sofa to complain and saw the answer. "Croft, the rug!"

"What? Where?"

"Behind you, that little throw rug. The corner is tucked into the floor." Croft turned to examine it. "Janie, you are brilliant!"

As he tugged on the rug a small section of the floor rose hydraulically. Beneath the rising floorboards was, of course, a small dark tunnel. My chest tightened almost on command. Croft stepped on the first step into the tunnel and some lights turned on inside. He shuffled down the stairs and held up his arm in invitation for me to follow. He smiled, knowing a tunnel was the last place I wanted to go, but I knew there was probably no other escape.

"Good job, sweetheart!" he said cheerfully trying to distract me from my neuroses, as I descended the stairs.

"Let's walk fast, can we?"

Croft laughed.

It was a short tunnel with a wood door at the other end. As we approached, we heard voices and Croft further hushed my silence. We leaned against the door to discern who was talking, but instead I heard crying and loud undistinguishable voices.

"Come on, let's go through," I whispered.

"You wait here. I'll go check."

"If you think I am going to…"

"Oh, okay never mind. I know you're not going to listen to me anyway."

The door was very heavy. We both pulled hard. I wondered if the weight of the door was the security. We slowly cracked it open to find another door. This one was metal. Croft used his thumbprint to unlock each of three deadbolt locks and then we pushed, but it took several tries before it budged.

As we finally cracked the seam, a gush of cool outside air passed through and aided our progress. We stepped through into a partial room that looked like it had been blown up. We could see dirt hanging down and sky above us. It was not a holo-turf room. The real sky stared back at us. People lay strewn across the floor, some of whom were bloody and some not moving at all. It was like a triage room with others running back and forth trying to give medical attention to those who needed it.

We stood there in shock for a moment until something drew me to a young girl who was crouched over a body on the floor. She looked up when she saw our shadow over her, and I recognized her as the girl from the GC council meeting. "Malina?" I stammered. I smiled at her but the tears in her eyes kidnapped the moment. She stood, in slow motion, to reveal a corpse, the lifeless body of our friend Charlotte Gage.

# 37 ~ Layover

"I get it," Delilah exclaimed. Foster and Bodhi looked at her in confusion. "Eagle Crossing, is that your name for what used to be La Crosse?"

"Sure, this is under what was once La Crosse, but we don't like to use the old city names anymore. We're all trying to start over ya know."

"Hi, are you Delilah?"

Delilah and Bodhi startled and whipped around to see an older man in a green shirt standing behind them. His sandy colored beard was course and thick in contrast to his bald head.

"Hi Dee, you don't know me, but I am friends with your uncle Croft."

"Uncle Crock?!" Delilah shrieked. Bodhi, Foster, and the man laughed. "Is he okay? Is he here?"

Foster put his hand on her shoulder, "No Delilah, he's been pretty busy. He is the one who just rescued your mother."

"Rescued from where? I still don't even…" Delilah yawned.

The tall man interjected, "Why don't you two get some rest first?"

"I'm not that tiiii…r..ed," Delilah insisted as she yawned again. Then laughing at herself, she relinquished her point. "Okay, I am, but I still want to know what is going on. Where is my mom, and why hasn't anyone come to claim me?"

Foster took over, "Sure, you need some answers. I'll give you a quick synopsis now and we can fill in the details later."

"Good luck with that," needled Bodhi.

"Your mother has been held captive for the last year. She was drugged into a coma, and it is very possible that she will not remember you when you see her."

Delilah felt her eyes swimming in her head with the information. "Okay," she answered. Bodhi leaned in toward Delilah, so their arms were touching, as a show of support. The gesture made her tear up as she looked up into Bodhi's eyes. His usual goofy personality stepped aside.

172

"But, okay, but wow…I mean, is she okay though?"

The tall man interjected, "It appears, last we heard, she doesn't have many memories, but she is making progress."

"Okay, but what about the years before that? You said she was held for a year."

"Your mother, well everyone actually, thought you were dead. We didn't even know you were at Indie City until recently."

Delilah squatted down and hugged her knees. "I don't understand," she whispered.

Bodhi leaned over to put his hand on her back. "She would have come for you, Delilah. If she knew, she would have come."

"It's a good thing you weren't with her when she was captured," Foster added.

Delilah stood up. "Who captured her?" Everyone stood silent waiting for her to answer her own question. "Oh right, so it must be my grandmother." She shook her head as she realized. "How could she do that to her daughter? How could she do any of what she did to…"

"To you," Bodhi finished her sentence. Delilah nodded.

"So, where did my grandmother hide her? She wouldn't have brought her to New Congress even though I was gone."

"No, you're right," Foster offered. "She was held somewhere in old Indiana. The Collection has a clinic holding facility."

"Okay then, what about Uncle Croft? Why didn't he come for me once he knew?"

"Your uncle, actually both of your uncles, are the ones who masterminded her escape over the last year."

"Both uncles? Wait, do you mean Uncle Braeden?"

"Yes, Croft couldn't have done it without Braeden's help."

"But Braeden is still living in New Congress. Why would he even help? He's loyal to my grandmother."

"Not since he found out about her kidnapping your mom."

"Dang it. I can't even think straight riiiiiight nooow," she yawned again.

The bearded man suggested they get some rest. Delilah, Bodhi, and Foster all nodded.

The bald man motioned for all of them to follow as he walked across the stone tiled floor.

Foster walked in a different direction, "You kids go with Hex and get some rest. I have a few things to do and then I'm going to take a nap too. I will catch up with you later this afternoon. Hey, and thanks for everything. Can't wait to talk cars with you later, kid." He slapped Bodhi on the arm and walked away. Bodhi beamed.

The tall man spoke as they walked. "Sorry, for this crazy welcome. This is not our normal way of doing things. Of course, we don't have too many guests. Muh name's Hexley."

Delilah and Bodhi answered together, "Nice to meet you."

Hexley cleared his throat and showed them into a huge room lined with doors. The walls between the doors were stone, and the ceiling, a calming sky blue. In the center of the room was a common area with tables and lounging couches under a canopy of hanging lights.

"This is the area most of the kids your age hang out. Delilah, you can stay in my daughter's apartment. She'll probably be out anyway, now that it's daytime. Why don't you wait here while I go talk to her? Bodhi, I'm pretty sure number twelve over there is empty. You can go check it out?"

Bodhi and Delilah stood awkwardly in the center of the room as Hexley whispered emphatically under his breath to his daughter, at door number twenty-seven. She wasn't thrilled. Hexley's daughter peered over her father's shoulder to get a glimpse of the girl that she was sure would ruin her life. Delilah pretended not to notice either of them. His daughter walked away and Hexley nervously gestured for Delilah to come over. He was wiping the sweat from his brow when she and Bodhi approached.

Before Delilah could say anything, Hexley blurted out, "We're all set. She would be happy to have a roomie for…a while."

Delilah tried not to roll her eyes. "Are you sure it's not too much trouble?"

"Oh no, she was very excited. Her name is Jocelyn, but her friends call her Jos. I'm sure you could call her Jos too. Well, I'll leave you to it. Number twenty-seven right over there. Have a good rest." He turned and quickly skip walked for the exit before his daughter could catch him again.

Delilah turned back to face Bodhi, "I guess this is it. Sleep tight." Delilah looked nervously into Bodhi's eyes. He squeezed her hand and tried not to laugh as he walked away.

"Have a good nap," Bodhi yelled as he made his way across the common area. Delilah could hear him singing while he opened the door, "Delilah Marieeee, is so very sleepyyyy…and I think she likes meee…" The door closed abruptly. Delilah smiled an amused smile, took a deep breath, and prepared to meet Hexley's daughter, whom she would henceforth refer to as "the offspring".

# 38 ~ Wounds

Taurus took an intentional breath. "You know Trey?" He swallowed hard to fight back tears. "I have so many questions, but first we need to get my other son. That's my Howard out there."

Braden tried to speak to form a plan, but before any words left his mouth, Taurus was out the door and on a sturdy march to the center of the street where Howard was being held captive. Braeden tried to follow but Sabine stopped him. "Wait, if they see you with Taurus Roma the jig is up."

"You're right. I didn't think of that. What do I do, wait here and watch them both get killed?"

"I don't know. Just wait, we will think of something."

They cracked the front door of Farley's tavern wide enough to hear as Taurus's presence drew gasps from the forming crowd. One of the Collectors in black followed Roma's path with a sweep of his gun barrel. "Stop right there, Congressman. We don't want to have to shoot you."

Taurus's voice bellowed above the clamoring crowd, "Shoot me? You better be joking boy."

"Freeze! It's no joke. We have orders to shoot you if necessary."

"Whose orders?"

"Ms., Uh, Congresswoman Chandler, sir."

"Congresswoman Chandler ordered you to shoot me?"

"Anyone who gets in the way, sir."

"Well, if you don't want to shoot me, you better be letting my son go then."

"I'm sorry sir. That's a negative. We were ordered to bring him to New Congress Hall. He tried to kidnap her, uh, Congresswoman Chandler's granddaughter, sir."

"Kidnap? You don't believe that though, do you?"

"It doesn't matter what I believe. I have my orders." Taurus continued to walk toward Howard, careful not to look at him for fear that his son's condition would distract his resolve. "STOP! I mean it, sir."

"If you meant it, you would have shot me already. Now hand over my son."

The Collectors let go of Howard and Tilly, who fell on the ground, and quickly pointed their weapons at Taurus Roma's head. Taurus continued to talk with authority as he took several steps to the side. The Collectors echoed each step he took with two of their own so that the guns stopped only inches from his face. As he inched backward, he tried not to notice Braeden and Sabine sneak out from the front of Farley's. Taurus, unswayed by the Collector's threats, kept them talking and moving in his direction, as Braeden slunk in, to un-tie Howard's restraints. Sabine started to un-tie Tilly until she realized the girl was already dead.

Howard gurgled on the blood in his throat, but Braeden signaled for Howard to be as quiet as possible. Braeden got close and whispered as he released Howard's restraints, "Do you know where Sequoia is?"

Howard looked up and tried to blink away the blood that was running down his face. Braeden wiped Howard's face with his shirt sleeve, but Howard still didn't speak. Sabine quickly walked over and picked up Howard's legs as Braeden carried his torso. Sabine could see that Howard was smaller statured than Trey but was made of the same sturdy stock. She tried not to grunt for fear of distracting the Collectors as she lifted his muscular legs.

Sabine and Braeden slipped through the front door of Farley's unnoticed except for the crowd who nervously tried not to look and give away their position. As soon as Sabine shut the door with her foot, they all fell, exhausted on the floor. Braeden jumped up and grabbed a towel at the bar to wipe Howard's face and Sabine grabbed a glass of water on a nearby table. She first poured a little on his face followed by a wipe with the towel and then she gave him a drink.

Howard gulped the water and then spit some out, tinged with blood before he consumed the rest. Feeling around with his tongue, he produced a tooth on the end of his tongue he let drop to the floor. Sabine tried to quell the look of horror on her face.

"What happened to Sequoia?" Braeden prompted. "Is she still alive? Nod if you can't answer."

Howard cleared his throat. "I'm not sure," he coughed out. "Arggg!" He rolled on to his side holding his ribs with his arms wrapped around his torso.

Sabine looked nervously at Braeden. "I think he might have some broken ribs and I'm worried one of them could have punctured his lung."

"What can we do?"

"We can wrap his ribs, but if his lung is punctured, well…"

176

Howard rolled back onto his back and whispered in a weak voice, "Is there anything you can do for the pain?"

Braeden turned to Sabine. "This is a GC establishment. There must be some natural remedies or something in the kitchen."

"Of course," agreed Sabine. "This is a bar, with alcohol. There must be a tincture or something. I'll go look."

While Sabine was foraging through the kitchen, Braeden pleaded with Howard for more information. "I know you're in pain, but can you tell me anything?"

Howard struggled to sit up more, so Braeden propped Howard's head on his knee. Howard peered out from his un-swollen eye. "They took her."

"Who took her?"

"The spiders - Collectors, you know."

"Do you know where? Could you tell if she was still breathing?"

"It looked like she had been shot but it was hard to tell if it was bad. She wasn't conscious." Howard groaned in pain again.

Sabine burst through the kitchen doors with an arm full of thin cotton kitchen towels, scissors, a small jar with an orange-colored liquid and a gel-filled tube. "I found some fresh hemp juice. I mixed it with orange and carrot juice to cut the intense flavor. Here, have him drink this while I cut some strips to wrap his ribs."

"These towels aren't going to be long enough to do any good."

"Trust me."

Braeden watched in wonder as Sabine cut the towels in an oval spiral pattern, making one long strip out of each towel. "You're amazing. Where have you been my whole life?" Braeden said, a charmed smile on his face.

Sabine blushed and handed the strips to Braeden, "Wrap tightly, it's going to hurt, but it will feel better once they are wrapped." Howard winced at the thought.

Meanwhile, Taurus had backed up to a statue in the middle of the divided street. An older woman wrapped in a shawl noticed the trail of blood from where the Collectors had dropped Howard to the entrance of Farley's. She inched forward and using her shawl, wiped as much as she could from the street. Her son grabbed a few other onlookers in the crowd to step forward and cover the trail with their feet. Taurus noticed what was happening, beyond the barrels of the guns pointed in his face.

The deflection of his gaze alerted the Collectors who turned quickly to see the crowd closing in and growing. Taurus' heart swelled in the hope that the people were rallying for him. They were ready. Ready to do something, anything. They had had enough, and so had he. He stood tall like the proud peacock his mother had told him to be. In his loudest voice, he spoke, not as a politician with a memorized speech but as an answer to an unspoken question in the minds of the wanting crowd.

"I beg you to listen to me. We don't need to be frightened anymore. I see it now. I see you now, all of you, probably for the first time. I'm going to help you. I'm gonna stand with you and set things right. I know you may think I am saying this because of my son, but I promise you, I…"

The Collectors' weapons, which were beginning to glow in the waning light, nervously darted from person to person and back to Taurus as the people inched closer.

"…We are plunging forward and not looking back. There is nothing in our past except reminders of how to do things the wrong way. We are never going to be the United States of America again! This used to make me sad. I think of the flag-waving parades of my youth, and it used to choke me up, but we were brought up in an enchanted world where nothing was what it seemed. We talked about bravery, but we weren't brave. We romanticized war, until it landed on our doorstep. Until we saw our neighbors killed or worse yet, killed them ourselves. We let corporations trample us for years, feeling like we could do nothing about it."

"We didn't let it happen! You, the politicians, the ones who were supposed to fight for us and make laws to protect us, you let it happen." A man yelled from the crowd.

"You're right. I stood by. I even participated in the system. I caved on regulations to the point that the whole of the government is now one giant corporation who dictates how we all live. I did this, you're right."

"But that's why we fought before. Things were supposed to be different after the war, but here we are again. Nothing has changed. In some ways it's worse," the same man yelled back.

"I know you may not trust me. I wouldn't either." Taurus stared at the ground, "I talked about change, but I never felt it, the way you all feel it. I watched you, from my high tower for years. I sympathized but I never really empathized with you. I get that now, but I am telling you, the ice is too thin not to act. The cracks grow bigger as we sit by. I know you want to believe in something. I want to believe too."

A few in the crowd tried to clap. "Shut up! All of you!" one of the Collectors yelled, feeling the situation spiraling out of his control. He lifted his dark visor, as the night overtook his vision. "We'll take you all in if we have to."

The old woman stepped forward, walked right up to the Collector, and looked into his eyes. "Think about what you are doing. You don't need to do this," she whispered.

"Back up!" he yelled in a panicked voice.

"I don't think so!" She grabbed the gun barrel and held it up to her head. "What are your convictions now? Shoot me if you must, but be ready, this will not end here."

"Listen ma'am, I don't have an issue with you. I had orders to find these two kids and arrest them. But if you get in my way, I…"

178

"What could those kids possibly have done?"

"It doesn't matter. Those are my orders, and it's not my job to question them."

"But it is your job, or it should be your job." She turned to the crowd. "We spent too many years not asking questions. When we finally began asking, no one felt they needed to answer. Those questions led to the revolts. But here we are on the other side of that war with the same questions. We need to keep asking the questions until we find our own answers and not the answers someone else tells us are correct." She turned back to the Collector, "So what are you gonna do? If you want those kids, you are gonna have to shoot me. Or," she paused, "or you can ask yourself the questions that are poisoning you from the inside out right now. Why should I shoot this woman? Why should I take these kids in to be tortured or killed? Can I trust the motivations of the person who ordered such a thing? Should I be loyal to that cause without stopping to examine whether it is right or wrong?"

The crowd instinctively stepped closer. The Collector, whose gun was on the old woman, nervously surveyed the sea of faces looking for the answer to the growing questions in his gut. The crowd stared back with fear and anger and one emotion he knew he could not fight--resolve. He held his weapon up in a surrender motion and then set it on the ground. As he stood, he thought about the implications of what he had done and the wrath that awaited him from both sides.

"What are you doing?" yelled one of the other Collectors.

"I'm not shooting that woman," he answered in a quiet voice of resignation.

"Fine, I will." He pointed his gun toward the old woman and the crowd lunged and pushed the remaining Collectors to the ground. Shots were fired, but no one was hurt. Several of the crowd secured the Collectors' wrists with belts, while the youngest in the crowd ran through the street throwing rocks at suspected cameras and the orange city lights which had begun to turn on in the dusk. The people of New Congress City had acted. It was a small victory, but it was enough to solidify their conviction.

Taurus stood still and silent, amazed at the tenacity of the crowd and unsure what to do next. The Collector who had relinquished his gun, stood meek and astonished that he was still standing. The old woman approached him and held out her hand, "Hi, I am Katherine. A lot of people call me Granny Kate, but it's up to you."

He took off his helmet and head gear and then put his hand in hers, "Hi Katherine, my name is Levi, but my friends call me Sugar."

She chortled, "Nice to meet you, Sugar."

"You're very brave, Katherine."

"So are you, Levi. We're keeping it formal then, huh?"

"No, you can call me Sugar, but I feel like, respectfully I should call you Katherine."

He felt her compassion as she examined his eyes, "You made a good choice young man."

"We'll see."

"You seem, kind. Why on earth would you be a Collector?"

"For all the wrong reasons, maybe someday when I can call you Granny Kate, I will tell you."

She smirked. Then the man who had been heckling Taurus tapped her on the shoulder and pulled her aside, "We can't trust him. What are you doing, ma?"

She leaned in with a loud whisper, "This boy has a story. Why don't we wait and see what happens?"

"It's your call, yer the one that almost got yer head blown off. Either way, we gotta go. We're gonna take the other Collectors to the farm."

She cautioned against it with her look. Then, she stepped back, "Sugar, this is my son Collin."

Collin held his hand out, "Nice to meet you. Thank you for not killing my ma. It takes a lot of guts to do what you did. It's not easy to go against orders. How do you feel?"

"Unemployed."

"So, I guess you really are one of us then." They both chuckled in solidarity." Would you do me another favor now? Would you take my mother home, so I can finish business here? She's had enough excitement for one night."

"That, I can do."

"I'preciate it. But," he bent to pick up Sugar's gun. "I think I'll be keeping this with me."

"What if we run into…"

"Trouble? Ha! You won't find anything out there that'll give you more trouble than that sweet little lady standing next to you." Katherine smiled her best beguiling smile. Collin then kissed his mother on the cheek and ran to Taurus. "We got this. Go check on your son."

Taurus, still in a daze over the events had almost forgotten his son was hurt. He stood silent, feeling the pull of the situation as equally as his injured son, a conflict that was new to him. "Seriously, go now," Collin insisted. Taurus thanked him with his expression and made a dash for Farley's. "Hey," Collin yelled. Taurus looked back over his shoulder. "I'm not letting you off the hook. We stood up for you today. Now remember your promise and stand up for us."

"I will. You have my word." Taurus turned to run to Farley's. "Wait," Taurus yelled back.

"What?" Collin answered.

"Don't drink the water?"

"What? Why? It's been off and on for days while they've been working on the pipes in town. What is going on?"

"Just don't drink the water. Spread the word. It's not safe. If you know anyone on the outskirts of town that has a well and doesn't sublet their land to the government, then that is where you should go."

"Okay, thanks Mr. Roma. Now go."

As he reached the front door, he heard three shots. He didn't look back.

# 39 ~ In My Wake

Croft started performing CPR. I stood motionless, not wanting to believe it. The room was silent. I was caught in a bubble I couldn't escape, watching the workers hustle and bustle around me.

My eyes glazed over until I could no longer see Croft's head. I was in the room where I awoke after my rescue. However, this time I knew it was my home. It felt like my home. Sage and I were sitting on our knees looking out one of the big windows to a grave marker below. Heavy sadness. Suddenly we heard a crash behind us. I turned around and saw my mother's face. Maybe somewhere in my experience I had cultured the thought of mothers being caring and kind and so I expected to see a warm and loving look. Yet, though she looked young, her face was chiseled.

She held a shattered frame with a picture of her and my father in it. "Time to stop moping around," she blasted. I felt the shock on my face. "Jane, you're going to have to pick Braeden up from pre-school."

"I know, I already do, every day." I felt her disapproval.

Sage spoke up, "Who is taking me to soccer practice? Dad always did, but…"

"Well, obviously not anymore," snapped mother. "I guess you're stuck with me."

I reached for my mother's hand, and she pulled it away. "She didn't mean anything by it, mom. She just misses dad. I'll take her."

"Well, she's going to have to toughen up. We all are."

Tears burned my eyes. I rubbed them to clear my vision and as I came out of my cloud, Croft was yelling my name. "Janie, Janie!" I stood in silence. He was vigorously pushing on Char's chest. "Janie, get some help."

The girl, Malina, who had been attending Charlotte spoke, "Mr. McAvoy, we have all tried. Several people worked on her. I already sent someone to fetch a cot. I'm sorry sir, she has been gone for a while."

The tension in Croft's arms released as he dropped his head. He made no sound. I wanted to hold him and comfort him, but I couldn't move. I was in shock. I couldn't make my body do anything. Croft pushed his thumb and forefinger deep into his eye sockets trying to caulk the drip.

His demeanor changed and he spoke softly as he stood to face me. The redness in his eyes only intensified the blue. He blinked hard and his eyes mesmerized me so that when he spoke, it startled me. "Have you been somewhere else?" I nodded. "I thought as much. She is gone, honey." I looked at him quizzically. "Char. Char is dead."

Though I thought I was aware, the moment finally came back to me, and I felt a hard, hollow pressure deep in my chest. Suddenly I knew why I flashed back to my mother. Char had been a mother for me in my short new life. She was the warm eyes, the caring voice, and the understanding that I had been missing for most of my life. And now she was gone.

I knelt beside her and touched her face. It was an honest face with several lines of wear and worry, but mostly lines of laughter. Her expression was light and peaceful, almost blissful. My eyes filled with tears. I had to blink, and my tears fell on her face and rolled down her cheek. Croft scooted closer to me, but I couldn't avert my gaze.

Still beautiful, she was the exemplar of clean, healthy, purposeful living. She was the epitome of everything I wanted to be. Yet, there she lay, dead to the world. All her expressions and memories wiped from the planet in one moment. Her vault of knowledge and experience extinguished from the world forever. I was empty.

I swallowed hard, almost heaving, and turned to Croft. "She didn't have to die. She could have stayed with us, and she would still be alive."

Malina chimed in behind us. "She sounded the city-wide alarm." She cried as she spoke. "If it wasn't for Ms. Charlotte, we would probably all be dead now. It's not fair, at all, ever, but she saved hundreds of people."

"What exactly happened to her?"

"She blew some charges up above on a large group of Collectors and a piece of the ceiling fell on her. She tried to get out of the way, but she wasn't fast enough."

I turned to look back at Char and only then did I see the number of bodies strewn about the room. Only a few GC, the rest were all Collectors.

"Are they still in the area? The Collectors?" Croft asked the girl.

A man walked up behind Croft. "We got 'em."

Croft turned, "Oh hey, DeWaun. We're secure then? We accounted for all of 'em?"

"Yep, sure did. Well, we didn't. That big man you brought with you did. He took out about twelve of them with his bare hands."

"Trey?" inquired Croft.

"Yeah, that's his name."

It was selfish of me, but I didn't want Trey to be the hero. I couldn't put my finger on why it made me so uncomfortable. Maybe if he was the bad guy, or at least not the good guy, it would be easier to compartmentalize him into a quick mistake, a blip in my radar that disappeared when needed.

Then, as if on cue, the blip walked into the room. Croft walked up to him, smiled a generous, thankful smile, and congratulated him on a job well done. Trey's sparkly white teeth dazzled in the natural light. I felt like a heel, but I didn't want to be generous or thankful. I wanted him to leave, and I wanted Charlotte back. The venom in my heart bubbled, and I felt woozy. Then, right as Trey walked over to give his condolences, I threw up all over his shoes.

Everyone froze and in a cathartic burst Trey doubled over in hysterical laughter. Croft asked if I was okay in a smirk and when I nodded, he broke out in laughter too. They both laughed so hard, tears slid down their faces. I wanted to be mad at them both, but the more I tried to hold it in, the sicker I felt until finally I started laughing too. The frenzy of the room stopped and focused on us. A wave of giggles commenced.

Croft spoke up, "We okay, everyone? I mean, we can't undo this. We can't bring back Char, or any of the others, but we can honor her and all the rest by not falling apart right now. We can stick together. We can remember and move on. That is what Char would want us to do." A glimmer of warmth and charity spread through the room, and small groups nodded and hugged.

I took a deep breath, and then Trey put his hand on my back. I am sure it was in solidarity, but I instinctively swatted his hand away. Awkward silence filled the space again. I wanted to disappear, but there was no place to go. Croft looked at me, confused. He had no idea how betrayed he was, but his expression still hurt.

"Man, there are some big flies in here," Trey offered to lighten the mood. Nervous laughter led to small conversations until everyone was back to business as usual. Trey approached Croft, "Can I talk to Janie alone for a minute?" Croft nodded silently and genuinely at Trey before he turned his questioning gaze to me. A dagger hit my heart as I knew he knew. He definitely knew.

Cautiously Trey approached me, "Janie, can I have a minute of your time?" I stood frozen and stupid. If I left to talk with Trey, that would surely be an admission of guilt. Croft would see right through it. "Hold on one sec," Trey excused himself, walked across the room and grabbed a towel on the floor next to one of the bodies, to wipe his shoes. I could feel Croft's eyes burning through me, but I couldn't look at him. I couldn't confirm his hurt.

In what felt like a moment of exasperation, Croft walked away to converse with the other Sentries that had gathered to make sure everything was secure in the area. I felt myself crumbling from the inside out, but I had to hold it together. Trey came back, "Walk with me please." I didn't move. "Please Janie!" he pleaded as he took a step forward.

I followed him through the rubble and suddenly all I wanted to do was to look at Croft, to have him flash those beautiful eyes at me and let me know it was okay. He did not look. There was no absolution.

We walked into another dark, dank tunnel. My chest tightened and I wished Croft were there to soothe my insanity. No salve. I was alone in my fears and self-loathing. Finally, the tunnel opened into a kitchen area. Food was out, as if it was being prepared but the room was empty. Trey stopped, "I know this may not be the best idea, with frying pans in here and all, but I need to talk to you."

I stood there, resigned in my fate that I was going to lose everything I had rebuilt in my short new life. "Janie, we didn't--do it!" I looked at him shocked, wondering if we were thinking of the same thing. "We didn't, ya know, go all the way."

"What do you mean? You said…"

"No, I didn't say exactly that."

"Yes, you did. I asked and you…and you…didn't say anything. WHY DIDN'T YOU SAY ANYTHING?! You let me believe this whole time that I was a whore? Sure, a drugged-up, out of my mind whore, but still a whore?"

Trey laughed, "Janie, you are not a whore. Look, we did some stuff okay. Yes, I liked it. I'm a man, what can I say? Kick me, punch me, do what you have to do. You have to believe me though, I didn't know you weren't in your right mind, and I didn't know you and Croft had a thing. I thought he just had a crush on you, like everybody else does. I didn't know you had feelings for him too. That's why we stopped. You called me Croft."

"I did?"

"Yes, and then you passed out, so I let you sleep. I wanted to tell you when you asked the next day, but I was still trying to figure things out myself. Then you ran off and wouldn't let me explain any further. I guess I liked the idea that you thought the worst. It made me feel a little better after you ran out acting like sex with me was the worst thing that could happen to you. I'm sorry, okay?"

I was still angry, but I was also relieved. I was thrilled in fact, that I had nothing, well not as much, to be ashamed of and nothing to keep me from Croft anymore. "So, we…didn't?"

"Nope."

I jumped up and put my arms around Trey's neck. "Thank God! I mean, I don't want to offend you, but it is a relief." We both laughed. He spun me around, and as he sat me down, he kissed my cheek. It was sweet, but the feeling quickly changed as the hair bristled on the back of my neck. An overwhelming panic ran through my body. Looking up, I saw Trey's smile slide off his face. I dropped my arms from around his neck and immediately turned to see the confirmation of all my fears.    Croft.

# 40 ~ Discoveries

Damien walked faster as he approached Sequoia's room. He paused when he reached the door. Even as a personal assistant, he was not allowed to enter family rooms without permission, but Aviva had not returned to her office and Sequoia acted suspicious. Damien thought he heard noises in the room but was too nervous to enter. He knocked and waited. Suddenly he heard banging and muffled yelling.

Damien opened the door cautiously to a pile of books on the floor and a large purple stain on the carpet. "Mrs. Chandler? Are you in here?" he asked with trepidation. A loud thud hit the closet door. Damien jumped and scurried toward the closet when, in an explosive burst, the door crashed to the ground with Aviva on top of it. Her skirt was ripped up the side and the top buttons on her blouse were stretched and pulling the fabric. Her face was crimson, and her snow-topped hair was stuck to her head from perspiration. She glared up at Damien from the floor.

"Are YOU going to help me up?"

Damien cautiously stepped toward his doom. Aviva, who was not a heavy woman, almost pulled Damien to his knees as she hoisted herself to her feet. "Where have you been?"

"I...I...was on my way back to see if Miss Sequoia liked the drink."
"Look around, Einstein. What do you think?"

"No ma'am."

"No ma'am," Aviva repeated in disgust. "Find her! Search the house."

"Ma'am, she is not in the house."

"What?! What do you mean?"

"She was heading for the fourth-floor habitrail a few minutes ago."

"And you let her go? Are you mad?"

"I didn't know ma'am. I'm sorry."

"Put out an alert. I want that student union and the grounds searched. If she is not there, get the Collectors on it. She is to be brought to me. Anyone who gets in the way, shoot them."

"Shoot them?"

Aviva glared her confirmation. Damien scampered out of the room until Aviva screamed after him, "DAMIEN!"

He appeared at the door. "Yes ma'am?"

Aviva grabbed the books from the floor and shoved them at Damien's stomach. "Here, throw these in the fireplace."

He was confused but didn't dare show it. "Yes, ma'am."

As he darted down the hall, he pushed a button on his earpiece and began talking. Aviva was still a furious mess. Various staff looked her in the eye to silently ask if she needed help as she stomped down the hallway. Her eyes were lasers, cutting her path and warning all not to approach. At first, she thought about going to her bedroom to freshen up but decided instead to go to her home office in the mansion. She entered and shut the door with more force than she anticipated. Once inside, Aviva felt an intense burning behind her eyes. She tried to rub them, but nothing helped until a solitary tear slid down her cheek. She was mortified.

Frustrated, she walked across the travertine floor to the washroom. The sight of herself in the mirror angered her more. She leaned in and splashed water on her face. It felt so good that she didn't care that her blouse was soaking wet. She grabbed a washcloth from a basket on the wall and ran it under the warm water, wrang it out, and applied it to her face, breathing in the warm steam. Throwing the washcloth in the sink, she turned slightly to dry her face and was startled by a hand on her leg.

She took a deep breath and dropped her head like a schoolgirl in heat. A voice whispered in her ear, "Nice! Wet tee shirt contest and you didn't even invite me."

"Hayward, I told you not to sneak up on me like that. I nearly clubbed you with my brush."

He grinned, "You are a fright, a sexy fright, but still a fright. What happened to you?"

"My granddaughter locked me in her closet."

He spit out a laugh, "What? No…"

"It's not funny," she fumed.

"It's a little funny."

She tried not to smile, "Not if you knew the circumstances."

"Why don't you tell me all about it?" he teased as he slid his hand farther up her thigh to the top of the newly ripped slit in her skirt. "This is a good style for you. You should wear it more often." She gave him a look that indicated he had gone too far, a look that only a lover would know.

Hayward Dawkins, seventeen years her junior, was suave in a calculating way, which Aviva enjoyed. Hayward was also very wealthy, so he didn't need Aviva for her money, but he felt at ease to spend her fortune more freely than his own. He was, at the time, the only person who could penetrate her thick-skinned exterior. Sometimes Aviva would look in the mirror and wonder why she wasted any time with Hayward. He would never be her great love, but he would suffice. A warm body at night had a way of forgiving a thousand other shortcomings.

He picked up Aviva's brush to brush her hair. Feeling her question, he answered before she could ask. "I like it shorter. It's sassy."

"I was going for serious. Sassy isn't exactly my style."

"That's why it's good for you. A little sass never hurt anyone." Aviva intentionally rolled her eyes. Hayward set down the brush and turned her around to face him. "Now, let's get these wet clothes off you, shall we?"

Aviva swatted his hand as it approached her buttons. "Hay, I can't. I have a situation on my hands."

"I can put a *situation* in your hands if you like."

"Keep it in your pants. This is going to have to wait." Aviva walked past him to her desk. She tapped on the desk com and spoke, "Ingrid, bring me a change of clothes." An ethereal voice answered in confirmation.

Hayward was immediately behind her. He wrapped his arms around her waist and began kissing her neck. "Since you have to change anyway, shouldn't we get this off of you?"

He tried to slide her shirt off her shoulder. Aviva looked at her bare shoulder and had momentarily thought about giving in when the door to her study opened after a brief knock. Ingrid, in the traditional burgundy uniform entered the room carrying several hangers full of clothes. Aviva stepped away from Hayward, disgusted that he tried to compromise her in front of her staff.

"Next time, wait until I answer, Ingrid."

"I'm sorry Mrs. Chandler. I didn't realize you had company."

"I don't!" she barked in an emphatic voice over her shoulder, cueing Hayward to make his exit. He walked past Ingrid and turned to blow a seductive kiss in the air to Aviva as he walked out. She smiled to herself and then bit her lip in disgust at her own weakness.

"Ingrid, have you heard anything from Damien yet?"

"Um, there's a problem in the domestic district."

"What do you mean, a problem?"

"Apparently there…"

Suddenly Damien burst through the door, "We found her!"

"Get out, Ingrid," Aviva barked and then turned her attention to Damien. "Where is she?"

"She has been captured, but not without a struggle."

"What does that mean? Spit it out!"

"She is being brought to the medical wing. She was shot."

"Shot?!"

"It looks like she was trying to run from the Collectors with a few other fugitives."

"Let me guess, that Roma boy was one of them."

"Yes, I believe so. One girl is dead--not Sequoia," he corrected quickly. Also, Mr. Roma's son has been captured."

"Good! Now maybe I'll have a little leverage. Let me know when my granddaughter arrives."

"Yes, ma'am," Damien answered in a perky tone, excited that he hadn't disappointed her again.

Aviva quickly changed into a taupe pant suit that Ingrid had brought her and sat in her desk chair tapping her finger on the desk. Finally, the peace and quiet she needed to devise a plan to tie up all the loose ends that flailed about and threatened to choke her.

# 41 ~ The New Plan

I would never forget that look. Ever. Croft's shoulders drooped as his hopeful intentions left his body. I knew he thought the worst, but I couldn't verbalize that he was wrong. I didn't have feelings for Trey, but I couldn't confirm that I was blameless. "Croft," I whispered listlessly. He turned and started to walk away with a look of defeat that I hated myself for causing. I ran after him, but I knew I couldn't appease his wounded heart. The fact was, I was complicit. I stopped and let him walk away.

Trey walked up behind me, "Let me talk to him, Janie."

"Um, no! That would not be a good idea. I need to talk to him. I just need to wait for the right time."

"I think now is the right time."

"It's not your call to make. I am the one that owes him an explanation, not you."

"I understand, but I don't want him thinking what he's thinking."

"What, that he has a reason to distrust me? Well, he does."

"No, he doesn't Janie. Why do you always think the worst of yourself?"

Frustrated, I lashed out, "Ya know, Trey, I don't know. I don't know if I always think the worst of myself. I don't even know how I think of myself. I do know that I have caused chaos in pretty much everyone's life I have entered. I know that the Collectors found this place because of my blood. I know that Char is dead because of me. And now, I know the man I love, that I have loved for years, has confirmed it. I am a virus to those who love me. I know…"

I stopped, realizing that I had admitted I loved Croft. I couldn't remember all our history, but I knew I loved him. I knew that I would go to any lengths to prove it to him. Yet, lingering in my gut I also knew he might never be able to love me again, whether I tell him the truth or nothing at all.

I felt more alone than ever. Trey was talking at me, but I tuned him out. "Please just go and promise you won't talk to Croft." Resigned, he nodded his head and walked past me through the kitchen. I felt worse for having hurt his feelings and involving him in my drama. I had not really thought of how I had hurt him too. Was there anyone immune to my tidal wave? I called after him, "Trey, I'm sorry!" He paused, didn't look back and kept walking.

I hadn't realized I was standing in the tunnel. The pressure of the place closed in all at once. I needed to get out of there. I needed a plan. I had to get out of my head and concentrate on finding my family. Plus, if the Collectors could still track my blood, I was putting everyone else at risk.

I ran through the tunnel until I came to the room with the hole in the ceiling. People were still around, but all the bodies, including Char's, had been moved. Croft was nowhere in sight. Chul-moo, whom I had met in the GC council room, saw me and approached. "Ms. Jane, can I help you? You look like you are lost."

"I am. I need to get to my room."

"I will walk you there." We walked through a system of tunnels and rooms until we came to Turf-dome. Finally, a familiar place but it felt foreign to me. Those I cared about were missing. "Ms. Jane, how are you doing with your memory?"

I guffawed. "I get little pieces here and there, but for the most part, it is still a big dark hole."

"Hmmm, I understand. Have you tried meditating?"

"Mmm'no, I don't really know how. Besides, being alone with my thoughts is the last place I want to be right now."

"I understand. Soldiers have similar complications, but meditation is not about thinking. It is about letting go of your thoughts and communing with your higher self. You may find some answers there."

"Maybe, but as blank as my mind is in some ways, I can't let go of the clutter that is in there now. I don't know for sure, but I think I am the type of person that can't sit around and wait for things to happen. I am pretty sure I need to do something, anything to get out of my mind and to find my family."

"I may be able to help you with that."

"You can?"

"Can you find your way to your room from here?"

"Yes."

"Gather the clothes you need and prepare. I will meet you there at seven tonight."

"Seven? Why so late?"

"We need to leave at dusk so we can travel in the darkness." I nodded. "Do not tell anyone. Croft would not like my interference."

# 42 – Patching and Purging

Braeden jumped as Taurus burst through the door. Sabine was applying the bandages to the torso of a wincing Howard. Taurus knelt down, "Howard, my son. Are you okay?"

"Okay," Howard offered through his gritted teeth.

"Is he okay?" he asked to Braeden.

"He probably has some broken ribs. Sabine thought he might have punctured a lung, but his breathing has stabilized, so that is probably not the case.

"Can he be moved?"

"I don't know. Can you move, Howard?"

"Help me sit up more," Howard strained. "Ah…ooo…okay, that was about as bad as I was expecting. Man, my head hurts almost as bad."

"Well, it looks like you were probably kicked in the head and face a few times," offered Braeden. "Are you dizzy?"

"No, just sore, I think that stuff your friend gave me, helped."

Taurus interrupted and gently grabbed Howard's arm. "As much as I want to hug you, I don't want to hurt you, but I am glad you are okay, son." A tear formed in Taurus' eye that echoed the many tears he had seen shed that day. "Listen though," he said, wiping his eyes. "We have to move. We have a little cover of darkness, but I'm sure the surveillance cameras got an eyeful before they went out.

Braeden stood up to peer out the window. He had to squint to see in the darkness, but the street looked empty. "What happened out there? Where is everyone?"

"It's a long story. A good story, but a long story. Right now, I need to get him out of here and get back to do some damage control, if it's not too late, before your mother gets wind of the situation."

Sabine interjected, "Mr. Roma, you can't take him home. He's a fugitive. I'm not even sure you are safe. I know a place you can take Howard."

"Where?"

"There are several GC safe houses around the city." She turned to Braeden as if Taurus were not there, "Can we trust him?"

"If Croft trusts him, then that is good enough for me."

She smiled and turned back to Taurus. "The safe houses usually have a GC marking. Several I saw had light fixtures with an ornate metal leaf design around them. Sometimes it's as simple as a green doorbell. I haven't been to this part of town before, but it also looks like most of the red door establishments may either be safe houses or a link to one."

"So, I just go waltzing down the street looking for a sign and then ring the doorbell. No offense, but I don't think they are going to let us in."

"Of course not, you will have to give them a code or a token of the GC lifestyle."

Braeden interrupted, "Sabine, why don't you go with them to help them find a place. I need to go home and gather my things before we leave town anyway." He looked at the time on the wall. "It's about eight-fifteen. Meet me back here at nine-thirty. If you can't get in or it looks compromised, go back to where you end up taking Howard, and I will find you." She looked at him sheepishly.

"Are you okay with this idea?"

"Yes, it's a good plan," she answered. "But what if something happens? What if you can't get back?"

"I know what you're thinking. I can handle my mother. I will get back."

Taurus jumped in, "Okay, you go first. It is still probably better for us all not to be seen together."

"Agreed." Braeden, who had been sitting on the edge of the booth seat stood to leave. Sabine instinctively stood with him. He gently grabbed her face and marveled at the contrast of his pinkish skin, next to her olive tone. "I will come back for you." He wanted to kiss her, and she wanted him to, but instead he just tilted his head to the side and smiled. She smiled her widest smile to date and then ran her hand along his arm as he walked away and out the door.

Braeden walked quickly through the dark streets. The city was eerily quiet compared to what he had witnessed earlier in the evening. Occasionally he would catch someone peering from a window, but no one ventured outside. Once he came to a more familiar part of town, he noticed the distinct contrast of city streetlights, but still very few people on the streets. He jumped on the sidewalk conveyor to get him to the outer spokes of the Inner-City Track Line. Taking the elevator up to the transport pod, he noticed a crowd around Line #15.

Braeden pressed his face against the glass of the elevator. It looked like a small group attacking a Collector, but he could not believe it was true. He tried to put it out of his mind. He had to be quick. Too much was on the line to lose focus. He boarded the pod, and with no other pods on the spoke

194

that night, he was quickly at Line #7. As the pod slowed into the dock at the New Congress Hall of Statutes, Braeden saw a flurry of activity. Aides rushed through the halls. The cylindrical building was illuminated by bright yellow office lights. Braeden looked up at the starless sky and wondered what it would be like to live where the stars still exist in the sky.

Though the trepidation of seeing his mother was in the back of his mind, he was filled with a new hope. Braeden was so anxious to see his sister and make sure she was okay. He was even ready for the possibility of having to live his life on the run. Yet, the idea of having a friend, a special friend and companion, accompany him in his new life was more than he had ever wished for himself.

The pod doors opened, and Braeden stepped out. The usual congressional guards had been replaced with black-suited Collectors. As Braeden walked by, instead of the standard greeting afforded to a Chandler heir, the Collectors stood stone-faced. After he passed, he glanced back to see them tapping their ears and talking into their helmet coms.

His pace quickened until he reached the tunnel to Chandler Manor. He stood still waiting for the retinal scan, half worried that his entry might be denied. He didn't realize he had stopped breathing until the entry light turned green, at which time he exhaled with relief. Braeden tried to be nonchalant as he waltzed through the foyer and into the library at the far end of the hall. A large fire in the fireplace caught his eye.

Berating himself for being distracted, he decided to check it out. The fire felt nice after the cool fall evening air. As he warmed his hands, he noticed the source of the fire was not logs, but big books. Braeden had seen his mother burn many books. While it disgusted him, this was nothing new, so he put his hands in his pockets and readied to complete his mission. Before he could turn to leave, a voice restored the chill to his blood.

"Braeden, s'nice of you to make an appearance this evening." Braeden stood motionless facing the fire. "I half wondered f'you were coming back."

"Well, I'm back, mother," he snarled, still not moving.

"D'your *girlfriend* go home, or is she moving in now?"

He turned defiantly, "Really mother. You just met her, and you are already asking if she is moving in?"

"I dinnit know, yer don't seem to be yerself lately. I didn't know what to expect or who to expect or what was expected. I just expected--I don't know." It wasn't like his mother to ramble on.

"Well, you can expect that if we are going to live together, I would move out rather than have her move in." Braeden hated conversing with his mother, but the charade of Sabine as his girlfriend was something he secretly enjoyed. Aviva opened her mouth to speak but he cut her off, "Save it mother. I'm tired. I'm going to bed." He whisked past Aviva waiting for her to try to stop him. Instead, she stared straight ahead and swirled the ice in her bourbon glass disapprovingly.

Braeden thought about getting back to Sabine and quickened his step to get to his room. His bedroom door was ajar, and a light peeked through the crack as he approached. Cautiously he walked into his room to find a Collector, holding an axe, lying dead on the floor. The carved metal door to his closet was marred, with axe marks. The Collector's face was blue, and his hair smelled burnt.

Braeden was relieved the armed security system for his closet worked, though the electrocuted Collector on his floor, made him queasy. He wasn't the type of person who could delight in anyone's death. Carefully, he stepped over the body, simultaneously kicking the axe away from the man's hand. Braeden worried that it would be hard to bring his heart rate down to match his scanner after the evening he had, but he concentrated and made the match. The door, because of the tampering did not open as smoothly as usual, and he had to push it the last few inches to squeeze through.

Once inside, he quickly opened the secret compartment and grabbed his bag of supplies. He threw a winter coat into the large duffle, then ran down the hall to Sequoia's room to grab some extra clothes for Sabine. He hated stealing from Sequoia, especially when he didn't know what had happened to her, but these were not usual circumstances. Assuming Aviva had her locked up somewhere, he was torn between searching for her or coming back for her later. He would let circumstances decide for him.

Braeden left Sequoia's room and jogged to the back stairs that were closest to the garden exit. As he reached the bottom of the stairs, his mother appeared with a fresh glass of bourbon. She wore toffee colored silk pajamas with leopard trim. Braeden had never seen his mother in pajamas since they had lived in New Congress. He couldn't believe she would be anything less than formal anywhere other than her bedroom. He thought she must be verging on intoxication or a breakdown, though that also seemed implausible.

"There's been a situuuation." Aviva splattered her words. She chortled to herself, thinking about Hayward's earlier comment.

Braeden raised his eyebrows, "Are you drunk?"

"Why, because I giggled?"

"Um, yes that is why. You don't even say the word giggle, let alone do it."

"That'sss…preside the point. Don't cha know." Braeden wanted to laugh until he reviewed all that she had done. Her performance wasn't cute. It was pathetic. "And," she tried to exclaim emphatically, "you said you were going to bed."

"I changed my mind." He corrected course to walk past her, but she sauntered in front of him.

196

"Like I said, there has been a sit-u-a-tion," she enunciated slowly as she shook her already empty glass of ice in front of his face. "In fact, a couple-uh situations. It seems your friend Charles caused a problem at one of the TRCs."

The blood rose to Braeden's face. He thought about silently walking by, but he couldn't push the hatred down any longer. He tried to grasp a fond memory from his childhood to save her from his wrath, but he couldn't find one in time. Braeden leaned in as close as he could without fainting from the smell of her alcoholic breath. "If, by a *problem* you mean my sister being kidnapped, drugged, and held captive for over a year, then you are right. There is a problem." He wanted to say more, but he stopped.

Aviva dropped her bourbon glass, and it shattered on the step. Several nearby staff came rounding the corner to see what happened. She stopped them short with an outstretched hand. Glaring at Braeden, she decided to play the drunk card. "Oopsie! Really, Braedenenen I don't knooooow…"

"Drop the act mother. You know exactly what I am talking about. You're drunk, but you're not that out of it. You can relax though, Charles is not your concern anymore, and neither am I." He sidestepped her and opened the door. He turned back to speak, "Goodbye, mother. Now that I have my sister back, you have nothing to hold over my head anymore."

Braeden stepped through the door and as it was closing, Aviva mustered the steadiest voice she could, "Sequoia will be disappointed to hear that." The door shut. Braeden turned and pressed his face up against the glass door. Aviva's glassy eyes stared back. Braeden tried the door, but of course it was locked. He tried the retinal scanner outside the door, but it wouldn't clear him.

Aviva turned and walked away while barking orders at her still-frozen staff to clean up the mess she had left. Braeden ran his hands through his sandy hair. He felt ripped in half. Sabine was waiting for him, but so was his niece. He couldn't leave. He ran to the gate that exited to the street bordering the park, with a plan to stash his bag and then go back for Sequoia.

The guards at the gate questioned him, but he pushed through, throwing a handful of government coins up in the air. As he reached the street, he noticed a large black vehicle with darkened windows approaching. Cars were unusual in the city, but at night, they were rarely seen. He thought it must be one of his mother's fleet. Setting his bag down at the curb, he stepped out in front of the vehicle.

To his surprise, the vehicle came to a complete stop and the driver's window rolled down. The driver yelled out, "Is everything okay, Mr. Chandler?" Braeden approached cautiously. As he reached the window, he realized the driver was the security guard that Red had brought into their meeting at the Red Horse Inn. He flashed Braeden a sly smile and showed him three fingers on the side of the door. As he motioned with his eyes, Braeden took it to mean there were three other guards in the vehicle.

"Oh, you're hurt," the guard said in a surprised voice as he winked. "Get out and help him." The passenger side doors opened, and the guard whispered to get down. Braeden bent down and held his leg to play the part. Two of the guards approached the driver's window and Braeden heard a high-pitched noise in the vehicle. As the guards moved toward Braeden, the driver motioned for him to move back then shot each guard with an electrical pulse. They dropped to the ground shaking and convulsing, and then nothing.

The faux guard told Braeden to come around to the opposite side. Braeden opened the passenger door and another body fell out. He wasn't sure if they were alive or dead and he didn't want to ask. The guard yelled out, "Mr. Chandler, you should probably ride in the way back."

"Oh right, in case anyone sees me. Thanks man," he reached across the seat. "You can call me Braeden though."

"Fine, now get in before someone sees you." Braeden walked to the back of the vehicle and opened the hatch. A breath of the cold night air almost choked him. Sequoia, bloody and moaning, was curled into a ball in the back end. Braeden quickly jumped in and shut the hatch. The vehicle went a few feet and stopped so the driver could grab Braeden's bag and throw it into the back seat "Thought you might need this."

"Thanks, yes. Thank you. Now go!"

# 43 ~ And Stuff

Delilah had a restful sleep. Having no daylight to judge the time, she opened the front door of Jocelyn's apartment to find Bodhi asleep on a chair he had dragged over from the common area. When he heard the door, he jumped up, wide-eyed, like he had never been asleep. Delilah burst out laughing.

"Fancy meeting you here, Miss Delilah. Come on, I have a cool place to show you." They walked through several tunnels and rooms, jabbering away like chums, before they came to a rock face that opened into a large cave. A small stream that widened in the middle flowed through the cave. Families were playing in the water.

"Wow, an underground pool. How does the water get in?"

"Right?! This is one of the remaining tributary thingies left over from the Mississippi.""The Mississippi River?"

"Yeah, I didn't realize 'til after we were through it, but that dried-up riverbed we drove through used to be the freakin' Mississippi."

"But Foster said the water was damned, and they were going to release it."

"There's still some deeper, stretches of the river that flow. I heard someone say that even the areas that aren't dammed are mostly dry, except for spring fed sections. Crazy right?"

Delilah still wasn't sure if Bodhi intentionally tried to sound less intelligent than he was, or if his personality just took over his brain. Either way, she thought it was cute.

"Wow, I never thought about all that before."

"Well, that's why I'm here. I will be your tour guide and teacher for the afternoon."

# 44 ~ Forward, Reverse

"I don't think Croft cares where I go right now, but I won't tell a soul."

Chul-moo looked at me confused and walked across Turf-dome to the blue hallway. I skip-walked briskly back to my room to ready myself for the trip. I was so conflicted. I didn't want to leave Croft, but I didn't yet know what to say to him. I couldn't stay, knowing my presence was a danger to the people of Fox Island. They had sacrificed enough for me.

On the way back, I walked through the big white room where I first met Char. I could almost see her standing there with her gentle smile. My heart hurt. I wanted to sob, but I tried to stop myself. I bit my lip so hard I tasted blood. As I was approaching the hallway to my room, I passed Trey with a group of admirers. He was smiling and humbly receiving their congratulations for the quick action he took in the skirmish. He looked up with a wounded smile as I approached. "You okay?"

I smiled gratefully and lied, "Yes, you?" He nodded and continued.

I spent most of the day gathering clothes and supplies. I didn't know what I needed to take or how much, so I grabbed everything I could, which were pretty much all my possessions. I took a long shower and a short nap, though I wished I had taken a short shower and a long nap. I walked through the bathroom one more time to see if I had forgotten anything. Next to the washbowl sink on the vanity something caught my eye. It was a silver ring. The top of the ring twisted into a Celtic knot, covered with small tourmaline stones, and imbedded in the center of the knot was a square cut diamond.

I knew instantly, it was my wedding ring. I rolled the band between my fingers, trying desperately to remember anything about wearing it or the man that gave it to me. I walked to my bed and sat down.

Putting the ring on my finger, I was instantly transported. Sunshine on my hand made the ring sparkle against my tan skin. Looking forward, I saw a large lake. It was so big I couldn't see the other side. I would have thought it was the ocean, but it smelled fresh and not salty. Between the

200

lake and I, stood an archway made of driftwood and bent branches. Tucked into the branches were white spiraea blooms, dog-wood and white-rock roses. It was strange, I could name all the flowers, like I had remembered picking them.

Underneath the arch was a small platform with a lavender carpet. I scanned to my right and saw Croft. He was a vision, barefoot in the sand and wearing a tan linen suit with a purple flower on his lapel. His white button-down shirt was open at the neck and his eyes mirrored the water and danced in the reflection. He was smiling so sweetly, I wanted to melt.

I caught my breath but felt guilty for feeling so attracted to him. As I smiled back to him, another figure stepped into my view, blocking Croft. Anson, who I must admit was dazzling. A younger, shorter haired version of his big brother, he wore the same thing as Croft but all white. His light hair caught the sunlight like jewels caught in a net.

"You ready?" Anson had a lovely quality to his speaking voice. I could almost hear it. I felt myself smile big and it made my heart happy. It seemed as if I loved Anson, and he loved me. Maybe I had just tried to block Croft out of my conscious world to let my love for Anson blossom.

I tried to squeeze my eyes shut to bring myself back to reality. The happiness hurt when I thought of it too long, because I knew the end of the story. When I opened my eyes again, I was still staring at my hand. Still outside, but I was not at the beach. I was sitting on a log, surrounded by trees, but there were ravines on two sides. It felt very high.

Underneath my hand was another hand holding mine. I looked next to me and was surprised to see that it wasn't Anson, but Croft. "You don't have to take it off," he said. "You were married for almost twelve years. I have accepted that. It doesn't make me insecure. It's okay, Janie."

"I just don't know how long it is appropriate for me to wear it. It's hard to believe it has been three years since..." He squeezed my hand. I felt sad, but relieved. I instantly hated myself that I felt that, but I did. "I might have even taken it off before, but I love it so much. It's so beautiful. Anson did have great taste. I couldn't have picked out a better ring for myself."

"My little brother did have great style, but I picked it out."

"What?"

"Anson had dragged me ring shopping with him several times. We went to the same three stores, again and again. He kept hoping he would find the perfect one in a new shipment. Finally, I had to do something. It wasn't an easy task, you know, watching my brother pick out a ring for the woman I loved. I went to that jewelers' down at the corner of Elm and Hazelton. What was that little old man's name? Gino, that's it. Anyway, Gino and I sat down together and designed that ring. I thought of everything you meant to me and what I would want to give you if it were me that was lucky enough to have your love. A part of me always secretly hoped you would realize it was really from me. I hoped you would see in it what I saw--see in you. What a ludicrous idea."

"Not ludicrous."

He shook his head in self-disgust. "I told Gino to place it in a prominent spot where Anson was sure to find it, the next time we went to that store. He walked by that damn ring twice until I finally said, "Hey, what about this one?" He looked at me with a big grin and nodded. I shook his hand, but I wanted to punch him in the gut."

I giggled and the vision faded. Of course, it would have been Croft to design the perfect ring for me. It was a lovely and briny thought at the same time. Still, I wondered where the ring came from. Croft must have left it in my room. What did that mean? Either he wanted to remind me that I kept stabbing his heart with my indecision or he wanted me to know that despite everything, he still loved me. I mean, he loved me even after I had married his brother. Maybe he wanted me to know that we were paired for life, no matter what.

Surprisingly, there was a knock at the door. It was only 5:30 p.m., so I knew it couldn't be Chul-Moo. Since Char was gone, there were only two people it could be. I cautiously opened the door. Croft, my first choice, the one who should have always been my first choice stood silently before me. I looked at him hopefully. He looked stern. He glanced down at my hand and saw my ring. Stupid! I wanted to kick myself, but then again, he had left it for me.

"Your trip with Chul-moo has been postponed," he said matter-of-factly. I tried to look surprised, like I didn't know what he was talking about. He didn't buy it. "We got word from your brother Braeden. He has Sequoia, but she has been hurt. Chul-moo and Chauncey, Char's brother, are going with me to get them. They may have some trouble getting here on their own."

"What?" I had too many questions to verbalize. I didn't want to be scared so I went for grit. "I am going with you."

"No! You're not!"

Gritty rage. "You can't tell me not to go! You're telling me my daughter is hurt and my brother is helping her? I am going! I was going to go with Chul-moo to find them tonight anyway."

He rolled his eyes as if I was a nonsensical child. I wanted to jump out of my skin I was so infuriated. "It's MY family. I'm going!" His eyes flipped up to meet mine. Instantly I felt the sting of the implication that it was my family and not Croft's that needed rescuing. Even though they couldn't ever truly be his family, he was there, offering to risk his life to go and get them. When had I ever deserved this man's love?

"I'm sorry Croft, I didn't mean…"

"Janie, you can't go. It's too dangerous for you."

202

I hoped I had misread him. "I don't care about me." I resigned myself to the inevitable. "I just want to see both of them and make sure they are all right."

"If you come, it would be dangerous for us too. If there is still any tracking solution in your blood, you cannot go to a Collection. You would be found instantly."

"But I'm putting everyone else in danger by staying here."

"Yes, you are." He glanced down in defeat. It was a look of his I had not seen before and didn't want to see again. "Chul-moo has a bunker a few miles from here, just north of the main city."

"Bunker?" My throat closed in anticipation of being underground in a closed-in space.

Always able to read me. "Don't worry it's not underground. It's a tree house. Smaller than where you grew up, but you will be comfortable there. It's more of a look-out tower than anything. He and Chaunce have put a lot of protections in it so no one will be able to track you there."

I knew he was right. "How will I get there?"

"That's the hard part. We may have a solution for you after you are another day out or so, but getting there is a problem. Once you are in the open, they will be able to track you much easier." He paused for a long minute. "Trey is going to take you. I have already talked to him about it. I didn't figure you would mind." Then abruptly he turned to walk away.

"Croft! Wait!" He turned back and his eyes were tortured.

"I have to go," he said breathlessly, with almost no tone to his voice.

I was killing him little by little. "Croft, it's not what you think. I mean, I guess some things happened, but I didn't know what was going on." I stopped. I sounded ridiculous. He would never believe that I didn't willfully partake in some affair with Trey.

He shook his head and started to walk away again. I grabbed his arm. "Croft, please! I don't love T...anyone else." I didn't even want to say Trey's name. I wanted him to think Trey was that insignificant to me. "I love you!"

Croft turned and took my hand off his arm. His reaction expanded the hole in my heart. He stared at his feet, not wanting to make eye contact with me. Then tersely he grabbed my face, glared at me, and angrily kissed me. Stupefied, I tried to pull away, but he wouldn't let me. I pushed on his chest, but when I realized he wasn't going to stop, I put my arms around his waist and pulled him closer.

The kiss transformed into something softer. Cayenne turned to sugar. His arms slipped down around mine and I briefly felt that I had my Croft back and that all had been forgiven. He kissed me gently and beautifully. I never wanted to leave that moment. But, as with all such moments, the winds changed. He stepped back, looked down, turned, and walked out without another word.

I leaned on the wall for support. In all realities, it could have been the last time I would ever see Croft. I wanted to hurt myself for what had I done to that poor man. I had to stop. I had to re-focus. I was finally going to get to see one of my daughters and my brother. The anticipation was unbearable. I couldn't categorize it because it wasn't the hope of seeing their faces again or reminiscing. It was the hope of meeting them for the first time in my new reality.

I didn't know if I would instantly love them, or if I would have to get to know them again, like I did Croft. Either way it was so unfair to both. They, as well as my other daughter, and Croft and Anson, and Sage, and Char, and Trey, and everyone else who mattered to me, had done nothing to deserve being dragged in the wake of Janie McAvoy.

I couldn't wallow any longer. A plan of action was what I needed. The past would only drain me of my determination to set things right, so I was going to leave it where it belonged. I turned to go back to packing and saw a camouflage duffle next to my door. Croft had probably set it there and I hadn't even realized.

Inside the duffle were flashlights, dried fruit, nuts and jerky, a water pouch, and a thin winter parka. There were also a couple of techno gadgets that I was sure Trey would know how to use and a book, The Poems of T.S. Eliot. A white satin hair ribbon that looked familiar marked a page. I opened it and read.

*We shall not cease from exploration*
*And the end of all our exploring*
*Will be to arrive where we started*
*And know the place for the first time.*

That was my credo. Croft, in all his hurt and anger still gave me something to inspire me. A pinnacle of unselfishness, he would never forsake me.

I threw my clothes and personals in the bag and set off to find Trey. Before I could even get to my door, there was another knock. Perhaps Croft had come back to kiss me again. The thought made me warm all over. I opened the door to find the only other possibility, Trey.

Without an invitation he walked past me and stepped in. "Listen Janie, I know you won't be too keen on this, but I need to take you away from here."

"I know," I said solemnly. "Croft told me."

"He did?"

"I was going to leave anyway. This was not my plan, but I accept it."

"Wow, okay, that was easier than I thought. He said I had to tell you, but he was sure that it would be okay with you. I tried to talk to him, but he didn't want to listen."

"I told you not to. What did you say?"

"I just said that you didn't remember jumping on me and kissing me and…"

"You said what?!! Oh my God, I told you not to talk to him."

"Janie, I was trying to be truthful without revealing too many of the details."

"Really, Trey? That was you being discrete? You couldn't word it any better than that? Or better yet, you couldn't have kept your mouth shut?"

"Janie, I was trying to make things better."

"Mission not accomplished."

"Okay, okay, I get it. I'm sorry." He took a deep breath and tried again in a calmer voice, "I'm sorry."

"S'okay," I muttered, not feeling the charity behind the forgiveness. "Croft told me we are going to a tree bunker that Chul-moo designed. What is the plan?"

"Yes, it was where he was originally going to take you after the rescue, but your sister insisted on your family's home. They thought the place would help jog your memory."

"Maybe with more time it would have, but that is neither here nor there now. How do we get to Chul-moo's?"

"Well, the idea is to get there as fast as possible because you will not have any real protection in the open. My first thought was to try to get the GC rig, but I think it is too dangerous and the Collectors may have even found it by now. I found an old dirt bike in a room they call the un-recycle bin. Char's brother Chauncey tuned it up and got it running while I welded a little tow behind cart to carry the gear."

"Okay, so when do we leave?"

"Ideally, I would like to wait until the middle of the night since there would be fewer possible patrols, but I think the sooner we leave, the safer it will be for you and everyone here."

"I think you're right."

"I got your bag."

I followed Trey to an outcropping that looked like a loading dock with no door. I could see trees in the fading light and an orangey glow from the nearby city. We walked the huge expanse to the bike and trailer. "Do they leave this open like this? I mean someone could walk right in."

"You'll see. Oh, and if you have a coat, you'll want to put it on. It's cold tonight."

I dug for the coat Croft had left me and put it on. "Okay, ready."

"You're going to have to put your arms around my waist. Can you handle that?"

"I'll try to resist the temptation," I said wryly.

"That's not what I meant. I meant because you are mad at me."

I jumped on and dug my arms into his gut spitefully. We pulled close to the entrance and then Trey pressed a clicker he had in his pocket. What appeared to be a clear film in front of us dissolved into little light crystals that vanished into the air. We drove out of the bay and Trey hit the clicker again. I glanced behind us and there was no opening, just the illusion of rock face or a large boulder.

"Trey, I've been meaning to ask you something."

He glanced back to hear me better. "Yes?"

"You told me I could feel other people's emotions and pain. Why can't I always? I mean, sometimes I feel completely blown away by what people say and how they act."

"You're not a mind reader, Janie. You are just more perceptive than most."

"How do I know when it is my emotions I am feeling and not someone else's?"

"The first step is being aware. You'll get better at it over time."

"Is it possible that someone else's feelings toward me could amplify my feelings for them?"

Trey's grin bared all his teeth. "Are you trying to tell me something?"

"No! See, that is what I mean. I wasn't thinking that at all."

"Okay, jeesh! I guess it's possible. Can you sense what I am feeling right now?"

"Aggravation?"

"You got it. Now hang on would ya?" We sped along quickly, but not quietly. The wind taunted me and froze my ears and nose, but my body was warm, wrapped around Trey's torso. I dared not like it too much. We had only been driving for several minutes when the bike began to sputter. Trey revved the engine with a twist of the handle, and it evened out for only a few seconds. Then it gasped and died. "Damn, gas guzzling, piece of shit." He pulled out a gizmo with a small screen from his pocket.

"How far?"

"We have about a mile to go. We're going to have to hoof it."

"You mean walk?"

"No, I mean run."

# 45 ~ Farm Delivery

Braeden stroked Sequoia's hair. She was sweating and non-responsive. He lifted her light coat to see the wound. It was much higher on her left side than he had hoped. He yelled to the front, "It is so dark in here. Is there some type of light you could turn on?"

"Tap the ceiling," the guard yelled back.

Braeden choked as he saw the extent of the damage. The tissue around the wound was beginning to dissolve. It was more than a bullet or a laser that had penetrated her skin. "Is there some type of medical kit or something I can use to stop the blood?"

"You don't want to touch that Mr. Chandler, uh Braeden. She has been shot with a virus pulse."

"What the hell is a virus pulse?"

"It's a new weapon that breaks the skin with a bullet which is contaminated with a flesh-eating virus. You can be near her, but do not touch the wound."

"What is the treatment for something like this?"

"There is no treatment."

"Then how am I supposed to help her?"

The car stopped so the guard could turn around. "Braeden, I'm sorry, but there is nothing you can do. It is just luck that we ran into you on the road so you could say goodbye."

Braeden's eyes filled with tears. "I don't understand. There is nothing I can do?" Then with a flash of hope, "Is there something my mother's doctors could do?"

"No, I'm sorry. They were not even supposed to be using those weapons yet from what I understand of their conversation earlier. The hot shot that was next to me was the one that thought they would be fun to try out, ignorant bastard."

Sequoia moaned in pain. Braeden pulled her jacket down over her wound and tried to attend to her. "Sequoia, can you hear me? I'm sorry.

207

I'm so sorry I let you stay here. I'm sorry I didn't protect you earlier." Her body which had been tense with pain, relaxed and Braeden knew instantly she was gone. How was he to tell his sister, who had already lost her children once, that he let her daughter die?

"Hold on!" the guard yelled from the front. Braeden noticed a light growing behind him. He turned to see headlights approaching fast. He braced for impact, but the guard accelerated, and Braeden was knocked against the back windows. The blood from Sequoia's body traveled faster across the back end of the cab as the middle of her body was beginning to melt away. Braeden shuddered at the thought of the wound and was thankful she had passed before too much more pain.

He kissed his fingertips and then touched them to her forehead one more time before climbing over the seats to the front. The vehicle was speeding through streets with odd groupings of people that had to lunge out of the way.

"Careful, can we please not kill anyone else tonight?"

"That other truck is right behind us. We have to move, but I will try to be more--wait, hold on, I have an idea." The guard sharply turned right, down a side road that looked like it led to nowhere.

"Where are we going?"

"The old interstate, it's not equipped with driving sensors, so I am hoping their vehicle won't be able to function out of the city."

"What makes you think this one will?"

"Because this is a GC rig."

"But my mother has cars that can drive in the country."

"Yes, your mother does, but do you think all of her goons do?"

"True, but if this is a GC car, how did those guards and my niece get in the car with you?"

"I was leaving a meeting with James, the one you call Red, and some other council members. I had a contact that was going to get me in with the new added security detail at the mansion. I just happened to pass by those three carrying a girl. They flagged me down. I didn't even know it was your niece until I heard them talking. They assumed I was the ride they were waiting for, so I didn't argue. We were on our way to take her back to the mansion when I saw you. Now buckle up!"

Braeden put on the seat belt. The guard accelerated and plowed into barrels at the entrance to the old interstate sending them scattering. The car behind them rolled to a stop. Braeden saw, in his side-view mirror, several Collectors get out and push the car back. "Great idea, it looks like you were right, but how are we going to get back into the city? I still have friends I need to get to."

"You mean that little brunette friend you were with earlier?"

Braeden smiled slyly. "Yes, that's the one, and others."

"Where are you meeting them?"

208

"Somewhere near Farley's tavern."

"I'm not sure if we are in range for this to work, but let's give it a try." The guard touched a green button on the dash and spoke, "Clearance please."

A voice answered back. "Identification?"

"Tango eight, four, lima, niner uh…pumpkin."

"Pumpkin?" Braeden whispered.

"Whatever is in season," the guard whispered back.

After a pause, the voice answered, "How can I help you, John?"

"I have Braeden Chandler with me." Several muffled voices conversed. "He needs to find his friend," he looked to Braeden for confirmation of her name.

"Sabine," Braeden answered. "She is GC."

"And Taurus Roma and his son," Braeden added.

More muffled tones. "Hold on John," the voice answered. After a long pause, the voice returned. "We found them. They are at a safe house. Where are you now?"

"Heading east on the old interstate, mile marker, uh one six four."

"Okay. Take the second exit you come to. It's going to look quite desolate when you get off the road. Go north about eight miles. You will see a Chandler Farms sign. Don't worry, it is a cover. When you get to the barn, ask for Grandma Kate."

"Roger that. Thanks."

"John, one more thing, you have the Chandler girl, yes?" He looked at Braeden apologetically, "Um yes, but she, just passed."

Silence on the line. "Oh, the young Roma will be very sad to hear that."

"I'm sure he will," Braeden whispered to himself.

Braeden berated himself again for not having acted sooner to get Sequoia away from his mother. He wondered how Aviva had turned so cold that she would not flinch at disposing of her children and grandchildren. He didn't remember much of the sweet, loving mother his sisters had told him existed when he was a young child. He convinced himself that it must not have been true. No one could change that much.

The sound of gravel on the road roused Braeden from his contemplation. "Where are we?"

"We're almost there."

Even just a few miles outside of the city Braeden couldn't believe how dark the skies were and how bright the stars. The trappings of his Collection upbringing were beginning to fade. If it were not for the horrible death of his niece, he could have thrown his whole youth away in a nice, neat package, but he was sure to be haunted for years to come.

They pulled up to a faded red barn and opened the car doors. Several people rushed out and told them to stay in their vehicle. John, the guard told them he was looking for Grandma Kate.

"Very good," said an older stocky man with a boyish face. "We've been expecting you. You can leave the car. I will park it for you."

"We have some precious cargo in the back." John leaned in to whisper so to not upset Braeden. "We need a fire, soon, and a decontamination procedure in the back."

The man winked discretely, "We'll take care of it."

Braeden heard every word. He glanced one more time to the back, cargo area and said a silent prayer for his niece. As they walked to the barn, Braeden noticed the rest of the group scurrying about. "Quickly, get into the barn," one of them urged.

"Why, what's going on?"

They pointed to the northwest as three headlights descended on their position.

# 46 ~ Souped Up

Croft, Chul-moo and Chauncey had been traveling by night and resting during the day. The trip to New Congress was about two hundred sixty miles but, for safety reasons, they couldn't travel long distances at a time.

Chauncey was driving what he liked to call his jalopy. It was a 2022 small OTR vehicle that had been retrofitted like a camper. Chul-moo had added holo-technology, but it only worked when the vehicle was still. Chauncey's fresh coat of camouflage paint was added as an extra precaution.

Croft had built a fire to warm up some leek and potato stew. Chauncey stepped out of the trailer, "Is that a good idea, with the smoke and all? We have the solar cooker inside."

"I know, I just miss campfires. I waited until dusk to hide the smoke a bit."

"Well, it smells delicious. You always have been a natural cook."

"Thanks. Chul-moo still napping?"

"Yeah, he is out of it."

"While I have you alone, I wanted to tell you how sorry I am about Char. I feel like I lost a sister too."

"Thanks Croft. I know she also thought of you like a brother. In fact, I think she liked you more than she liked me," Chauncey laughed. Croft smiled sadly. "She sure thought the world of Janie too." Croft sat silent, staring into the fire. "Are you okay? I mean, is everything okay with Janie?"

"Long story, I'm not sure what else to say at this point."

"Croft, you two have been pulled apart repeatedly for the last twenty years, but you always manage to find your way back to each other. She's made a lot of progress, but it's only been days. Give her some time. You'll see."

Croft nodded and tried to change the subject. "Sitting by the fire reminds me of camping with my dad when I was a young boy. We spent hours fishing and frying-up the fish. My mother would read in the tent while we fished and then she would make a loaf of blueberry bread on the fire to go with the fish. It was amazing. I can taste it now."

"Did you ever think things could change so drastically? We had pretty comfortable lives, and we traded all of it."

"It's not like we had much choice, but living a simpler life agrees with me. No matter the outcome, it was still worth the trade."

"I know, I'm with ya, I just always hoped I could share those things, from my upbringing with kids of my own someday." The lonely part of Croft's heart sank a little deeper. He thought of Janie and her girls and what type of life they might all be able to have with each other and where he could fit in. At the back of his mind was the nagging memory of his brother. They would always be Croft's borrowed family.

"I didn't mean to bring up a sore subject, Croft."

"No, it's okay. None of us are where we expected to be. The country, if you can even call it that anymore, is certainly not where we thought it would be. I know, I'm arguing your point now, but it's just too much sometimes, you know. We have all been through a lot, and for what? We spent decades trying to live on less. We watched people drown in poverty and hunger. Even when we were modernized and civilized, we didn't take care of ourselves or each other. We had another goddamned war and it changed nothing!"

Croft was not one to complain, so Chauncey knew Croft's outburst was about more than politics, but he thought it best to keep him distracted. "You're right man. Nothing came of CW II because there was not one unified rebellion. The people had a thousand reasons to rebel, but that's not even why we went to war. I guess it was the overwhelming greed of a few, that pushed us all over the edge for different reasons. We still knew that a war wasn't the answer, but they made it flippin' impossible not to war."

Croft resigned his earlier position and fell back into himself. "It's always possible not to war."

"Is it? I don't know anymore. When the politicians couldn't agree on even one darn thing, it was inevitable that it would trickle down to families and friends. I remember, you couldn't even go to the grocery store without somebody having a tiff about something and pulling out a gun."

"That's true. Everyone I knew had at least one weapon, if not a stockpile."

"Those bastards knew exactly what they were doing. Give 'em weapons, let 'em kill each other off. They played on everyone's fears and irrationalities, and we believed the garbage from all sides. We actually believed we wanted to war with each other."

Chul-moo burst through the camper door, which was uncharacteristic of him. "What's for dinner? Smells yummy."

Croft and Chauncey looked at each other. "Yummy?"

212

"Heh, heh, I feel, I don't know, silly."

Croft and Chauncey questioned again, "Silly?"

"I think you slept too long." Croft added.

"Maybe. I've had this tingling in my ear for a few hours now. I tried a Thieves mixture, but it's not helping."

"Try some of Croft's stew. It's, yummy."

Chul-moo laughed and sat on the fallen tree shared by Croft and Chauncey.

"We should probably hit the road soon, boys," Croft said as he put out the fire. "We'll save the world tomorrow, hey Chaunce?"

Chauncey gulped the rest of his soup. "You got it, chief."

Chul-moo jumped up, surprised since he had just sat down. "Eating on the run like a drive through."

"Yeah," Chauncey added. "You know you're old when you can remember fast food."

The three laughed, cleaned up their site and hit the road.

Darkness was upon them quickly. Chauncey had installed headlamp diffusers on their OTR rig. The lights still lit the road, but from a distance the diffused light was undetectable. "How far will those diffusers work?" asked Croft.

"Anything over a mile and we are good. If we are close to a tree network, anything above a green ping will turn the lights off automatically."

"Wow, you can do that?"

"I guess so, apparently I did."

"Are there anymore tree networks between here and New Congress? Wait, let me rephrase that. Is there anything between here and New Congress?"

Chauncey laughed, "Naw, not really."

Chul-Moo, who was driving, chimed in, "I hear there are still Kentucky wild men roaming around."

"It's possible," answered Chauncey. "But they are not going to bother us. They want the Collections to fail more than we do."

"I don't want the Collections to fail," rebuked Croft. "I just want *something* to work."

"Here-here to that old friend," agreed Chauncey.

The three had been driving for several hours when they noticed signs of city life. Garbage was dumped in empty lots and yards.

"Those morons! There is no reason for garbage anymore," bellowed Chauncey.

"They don't care, out of sight, out of mind, as we used to say. It's not the people who don't care, it's the government," said Croft. "There is no money to be made in renewable energy and reusable products. Well,

213

technically there was when we were capitalists, but they sure missed that boat."

"Fellas, I don't know if you noticed but the city lights are getting brighter. I'm thinking we should stay north of the city," Chul-moo interrupted. "We could ditch the rig at one of those abandoned farms ahead and take the scooters in to the edge of town.

"Um, Chul, did you see that sign?" Croft asked in an ominous tone.

Chul-moo turned back to glance at Croft. "Do you mean the one that said *Chandler Farms*?"

"Yes."

"Nope, didn't see it."

# 47 ~ Buffet

Delilah ran her hand along the bumpy rock walls of the cave tunnel. "It's a little stuffy in here," she yelled back to Bodhi over her shoulder.

"Dude, the echo is a little loud in here when you yell too," he whispered in her ear and startled her. She jumped and screamed. "Don't worry, there is a bend coming up and then we are out."

As they passed the bend, Delilah could hear voices that sounded like the children playing on the playground inside Indie City. They stepped out of the tunnel, into a gymnasium that looked like it had been built with a variety of cinderblock. Bodhi ran for the wall with equipment storage and grabbed a basketball from the rack.

"One-on-one, what'cha say?"

"I don't know how to play, but sure," Delilah shrugged.

"First we have to teach you some dribbling skills." Bodhi dribbled the ball slowly to show her the technique. He was chatting away about rules when Delilah suddenly stole the ball, dribbled it down court and made a basket. Bodhi's mouth hung open, dumbfounded until the shock wore off. He ran up to meet her. "Delilah Marie is a hustler!" Delilah dribbled around him and shot again. "Okay, now you're just showing off."

"I used to play with my dad, but at Indie City my friend Ahanu taught me some skills too."

Bodhi took the ball back, with designs on challenging her, but their smiles faded quickly when they saw Foster sternly making his way through the teens at the other end of the gym, heading in their direction.

"Come on kids. We have some news," Delilah and Bodhi ran to Foster as he summoned. "We're going up top."

"Is it safe?" questioned Delilah.

"It is where we're going." Foster led them out of the main gymnasium doors into the bottom level of an old department store. The lights were bright, and it was stocked like a store still in business. "We need to grab a few things for you while we are on this level." Foster pointed, "Delilah, go get some jackets and warmer gear for the two of you in the hunting section there. Bodhi and I will be over there in sporting goods."

"Okay," Delilah answered confused. She grabbed a cart, put one foot up and scooted herself quickly across the store.

"Listen Bodhi," Foster talked in a whisper, "we need to get Delilah to Euro City. Word is out that her mother is on her way there shortly."

"For real?" Bodhi bent low to avoid Delilah's questioning glance. "For real?" he said again in a whisper.

Foster smirked, "Yes, but listen, you and I are going on up to the old satellite installation. Ryker tells me you are a cracker jack and after seeing what you can do with a car, I am thinking you are the man that needs to go with me."

"But what about Delilah? I can't leave her. I promised Ryker that..."

"That you would get her to Euro City and then try to hook up the satellite, I know he told me. But we are running out of time. Euro City is on the west shore once we get into old Michigan, but the satellite launch is way across the mitten. I'm thinking--we all are thinking, the satellite is what is going to turn things around for us and we need you to help."

"I thought Euro City was southeast of Chicago."

"It was but they had to move it farther north because the Collections and the local wild ones were getting too close."

"How do you move a city?"

"You'll see."

"But what about Delilah?"

"We're all going together until we get to a place called Cherry Beach. Then Hexley and Joselyn are going to take Delilah to Euro City."

"Delilah's gonna to love that."

"Love what?" Delilah inquired innocently as she spun the cart in a circle.

Bodhi refused to answer and raised his eyebrows at Foster. "G'head, tell her."

Delilah's reaction was exactly what Bodhi had feared. "You're leaving? And I have to go with Hexley? And the offspring? Are you serious?"

Foster tried to explain why Bodhi was so needed, but it didn't appease her. "Sure, I know you're disappointed Miss Delilah, but your mother is going to be waiting for you in Euro City, we hope."

Delilah's face brightened, "What? She is?"

"Yes, and we need to get you there safe and as soon as possible."

"When do we leave?"

"In about two hours. We're going up to eat right now and pack."

Delilah's head spun with the thoughts of seeing her mother, until Bodhi grabbed her hand to walk her up the still escalator stairs. Once she felt his grip, she gazed up into his eyes and felt a sting of sadness. "Is this okay with you?"

216

"No, but I know it's what we have to do."

Delilah squeezed his hand reassuringly. "You know, everything seems better after you eat."

"Buffet is on me then. After you mi'lady."

Bodhi chased her up the stairs, followed by Foster. As they reached the top of the stairs, the mood of the room had changed considerably. The ground level of the department store was dark except for the afternoon sun reflecting on the rows of tipped over clothing racks and broken display cases. The room had obviously been ransacked.

"Watch your step," warned Foster as they stepped off the escalator onto the cluttered floor. "We leave it like this in case someone comes snooping around." Then Foster reached up to the darkened *DOWN* sign above the escalator and put his hand on the glass. An extension of the wall appeared, covering the entrance of the escalator behind them. "Follow my footsteps and try not to disturb anything."

Foster stepped on clothing and shopping bags where he could, so as not to leave a trail in the dust that covered the floor. Delilah, whose legs were shorter than both Bodhi's and Foster's, tripped on a rack of hooded sweatshirts and tumbled to the floor. Bodhi snorted and they both laughed. Glaring at them, Foster tried not to smile but couldn't resist.

Both men helped Delilah up, but her foot was still stuck in the sleeve of one of the red shirts until Foster pulled it off and handed it to her. "I guess you were meant to have it."

"Can I?" she squealed. Foster nodded. "Woo hoo. Thank you, they look so cozy." She unfolded the shirt, "Wisconsin Badgers. We're in Wisconsin?"

"What used to be Wisconsin, now it's just handfuls of small GC towns trying not to get swallowed up by the Collections," lamented Foster.

"Do you think that is what will happen to everyone? Do you think it's possible that we all will have to be in a Collection, again?"

"Bite your tongue girl," Foster chuckled. "Seriously, the GC is growing and for every new Collection city that forms another one crumbles. Still, not much is going to change until we take down New Congress City. I hate to say that because I know you have family there."

Delilah tried to change the subject, "So, I thought you said there was food up here."

"One more level," answered Foster, as Bodhi's stomach growled audibly. The three laughed as they made their way up another frozen escalator.

As they neared the top, Delilah's nose remembered the smell of Mexican rice and beans. She hadn't had any food besides 'pure American food,' as her grandmother called it, since she had been with her mother and father. It made her disgusted to think of Aviva's prejudices, but she refocused on the food. "Smells delicious."

"Mmm hmm," added Bodhi.

The third floor of the department store was lined with floor to ceiling glass, mirrored from the outside. The center of the space held a large bar island with a grill in the middle. Thirty mismatched tables and chairs scattered about the room, filled with residents of the underground ghost city of Eagle Crossing.

Delilah looked at Foster amazed, "Is this a restaurant?"

"Sure, it's as close as you will find in any non-Collection. However, true to the GC lifestyle, no one pays for food. We all help grow the food, cook the food and serve the food to each other."

Delilah got suddenly introspective, "Do you think society can ever be that way, like really help each other and not just try to take from each other?"

"I don't know Delilah. I would like to think we can. All I know is that we can't give up on the idea of a better life just because we can't yet conceive of how it could happen."

Delilah contemplated Foster's words and smiled, "Yes, that makes sense. My father used to talk that way."

Foster grinned and patted her on the shoulder proudly. He wished he had known the joy of a daughter like Delilah. "There is a buffet on the other side of the bar. Go grab a plate and eat a good meal, you two. We have another long night ahead of us."

"What do you mean, 'we?'"

"Yes, I'm going to take you."

"Yay!" Delilah hugged Foster tight around the neck.

"Now go eat."

# 48 ~ To the Trees

We shoved the bike into a bush. "I'll carry the bags. Can you carry yourself?" Trey asked.

"Yes, but I can carry a bag too."

"If you're sure."

Trey handed me my duffle and started to run. I liked that he had confidence in me, but feeling its weight, I regretted offering. I was surprised at how fast I could run with healed feet and a well-fed body. I amazed both of us at how quickly I had caught up. It was dark, but the waning moon and the nearby city made it easier to run. Suddenly my feet slid on the underbrush, and I realized we were going down a hill. Trey stopped abruptly in front of me, and I ran into the back of him. He grimaced.

"Janie, it gets steep right here. Give me the other bag in case you fall. I don't want the weight pushing you down the hill. You are going to want to hang on to the trees as we work our way down."

"Were we going to ride down this hill?"

"No, we were going to have to run from here anyway. But it's not too far now."

"Okay, good."

We slid our way down the hill, purposefully running into tree trunks when the momentum threatened to carry us away. I managed to stay on my feet, though Trey carrying all the bags, fell three times. I could barely see the horizon, but it felt like we were leveling out.

Once on a flatter surface, we walked through a small stream. As my eyes adjusted to the darkness even more, I realized in front of us was the other side of the gorge we had just descended. I tried to squelch the sinking feeling of having to climb the steep hill.

"Janie, we're not too far from a Collection. There could be patrols so we need to hurry. We are going to have to climb a bit. Use the tree roots to pull yourself up if you need to."

We pulled and wrestled our way up the hill. My fingers felt raw. Trey stopped at the base of a very large tree that was growing up out of the side of the hill and held his watch up to it.

"We're here." I looked up and saw only black trees silhouetted against a navy sky. He wedged the bags in the crook of a small tree and reached for my hand to pull me up next to him. He had me push on the tree bark, and a seam cracked on the tree, much like the one at Fox Island, and a pressurized door popped open. He pushed me inside to a landing, followed me in and shut the door.

"What about the bags?"

"Don't worry. We'll get 'em."

We climbed a rope ladder suspended inside the trunk. The climb was tough, but I moved quickly because the space was tight. "You okay? I can feel your shallow breathing."

"Yes, I'm not too fond of tight spaces."

"Right, I knew that. Look up, we're here." Five more rungs and then I stepped into a huge room. A soft light filled the whole space. The floors, walls and ceiling were all various shades of beautiful, natural wood. Large windows replaced the top half of each wall, except for the kitchen and bathroom area.

I walked to the windows and could see starry sky and treetops in every direction. Trey sauntered up behind me, "Don't worry. We can see out, but they can't see in."

"Like the holo-turf?"

"Yep, exactly. We need to get the bags." I followed him to a door on the wall that looked like it led out into nothingness. Once he opened the door, I could see a deck that wrapped around both sides. At the corner of the deck was a pulley system. Trey lowered it down until it hooked the bag handles. Once we got them into the tree house, I went back out on the deck. I couldn't remember a time I had been so high above the world. Trees filled the landscape in every direction except for the orange glow from the distant city. It seemed so benign for a place where the Collectors were probably plotting to kill me.

Trey peeked out and reminded me to be silent outside. Even though no one could see the tree house, I could still be heard by anyone in the area if I made a noise. Not wanting to take a chance, I stepped back into the warmer room, where Trey had stoked up a fire in the fireplace.

After I warmed up, I took a quick shower, threw on some shorts and a soft cotton shirt, and ran my fingers through my unmanageable maze of wet hair. I braided it sloppily and stepped out of the bathroom to see Trey sitting with one leg up on the couch. He was eating some biscuits with honey.

"Mmrrryyyou hungry?" he asked with biscuit still in his mouth.

"Yes!" I laughed. "What's for dinner?"

"Well, biscuits and honey, obviously, and some beautiful strawberries and…"

"Where did you get strawberries?"

"Check out the kitchen drawers."

The other side of the kitchen island was covered with drawers that pulled out. Each drawer lit up inside and showcased hanging hydroponic plants like berries, beans, herbs, and spinach. It smelled wonderful. As I closed the drawers an internal misting system turned on as the light dimmed.

With goodies in hand, I ambled back to the couch and sat at the opposite end from Trey. I could tell he wanted to say something, but he let it go. I scarfed down three biscuits, a handful of strawberries, and some nuts. We toasted it all with a glass of dandelion wine that went straight to my head.

"So," Trey said with uncertainty. "There is only one bed. It's a pretty big one, but I…"

"I can sleep on the couch."

"No, I was going to offer, but then I thought we are both adults. There is no reason why we can't both have a comfortable night's sleep."

I thought long and hard and then longer and harder. "Okay, but…"

"Janie, you don't have to worry. I won't touch you."

"That's not what I'm worried about. If I touch you, you must push me away or run. I don't want to take any chances that I might lose my mind again."

Trey laughed.

"I mean it! Even if I tell you I am in my right mind, don't believe me. I can't be trusted around you."

Trey's smile bared his teeth from top to bottom. "I am pretty irresistible."

"Good night, Trey," I said exasperated. I walked to the bed, scooted as close to one edge as I could, pulled the covers up to my neck and fell asleep.

# 48 ~ Cruisin'

Delilah napped, off and on, as the low flying cruiser zipped around trees and houses and over rivers and ponds. Foster had been driving, but Bodhi was itching for a turn. "I had no idea the GC had any flying vehicles."

"Newly acquired, but they are more like gliders. We have two now. Let's just say they were parked, and their owners were detained."

Bodhi grinned, "It's so cool to be in one." He raised his eyebrows at Foster, "It would be even cooler to drive one."

Delilah yawned and sat up in the back seat. "It sure is a smooth ride."

"Delilah Marie had a little nap-eee."

She giggled, "Are you really going to let him drive this?"

Bodhi leaned toward Foster with anticipation. Foster slowed the vehicle and let it lightly touch down. Delilah tuned out again as Foster explained the controls, losing herself in the idea of seeing her mother. Years of loss tried to creep in her thoughts, but she had a newfound hope to keep the demons away.

Bodhi and Foster switched places. Delilah leaned forward to tap Foster's shoulder, "How much further do we have to go?"

"We are already near the Chicago ruins, so I'd say we have about seventy miles to go."

"Wow, this thing is a lot faster than you'd think."

"Yes, it is," cautioned Foster to Bodhi.

"I got it, I got it." Bodhi pulled up on the joystick and the vehicle hovered a foot off the ground. As he pushed the button on top of the stick and pulled back, the vehicle lurched forward and sped away. Delilah was thrown to the back of her seat.

"Woo hoo!"

Foster was not amused. "Just keep your eye on the terrain monitor. Especially at night, it is much better than looking out the window."

Bodhi learned quickly and was flying with ease around obstacles. "The best thing is there is no traffic to watch for. Ha, ha. This is freakin' awesome."

"Sure, it's fun, but we are coming up on the outskirts of Chicago. We need to be cautious here."

"Why, I thought the Collection in this area is farther south?"

"It is, but there are still groups that inhabit many of the bigger cities."

"Why do people stay there?" Delilah asked innocently.

"Why did you stay with your grandmother as long as you did? Fear. People always fear the unknown. Plus, fending for yourself has to be better than living in the Collection."

"Wow, look at that!" Bodhi marveled at the city skyline growing in the southeast. Many of the outer buildings had been destroyed in the war, but surprisingly most of the inner city still stood. "So, tell me again, how they moved Euro City."

"I don't think I told you in the first place," quipped Foster.

"Funny. Are you going to tell me or not?"

"Not."

Delilah laughed at their banter. Bodhi rolled his eyes, "Have it your way, then."

Foster glanced at the horizon monitor and then leaned forward and looked around.

"What? What's wrong?"

"You need to stay west until we get a little south of Lake Michigan."

"I am, but what's up?

Foster shook his head, "Nothing. I don't know. I thought I saw something cross our path up ahead."

"What sort of something?"

"It was big, maybe a vehicle."

"What?" Bodhi and Delilah both exclaimed in unison.

"I'm not sure. It could have been a shadow. You watch the monitor, and I will watch the road. Delilah, why don't you scan back and forth between the two?" Everyone was on high alert and sitting on the front edge of their seats.

"Why don't we all put on our safety belts? Bodhi, keep your hand on the joystick and hand me the belt with your other hand. I'll buckle you in," said Foster.

No sooner had Foster clicked Bodhi's belt, than the cruiser felt like it hit a brick wall. Stopping abruptly, the vehicle stood up briefly on its nose and then flopped over on its top. Delilah and Bodhi felt their belts dig into their necks and stomachs while they hung suspended from their seats. Foster, however, was a crumpled mess on what used to be the ceiling of the car.

Delilah screamed, "Oh my God! Foster didn't have his belt on!"

Bodhi, who was slightly delirious from hitting his head on the window, shook his head to clear the fog. He clamored to undo his belt and then crashed on to his hands and knees. "Wait Delilah, hold onto something and I'll undo your belt." She tried to brace herself on the seat but fell equally as hard when he undid her belt. Bodhi then slid back into the front seat to check on Foster. His lower body was rolled over onto his neck and head. Squeamishly, Bodhi checked for a pulse and then bowed his head.

"He's dead?" Delilah screamed. Bodhi nodded. "I think his neck might be broken."

Delilah looked around panicked. "But what happened? What did we hit?"

"I don't know, nothing that I could see."

"We had to have hit something. It felt like we hit something."

"I know, but there was nothing there. I'm telling you, there was nothing on the scope."

"What do we do now?"

"Well, gather as many supplies as we can. This is not the best area from what Foster said. We need to get out and move fast." Bodhi grabbed the terrain monitor and a few other items from the floor.

"Is the cruiser still working?"

Bodhi tried a second time. "Nope, not a spark." Foster's bag had wedged between his lifeless body and the door. Bodhi gingerly reached around him to grab the bag and handed it to Delilah. "Here, this one is lighter. You take it and I'll take our big bag. Grab our coats first. The windows are already steaming up. I think it's a cold one out there tonight."

"What about Foster? Are we just going to leave him here?"

"M'yah. What else can we do?"

Delilah began to cry because she knew the answer. Bodhi kicked out the driver side door and a gush of cold air filled the cab. Delilah couldn't imagine a worse scenario. Cold, lost and no way of rectifying either. Bodhi pulled the bags out first and then Delilah. As they stood and looked around, the decaying outer city formed nightmares in both of their minds.

"Look, did you see that?"

Delilah moved in closer to Bodhi. "What?"

"...that blinking on the road. There, look." Bodhi jogged a few paces until the terrain monitor flashed and died. He glanced down toward his feet and saw a thin green laser graze the front of his legs. He dropped a stick through it to test it.

"Stop!" Delilah yelled in a whisper. "What are you doing? What is that thing?"

"I think it's like an electrical trip wire or something."

"Well, if it's a trip wire, that means whoever set it, is probably not far away."

"Good point, let's go."

224

# 50 ~ Close Calls

I awoke to the smell of warm tea. The sun was rising and filled every window with a panoramic painting of a peach and pink sunrise. Trey was sitting on a window bench across from the bed. "Your skin glows in the sunlight."

I tried to ignore the admiration in his voice. "I'm pale, that's what happens."

He nodded. "Did you sleep well?"

"Well enough, I guess, for having someone who snores like a chainsaw next to me."

"I don't snore!"

"Do too."

"Oh, I see. This is payback for letting you believe..."

"I hadn't thought of that, but that's a good idea." Trey smirked. I think because he didn't know what to say next. "So how long are we staying here?"

"Unfortunately, we need to leave around dusk, so you may want to sleep a little longer. I have already seen three patrols in the area this morning. Even though this house blocks the signal of the tracking solution, I think they may have been able to pick up our heat signature last night which means they will keep combing the area. I'm afraid that the longer we wait, the harder it will be to leave."

"Do you think my blood will be clean enough by then?"

"Well, it will be cleaner than it is now, let's put it that way. Croft gave me some supplements for you to take during the day today that he thinks may help. The theory is that they will bind to the amino acids in your blood that carry the tracker and surround it, so it lessens the signal."

"So, it won't hurt me?"

"No, but one side effect is you will be hungry most of the day because it blocks some food absorption. In small doses it's not dangerous. You also need to spend some time in the sun, because the UV light speeds up the process."

"So, sleep, eat, and lay in the sun for the day, I think I can handle that. And I can be outside?"

"You are safe on the deck." I sat up and stretched. As the covers fell from my torso, I noticed my shirt had wriggled up exposing my stomach. I looked up to see Trey staring.

"Sorry, can't help it." He jumped up, embarrassed to be caught and went to get the supplements and some water. After freshening up and dressing, I met him in the kitchen to eat and take my first dose.

"Wow, I feel a little queasy already."
"No offense, but you already baptized my boots, and I don't have shoes on, so if you need to make a run for it, go now."

"Very funny, it's not that bad."

The sun was completely up and warming the whole room. "I'll be on the deck." I grabbed the poem book Croft had given me and headed for the door.

Trey wadded up a soft yellow blanket and threw it at me. "Here, you might need this. The sun is deceptive."

As I opened the door to the wrap-around deck, I realized Trey was right. It was a true fall morning, bright and crisp. I wrapped the blanket around me and set my book on a side table next to a green wicker love seat with a thick yellow and orange striped cushion on it. I walked the whole length of the deck. Even in the daylight, it was still mostly treetops in every direction except for the miniature buildings of old Fort Wayne in the distance.

Careful not to make noise, I tiptoed back to the outdoor loveseat and curled up with my blanket and T.S. Eliot book. A second page was dog-eared:

*It is not to ring the bell backward*
*Nor is it an incantation*
*To summon the spectre of a Rose.*
*We cannot revive old factions*
*We cannot restore old policies*
*Or follow an antique drum.*
*These men, and those whom they opposed*
*Accept the constitution of silence*
*And are folded in a single party.*
*Whatever we inherit from the fortunate*
*We have taken from the defeated.*

Next to the text were handwritten scribblings that felt familiar. I had not written anything since I had been rescued, but I was sure it was my own handwriting. They were a combination of my thoughts and what looked like notes for one of my classes with references to pages in other books. This must have been my book that Croft had kept for me. I wondered how many other things of mine he had been safeguarding for me during my captivity. I held out my left hand and let my wedding ring dazzle in the sunlight. It felt right to keep it on.

I'm not sure how long I had been sleeping when I heard voices below. Quietly, I stretched to peer over the side of the wicker through the slats in the deck. As I leaned forward my book dropped on the decking. Conversation burst from the forest floor.

"Shh, what was that? Did you hear that?"

"Hear what?"

"Something up there in that tree."

Suddenly a gunshot whizzed by the deck. I stayed frozen, barely breathing. I could see Trey pressing his face to the glass in panic. I mimed for him to be quiet.

"Stupid, what are you doing? Don't waste the ammo. There is nothing up there. It's probably birds or something." The conversation on the ground continued. I didn't dare try to look again to see how many. I stayed motionless until I could tell the patrol had moved on. Trey was a statue until I sat up. Cautiously, I grabbed my book from the deck and stepped inside.

As soon as the door closed Trey ran up to hug me. His bare chest was warm from the sun. I cautioned myself. *Don't like it. Don't like it. Don't like it.* I tried not to hug him back. I kept distance between my arms and his sides and just patted him on the back.

"My God Janie, I didn't even know what to do. I must have nodded off on the couch and the next thing I hear is a gunshot." He released the hug but grabbed my arms. "I couldn't breathe until I saw you move out there."

"I'm okay. I made a noise right when they happened to be walking by. It was dumb. I'm very lucky. I think I have had enough of the great outdoors for today." As I spoke, I realized the sun had already crossed over the house and was beginning to set. "Oh no, it's almost time to go, isn't it?"

"I'm afraid it is. Everything is packed. Why don't you take another supplement and I'll fix us something to eat before we take off? You are going to want to dress in layers, a lot of them."

# 51 ~ Lights and Lights

Braeden stood nervously in Katherine Cleary's barn surrounded by a sea of whispering GC. All were anxiously craning to see the growing headlights through a small slot in the wood. Surreptitiously, fingers intertwined with Braeden's and squeezed his hand. Braeden was so focused on the drama it startled him until he realized they belonged to Sabine. He reached around with his other hand and pulled her close to kiss her strongly on the top of the head. "I'm so glad to see you. I wasn't sure I would be able to find you."

"I wasn't sure you would either." She smiled and her dark eyes twinkled in the aura of the low hanging light bulbs scattered throughout the barn.

Braeden pulled Sabine around in front of him and wrapped his arms around her so he could bend down and whisper in her ear. "Does anyone know who is coming?"

"No, that's why everyone is on high alert." Sabine motioned to show Braeden the number of firearms in the hands of those surrounding them. Hearing the musings and questions in the crowd of why he was there, Braeden tried not to make eye contact with anyone else besides Sabine.

Comments burst from several men in the back of the room. "Shh! Shh! Someone is trying to get through. I can't hear over all the chatter."

"If they were GC, they would have a call sign or at the very least their vehicles would register on our network."

"Wait, wait that is code. If they are GC, they must be old timers because we haven't used those codes in years."

"Or maybe it's someone trying to hack into our system."

"Shut it down. Shut it down now!" yelled Katherine as she entered from a stable door in the back.

Braeden was surprised to see an older woman amidst the men about the room. She was small, but mighty. He was about to ask Sabine where Taurus and Howard were when the crowd began to cock their guns and arm their lasers. Most of the crowd took defensive positions around the barn, covering windows, exits and holes in the walls. Braeden and Sabine stood alone in the middle of the room.

"Get down you two. You need to take cover if yer not armed," whispered Katherine gruffly. Sabine pulled Braeden in front to an empty horse stall to watch the action through a swing door at the bottom of the wall used to shovel in hay from the outside. Sabine pushed the door slightly askew so they could see outside. Braeden glanced about the stall noticing the reins and other tack hanging and wondered at the physical labor of such a life until Sabine tapped him to refocus on the action in front.

As the headlights turned on to the dirt road leading to the farm, they split, and it became obvious there were three separate vehicles. Dust flew out behind the motor bikes and as they braked on approach, the taillights illuminated a red dust cloud. Sabine could taste the dust that plumed around them and seeped into every nook and cranny of the barn. When the dust settled, three male figures stood backlit by their headlights.

Grandma Kate, whom Braeden still hadn't met, leaned on the men in front to peer out of a large knot hole and whisper yelled across the room, "Flip that switch!" A loud bang, belonging to what Braeden thought was a defunct generator, startled the crowd as it turned on, blinding the three men out front. Several laser points danced on each of their chests, with even more guns in waiting. As the three men lowered their raised hands that were shielding their eyes from the bright lights, Braeden stood to speak, but hit his head on the wooden gear hook on the wall. Dizzy from the knock, he stumbled out into the open floor of the barn and winced as he tried to yell again. "Stop! Don't shoot!"

A voice from the crowd answered back, "Shut up and get down. We're not going to shoot you, ya fool."

"No, I mean don't shoot *them*!" Braeden tried to stand but the sting of his injury kept him hunched over trying to recover. "They are GC! That is Croft!"

Through the barn wall, Braeden could hear Croft's voice in return, "Braeden? Is that you?" Croft stepped forward, holding his hand up to buffer the harshness of the lights.

"Don't take another step!" Katherine warned through a knot hole. She turned to look at Braeden. "Are you trying to tell me that is Croft McAvoy?"

"Yes, it is!" yelled Croft from the outside. Katherine walked over to the flood light switch and turned it off. Sabine hadn't realized until it stopped, but the hairs on her arms and neck had been standing on end with the buzz of the electrical current. Croft put his arm down. Chauncey and Chul-moo inched up close behind Croft as all three stepped tentatively forward. Katherine motioned for two men to slide the hefty barn door to the side.

Braeden shook off the stinging haze in his head and pulled Sabine out from the horse stall. The crowd that had been gathered at the front of the barn parted as Braeden stepped forward. When Croft breeched the subtle bulb light of the barn, the reflection caught in the corners of his eyes showing tears.

"Croft!" Braeden plunged forward in joyful exasperation and wrapped his arms around Croft. "I can't believe you're here! I got your message!" He stepped back and scrutinized Croft's face, "You got her? You got Janie?"

Croft put his hands on the top of Braeden's shoulders reassuringly, "I got her!" The emotion caught in Croft's voice.

"She is safe then? Oh God, you didn't bring her here, did you?" Braeden peered behind Croft to make sure neither of the other figures was Janie.

"No, she's not here. She is--well, she is safer than--let's just say she's in good hands. She is being transported to Euro City."

"What? Is that safe?"

"She had to be moved. They found Fox Island, Braeden."

Katherine pushed rudely through the crowd and interrupted, "What do you mean, they found Fox Island?" Croft, dumbfounded, stared at her for the interruption. "Sorry, my name is Kate...Katherine Cl..."

Croft confirmed before she finished, "Cleary," as he shook her hand. My name is Croft..."

"McAvoy," she finished for him. They smiled in mutual appreciation of each other's reputations.

Braeden, dismissed, talked mockingly to the air, "And I'm Braeden Chandler, nice to meet you."

Katherine spun on her heels as the crowd fell silent. "So, you're Chandler? I figured. Roma was filling in the details for me."

Croft interjected again in the disjointed conversation, "Wait, so Roma is here?"

"Yes," answered Kate. "He's with his son up at the house."

Croft's face brightened in anticipation, "If Taurus and his son are here, does that mean you have Sequoia? The last I heard on the wire was that she had left town with him."

Braeden swallowed hard, "She is gone, Croft." The fresh scar opened inside his chest, "Sequoia is dead."

Croft shook his head in disbelief. "Dead? She can't be dead. I came to get her, and you. I promised Janie I would bring both of you home. How? What happened? How is she dead?" Croft felt the cold night wind was the only thing keeping him on his feet. He blinked and silent tears slid from each eye.

Braeden hugged Croft again and bit his lip to squelch the noise of his sobs. "I'm sorry. I am so sorry. I should have protected her. I should have gone for her sooner. I got there too late."

Croft stepped back in sudden anger, "What happened? What did your mother do to her?"

"It wasn't, well indirectly it was, but she was shot by one of the spiders. It was a new weapon they developed that kills the skin around the gunshot wound."

Croft felt a punch to the gut. "Oh my God! Where did it, I mean, where is she?"

Braeden pointed to the oversized truck he had arrived in with John, the faux guard. "She's in the back." Croft turned to pay his respects when Braeden grabbed his arm and stopped him. "Don't. Stay away from there, you don't want to see."

Croft almost vomited as he strained to confirm the blood that had begun leaking out the bottom of the car's hatch door. Braeden's stomach lurched but before he could speak, one of the many gawkers still in the barn walked past them and sprayed the spill with a fire extinguisher. Katherine walked between the men and turned them around. "Let's go inside boys."

When Braeden turned away, he noticed Sabine who had been standing at the edge of the barn crowd. "Oh my gosh." He ran to her in apology. "I'm so sorry…" Braeden tripped on his words as he dragged her over to see Croft and Katherine. "We got so wrapped up, I forgot to introduce you. This is Sabine." Braeden brightened as he spoke her name.

Croft wiped his eyes with his shirt sleeve and grinned at Braeden's change. "So nice to meet you in person." Croft hugged her warmly and winked at Braeden. "I guess everything worked out, then."

Sabine answered, "Yes, I guess it did *Charles*."

Katherine invited the three of them to her house, a little more than walking distance from the barn. "Come on we'll take the buggy." Croft looked around, realizing he had completely abandoned Chul-moo and Chauncey. "If you are looking for your friends, they are down in the pit with the rest of the boys looking at some security issues we have been having.

Croft laughed, "Of course they are, I guess I won't worry about them."

"Come on then. Your other friends are anxiously waiting for you too." Katherine glanced back at Braeden and Sabine walking arm in arm and grabbed Croft's arm, "You're stuck with me I guess." They chuckled like old friends. "When I woke up this morning, I wouldn't have thought I'd have two Romas, a Chandler, Croft McAvoy, and two run-ins with guns all in one day."

"Two run-ins?

"Long story, I will explain later."

Katherine led them past the barn to a flat-bed semi-trailer attached to an old farm tractor with chains and ropes. The trailer was covered with a makeshift awning made from an abandoned garden pergola and tarps. In the middle of the trailer were two couches and a table with an in-progress checker game on it.

Croft smirked. "This is the buggy?"

"This is the buggy." Katherine lowered a wooden step ladder from the side. "Climb on board."

As they rumbled up to the house, a commotion stirred outside. Katherine stopped the tractor and hop-stepped to the people standing around. Croft, Braeden, and Sabine arrived at the group in mid conversation.

"Did they go by themselves?"

"No, Sugar took them."

"Well, that's a good choice. See I knew that young man would come in handy."

"I know, ma. You were right."

Croft joined in, "What's going on?"

"Seems your friend and his son are gone."

"Gone?"

"Apparently one of Howard's wounds was looking bad and he was running a slight fever, so they decided to try to go back to the city for medical help."

"Is there no one here that could help him?"

Katherine's son jumped in, "Sure there was, but I got the feeling he thought our remedies were a little too back-woods for him."

Croft looked to Katherine.

"Biscuits, where are my manners?! Collin, this is Croft McAvoy. Croft, this is my son Collin Cleary." The men shook hands. "And this is…"

"I know who this is, ma. What is he doing here?"

Braeden intervened on his own behalf, "Hi, I'm Braeden. Unfortunately, my last name happens to be Chandler. Do you know who my sister is?"

"Yeah, what's your point?"

"I know you have no reason to trust me. However, if you know that my sister is a good and decent person, could you believe that maybe her brother is too?"

"The difference is, she hasn't been living the high life in the mansion that takes up an entire city block. She has been imprisoned by your mother."

Croft stepped into Collin's line of view, "Collin, he is a good kid. You have to understand, he's been imprisoned in other ways."

Collin stepped back and scrutinized Braeden in silence for a moment. "Hmm, I guess I could see that." He thought for another moment and then extended his hand to Braeden who took it willingly. Braeden then turned to Sabine to introduce her but was cut short by Collin. "No, no, I already met the pretty lady. We were having a nice chat over mashed potatoes before all of you showed up."

Croft lamented, "I was hoping to get to talk to Taurus, but if he makes it safely to his house, I'm sure his personal physician will be much better for the kid."

"IF!" Katherine clarified. "I have plenty of beds. I want you all to get a good night's sleep and then I'll call all the boys in for a strategy meeting."

Croft nodded and yawned, "I'm not even going to argue with you."

Katherine smiled and led them through the house to a wide staircase where framed photographs lined the walls. At the first landing, Sabine noticed a shelf with figurines of cows and pigs. "What are those?"

"Cows and pigs," Katherine answered drolly.

"I mean, why are they there?"

"They're knick-knacks."

"Knick-knacks. Hmm, I think my grandmother used to have knick-knacks."

Katherine guffawed, "Yep, that's what grandmothers do."

"But what are they for?"

"I guess to remind me of the people that gave them to me or some special time in my life."

"Oh. It's weird to see people, besides rich people, who own *things*."

"You're right, they serve no purpose and have no real function. I just like them."

The stairs ended into a hallway in either direction. "Take your pick." She then pulled a rope hanging from the ceiling that lowered another small staircase. "There's one more up there."

Sabine debated but decided to share a room with Braeden. Croft winked and slapped Braeden on the back of the head as they stopped at the first bedroom door. Braeden smiled and followed Sabine into the room. Sabine nervously busied herself in the bathroom while Braeden undressed down to his undershorts and tee shirt and crawled under the covers. He was thankful for the double sheets to lessen the abrasion of the wool blanket on the bed.

Sabine opened the door to the bathroom and Braeden tried not to gasp. She turned off the light and embarrassingly skipped to the bed and slid under the covers. Braeden let his eyes adjust to the darkness until he could see the features of her face outlined in the reflection of the faint moonlight through the window.

Sabine's heart fluttered as she lay still on her back, not knowing what to do. She berated herself for climbing into bed with a man she had just met, but she wasn't sorry once she realized it was more her mother's voice than her own. Braeden sensing her tension leaned in to kiss her on the cheek and then the forehead. She relaxed and he put his arm around her waist.

234

"Wanna spoon?" Sabine giggled and turned her back to Braeden so she could cuddle in. He pulled her close for a perfect fit. "Good night," he whispered, and nodded off to sleep.

Croft chose the attic room because it had a skylight. Not bothering to undress, he plopped down on his back and inhaled the familiar scent of old quilts and cedar. As he gazed at the clear, star-filled sky, his mind drifted back to Janie. He felt like he hadn't thought of her in a while, and it felt foreign to him. His heart pinched at the thought of her with Trey.

Croft wondered if he and Janie were meant to be together when the universe had worked so hard at keeping them apart. He tried to imagine a life without her and her family and choked on the implications, even while his conscious mind was fading with fatigue. Sleep knocked on his eyelids as he tried to figure out how to tell Janie about Sequoia. Suddenly he had a thought. Now that he had Braeden, if he could find Delilah and bring her back, maybe it could lessen the blow. A plan could be made in the morning. In the moment, he had to rest. The day was too heavy to continue.

# 52 ~ Getting Help

Sugar cautiously snaked the faded blue pick-up truck through the outskirts of New Congress City. Taurus lay next to his son on an old mattress in the bed of the truck. The two quilts covering them were not enough to keep out the chill of the frigid night.

Through his chattering teeth, Taurus tried to talk to Howard to keep him from succumbing to pain that was ravaging his young body. "I'm so p-p-p-proud of you s-s-s-son for helping that little Chandler girl. I sure hope she is okay."

Howard was in too much pain to respond with more than a smile. Taurus poured more of Katherine's distilled alcohol on the ugly wound on his son's head, hoping to extinguish any infection. Howard lurched up and grabbed his still aching ribs from the contortion.

"Oh no, oh my boy I'm sorry. It was looking so bad."

Howard's weak voice could barely be heard above the wind and motor hum, "It's fine dad."

"It's not fine. I should have b-b-brought you home sooner. I think your wounds may be more severe than we thought, but my doc can fix you." Taurus turned away to acknowledge to himself, "We just have to get there."

Coming up on the gated congressional housing community, Sugar decided the antique truck would surely look out of place. He pulled into an alley and got out to talk to Taurus. "Do you have someone that can drive your car to meet us here?"

Taurus rubbed his head befuddled, "Trey and Howard's mom passed when the boys were young, and the second Mrs. Roma didn't work out so well."

Howard managed a disgruntled, "Hmph."

"Isn't there anyone else that can help – a friend, a staff member, somebody?"

236

"Well, now that you say it, I could have our housekeeper come and take us to doc's house."

Sugar offered Taurus his Collection phone. "Here, you can use this."

"What if they have found you out by now?"

"How would they do that? Kate's son took care of the other Collectors."

"Oh right, I forgot. Okay, let me see that thing." Taurus quickly dialed. "Hello? Steph?"

A hushed voice answered, "Oh my goodness, Mr. Roma, are you okay?"

"I am, but Howard isn't. I need you to come pick us up." Muffling sounds followed by silence was his only answer. "Steph, are you there?"

She spoke softer still, "I'm sorry Mr. Roma. There is a bit of a problem."

"Problem? What problem?"

"It's Mrs. Chandler, sir. She is here." Taurus froze. "Mr. Roma, are you still there?" The panic rose in the housekeeper's voice, but she managed to keep her volume down. Sugar, seeing the panic on Taurus' face, grabbed the phone.

"Hello, this is Stephanie, yes?"

"Who is this?"

"I am a friend of Mr. Roma's. Are you able to come get him?"

"I don't know. She is grilling the whole staff. We are kind of in a lock down."

"She who, Chandler?"

"Yes. Wait, hold on." The phone was muffled but Sugar could still hear voices in the background.

A harsh voice crackled in Sugar's ear. Sugar put it on speaker but cautioned Taurus to not make a sound. "What are you doing in here?" the voice demanded.

"I was going to make some coffee for you Mrs. Chandler."

Skeptically Aviva agreed it was a good idea. Her head was still swimming from its bourbon haze. "Well, get it done then girl and then back to the foyer with the rest of the staff."

"Yes mam." Stephanie grabbed the phone she had dropped into her apron pocket. "Hello, hello, are you still there?"

Taurus answered, "Yes, Steph. I am sorry. Are you okay?"

"Yes. I don't think she is going to let me leave, but I have an idea. Tell me where you are." Sugar explained their location. "Okay, I have to hang up now, but I am sending help."

"What do you mean?"

"You'll know it when it arrives. Mr. Roma, I am scared. That woman, she is…"

"I know Steph. You listen to me, do whatever you have to do to stay safe. Okay?"

"Okay Mr. Roma, Taurus, be careful and don't come home." Her voice indicated an intimacy that even Howard, in all his pain was shocked to hear.

"Goodbye Steph."

The phone cut off and Taurus stood shivering in the night air wondering what would become of his staff and his son. Sugar told him to get in the cab of the truck where the weak heater took the chill out of the air. Taurus refused to leave his son alone and instead got back into the truck bed and wrapped his arms carefully around Howard. He sang softly in a honey filled baritone, the words of a lullaby he had sung to both of his boys when they were children:

*The sun can shine and linger on,*
*But matters naught when it is gone,*
*Your little hand that holds my heart,*
*That makes you strong, that makes you smart.*
*It's in that hand my hope resides,*
*To lift the moon, to change the tides.*
*Alora-dee, Alora-dum,*
*It matters not what you become.*
*Just that you were, and that you are,*
*For that's the greatest gift, by far.*

Sugar leaned on the side of the truck, listening, and let his gaze drift to the dark sky, begging to let its stars shine through the city glow. He contemplated his life's choices, knowing there was no going back. Sugar's fate, and the fate of his new friends rested in the decisions he made from that point forward.

A gravel sound, amplified by slow tires, interrupted his reflection. Lights turned in at the end of the alley way. Sugar put his hand on his holster carrying the weapon Katherine had given back to him, in trust. The dark car came to an abrupt halt. A medium sized man with light patches bleached on his dark skin jumped out of the car.

"Don't shoot. Steph sent me."

"Who are you?"

"I'm her brother."

Taurus jumped up and ran towards him. "Poppy?" Seeing the man run towards them made Sugar anxious. Taurus patted him on the shoulder. "It's okay. I know him." Sugar relaxed but stayed vigilant.

"Aw man, Mr. Roma, it's a mess out there. Collectors are everywhere in the Congressional Village. My sister said Chandler is at your house right now."

"She is. Are you still working for the Heath's?"

"Yes. They are pacing a path in their new carpet though. Little Tilly is missing, and they haven't been able to find her."

238

"Oh my God, Poppy, they don't know?"

"Know what?"

Roma pulled him aside so Howard wouldn't have to hear it again, "Tilly is dead. She was with Howard when the Collectors got her."

Poppy, nicknamed for the flower shaped white birthmark over his left eye squinted to shake off the bad news. "Aw no, poor Tilly, such a sweet girl. Why were the Collectors after her?"

"She, and my son were helping Chandler's granddaughter Sequoia. They are all good friends you know. Aviva finally flipped out on Sequoia apparently, and they were helping her escape when they were caught. I think the Collectors broke Tilly's neck."

"Mr. and Mrs. Heath, you know they aren't perfect, and I certainly don't agree with their politics, but they loved that little girl."

"I know they did."

"So that is how your son got hurt too?"

"Yes, he has some broken ribs and several head wounds. One of them is looking sketchy and he is getting worse by the minute."

"Well, let's stop standing around shooting the breeze and get him to a doctor. Can your doc be trusted?"

"Yes, but we need to get him there without being seen."

"It is only a matter of time before they get to your doctor, and to the Heath's. I'm gonna take you someplace else. You have to trust me."

Taurus wrung his hands nervously. "Okay."

"Let's get your son into the Heath's car." The three men carefully lifted a sweating, moaning Howard into the back seat of the Heath's sedan. Taurus sat in the back with Howard's legs on his lap. Sugar rode in front with Poppy, who put the security screen up for the back seat in case they were stopped. Sugar asked about the truck. "Leave it. You are not getting farther in or out of the city with that thing tonight."

Poppy turned left at the end of the alley away from the Congressional Village. After several neighborhoods and another shopping district, Poppy drove them up the side road of a large grass covered hill. As they pulled around an embankment of trees an eight-building campus sprawled out in front of them.

"The University?"

Poppy remained silent as he pulled under the overhang of a building with an unlit red cross on it. "Wait here." Poppy jumped out of the car and approached the sliding glass doors. A red warning light shone down on him from above and three men in scrub suits, but holstering weapons ran out of the building, surrounded Poppy, and searched him. Sugar nervously tapped his foot as he watched Poppy animatedly tell the story of how and why they were there.

The men looked up suspiciously. The silly side of Sugar's nature wanted to wave and smile, but knowing it was not the time or place, he refrained. Poppy jumped back in the car.

"Well?"

"They are letting us in. Hold on."

One of the men motioned for Poppy to drive to a large metal door that opened. The three men ran to the vehicle, wheeling a stretcher. Taurus tried frantically to explain what had happened as they lifted Howard out of the back seat. Busy with tasks, they appeared to not be listening, so Taurus raised his voice. Finally, one of them stopped and grabbed his shoulders. "Mr. Roma, we need to get your son in for treatment. It doesn't matter what happened. You have been cleared now so we need to get him upstairs." Taurus ran alongside the stretcher to a large elevator across the room. His body ached with age and exhaustion, but he sprinted the best he could to keep up. Poppy and Sugar followed.

The elevator took them to the top floor of the glass building. As they exited, Taurus could see miles in every direction. New Congress City was a mosaic of light and dark. The Congressional Village and several other gated communities still had power, as well as the city center, but the rest of the city was in total darkness. Taurus shook his head. "She cut the power. I can't believe, she actually cut the power. It is a cold night out there."

"Mr. Roma? This way, please." Taurus turned to see a tall slender man, with a jet-black comb-over and large dark glasses wearing a doctor's coat and then noticed his son was gone.

"Howard!"

"He is being cared for. Come to my office."

The doctor's heels clicked and echoed at an agonizing pace down the long empty hallway of the Charlemagne University Hospital. His long strides, not expected of someone in the business of saving lives. He stopped at a green door, "Come in gentleman." It was a plain office, with a brown desk and two extra chairs. "Have a seat. I understand you may have some questions."

"I thought the University was closed?"

Ignoring the question, the doctor answered in an affected slow drawl. "My name is Dr. Vincent. May I get you some coffee or a lemonade?"

"No, no thank you. I need to know what is going on in this place and where my son is."

"Yes, of course." He poured himself a cup of coffee from the pot behind his desk and, slowly emptied three sugars into the ceramic mug, ceremoniously stirring with his silver spoon. "The University is…officially closed. Yet, you can see that both the campus and hospital are quite functional. We run on sort of a skeleton crew, especially on a night like tonight when our residents are busy with other, shall we say, pursuits."

Sugar, impatient with the man wasting time spoke up, "Cut the crap doc. What is going on here?"

Dr. Vincent eyed Sugar, who was still in his Collector's uniform. "Young man. You are the least welcome of your party, so I would suggest you employ some decorum and have a seat."

"He is with us," Taurus defended. "He's just in costume."

Unconvinced, the doctor continued, "As for your son, he is in our nano lab. A new instrument is rebuilding his abrasions from the inside out. As new layers are forming, a light chemical wash is alleviating any infection that might be forming. Once that is under control, we will do a full body scan."

"How do you know all that? We just got here." Then Taurus noticed a small earpiece in the doctor's ear. The doctor smiled and said nothing.

"Okay, so how is it that this place is open? There has not been funding for it in years."

"Oh, I assure you Mr. Roma, there has. Mrs. Chandler writes a monthly check to the hospital for um, I guess you could say, research."

"So, she is funding the University?"

"No, that is all being done underground. The professors are not paid. That's one thing that hasn't changed much. Any expenses are covered in the residual of the hospital check. Sir, we are not churning out degrees here. Students will leave with knowledge and experience, and I dare say more than any degree bequeathed here to date. We're not about to hand students a slip of paper that tells them they are prepared for a future none of us can predict right now. Mrs. Chandler doesn't even know about the students."

"Do the doctors work for free too?"

"Mostly. They are given an apartment in the student dorm and all food is provided by a donor."

"What donor?"

Poppy, who had been quietly reading over the doctor's credentials on the wall, turned to the group, "The GC of course." The three men gasped in his direction, none of them sure if the other should or did know of the GC. Dr. Vincent scanned their faces and relaxed his shoulders.

"Well, I guess that puts the pepper in the gumbo. So y'all are GC then?" His gentlemanly manners relaxed with his speech as he leaned back in his chair and put his foot up on his other knee. "Even the great Congressman Roma? Hmm, very interesting."

"Titles are not important right now," insisted Taurus.

"Oh yes'sir, I think you will see they are, especially after I show you the lab." Dr. Vincent led them to a keyed elevator. Once inside, he spoke. "There are no cameras in the lab, but there are speakers. You must not say anything, anything at all until I speak directly to you and tell you it is safe. Do you all understand?"

Already afraid to answer, Taurus, Sugar, and Poppy nodded their heads. Upon leaving the elevator, the doctor took them down a long hallway with glassed in labs on both sides. One side was filled with microscopes and computers. Giant metal mixing vats filled the other. At the end of the hall, he turned and motioned to remind them to be silent. As he opened the door, Taurus covered his mouth to keep from gasping. Ten rows of sedated patients strapped to their tables filled the room. Each row was at least fifteen beds long. Taurus and the others tried to quell the questions in their minds as the doctor took them to the end of the second row and pulled back the sheet that was cradled up under the chin of the patient.

Taurus' eyes popped and looked questioningly at the doctor, who nodded in confirmation. Poppy and Sugar strained to see around the two and discover who was on the bed. Then the doctor simply walked through the men, back to the elevator where they had come from. The doctor waited until they were back at his office before he spoke. "Okay."

The men let out a collective breath and all clamored to speak, but no voice could overshadow Taurus' bellow. "What is that place and what is *she* doing here?"

"She who?" asked Sugar.

Poppy turned to him after realizing for himself. "That was Aviva Chandler's daughter."

"What, are you sure? I thought she was rescued."

Taurus spoke, "No, that is her other daughter, this is the middle one, Sage, I think is her name. How did she get here?"

"I don't know what happened to her exactly," answered the doctor. "She arrived a few hours ago. We had to fix her up quite extensively before we put her under."

"But why are you keeping her unconscious, and what about the rest of those poor people in there? Why are they there?"

"Those aren't just any people. Those are Sentries, the former staff of the entire University to be exact, plus some others. Some of them are my very good friends."

"Then why the hell are they all being sedated in there? Out with it, doc!" Taurus's large presence was undeniably frightening when he was angry. "Wait, is this one of those places Braeden was telling me about? A TRC or something I think he said, where they drug people into submission?"

"Yes, well it was. As far as Mrs. Chandler knows, it still is. However, we have not been giving them the strong drugs for weeks. They are only still sedated now for the show."

"The show for what?"

"For Mrs. Chandler's visit tomorrow, to see her daughter. After that we are ready to start waking them up. As far as she knows, they are all still under the influence of the little cocktails she had the last staff develop before she killed them off. I guess she didn't realize when she recruited from the city hospital how many GC, or supporters work in health care."

"What are those big vats for that we passed?"

"Well, that is another story. Are you aware of the flush?"

"Hm, yes just recently."

"Well, this is where the drugs for the flushes are, or used to be manufactured."

"What do you mean used to be?"

"It's now a placebo. Mrs. Chandler just ordered the largest flush ever in Collection history, but we have been weaning the general public off the drugs in the last two flushes. Have you noticed how the people on the street seem to be waking up, if you will?"

"Yes, now that you say it, I have noticed."

The doctor touched his ear and then held up his hand to stop Taurus. "Come with me Mr. Roma. Your friends can come too." Dr. Vincent led them down a different hall to a residential wing. As they walked into the room, Taurus was relieved to see Howard sitting up in a bed with a smile on his face, sipping a hot liquid. He ran to his son's bedside.

"Oh, my boy, you look so much better."

"Dad," his voice was finally unaffected by pain. "I was wondering where you were. I feel better." Taurus noticed Howard's face and head were almost scar free. He ran his hand over Howard's head and then kissed it while he choked back a tear of thankfulness. Howard reached up to hug his dad and grimaced slightly.

The doctor offered an explanation, "We were able to repair his ribs with a regenerator, but the tissue holding them is still going to be sore for a few days. The good news is, there is no infection."

"I can tell. I can't believe how you fixed his head."

Howard laughed, "I don't know if you can really fix this head."

Taurus laughed boisterously and grabbed his son's chin in appreciation for his sense of humor returning. "Now you need to get some rest, son. It's been a long night."

"Actually," the doctor interrupted, "you are all going to need to leave. Mrs. Chandler is coming tomorrow, or maybe even tonight the way things are going and y'all cannot be anywhere in the hospital when she arrives."

"Where are we supposed to go? And why do you keep calling her Mrs. Chandler like she deserves some type of respect."

"Let's call it self-preservation. Don't worry though, we're not gonna kick you out in the cold. We have some student housing available. It's about as pretty as a snake in a knot hole, but you will be safe and comfortable for now. The nurse is bringing you all something to eat and then you need to skedaddle. Someone will be here shortly to escort you through the underground passage."

Taurus reached for Dr. Vincent's hand. "Thank you, doctor, I can't thank you enough."

"My pleasure. Good luck."

"Wait, what happens now? I mean, what happens when all those people wake up?"

"Anarchy."

# 53 ~ What Happens at the Table...

Croft awoke to the smell of bacon. He hadn't realized how much his stomach still yearned for meat after so many years on the leaner GC diet. Following the aroma, his nose led him to the large Cleary kitchen. The perimeter looked like a typical kitchen, but the spacious room was filled with two ten-foot wood plank tables accompanied by wooden benches. The cork kitchen floor was warm under Croft's feet. Katherine was cooking and turned to see who the footsteps belonged to. "We host a lot of meetings here."

Croft smiled, "Well, you sure have the room." Glancing to see both tables set with placemats and silverware he asked, "How many are you expecting today?"

"Looks like a lot."

"Can I help you?"

"Sure, I think the muffins are done. Do you want to grab those for me? There is an oven glove on the counter there."

Croft walked to the three side-by-side ovens. As he opened each one, the smell of warm blueberries overwhelmed him. "Mmm, these smell heavenly."

"They taste heavenly too," Katherine quipped eternally proud of her recipe. "So, have you decided what you're going to do next?"

Croft set the muffins on the granite slate above the ovens and walked over to stand next to Katherine. "I have to find a way to tell Janie about her daughter. The only way I can think to do that is to go find her other daughter and take her to be with her mother."

"Other daughter, I thought the other one was killed in a car crash?"

"Where did you hear that?"

"On the weekly news address in town, a few years ago."

"I'm sure her grandmother pitched that story so she wouldn't have to answer questions about Delilah's disappearance. Apparently, she has been in Indie City for the last couple years. I need to go get her."

"We're going with you." Braeden's voice startled Croft from behind.

"Good morning. Listen Brae, I don't know if I can even find her but now that I found you, I don't want to take any chances with getting you safely to Janie. I am going to talk to Chul-moo and Chauncey and see if they will take you to Euro City. I will go after Delilah and try to meet you there."

"You're not going by yourself."

"No, he's not," Katherine added. "Come here boys." She wiped her hands on a dish towel and sat down at the head of one of the tables. Croft and Braeden joined her. "I've been doing some planning of my own. I don't like what is going on around here. I'm afraid we are in for some riots and who knows what else, pretty soon. I want Collin to leave."

"What about you?" Croft asked. "You can't stay here by yourself."

"I have a whole crew here, if I need anything, but if Collin stays, I know he is going to try to be brave, standing up for somebody and do something stupid. Even though everyone calls me Grandma Kate, I never had any grandchildren. Collin is all I have left, and I want him to have a better life. He is only twenty-four. I want him to go somewhere with a future. Somewhere where he can live his life."

"I'm not sure where that somewhere would be, but I don't think he is going to leave you anyway."

"He will if he is needed. You need to make him think he is doing you a favor and that you can't go without him. He is an expert navigator. Make him think you need him for navigation."

"If that is really what you want Katherine, I will try."

A loud crowd of men burst through the kitchen door. Chauncey and Chul-moo blended in with the raucous men. Katherine laughed, "You boys smell of beer and all-night shenanigans. I wondered if you fools were ever going to sleep."

Chauncey answered, "I think we had just decided it was a good idea a few minutes ago, then we smelled breakfast."

The crowd laughed and settled in around the tables. Croft was elevated with the jovial company of good solid folk. Dishes clinked, food slapped on plates and shoveling of food commenced. The conversation grew louder and louder until it suddenly came to halt. All eyes focused on Sabine who stood at the bottom step of the back stairwell. She wore athletic pants and an oversized white button-down shirt, which Braeden recognized as his, tied up around her waist. Meekly she spoke, "Sorry to interrupt." She looked at Braeden, "Someone delivered your bag to the room. I hope you don't mind."

"Mind? My clothes look way better on you than they do on me."

Her wet hair was tousled in a loose bun on top of her head. The crowd of men stared dumbstruck until Katherine spoke, "Dear Lord, don't be such men. Come on, Sabine, I have a spot next to me." Conversation

246

resumed as if on Katherine's command. Sabine sat down and immediately searched for Braeden's eyes across from her. He smiled and stretched his feet to touch hers under the table.

"Sleep well?"

Sabine couldn't take her eyes off Braeden to answer Katherine. "Mmm hmm, I mean yes."

Croft scooted closer to Braeden and tried to talk lower than the crowd to his small audience. Katherine, who was flanked by Sabine and Collin, leaned in for the scoop. Croft told the tale as if for the first time. "Listen you two, I want you to go on ahead to Euro City. Braeden, I know you want to get to your sister, and she needs you. You could be the missing link for her. She remembered some things with Sage before…" Croft stopped short realizing he hadn't told Braeden of his other sister's fate.

"Before what?"

"Braeden, I'm sorry. With everything going on, I forgot to tell you what happened with Sage." Braeden's face grew pale enough to highlight a few of the sudden freckles around his hairline. "I can't say for sure, but she was either captured or killed." Croft continued to tell Braeden the story of the night he rescued Janie for a second time from the family tree home where Janie and her siblings had grown up. Braeden's face contorted with every twist of the story. His elbows were on the table, holding up his head with fists full of hair.

Braeden's arms fell on the table when Croft finished the story. "So, you rescued one sister, but left the other?" Sabine grabbed his hands across the table.

"I know." Croft shook his head in disgust with himself. "It has torn me up inside ever since. But Brae, I didn't have a choice. I had to get at least one of them away from there."

Katherine chimed in, "It sounds to me like your sister Sage was the one that made the choice. It sounds like what she wanted."

The room of men, who had grown silent in listening to the tale, nodded in affirmation of Katherine's assessment. Braeden lifted his head to see an audience staring back at him. "Eat, please." He flicked his hand to the group who went back to softer conversation, hoping to overhear any details. "Sorry Croft. I know you wouldn't leave her on purpose. So, do you really think she is dead?"

Croft put his hands over Braeden's and Sabine's. "I don't know. I would like to think she is alive, but if your mother knows about Janie, I can't imagine how well she will hide Sage."

Braeden chuckled at his own stupidity, "Oh, my mother knows. You can be sure of that."

"How do you know?"

"Heh, well, I told her." The room gasped. "I know, I know, it was stupid. I was so angry, and she was threatening me, and I just wanted something to rub in her face."

"Don't beat yourself up, kid. I understand." Croft pulled his hands back and wiped the nervous perspiration from his palms on to the legs of his pants. "Once we get Janie settled and safe, we will make a plan to find Sage, I promise. For now, though, like I was saying, I want you and Sabine to go be with Janie and I am going to go find Delilah."

"Croft, it is too dangerous by yourself."

Croft felt his plan fall into place. "Collin, I heard you are pretty good with navigating the grid we have."

Collin raised his eyebrows, "Where did you hear that?"

"From everyone."

Collin eyed his mother suspiciously. "Okay, your point?"

"The point is I need a good navigator." He looked over to Chauncey and Chul-moo at the other table. "It looks like my guys are going to be busy here for a while so I was hoping you could go with me."

"Nope, no way! I'm not leaving ma, no matter how much she is trying to get rid of me!"

"I'm not trying to get rid of you son, but it looks like you are needed elsewhere. I will be fine. I have our new friend John and the other boys here to help me. It would be good for you to get out and see a little more of the world. You always wanted to see the Great Lakes, since you were a little boy. Besides, Croft needs you. The GC needs you."

Collin smirked at his mother and leaned in close. "Mom, I know these guys can take care of you, but…"

"Who is going to take care of you?"

"No, that's not what I was going to say. I don't know if I can leave you. You never know what might happen. I could never forgive myself if something happened to you while I was away."

Katherine hugged him tight. "Oh, my Collin, I am going to miss you more than you know. I don't know if we have ever spent a whole day apart. But sometimes missing folks is what lets us know how much we love 'em." Collin squeezed his little mother and gritted his teeth to keep from crying. Katherine finally pulled back, "All right, all right enough of this blubberin'. It's settled then."

After breakfast Croft helped Braeden and Sabine pack a few essentials in the seat storage of his motorbike. "Listen kid, stay off the main roads as much as possible during the daytime. And if I were you, I would stay to the east of Fox Island all together, but not as far east as New Fundamental. Chaunce put a better homing device on this thing, so you should register in the tree network if you are even close to any ghost cities." Croft pointed to a set of buttons. "If this is green, you are near the GC. If it is red, stop and take cover. I bet you are smart enough to know what to do with the yellow button."

"I got it."

"Okay, one more thing." Croft grabbed Braeden on either side of his face. "You take care of yourself kid and take care of that pretty girl." He winked at Sabine. "I don't want to lose anymore Chandler children. Do you hear me?"

"It's okay Croft. We will be careful. Do you have any message for Janie?"

"Just tell her I am the moth, and she is the flame."

"Too poetic and too tragic, do you have anything more light-hearted?"

"Ha, you're probably right. Tell her anyway please."

"Give me a hug, ya old fool."

"Old? You're catching up you know."

Croft hugged Braeden one more time. "That one's for your sister."

"You're not going to kiss me now, are you?"

"In your dreams, big fella."

Croft slapped Braeden on the back and hugged Sabine. Then stepping back, he watched until the bike disappeared in the distance. He carted his worried heart back into the Cleary barn. Collin was busy with Chauncey and Chul-moo updating his 2019 classic Corvette. When they were finished, the dashboard looked like an airline cockpit. Painted with mirrored chameleon paint, the car could virtually disappear into its surroundings. It was so smooth Croft wanted to touch it but didn't dare.

"Are we ready to hit the road pretty soon?"

"Yeah, but some news just came in on the wire. Delilah and a friend apparently made it to Eagle Crossing in Wisconsin. A Sentry from there was guiding them to Euro City, but their signal was lost around old Chicago."

"Chicago?! Holy Hell!"

"Yeah, it's not good. That's why Chul-moo added a few weapons to our ride."

"That's my boy. I'm going to miss you two." Croft grabbed Chauncey and Chul-moo around the neck. "Chul-moo, what about your rig?"

"We are having a pig roast and then the boys are going to take us out tonight after dark to bring it in."

"Pork? You're eating pork?"

"I know, can you believe it? I'm actually looking forward to it."

"Take it slow. You haven't had anything that heavy in years."

Katherine walked into the barn with a bag of food and water. "Some grub for the road." She was afraid to cry so she hugged Croft first and then Collin quickly. On her way out of the barn her voice cracked, "Keep in touch boys." She didn't look back.

# 54 ~ Burma Shave

Patterns of leaves danced on our bodies from the afternoon sun as we jogged through the woods. I couldn't help but laugh at how I was on the run once again. Maybe it was the rest, but I didn't feel as winded as the day before, even carrying my bag. I was getting used to being on the run. Trey's long legs kept a fast pace, but I didn't find it hard to keep up.

"Trey, are we almost there?"

"Almost where?"

"Where we're going?"

"Sure, only about 160 miles to go." I stopped running. It took Trey a few strides before he realized I wasn't behind him. He rolled his eyes and came back to me. "Janie, we are not going to run the whole way."

"That's a relief. What's the plan then?

"Come on, we're close." Trey started to run, and I picked up pace again behind him. Before long, the trees thinned, and we were abruptly running on open land. It felt strange to be out of the woods. Soon after, crumbling buildings rose in the distance--the shattered remains of a lifestyle I couldn't remember. I was momentarily lost.

The cool autumn breeze brought me back to my senses. I realized I had slowed down, so I pushed to catch up with Trey. "You still didn't tell me where we are going."

"Outpost two."

"What's an outpost?" As I asked the question, I glanced forward to three silos in our path.

Trey nodded ahead, "That's an outpost."

I guessed he was being cryptic for a reason, so I stopped asking until we reached the silos. A faded banner hung on the largest of the three that read, "Grover Cleveland's Army Will not be Silenced."

"Grover Cleveland? Ah, GC! Am I right?" Trey smiled. "So, what does it mean?"

"It doesn't mean anything anymore. GC used to use banners like these and old Burma Shave signs to display codes during the war."

"It reads like a pretty simple code. Did it work?"

"Well yes, considering no one had even heard of the GC back then. I still don't know how much of the Collection understands us or even knows about us now."

"So why is this an outpost?"

Trey grabbed my hand. Luckily, it didn't faze me. His touch held no more kryptonite. He dragged me to the area between the three silos to a large door that had no visible way of opening. My eyes scanned up the side to several green blinking lights around the top rim of the silo. "Green is good, yes?"

"Green is good." Trey traced the edge of the door with his hand until the seam became a glowing liquid. "Janie, check in your bag for a recognizer. It looks like a wristwatch." I dug through the bag and produced it.

"Yes, yes, that's it." Trey held it up to the liquid seam that appeared to catch fire and then cool to a light green. As the green chased its way around the edge, the door cracked open with a gust of stale air. The large door raised and disappeared into its framing. Inside was a showroom of cars. They were not just any cars but a fleet of super sleek Chevrolet Wildebeests, the last domestic made car of the United States.

"Wow, these are beautiful. Where did they come from?"

Trey eyed me with a devilish grin. "They were your mother's."

I couldn't help but laugh, "Okay, so how did the GC get them?"

"Croft wouldn't tell me. I don't think he was in a joking mood last time we spoke."

Even though his inference pricked my heart, I tried to ignore it.

"Anyway, he called them, "Aviva's back taxes," and told me where to find them."

"I suppose she does owe some restitution."

Trey looked at me intently, "Mostly to you!"

Trey had a unique way of defending me and making me feel guilty for my life all at once. I tried to de-funk myself. "Well, all right, let's go get my new car." I jogged to tag a car.

"Hold on, don't get in yet. I need to disable a few things. The satellite chips have already been removed, but Croft was worried there might be another type of sensor on them that registers when they are running." Trey pulled up the hood and mumbled to himself as he pulled plugs and re-routed wires. "That's it. We should be good to go."

"I see that they are plugged in, but where does this whole place get its electricity from?"

"There is a solar array on the roof of the silo. From the air it looks like a water holding tank."

"Is it true the Collections, or should I say my mother, are the only ones who have the capability to fly anymore?"

"They would like to think so, but no. The Kentucky wild men have some old crop dusters and the people left living behind the mid-continental wall out west have something, because lights in the sky are seen often by the folks on this side."

"What about the GC?"

Trey instinctively looked around like someone could be listening. His childishness was sometimes endearing. "You have to promise you won't tell. Much of the GC doesn't even know this, only the Sentries and a few others, like me. We have a rocket."

"What?!"

"Well, actually we have a shuttle. Moon Shuttle Fortitude, to be exact. It's one of the shuttles that was used to ferry people for moon cruises in the thirties. However, since Cape Canaveral and Houston are both under water it doesn't do us much good. Bodhi was right. We do need satellite hook-up. We are living in the stone age."

"That is impressive, but I was thinking of something a little smaller scale, like a plane or a helicopter."

Trey laughed sarcastically, "Yeah, we're working on that."

"Oh, so moon shuttle-no problem, but mention a small plane and that is out of the question. I can't believe people can just joyride to the moon now."

"Well, they can't anymore, but the possibility is there."

"Um, I hate to change the subject, but is there a bathroom in this place I can use before we leave?"

"Yes, but hurry. It's in the other silo through the door on the right. The only problem is you have to go through a tunnel before you get to it."

Of course. "I can do it. It's okay." I tried not to walk as if I was compromised by the urge, but I knew I looked funny even before Trey snickered under his breath. To my surprise there were no security lights or secret entrances, only a doorknob. The tunnel was tight but short. As I opened the door on the other end, the second silo showed a maze of office cubicles and old desktop computers.

The room was lit only by window slits near the middle of the silo. Anxious about what might be lurking in the dimly lit room, I ran to the bathroom. The light didn't work, so I propped a trashcan in the door. The side light through the door cast eerie shadows on my face in the mirror and made me look more haggard than I had remembered.

I moved the trashcan to get out of the bathroom and heard Trey's voice echoing in the giant office chamber. "Janie, come on. We've been found. We have to go - now!" Panic moved me faster than my body felt was natural. I met Trey at the tunnel entrance, and he yanked me by the arm through the tunnel.

"Which one are we taking?"

"Shhh!" He pulled me to a charcoal gray car that was running with a barely audible hum. "Get in and buckle up." As we breached the opening three Collectors stepped in front of the door. "Hold on, Janie!" The motor revved and we headed straight for the men. They jumped out of the way, but I was pretty sure we ran over at least one of them as our car was momentarily launched over an obstacle. The thought of it made me queasy.

Metal pings hit the back windshield and bumper. "What is that?"

Annoyed to answer, Trey snapped, "They are shooting at us."

The pings finally faded, but my anxiety didn't. I scanned the area. There was no rear window, only a screen displaying the rear-view camera. It appeared they were gone. "I don't see them. Do you see them?"

"No, but I didn't see where they went either."

I glanced out of each side window expecting to see something. An uneasy feeling crept up my spine and stole my breath. Trey was busy trying to dodge trees and small farm buildings but kept glancing over at me. "What is it? Are you okay?"

"Yes...no, I don't know. I have an odd feeling, like something bad is going to happen."

"I know, I feel it too."

Finally, through a maze of country shops we had wandered into, we saw a road. Trey sped up. Dipping down in a rut, we hit hard and then hurtled up on to the road and into the path of a large black semi-truck and trailer.

"Holy Shit, there's traffic!" He tried to crank the wheel and then remembered to engage the lateral wheelbase. The body of the car rotated and suddenly we were going forward on the road with the semi close on our heels.

Adrenaline pumped through my veins. I had to close my eyes. When I opened them again, I noticed light from the rear. Trey had found the switch for the back windshield. Though it let in the light, darkness was growing again in the shadow of the gaining semi. "Trey, it's getting closer."

"I know, I know." Trey leaned back and pressed his foot hard on the gas. My head slammed against the seat. The scenery whizzed by, but as fast as it felt we were going, the semi was closing the gap. "I have to get off this road. We can handle the terrain, but I don't think goliath back there can."

Trey veered off the road and once again, I could feel the chassis separate and rotate. We turned on a dime and the semi following us almost tipped trying to keep up. "Is this your plan?"

"What?"

"An obstacle course?"

Trey's agitated face broke a smile, "Yeah, an obstacle course."

He weaved in and out of light posts, buildings, and curbs in our path, avoiding roads whenever possible. The semi tried to stay as straight as it could while still following us but several times it looked as though it could tip. Finally, we came to a dry creek bed. Trey maneuvered us into the bumpy gulley and, surprisingly, the semi followed. Trey increased his speed and the semi followed suit. Low hanging trees were pummeling its sides, but it stayed on our tail. Trey's infectious smile took over his face as he laughed.

"What is so funny?"

"You'll see. Hold on." The creek bed turned and suddenly we were under a low bridge. The roof of the bridge cleared our car by only a few feet. I whipped my head around to watch what I knew was going to happen. I didn't see the semi plow into the bridge, but the explosion was fierce. Pieces of flying debris almost caught up with us.

"Ha! Serves 'em right. I guess we know where those Collectors went." Trey continued to laugh but I was immediately transported back to the death of my husband. The heat, the explosion, it was now seared into my brain. I still didn't have enough memories to piece our life together, but glimpses of his face turning toward me before the explosion made missing him more profound.

"…you know what I mean?"

I was brought back to reality in Trey's midsentence. He looked different somehow. The man that had wept over accidentally killing a Collector with his grandfather's knife was now a changed man capable of killing whenever necessary and almost without remorse.

"Don't look at me like that Janie. I know what you are thinking."

"No, you don't."

"Yes, I do. You're wondering why I'm laughing and so excited."

"Yeah, I guess that's part of it."

"It's not like I wanted anyone to die, even those creeps. But they were going to kill us if we didn't get them first. I only wanted them off our tail. We just lucked out with that bridge."

"Lucked out? Who are you? We could have died."

"Right, but we didn't. We win today."

"There, that is what I'm talking about. Winners? How do we win when others die?"

"When we don't die—that's how we win. Look, you can't have it both ways, Janie. People are going to die."

"I know, Trey, I just don't see why we need to celebrate it."

The car was silent for miles until Trey found the old interstate. "Phew, I wasn't sure if we would find the road again."

I didn't answer. The adrenaline had worn out my body. I could feel my eyelids closing as the road waned on. I reclined the seat and turned to face the window, pulling my knees up to my chest and hugging them. I drifted between images of Croft and Anson. I just couldn't justify how I could have lived my life that way, loving two men. It was a problem I no longer had, but the idea of it still bothered me.

Sleep felt good. I was dreamless except for when we would hit a bump on the road and my mind would wander through its few known and sordid details before I would drift off again. Sometimes a light in the distance would fly by and I thought I heard thunder once, but other than that I was out of it. I knew it was dark and I knew I was covered up with something warm, but I barely realized I was still in a car with Trey.

I'm not sure when we stopped or what time it was, but my eyes opened a few times with the bounce of being carried. I'm sure it was Trey, but I was too tired to even open my eyes enough to confirm. I had not remembered being laid down on a bed until I awoke to sunlight in my eyes and a gentle rocking motion.

The walls were knotty wood, and there was an open window with nothing but sky outside. Next to the bed a small nightstand with a crocheted doily held a glass of water and some tissues.

"G'morning sleepy head, we're here." I rolled over to see Trey propped up on his elbows, his bare chest reflecting the light. I might have rolled my eyes, but it was only to distract myself. I felt myself hating him a little bit for his attractiveness.

"We're where?"

"Euro City."

"What? When? How did we get here so fast?"

"It wasn't that fast. You just slept the whole way."

I tried to wrap my head around what he was saying when I heard water sloshing. I flung the covers off and stepped out of bed. "So, how did I get here, to this room?"

"You were so tired last night. I couldn't even wake you when we got here. I carried you in and put you on the couch on the main floor while I figured out rooms with the owner of this flotilla. There were thirty people in the room drinking and laughing, having a celebration and it didn't even faze you. You slept through the whole thing, the boat ride and even me carrying you up the stairs. There was only one room, so I hope you don't mind. That wooden chair over there did not look too comfortable."

"It's fine." I was too distracted by his mention of a boat ride and the sound of the water to care. Trey began to feel like a nuisance to me. I didn't want to have to deal with him for a while. "Thanks for taking care of me last night…"

"You're wel…"

"…but I need to be away from you for a while."

"I understand." He walked to the chair to grab his shirt.

His hurt expression gave me pause. "No, I didn't mean you had to…"

"It's okay, I need to find some other clothes and talk to a few people anyway. If you leave, remember we are on red flotilla number nine." His head hung low as he left the room.

Flotilla, there was that word again. I walked to the window. As I reached the sill, I could see water in every direction. I put my hands on the sill and looked down. The side of the red building disappeared into water. *Red flotilla number nine* I repeated to myself as I left the room and ran down the stairs.

A door at the bottom of the stairs opened into a large room that looked like the lobby of a hotel. A tall man with black slicked back hair and a black handle-bar mustache stood behind the counter. His white shirt sleeves were rolled up to his elbows and he wore suspenders and a garter around his arm. "Good morning, miss. I hope you slept well."

I scanned the nineteenth century furnishings in the room. It felt like another time. The walls were red velvet brocade and faux oil lamps hung everywhere over lace covered tables and ornate chairs. A bar on the far side of the room was home to seven brass beer taps and large portraits of ladies in ball gowns lined the wall behind it.

"Where am I?"

"Welcome to *The Golden Corset*. Technically we're housed in red flotilla number nine, but we still like to name our restaurants."

A slight feeling of relief that I was not completely crazy released my shoulders. "Oh, this is a restaurant?"

"Restaurant, lodge, party pontoon, whatever you want to call it."

"Pontoon, so we are floating, then? I saw water out my window, but I could hardly believe it."

"Sweetheart, do you not know where you are?" His tone felt condescending.

"I wish I did."

"You are in Euro City."

"I guess I knew that, but the water confused me."

He laughed and walked around the counter. "Let me show you. I'm sorry, my name is Samuel. Samuel Shakes." He turned and held his hand out in greeting.

"Hi, Janie McAvoy."

His hand stopped shaking mine and he scanned me up and down. "Are you..."

"Yes, I'm Janie McAvoy."

He started shaking my hand again. "I'm sorry. Nice to meet you, mam, real nice to meet you. I thought you were..."

"I was, but I was rescued." Croft's face fluttered through the back of my mind.

"Well, Ms. McAvoy, let me show you Euro City." He draped my hand around his arm and led me through the front door. A bustling city with composite slat streets and tall colorful wooden buildings spread out in every direction. I looked at him still confused. "This way, you'll see." We walked around the side of the red building to a path with a railing. As we wound around the building, the path turned into a balcony over the water. I looked up at Samuel again.

"This is the edge, mam."

"The edge of what?"

"Euro City, the greatest floating city ever built."

"The whole city floats?"

"Yep."

"Show me more."

Samuel took me back around to the front of the building. "You might like to go to the town hall, huh?"

"Sure, I guess."

Cute little shops and carts full of fresh fruits, vegetables and other small trinkets lined the way. People meandered through the street taking what they needed from each bin. At the end of the path was the town hall, a copper-roofed building in the city center. I was caught by the beautiful small aqua tiles surrounding the door. They reminded me of Croft's eyes. I think I sighed out loud.

Samuel held the door for me. Inside, was a digital display with images of the war. The slogans, "Don't ever forget" and "Re-set humanity" kept popping up. I stood mesmerized by the slide show, watching a reality I must have lived, but couldn't remember. I was so frustrated with myself. Just as I was about to turn away, a picture of a woman with long blondish hair, wearing grey riot gear, spray painted with red words, flashed on the screen. It was me!

I looked different, younger, and not so tired and worn by life. Scrolling over my face were these words:

*My friends, my tenacious warriors, we tried peaceful protest. We tried to support the few elected officials who weren't corrupt. We then set our sights on bringing down the old order, but we are still branded with the capitalist price tag that warped our souls and continues to kill our planet in its aftermath. Now, you may think it is time to celebrate and relax, but even though the state bombings have stopped, we have won nothing! This sick society, that we helped create, is seeping back into our collective consciousness. We must un-create it! Remember, the enemy is not our neighbor, or even the government. The enemy is within. I wish I could say we can fix it with protest or fighting, but we fix nothing until we fix ourselves. We all must be responsible for the hate we still hold in our hearts. I most of all.*

*~J. McAvoy, 2044 GC Peace Summit*

That uncomfortable feeling of responsibility crept in, seeing my words in print. How does someone live up to that? It was followed by a parade of pictures with the caption, SENTRY HEROES. I choked up a little to see Croft's face and Char's and Chul-moo's and a young picture of Anson and even of myself.

Samuel, seeing I was visibly shaken, put his hand on my shoulder. "There is time for politics and regret later. Come, I think you will want to see this." I followed him around the screen to a row of smaller screens lining the back wall of the octagon shaped room. We sat down and Samuel spoke to one of the screens, "Social network history - Janie McAvoy." Suddenly the screen in front of him turned on. It was tiled with thumbnail pictures. "It's not everything, since we don't have internet, but it's a pretty good database. Touch one."

As I touched a picture, it enlarged. Staring at me was a picture of Anson holding our two girls as toddlers. I studied it carefully for memories attached to it. Frantically, I touched the tiles, bringing up picture after picture. My eyes were so filled with tears, I had to blink continuously to clear my vision. Why couldn't I make myself remember?

A hand touched my shoulder. I jumped and turned. It was Trey. He had an odd smile on his face. "I need you to come with me, Janie." I shook my head. I wanted to stay and pour over my life and look at my family and remember. "Please," he said.

Reluctantly, I stood. I thanked Samuel and told him I would be back in a minute. As we approached the entry screen, I could see two pair of legs beneath it. Trey's smile widened. I walked around the screen to see a man and woman. She was short and pretty with dark hair and eyes. The man next to her dropped her hand and took a step forward. He was tall and familiar. His hair was almost the same color as mine. It felt like I knew him. He smiled and started to cry. "Janie?"

# 55 ~ Recognitions and Regrets

I knew his face, but not his place.

"Hi," he said tentatively. "You may not remember me."

His voice was familiar. "I'm sorry, I know I should, but I don't."

"Janie, it's okay. You have nothing to be embarrassed about. My name is Braeden."

I should have been overwhelmed with recognition of my own brother, but I only knew his name and a few childhood memories of a little light-haired boy. "Hi Braeden," I said shyly. "You're my brother."

"You remember?" he said hopefully.

"No, I'm sorry." I paused. "I know your name, but I don't have much to go with it."

"It's okay. It's good to see you."

"It's good to..." I was crying, even though I had no past with him that I could recall. It was the invitation he needed to pick me up and hug me tight. His hug felt familiar, but I was angry with myself that I could conjure nothing more to go with it. I wanted to talk to him, but I didn't know what to say.

"How did you find me?"

"I knew you would be coming here."

"You did? I didn't even know I would be coming here." We both laughed and wiped the tears from our faces in the same way.

"Croft told me."

"You spoke to Croft?" The hope in my voice was unmistakable but immediately after I said it, I wondered if I had cause for any hope.

"I just left him last night."

"Where is he? How is he? Did he find my daughter?" Braeden's face dropped. I couldn't have known what was coming next, but on some level my heart knew it was terrible. He grabbed both of my hands and took a deep breath. I was barely breathing, waiting for what I knew would be bad news about someone I loved.

"Sequoia is dead."

Braeden's voice wavered with emotion as he retold the story of my daughter's death. A second death of a child I didn't know. I hated myself for not remembering Sequoia. I felt so much resentment. Our chance to create new memories was over. I sat on the ground, a useless lump of nothingness--no past, no future, no daughter. Everything that came after that is a blur.

For the next several days I slept off the remaining drugs in my system. I had hoped my memory would come back with their leaving, but it was a false hope. My only meal each day was dinner since it was the period of the day that I was most alert. Every dinner I spent with Braeden and his friend Sabine, who helped fill in some details of my life and capture. After dinner we would walk to *The Dangle*, an area with large four-person swings that swung out over Lake Michigan on the edge of Euro City, to watch the sunset.

The floating city had slowly been making its way along the coastline from old Chicago because storm surges in that area, had been rough. The city could be steered but only moved a few miles a day because of its enormity. Docked near a place called Cherry Beach, the giant barge had come to a full stop to make repairs. So, my brother kept me busy touring the amazing wooden and metal terrain of the city and taking short boat rides when the weather cooperated. We had almost made it around the entire city.

As my stupor lifted, managing Sequoia's death became arduous. My companions encouraged me to stay distracted by attending social gatherings in the city. Trey, to his credit kept crowds away from me when the buzz of who I was spread through the town. Trey and I didn't talk much, but I think he purposefully kept his distance for my sake. I felt sad for him. He hadn't asked to be a part of my circus. I'm sure he'd rather have been with his soybeans. Nevertheless, he was a loyal friend.

I wanted to move forward, but I was stuck. Still stuck without my memory, and without Croft. I finally felt safe but not yet comfortable. Braeden had told me Croft was trying to find my other daughter Delilah but every day that passed made me more anxious. I tried to self-soothe and took long evening walks through the city. I found the retelling library which was a gathering of classic books retold and re-written to preserve the stories until the originals could be found in abandoned libraries along the coast. Books seemed so insignificant and hugely important at the same time. I spent hours there.

It had been over a week with no word from Croft.

# 56 ~ Uncle Crock

Collin's corvette hummed along peacefully despite its age. Croft was driving so Collin could navigate a new grid system he had developed using the tree network and maps he had painstakingly loaded by hand into the car's computer. Some G.P.S. data remained in the motherboard but without the added benefit of an actual satellite, it hadn't worked until Collin booted up his new system that used stored memory and occasional input of landmarks.

"Nice job, kid. That is an impressive display. How long have you been working on this?"

"Three years."

"Nice."

"Thanks. I rebooted two more systems last night when we stopped. I couldn't sleep."

"You are your mother's son. Good for you. Any transmissions yet?"

"Not yet. We are getting close though. We passed a small ghost city a few minutes ago. They said the word on the wire was that Delilah's car lost signal near a place called Douglas Park, so they may be hiding out there. The Sentry that's with them is named Foster and he apparently is quite a survivalist, so I am sure they are okay."

"I've heard of Foster. I might have even met him once. The hard part, no matter his skills, is getting in and out of there without being caught by the wild ones."

"In about five miles, we should start to get a ping from their vehicle. Keep your eyes peeled for anything."

Collin and Croft scanned the landscape in every direction. Occasionally Collin would almost catch sight of his car in the mirrored facades of old office buildings, but he was pleased that his car's camouflage looked less like a reflection and more like a little blip or a bubble. Croft slowed so he could drive and scan at the same time. Suddenly he came to an abrupt stop.

"Why did you stop?"

"There, up ahead. That car flipped over in the middle of the road."

"We have a ping too, so that must be it."

"Please tell me Delilah is all right. I must take at least one daughter to Janie. How do you think the car flipped? It looks like it has hover capabilities. How does something like that flip?"

"Good question. I'm afraid of the answer."

"Do you see any bodies?"

"Yeah, one."

"That's what I see too, but he has white hair. I bet that is Foster. Man, I was hoping to meet him. So much for being safe with the survivalist. What now? Any ideas?"

"Drive slowly to the edge of the street." Croft maneuvered the Corvette to the curb with no incident. Just as they opened the doors, they were surrounded by a small group of young men, holding pipes.

Collin tried to shut his door, but one of the men grabbed the door while another one pulled him out. As Croft stepped out, the car automatically turned off and the full outline of the car became apparent. The crowd cheered and high fived each other.

"Hey there, fellas, it's okay. We were only passing through."

A scrawny boy with patchy facial hair and grayish skin stepped forward. "Naw, not okay. You won't be passing anywhere today."

"Listen, we had some friends who were lost in this area on their way to somewhere else. We're trying to find them. Can you help us? A blond girl and a young man."

"Yeah, we saw 'em." The other boys elbowed him in the ribs for confessing.

"Where? When? Are they okay?" begged Croft.

A short young man with long black braids stepped forward. "Hmm, probs. I can't say for sure. I'm thinking a ride in that sick car might jog my memory."

Croft was tired and not in the mood for games. "Have you seen them or not? It's urgent we find them."

"Okay, okay, don't freak out. Let's try this again. I'm Rooster, and my associate here, is called Night. We would like to, um, rent your vehicle, for free of course, b'cause it's a sweet ride, and also, it's cold out, and I don't wanna walk. For your services, we'll take you to see the blond girl and her dorky friend."

Croft and Collin shrugged their shoulders, knowing they didn't have much choice, and agreed to the deal. The two boys told the rest of their group to leave and then jumped in the back seat of the car. Croft and Collin stepped in slowly, still not sure the boys could be trusted.

"Turn over there past the park. You'll wanna head toward the river, that way. Let's hit it. I want to see how fast this sweet baby can go."

262

Rooster and Night regaled them with juvenile songs they had made up on their way into the downtown area. The buildings grew taller and taller until they eclipsed everything around them. As they turned the final corner, the silver sun was shadowed by a wide building with a sign that read Barack Obama International Library. The glass on the upper floors was gone, but the lower floors reflected pink in the hazy morning clouds.

"Home sweet home. Pull in the ramp next to the building," Night ordered.

Croft was still surprised as he drove into the structure. "You live in a library?"

"Don't act so surprised, old man. I can read."

"Yeah, we can read--you like a book," added Rooster laughing hysterically at his own joke.

After parking on the highest level of the ramp, Croft and Collin followed Night and Rooster into the building. At the end of the hall was a heavy metal door with two guards outside. Croft looked angrily at Night. Night just shrugged and smirked to Rooster. As they approached, Night motioned for the guards to unlock the door, and as Croft and Collin entered the room, Rooster and Night shoved them in and shut the door. Collin lunged to grab the door, while Croft cursed his age and injuries until he heard a whimper. Delilah was huddled in a corner crying with Bodhi's arms draped around her. They both looked up and Croft saw Bodhi's face was badly bruised.

Delilah lunged toward Croft, "Uncle Crock!" They both fell to the ground laughing.

"Awe, Dee Dee, I am so glad to see you." He pulled her back to check her over. "You are so grown up. I can't believe you're actually here." He hugged her again. "Are you okay? Are you hurt?"

"No, but they beat Bodhi pretty bad when he wouldn't tell them anything about the hover car we came in. I probably would have been next, but I think that weasel-y one with the braids has a crush on me."

"He's not going to touch you. I will kill him first." A weak and battered Bodhi stood to make his claim.

Croft and Delilah helped each other up and hobbled over to him. "You're Bodhi, the driver that Trey wanted so bad? I've heard a lot about you, young man. You have a lot of fans in the network."

"Yeah, too bad I don't have any here." Bodhi held his ribs when he chuckled.

"Thank you for helping this girl. But how did you come to be with Delilah?"

"Aw man, it's a long story that starts with big guys with guns and ends with, well, little guys with guns."

"Well, I can't wait to hear all the details. In the meantime, I'm so thankful you took care of my Dee Dee."

She beamed back at him, "Uncle Crock, I am so glad you found us."

Croft made introductions with Collin. Shortly after, the door opened, and some blankets and a bag of pita loaves were thrown in.

"Well, at least they are feeding you, I guess."

The room was large for a prison. Half of it, where Delilah and Bodhi had been sleeping, had green carpet and some blankets. The other half was parquet with a long table and chairs. A jug of water and other re-used bread bags were strewn about the table.

"So, bread and water for the prisoners, eh?" Croft smiled and stroked Delilah's hair. She put her arm around his waist and hugged him again. Collin and Bodhi sat down at one end of the table to talk about cars while Croft and Delilah sat at the other end filling each other in on the last few years of their lives.

Before falling asleep that night, Croft decided to finally tell Delilah about her sister. She wept silently into his shoulder. "I knew something was wrong, Uncle Crock. I don't know how to explain it, but I woke up from dreaming about her with a terrible pain in my stomach. I don't know if it's possible, but I felt like she was gone. I still can't believe it." They consoled each other until they each finally drifted off to sleep.

For the next seven days, they tried to devise a plan to escape but kept coming up with dead ends. Finally, the door opened, and Night stepped inside. A young woman with her hair tucked in a black beanie stood behind him with a pipe in her hand.

"You!" Night pointed at Croft. "We can't get that damn car of yours to work. You're gonna tell me how right now."

Collin stood, "Actually it's my car, and I'm not telling you shit."

Night took a step in Collin's direction. As he did, the young woman pushed the door back against the outside wall and knocked out the guard behind it. The other guard was missing. Night turned back toward her in a rage, and she swung the pipe in her hand around to blast him in the side of the head. He fell to his hands and knees. She yelled, "A little help here!"

Bodhi stepped forward with a smug confidence on his healing greenish face. "Allow me." Bodhi kicked Night in the gut until he dropped to his stomach and rolled over. His eyes fluttered in and out of consciousness.

"Come on, we gotta go," yelled the woman. The four prisoners, still in shock, left the room and followed her down the same hallway to the parking structure. She stopped them at the door. "God, I hate those guys. I'm sorry I couldn't get to you sooner. I've been trying to find a time when the asshole patrol wasn't all together. I don't think they've done too much damage to your car though, since they couldn't even figure out how to turn it on."

Croft pulled the keys out of his pocket and dangled them in the air. The whole group laughed. "Thank you, miss. My name is Croft."

"Hey, I'm Winnie. I wish there was more time for introductions, but your car is just through there, and the rest will be coming back soon, so you better go."

Collin chimed in. "Why don't you come with us? I don't think it's too safe for you here, now."

A shy smile crept through her face. "Really? I mean, yes. Hell yes! Any place has to better than here. If you're sure?"

Delilah grabbed Winnie's hand and pulled her through the door. "We're sure." They laughed like old friends as they ran to the car.

# 57 ~ Cherry Beach

The sun was not bright enough to be blinding, but it was light enough to wake Collin. Even though the internal temperature control had kept the car toasty, the windows were steamed up from the frigid temperatures outside. Collin sprung out to stretch and let in a blast of cold air, thoroughly rousing the passengers. Soon after, he jumped back in, rubbing his hands together.

"I'm glad we stopped for the night, but we should get rolling. We're only about twenty miles from Cherry Beach. That is the last place Euro City was reported."

"What do you mean, the last place it was reported?" asked Winnie. "Does it disappear or something?"

"It floats," answered Croft. The three in the back were equally amazed, even though Bodhi had heard that before.

The wind whipped and threatened to slide the Corvette off the road. Chatter in the car became fast and furious in anticipation of getting to Euro City. Abruptly, Collin made a sharp left and headed toward the lakeshore. "Croft, look is that it?"

"Out there on the point, by the end of the boardwalk."

Croft squinted, "I think it might be. Look at the size of that thing. Aren't we too far south though?"

"Yeah, but maybe they had to move it again. That has to be it." The car cheered. "Pull up over there by that boat launch. There are a couple of row boats we could maybe use."

Collin parked the Corvette just shy of the sandy beach and everyone jumped out.

As they got close to the water, Bodhi stopped. "So, a thought. Before I make the trip out there, on those raunchy waves, I have a job to do. I still need to make it across the state to the satellite installation."

"Why don't you rest here for the night and go tomorrow?" Croft offered.

266

"Not a fan of big water. I'd just as soon get my job done and then come back, on a calmer day."

Tears formed in Delilah's eyes. "You're going?"

"I'm coming back! You need to see your mom. I'll find some way to get there and get back lickity-split."

"No, I don't want you to go."

Collin, who had been pretending not to overhear spoke up. "I will go with you Bodhi. We can take my car. I may even be able to help you get it back online."

"Righteous! That is awesome. You would do that?" He turned back to Delilah, "There, ya see? Satellite posse engaged. Back in a jiffy." Winnie offered to go with Collin and Bodhi, not knowing anyone in Euro City. "Satellite posse, plus one badass," Bodhi corrected.

Bodhi leaned down to sing in Delilah's ear, "Wait for meee, Delilah Marieee." Delilah smiled up at him. "Now, go see your mom. I can't wait to hear all about it." He hugged her quick so he wouldn't be tempted to try and kiss her, then ran and jumped in the car with Collin and Winnie.

After they sped off, Croft and Delilah got in one of the row boats and pushed off. The water was freezing and made their hands numb. When they reached the end of the breakwater the waves grew angry and sloshed them around, almost knocking them out of the boat several times. Delilah was shivering so hard she could barely move.

Both Delilah and Croft marveled at the magnitude of the city as they approached. A doc-hand holding a bow and arrow, shot the arrow at the rowboat and as it hit, the soft tip expanded into a suction device. Croft tied the boat's line to the arrow line for extra security and several men on board towed them to the edge.

Croft followed Delilah up the metal stairs on to the platform on the eastern edge of Euro City. A few in the vicinity welcomed them and one ran into a building to get them some blankets. Croft told a brief story about who they were looking for. Faint recognition covered the face of the woman leading them into the city center. As they rounded the corner of Red Flotilla number nine, a large man coming out the front door almost knocked them over.

"Trey!" Croft cheered as he hugged him with generous relief.

"Woo, you're freezing, but you're here!"

"You made it! Where is Janie? Is she okay?"

"She's fine. I'll take you to her." With his words Croft could feel Trey had relinquished any claim he thought he once had on Janie. Croft was satisfied to let whatever happened between them die with the past. He was only minutes away from Janie.

# 58 ~ The Long Wait

It was the tenth day since Braeden and Sabine had arrived. I skipped downstairs and had a morning tea with Samuel before leaving to explore the city. The weather had turned cold again after a brief heat swell. I breathed deeply and could smell the falling leaves with the crisp breeze that whipped in from the lake and circled back from the shore. Most days I didn't feel the movement of the city, but the waves were lapping fiercely. The engineers had been working on beaching the city even farther south for the winter, but the struggle was evident that day with the waves.

It was early and the infant sun had barely breached the land. I jogged to my new favorite spot, a little café called *Sassafras* on the west side overlooking the lake. Even though no one charged for goods in the GC, giving a name to establishments had had a resurgence. Flotilla colors and numbers had become a little redundant and boring with the locals.

*Sassafras* was always exactly the right temperature to compensate for weather outside. Barstools lined a giant window, which drew crowds for the breathtaking sunset views, but fresh pumpkin muffins and hot cider were a new draw in the morning. It was surprisingly busy for so early in the day. The crisp air had forced many to seek out their creature comforts.

I declined a barstool for a spot on the faded burgundy couch in front of the fireplace. The plush took me back to the shirt that Croft was wearing the day he rescued me. I hugged my warm cider close and cuddled into the couch to feel its nap on my cheek. Closing my eyes, I tried to imagine his arms around me. Comfort sleep was starting to grab me when I felt a brush on my ear. Braeden plopped down next to me on the couch.

"Howdy sis, how ya doing?"

I chuckled. "Pretty good bro. How are you?"

"Sabine is still asleep, but I was restless. I thought I might find you here. What do you want to do today?"

"Everything and nothing."

"I couldn't have said it better. I'm restless and exhausted both. Maybe I was a bear in a former life. I'm feeling the need to forage for food and then hibernate."

"Go grab a muffin, they are delicious."

Braeden stood and hopped over the couch. As he passed the door a small crowd entered, led by Sabine and Trey. He raised his eyebrow in reference to Trey then kissed Sabine spritely and took a step back in shock when he saw who was behind them.

# 59 - Finally

I felt a breeze from the door and saw a crowd enter. As I stood to see who it was, my knees almost gave out from underneath me. Delilah! My Delilah! Different, but still her, I knew it. The moment froze. My daughter. I stared at her, motionless. I knew her. I felt her. I remembered her personality and wit. I remembered her darling toddler cheeks and infectious laughter. I remembered her thirst for knowledge and her creativity. Then with a force that nearly dropped me to my feet, I remembered her birth--and the moment I thought to have been her death. I remembered.

I wanted to smile, but my tears fought the urge. She stood still and quiet with a wounded look wondering if I, her mother, remembered her. I wanted to yell it, but the intensity of the moment pulled me back and I barely whispered, "Delilah, I remem..." Before I could finish, she was in my arms. We fell to our knees, hugging and rocking each other. I could feel everything. Her loss, my loss, her pain, my pain, but most of all our renewal together. Time held us in a vacuum as we were woven together with golden threads of something beautiful and intangible.

She pulled back slightly, putting her hand on my face, and whispered, "Mommy, mom." Her childish features were gone. She was a young woman. The missed years compounded in my mind. I would never see her awkwardness as she yearned to find herself in adolescence. I couldn't ask for those years. I could only claim the moment.

I put both of my hands on her face and whispered back, "Dee Dee. I love you so much. I have missed you so much." I didn't know until that moment--that aching pain, the emptiness that had been carving out my insides, it was her. It was the memory of her and the agony of missing her and her sister.

"I love you mom," she sobbed in my ear as she hugged me again.

"I love you, Delilah. I can't believe I have you back. I can't believe…"

She loosened her hold, "Mom, do you know about Sequoia?"

270

Sequoia, my poor baby, hers was a loss I still had to conquer, as if anyone ever could. I could feel her pain, dying alone, without her mother to hold her. Trying to soothe the gnawing and burning, I pulled Delilah in tight again to know the warmth of holding Sequoia once more. I gazed inward, remembering Sequoia's strange and wonderful eyes and delighted at her sparkling personality. Sequoia and Delilah were so alike and yet so different, and now one had to replace two. So unfair to both, Delilah would forever be half of the unit she once was. I stroked Delilah's hair, "I'm so sorry about your sister, Dee."

"I still talk to her in my dreams, mom."

"Of course you do, you should."

"Sometimes, I think her, and dad are both trying to communicate with me."

*Dad. Anson!* Another wave crashed and pushed me back from Delilah. "Mom!" she screamed a whisper. I could see her trying to talk to me, but I heard nothing. I was lost with Anson. My mind skipped immediately to the pinnacle moments of our lives to see if they were logged in my memory. They were there!

I remembered in more detail, the day we met, the day we got married and the look on his face when our children were born. I remembered little things, silly things of the everyday life of marriage. The way he smiled at me, the light freckles on his tan shoulders, how we would race each other to the mailbox to get the mail. I did love him. I loved him.

The memory of his love may have sustained me for a while, but more poignant even than our life, was the horror of his death. The explosion, the searing heat and the confusion of the event that changed my life forever. I felt, not only his death, but the ache of losing my children, who I thought had died too. I remembered the horrible burning smell and the feeling of utter helplessness.

Then, the speedy visions of the months that followed choked me in their intensity. I had sobbed so violently from the horrible dreams that I hadn't worked for nearly a year. The pain of losing my whole family in one fell swoop almost killed me. I wondered briefly how I had survived and then the third wave hit. Croft!

Croft had pulled me back from the fire. Croft had held me day after day until I fell asleep. Croft had paid my bills, and walked my dog, and fed me when all I could do was sleep to relieve the anguish. Croft had rubbed my temples when the mental and physical pain overtook me. He was my therapy.

Croft had taken long walks with me and planted a garden with me. Croft had helped me paint my classroom and stocked my shelves with books and stood by me while I got back on my feet as a teacher. Croft had driven me to rallies and picketed with me when our pay was frozen in escrow by the state government. Croft had wept with me when our former students had died in protest.

Croft had told me a million times that I was important and needed and that I could come back stronger than before. Croft had done all of that while mourning for his brother and for the marriage and children that should have been his.

When I finally looked up from my inner battle, Delilah's face was streaked with tears, but she looked comforted that I was back in the real world. I grabbed her hand and silently communicated that I was okay. She smiled and rubbed the top of my hand with her thumb. I scanned the room to find Croft. He stood in the same spot as when he had entered. He was a mess. His body was wrought with emotion, but he was as frozen as I had felt for weeks since I emerged from my drug cocoon. Silent, patiently as always, he waited, hanging on my next move.

What I felt for Croft was as complex as the planet itself. I had loved Anson and I was relieved about that, but I had also loved Croft. I still loved Croft. Anson and I had had a marriage, which was quite a different entity from love at times. A marriage based on love, but also an arrangement. We had agreed to a certain set of habits, a certain way of living and a certain way to love each other. It worked and it was beautiful in its entirety. But the love I had for Croft was a way of breathing. It was the knowledge that he was the part of me, and I was the part of him that no one else could ever replace.

I squeezed Delilah's hand again and then stood to meet the man that figuratively and literally saved my life. He used his whole hands to wipe away the tears from his face and then wiped them on his pants. I tried not to giggle. When his face was dry, his expression changed. He was no longer the tortured soul who had given the woman he loved to his brother. He was no longer the man who loved a woman who couldn't remember him. He was my Croft, and for the first time in over a year, I was his Jane.

The anticipation on his face was more than I could bear any longer. I walked to him, nervously, hoping he would reciprocate. He stood completely still until I reached him, questioning my state of mind, until he was sure. Then suddenly he laughed and swung me around. Burying my face in his hair, I whispered, "I remember. I remember everything."

He whispered back in a broken voice, "I know."

Neither of us could have said anything and the meaning would have been the same, but it was good to say it, nevertheless. He didn't set me down. He held me tight with my toes barely touching the tops of his feet and stroked my hair over and over. I breathed in his scent.

Slowly the cobwebs began to fade, and my insides filled with light to replace all the dark places. I tested myself while he held me, trying to recall various moments throughout my life and to my surprise, they were mostly there. The more recent memories, right before my capture, were the

272

fuzziest but there was no more searching. With the toxins gone, I could travel my brain's pathways with ease.

Finally, he put me down while holding me close to his chest. I released the embrace enough to look into his eyes. "I love you, Croft." His eyes reddened again. "For weeks I have come to love you again, but now I can also love the memory of you--the whole you."

"And Anson?" he asked with the insecurity of a child.

"I loved Anson, Croft. I think you already knew that. But maybe what you didn't know is that I also loved you too, through my whole marriage, I loved you too."

"I know Janie. I was too stubborn and stupid to just tell you how I felt in time."

"I was too."

Then he changed. "But Janie, you were meant to have the life that you did, as was I. Don't you see? It's all a beautiful puzzle how we reach the knowingness of each destination in our lives, but when we get there, we understand that there was no other possible way for us to arrive." I wanted to believe that he believed that.

I closed my eyes and inhaled the moment with all its nuances. Then, smiling broadly and confidently and with all the necessary drama of the moment, I grabbed him by the shirt and relinquished all our fears with a kiss. I swear I felt the earth stop turning.

Sounds of support chimed from around the room which made me kiss him deeper. The energy from the crowd of family and friends was electric. It felt like they wanted to clap, but instead, to give us privacy, walked arm in arm out of the room reminiscing. We paused to see Delilah get swallowed up in her uncle Braeden's hug and to see the woman I would come to know as my sister-in-law, Sabine, smile lovingly at my brother. Trey observed the scene from a respectful distance, but with a smile on his face.

In the days that followed, the torture of my past was slowly replaced with healing. A healing I had already experienced but which was more complete the second time. Tears were relieved by laughter, wondering by answers. We had yet to find Sage, but the word in the GC network was that she was still alive, and I knew with certainty if she were alive, we would find her.

Only one question still haunted me. What was my mother's next move? Of all the convoluted relationships in my life, none would plague me more than my relationship with my mother. I could not answer, in all my newfound awareness, the reason my mother had set out to destroy me and the world along with me. I, too, had lost a husband, and even more. Yet, my grief did not turn me into a monster.

I wondered which switch in the human mind either anchors and copes with life's tragedies or shifts and obliterates all in its path. Could that

273

switch be turned on in anyone? Could it be turned off once it was triggered? Only my mother could answer those questions for me.

# *Epilogue*

Almost every Sentry in the GC had visited Euro City, in the weeks following the recovery of my memory. Trey and Braeden had been inducted into the GC council and I had pulled away from most of the meetings to spend more time with my daughter. Croft was busy with council business, planning more rescues and cautioning against rash action without a plan.

The entire council decided to take a field trip to the old Meijer Gardens near the ruins of Grand Rapids. It was one of the last times we would be able to navigate the water before it froze. The trip up the coast was hard in the glacial wind. We traveled in dune buggies that Trey and one of his new friends had found on an earlier adventure. When we reached the gardens, everyone ran inside to warm in the arid room.

After a brief rest, we toured the overgrown grounds. I decided the crowd and all their talk of war was too much for me, so I wandered off by myself. I walked through the perennial gardens dotted with sculptures. Fall's grip had seceded to winter. What was vibrant and alive a few weeks before had begun to brown and fade with each new sprinkling of snow. The promise of spring seemed too far to grasp.

I trudged through the gardens, mourning the greenness until I made it back to the tropical conservatory. It was a beautiful five story glass building that housed exotic plants from around the world. The smell of all things fresh and alive was not wasted on me. The GC council appropriately met in the greenest place in all the north.

Even with its transparency, it was deemed safe. Several caretakers still lived in the tunnels safely underground and welcomed newcomers often. The Collections had not been able to take hold in the Michigan territory. In fact, the people in their pride had resorted to calling it Michigan again, as we had before the states collapsed. Not a state, but a collective way of being.

I sat on a bench at the outskirts of the meeting area, behind a large orange hibiscus bush, and listened to rationale for war and rebellion. It all seemed so out of place in such an intoxicating and luscious habitat. Staring at the ferns, I tried to refocus the negative energy in the room. I still had a lot to learn about myself and the empathic gifts I had. They were nothing mystical or magical, but just tools for how to understand myself and others. It was a quest that would take a lifetime to complete.

Still, the voices threatened to suck the vitality from the space. I was preparing to join the discussion when Delilah plopped down next to me on the bench. "Are they really going to go to war with grandma, mom?"

"I don't know, honey. We all want things to change, and grandma appears to be at the center of why it can't, but it's not a war with grandma. It's a war with ourselves and each other. We still can't seem to manage letting each other live in peace. We all know there is a better way, we just can't seem to get there."

"Why not? Why can't we simply replace the leaders we know are wrong?"

"It's complicated Delilah. First, not everyone agrees on who is right and who is wrong. So, if we just replace people like your grandmother, then the solution is no better than the problem. You can try to teach people to not be controlling or greedy, but absolute power always corrupts. It's the system that needs to be changed."

"So, if we get rid of all the tyrants, like grandma, then would we be left with a bunch of people still arguing about who is right?"

"That's entirely possible, which is why I don't want to make any rash moves until we have a solid plan."

"What do we do, then? Just wait around for grandma to keep doing horrible things?"

I smiled because I understood her point. I had been lying to myself because I was afraid of the consequences. I didn't have the luxury to be the rebellious youth I once was. I had responsibilities to my family. I needed to take care of my daughter, which I hadn't been able to do for years. Yet, what would I say to my daughter? How could I look into the questioning eyes of this beautiful intelligent girl, who had become wise beyond her years under someone else's watch and tell her I would do nothing?

"I'm not being clear, Dee, I know. You're helping me clarify it for myself. Still, there is a difference between defending yourself against an aggressor and being the aggressor yourself."

"Are you being the aggressor if you're helping people? Wouldn't that make you the defender?"

I nodded my head at the pointed intention of her words, "Of course you're right."

At sixteen years old she had more foresight than I. My experiences had made me cautious to the point of being too afraid to act, even too afraid to have an opinion. I knew what was wrong. We had let a few, with a lot, separate us and convince us they would take care of us, if we trusted them. We spent decades telling ourselves that it would all work out because we were too afraid to stand for something. We were too busy defending the status quo. It was easier to let someone else take care of it. We not only let others act for us, we let others think for us.

I stroked Delilah's golden hair and stared at the Lady Palm across the stone path from where we were sitting. Its shallow roots reminded me of how vulnerable we all are, but the clumps of stalks created a huge base, one that together made the plant strong and sturdy. *Strength in numbers.* I had my daughter, I had my brother, and I had Croft. And probably not just the whole GC, but a good share of the Collective.

"You are right, Dee. We need to stop being afraid. I need to stop being afraid."

I stood and picked up a dried palm frond from the floor. As I crumpled it in my hand, the fear dissipated. It was time to stand for something again. It was my vocation to act. I was awake now – completely awake. The door was open. I had only to step through.

# ✦ Acknowledgements ✦

A thousand thank yous to my editor and friend, Ellie Sharrow. Your expertise, gentle critique, and pointed questions helped me find my voice at an early age and refine it at a (*clears throat*) later age. You are truly invaluable.

Tons of gratitude, praise, and awe to all of my fellow teachers around the world. I see you. I know you. And even though I'm retired, I still want to be you when I grow up.

Eric, Owen, and Abby, you are my who, what, where, when, and why! Thanks for always having my back. I love you to pieces.

Thank you, Lydia, Nancy, Della, Sarah, Angie, Shelley, Katy, my first beta readers. Can you believe it's been ten years since you first saw this, y'all?!! Thanks for being my fam and my fans. Love you bunches.

Thank you, Shelley for being the best cover model, and for being such a great sport!

Thank you to my brother Bill, for always being there to encourage me and cheer me on.

Thank you to my amazing support group of friends and followers, you inspire me and lift me up every day.

## If you want more…

## Coming later in 2023
### *Re-Distribution* (the prequel)
## And in 2024
### *Re-Action* (the sequel)

For maps and more content from the *Re-Collection* world visit lwhallauthor.com.

Made in the USA
Coppell, TX
08 February 2023

12436360R10163